The Road to Sagarmatha

The Road to Sagarmatha

A Himalayan Adventure

Adam A. Wilson

Library of Congress Control Number:		2010917915
ISBN:	Hardcover	978-1-4568-1596-7
	Softcover	978-1-4568-1595-0
	Ebook	978-1-4568-1597-4

To order additional copies of this book, contact:
Xlibris Corporation
1-888-795-4274
www.Xlibris.com
Orders@Xlibris.com
89586

For my parents, Robin & Eileen,
the very best storytellers.

Without them,
The Road to Sagarmatha would not exist.

Acknowledgement

Grateful thanks to my family—Lynn, Aaron & Eva—for their love and support while writing the book, and Pam Hirson, for her wonderful editing voice that made the story whole.

Chapter 1

Aaron's Climb

May 14th, 2003. 12:52 pm.

"I'm sick and tired of being so goddamn cold!" Aaron exclaimed as he took another four steps, bent over his ice axe, and heaved for breath. At 29,000 feet, he was just a hundred yards from the top of the world and the lack of oxygen wreaked havoc on his senses. Besides the persistent whipping of the wind, all he could hear was the sound of his own labored breathing.

This is impossible! His head ached. The dull, throbbing pain that kept him up most of the night had become worse. *Just keep moving.* He focused on the summit. The 50th anniversary team had plowed on and was nearing the top of Everest. It was his job to photograph the event; he had to get closer. In spite of his miserable condition, he would not fail his assignment.

"Be quiet and still for a moment and listen to the world," he said out loud. His thoughts returned to his Buddhist training. He cleared his mind of everything except his breathing; calm, even breaths. Knowing the first team had reached the summit, his gloved hands fumbled for the knotted string that would unzip his wind suit, beneath which his beloved camera lay close to his hip. He pulled out the old single lens reflex Nikon, his first and favorite work camera. It was big and bulky, had an f-stop and shutter speed that was controlled manually, and it didn't require batteries. In the intense mountain cold, this camera was indispensable. More than any other piece of equipment he had, this one captured best the images that passed through the viewfinder and into the mirrors of Aaron's eyes.

Staring at the camera, Aaron realized the wrong lens was attached. He wound off several panoramic shots of the cloud-skirted peaks in the distance and then switched lenses belting the other one to his waist. A fairly large boulder lay not too far off to the left. Aaron figured it would make a perfect lean-to for him and a stabilized platform for the camera. Metal crampons crunched into crusted snow, as he walked his six-foot frame across the slope.

Despite the pounding in his head, Aaron stayed focused. The knob on top of his custom walking stick had been flattened out and a fine screw thread protruded from the top. As he leaned back against the boulder, he aligned the mounting hole in the bottom of the camera's body with the screw on top of the pole. *God this is taking forever.* Sensing little progress, he looked down and realized half way through that he had inexplicably reversed the process and began unscrewing it from the pole.

"You're pathetic," he scolded himself. "Come on, think! Righty tighty, lefty Lucy." He repeated the phrase until the camera was secured. Aaron leaned back against the waist high rock and straddled the pole between his legs; the next part would be tougher. In order to get the camera to his eye, he knew he'd have to remove his goggles and unclip his oxygen mask. The distinctive ripping of nylon loops gave way to the hissing sound of oxygen as he pulled on the Velcro strap and the mask fell away. Aaron took a deep breath and exhaled, then another, and another. *Not too bad.*

With a downward thrust he impaled the pole into the snowy ground. He grabbed his goggles, making sure to keep his eyes closed as they came off. The heavily polarized lenses had done their job, but now without the protective layer, the radiated light pierced through his eyelids. A soft painful moan escaped from his lips as he looked down and grimaced. While waiting for his eyes to transition, he reached out and grabbed the shaft.

"Now," he whispered. He came up off the boulder and stepped forward to balance himself. With eyes still closed he brought the shutter window up to his left eye. He opened it slowly, and kept the other one tightly shut. At first there was nothing but blurry snow. A quick angle adjustment brought the cluster of men standing on the summit into view. Without another thought, he shot and wound the film three times.

"Got at least three in the can. Now let's take a good look." From his viewfinder he could see the sons of Edmund Hillary and Tenzing Norgay hugging each other and congratulating the Sherpa guides who had accompanied them. Behind the climbers stood a metal tripod pole with flags fluttering from its mast. Aaron watched as members of the expedition attached objects to it. Aaron's own guide, Lopsang, had said that the Sherpas would perform a small ceremonial rite and place prayer beads along with family artifacts on the sterile aluminum flagstaff.

"For people of Nepal," Lopsang told Aaron, "Everest is 'Sagarmatha', mother goddess of Earth." Aaron pressed off several more shots. He could see that there really wasn't too much room at the top; the men had little room to maneuver. *How ironic, to have come all this way through such a vast expanse and enormous mountain range to end up clamoring for space that was probably no bigger than the top of a pool table.*

Aaron panned slowly to the right where he saw, only a short distance away, the second team. Between the two groups was the unmistakable purple-black parka'd figure of David Horton, organizer and leader of the expedition. Aaron could see Dave headed for the summit with two guides carrying the cell phone equipment. The telecommunications giant backing the trip wanted Peter Hillary to call his dad, Sir Edmund, back in New Zealand. Father and son would converse using "Telstar's" new service in Southeast Asia. Dave had constantly reminded Aaron how important that moment was and how he was expected to capture it on film.

"Get as much as you can for my magazines," Dave had said, "but get Hillary on the phone!" In all the years Aaron knew him, Dave hadn't changed one bit. But in spite of what he felt about Dave, he'd get the job done. He owed that to everyone making the climb.

After the necessary shots of the phone call, Aaron noticed a Sherpa fix his gaze down the mountain. When Aaron glanced down the Southeast Ridge, billowing cumulous clouds were heading for the summit. *This isn't good.*

The guide was alerting everyone to the danger coming their way. Through his viewfinder Aaron could see men gesturing that it was time to go, but he continued to shoot until his vision blurred and dizziness gradually overtook him. He reached for the dangling strap and settled the oxygen mask back over his nose and mouth, and then pulled on his goggles.

Hmm. Not much better. He was exhausted. Not sleeping for the last thirty hours and eating only peanut M & M's and beef jerky didn't help. *Even my hair's cold.* How long had he been above 25,000 feet? There was a reason it was called, "The Death Zone."

Aaron closed his eyes and willed himself away from where he was. He stretched his mind out of Nepal, back across continents and oceans, all the way back to California a month ago, in a bedroom with pink curtains and a small bed in the corner.

"Hello Daddy."

"Hello my little sweetheart. How are you?"

"I'm okay. Look at all the ponies I have."

"Yes, I see. You have quite a collection." The small plastic horses with doe like eyes and manes with matching nylon tails stood in front of him as he sat cross-legged on the floor. The little girl picked up one of them.

"This one's Bubble Gum, she's my favorite."

"How many do you have?" Aaron asked with genuine interest.

"Let's see, there's Bubble Gum, Angel Hair, and Buttercup." She enthusiastically named the little ponies and explained their different traits and personalities as Aaron listened intently. Hannah passed him a small brush along with one of the ponies.

"Daddy, you have to use the side of the brush for the tail."

"Wow," Aaron said, "multi functional brushes!"

"Oh Daddy, you're so funny." Hannah giggled as she got up and hugged him. By his ear she whispered, "I love you Daddy." Aaron lovingly squeezed her in return.

"Mommy says you're going to climb a mountain?" She turned and went back to her dolls.

"Yeah, a really big one. The tallest one in the whole world!"

"Can I come?"

"Oh, I really wish you could sweetheart. But the mountain is so far away it's on the other side of the world."

"I don't mind," she said in a very quiet voice. Hannah walked to the far corner of the bedroom where she pulled out a little doll. Aaron recognized the small, blue, funny looking doll that he hadn't seen in many years.

"Satchmo," she said, "wants to go, too." She handed the doll to him.

Suddenly, his head jerked in response to the whipping wind of the mountain. His eyes focused on the climbers lining themselves up on the path leading away from the summit. There was a sharp pain in his head when he came back to reality, but it vanished quickly, and along with it went the throbbing ache.

"That's better," he said as he pulled up the pole for a new shot. *Amazing.* The headache that had punished him for weeks was finally gone. *I'll finish up and get off this miserable mountain.* Adjusting slightly to the right, he noticed a climber about sixty feet away separating from the others and slowly walking toward him. It was Horton.

"What does he want?"

Aaron systematically shot and wound the film several times. He panned back to the summit and focused to shoot the items that had been left behind. Dave was getting closer and waved at him. He flipped down his goggles in disgust. "He really is one sorry son of a bitch." Aaron pushed off the boulder that had been supporting his weight and used the camera pole to straighten up. "Of all the people . . ."

A crushing spike of pain jolted the left side of his head. As his vision went black, the next jolt came. A neck spasm jerk-twisted his head to the left. With a low moan he doubled over. Blurred vision returned in his right eye, but the left saw nothing but black. As Aaron attempted to right himself, he fell forward, driving his shoulder into the ice-crusted ground followed by the whip snapping of his head against the mountain's slatty rock. He lay there, stunned.

What happened? He tried to get up. Nothing. *Am I dead?* His body was not working. He could sense the camera pole wasn't far and knew he would need it to get himself up. He managed to roll over so the boulder he had been sitting on was against his backside. After a moment to catch his breath he reached for the pole, but only the fabric of his glove touched the shaft. With his teeth, he pulled off the glove and extended his shoulder as far as it would go; he reached out and grabbed the pole. Two deep breaths, and then with great effort he attempted to lift himself.

Aaron had been physically strong all his life, but the effects of the climb had left him feebly weak. He closed his eyes and let out an anguished cry. The glove that had been in his mouth fell away. His arm bent slightly, gathering strength and with a final pull was able to bring himself up to the pole's side. He sat back against the boulder, lowered his head and brought his knees up to his chin. Quickly, he thrust his exposed hand into the wind suit's pocket and flexed his fingers inside. *At least there's feeling and movement.*

Aaron concentrated on breathing. Because his mask was off again, he had to bring in as much oxygen as possible. Positioning himself against the boulder had been a good decision. The rock was sheltering him from the accumulating wind. *Inhale, exhale. Focus. Concentrate.* The numbness on the left side of his body and the spiking pain around his eyes started to diminish. *Good. Keep breathing. Get control.*

Aaron thought he heard someone. The voice was so faint that he couldn't figure out where it was coming from. It sailed in and out of the wind. *Horton.* His mind shouted for joy. *Yes it was Dave! It must be.* With his eyes still shut, he could hear the crunching sound of boots approaching. Squinting, he could see from the shadows of his damaged retinas a figure looming over him. It was waving, beckoning Aaron to follow.

Consuming fear suddenly rose through Aaron. This apparition was not his salvation. It was death calling. *Oh God!* Aaron lowered his head once more to his knees. "That isn't Dave," he muttered. He began to rock back and forth. *Where is he? He was coming.*

Hands were pulling on his parka. He fought them off, kicking and thrashing.

"NO!" He hoarsely yelled. He flailed at the arms reaching for him and then balled up once more, gulping for air. Another attack and again Aaron repelled the monster that loomed overhead. It was close to him, shouting and cursing. Its foul breath was mixing with Aaron's own, poisoning him, and taking away his oxygen, smothering him. Aaron jerked his head back and forth. He had to get away. *Gotta get away. Run. Don't look back.* Aaron's mind propelled him; he was up and running, the wind rushing past him.

Then his fingers and toes regained their sense of numbing cold. Through his shuttered eyes he could see light. It was gray and fading like the last light after the sun had disappeared beyond the horizon.

Suddenly, he was back on Everest half buried in snow. The shrouded apparition was gone. His vision was still blurred in his left eye, but the blackness had drained away. *Where's the summit team?* He looked to his right and saw his trekking pole still planted firmly in the ground, but the camera was missing. *Who took my camera?* He stretched out his long legs and tried to get up but he couldn't move. He managed to bring his left arm to his mouth and with his teeth pulled back on the sleeve to reveal his watch. *Three-thirty. I've got to get . . .* And then it dawned on him.

Something had happened. *There was a storm. I fell. Someone tried to help.* Aaron curled his legs back up. Once more he tried to clear his mind. *Inhale, exhale. That's right, slowly.* Snow was falling; intense cyclones of white powder dancing up and down the summit ridge. His mind was slipping out of focus, like floodwater bursting through a storm damaged levy. He was alone. They had left him to die.

Chapter 2

Hank's Run

May 14th, 2003. 5:45 A.M.

AS USUAL HE increased his pace as he rounded the corner onto Osprey Drive. He sucked deeper and blew harder in response to the increased demand for air. He was half way through his daily run.

It was a 'get healthy or die' program. Jogging to slim down figured to be the least time consuming and most cost effective choice for Hank. At first, he stayed around the neighborhood, but now he was up to four miles.

Today's route had him out beyond the confines of his manicured development in suburban Orlando, and all the way over to Hunt's Creek where he helped coach his girls' soccer team. After successfully circumnavigating the enormous recreation area, he headed back to the neat rows of houses and palmetto trees.

A sprint to the driveway and then a fast-walk past his house was a cool down ritual that Hank was dependent upon. It signified his accomplishment.

"Boy, that was good." His right hand reached under his sweat soaked t-shirt where the gold crucifix hung from his neck. He tapped it twice.

"Thank you for being with me." He grabbed the newspaper from the lawn and banged it against his thigh. Time to hit the shower. As he took his sweaty body inside, the blast of cool air made him shiver. He quietly closed the door behind him.

Waking up this morning was a grumpy affair for Linda and the girls. Hank was long gone before his wife poured her first cup of coffee. And by the time she had Elisabeth and Eva ready for school, he'd already started his workday.

Hank's commute was an easy one, twelve minutes door-to-door. As senior comptroller for the Benson Hotel Resorts Group in Central Florida, it was his responsibility to reconcile the hotel accounts.

"Okay, let's see what came in last night." As he examined the screen, his right hand expertly tapped the keypad. "This looks good."

"Morning Henry," came the thick Latin American accent belonging to his assistant.

"Morning Charo," Hank responded.

"Some e-mails came in from West Palm after you left last night." West Palm was corporate headquarters for the three hotels in Orlando and a Holiday Inn Express in Texas. Hank quickly read the e-mails Charo had printed out for him. The home office never had any good news. The hotel industry, especially in Orlando, had taken a beating since 9/11. *Just keep paying the bills so I can pay mine.* He was keenly aware of the numbers and dreaded March when insurance was due, or November when property taxes were paid.

Hank decided to check out the news on Everest. He highlighted and clicked the book-marked site. There it was, the Himalayan range dotted with trekking tour, hiking gear and speaker's bureau icons. "50th Anniversary Team Succeeds," read the banner headline.

"Thank God," Hank exhaled with relief. As he read on, he thought about Aaron, his best friend and mirror opposite. There weren't many details except to report Hillary and Norgays sons' had reached the summit. Hank quickly scanned the article for other news. There was a brief description of a phone call being made, but that was it. It was Aaron he wanted to know about, to make sure he was okay.

"No bad news. That's a good thing." Hank confidently clicked out of the site and chuckled. "He gets to have all the fun while I keep the world safe for travel and tourism."

Chapter 3

Snowbound

May 14th, 4:30 pm

HYPOTHERMIA. AARON RECALLED the effects. It was, he had been told, a pleasant way to go. *Not that bad really*, he surmised. *Once the shivering stops and sleepiness sets in . . .* The wind whipped and the snow fell in wispy curtains of crystal powder, blanketing the ground in layers of white frosting. By sitting with his back against the boulder Aaron had both relief from the wind's velocity and a view of the ridge leading up to the summit. *It's so beautiful, and peaceful, too. Wish I had my camera.*

Aaron's life had always depended upon his cunning. Every one of his past near death experiences had an escape clause. "Can't wait to get back to a hot shower and warm bed," he whispered. *And a doctor, too,* he reminded himself.

What the hell happened to me? His mind was juiced with thoughts of his rescue until he commanded his legs to move, and they wouldn't. He couldn't even raise his arms. His body had failed him and so he remained right where he was, immobile in a fetal crouch. Aaron could only rock back and forth ever so slightly as the numbness of his extremities crept in. And then his fate became a crushing reality.

Alone, he thought sadly before a surreal peace settled over him. Fate had brought him here and left him to die. He visualized a moving walkway that would take him past the glass window of the universe. Eventually, he would have to step off, but for now he liked the view, and enjoyed the slow ride.

"It's so cold!" he shouted as reality returned. "Where's that bathing warm light they talk about?" He thought of the time, growing up in New England, where the winters were so cold and he'd never layer up enough. He was ten when they had the competition. Which of the neighborhood kids could build the biggest snowman? Everyone put a dollar in. The contest went on for hours as each kid's snowman grew in size and scale. It was almost dark by the time Aaron and his neighbor became the last two left. Another hour passed. In the end Aaron had won the money by outlasting his opponent. He had chosen girth over height. He kept building until his friend capitulated. Aaron's strategy won him the bet, but his hands were almost frostbitten as he stuffed the money into his coat pocket.

Now, I'm the snowman. Then, in the wind he heard children laughing and playing, and there was music. Aaron lifted his head to see the children all bundled in winter jackets with scarves, hats, and snow covered boots. Snowballs hurled through the air with all the excitement of a first winter snow.

The sound of a symphony orchestra was playing and the children's gloved hands formed a circle around him. Smiling faces glared at him as fogged breath mixed warmly with his own. With his one good hand, he reached into his pocket and pulled out the doll his daughter had given him. It was smiling too.

"Do you hear the music, Satchmo?" The happy little face looked back at Aaron and then amazingly its head turned and looked toward the summit. The children jumped up and down, and excitedly encouraged him to go toward the peak.

Once again, Aaron summoned his body to move. He staggered, pushing against the rock that had been his sheltered home. The children cheered and pressed themselves to his sides to help him move forward.

"The snowman cometh," he whispered. The music grew louder. He raised his arm allowing the doll to lead him on. His first steps were careful little movements; then quickly gave way to purposeful strides. *Am I walking?* There was movement, but no feeling. He looked at Satchmo.

"No matter, we'll go together and see what all the commotion is about."

Chapter 4

Linda's News

2 Days Later
Soccer Practice—6 pm.

PARENTS SAT ALONG the sidelines of the playing field as both boys and girls warmed up. Hank had them practice different ball skills which made his girls' team the most competitive in Orange County for "ten and unders." As he looked on, he smiled at the bobbing and weaving drills that were underway, the passing and dribbling styles that would move the ball so effortlessly up and down the field.

"That's it Elisabeth," he shouted. "Protect your ball!" Hank needed to be more encouraging to her. At ten, Eva was lanky and nimble and could keep her head up while bringing the ball down the field. Elisabeth was only seven and still working on the basics. Hank favored his younger daughter who reminded him of his own stubborn desire to keep up. As he watched the scrimmage from a flagged corner of the field, he noticed his wife's car pulling into the lot. Hank focused back on the game, but after a while looked over to see what was taking her so long. She was standing by the car and waving for him to come to her.

"Hey Jeff!" He called across the field to the other coaching assistant, as he pointed to the parking lot. "I'll be right back." Jeff gave a nod of acknowledgment and went back to the game. Hank handed his whistle to another soccer dad and started to jog toward his wife's car.

Can't she see I'm busy coaching right now? This was not like Linda at all. Once it dawned on him something was wrong, his cleats dug in. He sprinted across the grassy field and stopped just short of where Linda stood. When he saw her face, he raced to her.

"Linda?" He put his hands on her shoulders. "What's wrong?" Her eyes were very red, like she'd been crying for a while. When she looked at him the tears cascaded down her cheeks.

"It's Aaron, Hank. He's dead." Hank tried to replay what he had just heard, but it was impossible. He couldn't process it.

"Wh-at?" He looked at Linda with a hard squint. His head tilted to the side and his lips came together, slowly forming the rest of the question. "What'd you say?"

"He's dead Hank. . . Aaron's dead."

Chapter 5

The "U"

Coral Gables, Florida. 1981

HANK WALKED QUICKLY across the University of Miami campus keenly aware that the rain soaked walkway was an enemy to his flip-flop "suicide sandals." He was late for the resident advisor training session that had begun in Mahoney Hall. As he made his way past the lake he could hear Molly Hatchet's "Flirtin' With Disaster," through an open dorm window. Looking across the water he could see the metered diving platforms that towered over the aquatic center.

Directly across the lake was the Rathskeller, the school tavern. He smiled as he recalled the previous night, a "St. Pauli Girl" promo at "The Rat."

He passed the Lowe Art Museum and cut through the parking lot to the hall's entrance. The dorms on the north side of campus were very different from the '68 complex as far as residence halls were concerned. Built in the sixties, the squat seven story buildings with big windowed rooms had a floor pattern that lay out like a cross. In comparison, his dorm was one of four tower structures twelve stories high and built to house the entire freshman population.

Hank approached the conference room for the morning session.

Man, I love Mahoney. He had lived there when he first transferred from Broward Community College. Although he was happy to have gotten the resident advisor position this year, being assigned to McDonald tower wasn't what he really wanted.

As he walked through the open doors he could see the session had already started. Right away he went to the back row of seats, where he spotted a group of staff members from his residence hall.

The training session stretched on through most of the morning. Although the subject matter was crisis intervention and suicide prevention, Hank only half listened. He had a difficult time believing that anyone could become so depressed that they'd think about taking their life. According to his faith, suicide was a sin; an unfathomable action that led you down the path to Hell. Hank's life was strong on faith. It was difficult for him to imagine what depression even was.

As the session dragged on, the cross talk and whispering was getting out of control. They were losing focus.

"So who here thinks they know how to handle someone who's suicidal?" Hank looked to see who spoke. Right away he recognized the new Assistant Complex Director, Aaron Temple. He was tall, wore khaki pants with a black polo, and had blond hair.

"Does everyone here," Aaron began again, "feel they're capable of talking someone down from say, jumping off a roof?" Aaron moved to the middle of the room. "It's one thing to react to a situation where someone's been hurt. You've all had your First Aid and CPR training for that." Hank noticed that Aaron had everyone's undivided attention. He asked everyone, "But what about a situation of being there when someone's <u>about</u> to hurt himself?"

Aaron now stood directly in front of the semicircle of seventy advisors. Hank waited to see if anyone would affirm being comfortable enough to handle that kind of intervention, but no one did.

"Don't for a minute think that you won't ever get into that kind of situation as an 'R—A.'" Aaron paused for a moment. "Statistically, it's impossible for it not to happen. Factor in the freshman far away from home and family, from friends or that special someone. How many of you remember the day the girlfriend or boyfriend you've invested a lot of time in tells you it doesn't work anymore?

Or how about the expectation that you have to do well academically," Aaron continued, "but you're not. You've been partying too hard, you don't get along with your roommates, and you failed two midterms. Besides that, you've over committed yourself to athletics, student government, and Greek life."

Hank was surprised at how confident Aaron, who was not much older than any of the other students in the room, was with his presentation. Hank wished he could be half as good as this guy when it came to public speaking.

"So let's simulate," Aaron continued, "or imagine if you will, a scene that involves a student and an 'R—A' in a crisis situation." Aaron turned back to the dorm administrators and made a motion for help. Several got up from their chairs and proceeded to take instructions from him to move different pieces of furniture around the room. As the chairs and tables were being scuffed along the floor, the seated resident advisors began to talk amongst themselves.

"You!" Aaron's voice rang out from the middle of the room. His arm, hand and index finger fully extended. Hank's smile disappeared.

Oh no, he contemplated with dread. "Perhaps you can assist me in this little exercise?" Aaron had a ring announcer's smile on his face.

Shit!! Hank thought as he slowly rose from his chair.

The staff members whistled and cheered him on as he made his way to the center of the conference room. Anyone who had to "volunteer" for these types of role model scenarios were often taunted by those fortunate enough not to have been picked. Aaron's eyes stayed locked on him until they stood face to face. Aaron smiled as he shook Hank's hand.

"Your name?"

"Henry Longo."

"Ever done any acting before Henry?"

"I was in my high school production of 'Godspell'," Hank responded.

"Really? What part did you play?" Going for a laugh, Hank deadpanned, "Christ". Laughter came from the assembled crowd, but Aaron simply leaned closer and in a lower voice said, "Listen to what I say and follow my lead. After this, everyone's going to think you can walk on water as well."

"Great! Okay everyone, what you're going to see is a situation that quickly develops into an intervention. Now imagine if you will that we've set up a rooftop. It's McDonald Tower. Henry here is on duty and has just received a report that the stairwell door to the roof is open so he's going up to secure it." Hank sees Aaron gesturing to him to leave the conference room and wait in the hall. He gets to the door, but before going out, stops and listens to the rest of Aaron's presentation to the group.

"Now because the door is open, Henry here decides to take a look at the stars. At first he doesn't see the student who's stepping up onto the corner of the retaining wall." Hank watches, along with everyone else, as Aaron climbs up onto chairs that have been placed with several others on top of a conference table.

"Now," he continues, "imagine as hard as you can that we're all on the roof of McDonald Tower. It's late, and there is a young man who is contemplating ending his life." Aaron turned his back to everyone and yelled, "Okay Henry! Anytime."

Hank pushed the crash bar handle to the metal door and stepped out of the room. He allowed the door to close and was about to go right back in when he stopped. He froze with the consuming thought that he had no idea what to say. Hank's face reddened. *I'm going to make a complete ass of myself.* The "Assistant" Complex Director had picked him out because he was not paying attention and was now going to be made an example of in front of his peers. *This isn't fair.* He did not like being embarrassed, especially in front of the people he considered his friends.

At that moment, he decided to play it for a laugh. He was not going to be made a fool of. *I'll put this guy in his place.*

Hank pushed through the door and came back into the room. He could see his fellow resident advisors smiling so he knew right away they were not taking this very seriously. Most everyone on the staff knew that Hank had a good sense of humor and enjoyed the role of jokester. He liked being a comedian. It was his turn to make people laugh.

He started off with a little song to himself. "I know a girl, her name is Lori. Hey la-di-la-di-da." He hummed the second verse, as it was extremely vulgar and not meant for mixed company. Most of the staff had seen the comedian John Valby perform the song and many of his other "dirty ditties" at the Rathskeller a few nights ago and laughed at Hank's clever improvisation. Then, he looked up at the ceiling. "Beautiful night." He took a step and suddenly fell forward, pretending to have tripped over something. Looking back at the imaginary object, he quietly muttered an obscenity under his breath, audible just enough for most in the audience to hear. More laughter. He moved to the center of the room and focused on Aaron who was fairly high up and had his back to him. Aaron's arms were stretched out and fingers spread wide in a crucifixion-like pose.

"Hey buddy," Hank said, "you're not supposed to . . ."

"Don't come any closer," came Aaron's quiet response.

"Hey man, you need to come down from there. You could fall." Hank moved toward Aaron. The "slap-slap" of his sandals was the only thing heard in the now quiet room. Aaron turned around and shouted.

"Are you deaf asshole? I said don't come any fucking closer!" And then he begged, "Please." And with that, Aaron turned back again.

Hank was floored. He could sense that the audience was as well. It was not just the sudden burst of anger and profanity that had gotten both his and everyone's attention. What was remarkable was that Aaron had tears running down his face. He was genuinely crying. *How did he manage to do that?* Right then he knew that this play-acting exercise was not going to be a joking matter. He raised his arms up and opened out his hands.

"Okay, okay, I promise I won't come any closer. Okay?" It was the only thing Hank could think to say.

"Good." Aaron said in a much quieter voice. But then the anger in his voice returned. "Because if you do, I'm going to fucking jump! I'll do it. Don't you fucking think for a moment I won't."

There was a long pause. Hank was dumbfounded. A small part of him wanted to laugh at what Aaron was portraying, but a swift glance at the audience had him quickly conclude that the entire residential staff was into this unfolding drama. Even worse, the female members of his staff, some of whom he lusted after, were staring right at him. No one was smiling. Hank could feel their thoughts. "*Now what are you going to do, asshole?*" He looked back toward Aaron.

"Look, why don't you come down from there, okay? We'll talk."

"I'm staying right here," came the terse reply.

"Look. Whatever it is, it's not worth dying for."

Aaron turned to Hank. His face was contorted with anger. He raised his voice again.

"What the fuck do you know about worth, huh? You don't know what I've been through. Shit! You don't even know my name."

Although Hank was clueless, he remembered Aaron's instruction to him; listen and follow my lead.

"Okay. What's your name?"

"Aaron. Aaron Temple."

"Well my name's Henry. Henry Longo. My friends call me Hank."

"That's nice—Henry!"

"Do you go by a nickname? Or is it just Aaron."

"At home, they call me Aaron."

Okay, we're getting somewhere.

"And where is home for you . . . Aaron."

"Pennsylvania. Shamokin, Pennsylvania."

"Wow. That's a long way from here. I bet you miss home, huh?"

"That's a good one," Aaron said sarcastically. "You ever been to Shamokin? It's the shit hole of the universe. And so are the people who live there." After an audible sigh he added, "Oh God, I'm tired. I don't want to do this anymore." Aaron's body slumped. Hank could tell from the way Aaron casually lifted his head and gazed at him that it was time to make another suggestion.

"Well if you're tired Aaron, why don't you take a little rest. Why don't you come down from that ledge there and . . ."

"I can't believe I drank all that vodka. Fuck, I'm so shit faced." Hank realized that Aaron was leading him. *Damn! That's what I should have thought to ask next.* He had no choice but to press on.

"All the more reason to get down from there. You could lose your balance." Hank took two small steps forward. Suddenly, Aaron was erect and pointed a finger at him.

"I said don't come any closer. I'm warning you." Hank put his hands out once again. "I'm not, I'm not." He had a sudden burst of inspiration.

"Look, it's just that I'm tired, too. I just want to talk to you, but I need to sit down, okay?" He pointed to the other two chairs that were also on the table. "I'll tell you what. Why don't I sit right here and you can sit right there. Right on the ledge, okay?" There was a pause. "So Aaron. You're a freshman here at UM?"

"Yes."

"But you're obviously not very happy to be here."

"Obviously."

"Would you rather be home?"

"Nope."

"What school are you in?"

"Marine Science."

"Whoa. That's a pretty tough program."

"No kidding Sherlock," Aaron said angrily. "And it sure doesn't help that two weeks into classes my grandfather . . ." Aaron sunk his head into his knees and cried. *Unbelievable, he's not crying, he's sobbing!* Even more amazed, he could hear a few sniffles coming from the audience.

"Your grandfather died?"

"Yes. I missed almost two weeks of classes. I haven't been able to catch up."

"Have you gone to Dean Starks and explained the situation?"

"I don't come from a family that makes excuses. My mom and dad are paying a lot of money for me to come here. I can't fail them. I can't!"

"You're not going to fail. You can get help."

"Yeah, I suppose so. But what about this?" Aaron reached behind himself and pulled an envelope from his back pocket. His crying had ceased and was now replaced with a sullen expression.

"A letter? Who's it from?"

"My girlfriend. Wanna read it?"

"Well uh . . ." Hank was confused. Aaron nodded at him. It was a cue for him to do something. "How about I sit next to you and you can read it to me. It's kind of personal, isn't it?" Aaron stared blankly at Hank. He was pinching the envelope between his thumb and forefinger, allowing it to play back and forth.

"I don't want to read it," Aaron said. "You read it." He dropped it onto the table beneath the chairs. Capitalizing on an unexpected idea, Hank quickly said, "Actually, I'm kind of freezing up here on the ledge. Let's get out of the wind." Without waiting for a response, Hank dropped himself cross legged onto the table top.

Aaron slowly got down from the chair and sat next to Hank. He placed his feet on the table and brought his knees up to his chest.

"Go ahead, read it. It's a barrel of laughs." Hank pulled out a sheet of stationary from the envelope. He was surprised to find an actual letter written on floral stationary. It was written in cursive and addressed to Aaron. He took a moment to scan through the note and then read out loud.

"Dear Aaron,

It's difficult for me to tell you that you should hold off on the planned visit to Atlanta to see me. I've been overwhelmed with schoolwork since I started the nursing program here at Emory. I must also tell you that I'm contemplating not going home for Thanksgiving and instead, I plan to stay with my grandparents who you know live not far from the university. I am amazed at how much my life has changed since coming here. I feel like a totally different person. I'm sure you do, too." Hank wanted to stop, but Aaron nudged his shoulder to continue. "I know we said that the love we have for each other would last through this long separation. You know that since our junior year I have always held a special place for you in my heart, and always will . . .'"

"You can stop there," Aaron said dejectedly. Hank put the letter back in the envelope and handed it back to him. Aaron began wiping away the tears from his eyes. A remarkable silence followed. The two of them looked out at their audience. *Oh man, now what do I say?* This was the moment where Hank was supposed to advise this pathetic character that Aaron had made pretty realistic. He too had been the recipient of a couple of 'Dear John' letters over the years. They were tough to overcome.

"Hey man, you'll rebound," Hank finally said. "We all do." Aaron chuckled.

"That's easy for you to say. You ever been pissed on like that?" Aaron looked down at the letter.

"Man, I loved her! We've been together for two years. Two years! Junior and senior prom, vacations at my folks' place out on Cape Cod. I had so much invested in her." Aaron brought the letter up to his eyes. "And this is all that's left." He looked at Hank. Once again, he knew he had to say something, but Aaron's little testimony had struck a nerve. All of a sudden, he didn't want to talk.

"So, you've been dumped too?"

"Yes, I have," Hank said quietly.

"So there you go. You know as well," Aaron said, somewhat triumphantly. Hank locked eyes with Aaron.

"Look man, you've had a lot of bad luck."

"Sometimes I think God's smacked a bull's eye right onto my forehead."

"Nobody's trying to punish you man. It's just you doing it to yourself. Shit happens! You gotta suck it up and move on." *Shit happens?* Hank contemplated this sage advice. *Great! Just great. My wonderful theory of life on this planet.* Hank noticed Aaron blankly staring at him. *I should say something.*

"Really?" Aaron finally said. "That's it? Your theory of life?" Aaron looked out at the staff and rolled his eyes. Laughter broke out everywhere. For Hank, it was the moment he needed to assemble his dignity. He did not mind the laughter. It was good-natured. There were head nods and confirmation by his peers that he was on to something. Hank hopped off the table. The mood had lightened and it prompted him to add depth to his fall back wisdom.

"Look. What I meant to say is that we all have a plan. Every one of us does. We set goals; we focus on the big picture. We're always trying to win the big game." Hank was talking to Aaron and using the room in front of the table to walk in a circle. "I think life is like driving down an open highway. All you want to do is just cruise in the fast lane. So each of us is traveling down our own personal highway and it's a nice, smooth ride. But even the straightest road is going to have obstacles that'll slow you down."

"Like what?"

"Like . . . rush hour traffic, or maybe an accident. Hell, sometimes it's so bad you have to get off the highway and detour around the problem. But you'll do it; you'll find an alternate route. Do you know why?" Aaron looked at Hank and shook his head. "Because it's your road of life! It's your personal destiny. The road keeps on going, for as long as you can imagine.

You have to have faith that there's a lot more for you to see and more things for you to do along the way before," Hank's voice trailed off.

"Before what?" Aaron asked.

"Before you run out of gas." A ripple of laughter ran across the room. Both Hank and Aaron ignored it. "Look," Hank continued, "right now I'd say you've got engine trouble."

"But it's a brand new car!"

"You're still under warranty. It can be fixed. Trust me."

"So what am I driving?" Huge laughter erupted from the gathered staffs.

"You're driving a Trans Am. Sleek. Black. You look great in it. Right now all that's happened to you is you've had a blow out—maybe a couple of blowouts, and the radiator has overheated. But the road hasn't ended, not for you anyway. Not now. You've got to get the tires fixed and continue on. I can tell that you've had some bad breaks, but listen; you didn't cause the accident! Find a way to get going again. Get yourself back up to seventy-five miles an hour. Just past the breakdown are the good grades you've got to drive to. Up the road ahead is graduation and the job that you want. At the next overpass is another girlfriend that will be even greater than the one that's left behind. Hey man, you're driving a Z-28 with the T-Tops off. The girls will be lining up!"

To Hank's amazement, there was laughter and applause. Aaron had been curled up with his head between his knees. Now, there was a smile on his face. Hank knew he had done a good job.

"I've got to tell you," he said as he stuck out his arm in a gesture to let Hank pull him off the table. "I thought I was too far gone." Aaron turned to look at the imaginary ledge he had been standing on. "But you brought me back." He turned back to his scene partner and looked straight into his eyes. "Thanks . . . Hank."

"C'mon," Hank said. "Let's get out of here. I know a lot of better places than on the roof of McDonald Tower." The two of them exited the scene amidst a roomful of applause. "By the way," Hank said loud enough for everyone in the room to hear, "how did you get up here? That door is always locked." Hank could see that he had caught Aaron off guard. He stumbled for something to say.

"I . . . I don't know. It was just open I guess."

"Really? I think I'd better write an administrative report." Hank looked over in the general direction of the '68 staff. A sly smile emerged. "There are certain staff members who have been reported using their master keys to get up here to work on their tans." He didn't have to say anymore as the two of them looked in the direction of a couple of '68's female staff members seated together, Tracy and her friend Lauren. The two lowered their heads and turned guilty red as a heckling chorus of whistles and jeers descended upon them. They both heard the applause as they passed through the door and into the hallway. When the door closed and they were alone, Aaron said, "Hey I liked your analogy, the highway and driving stuff."

"Thanks."

"Just to let you know if it were me, the car would be a '67 Bonneville, convertible. That Trans Am you had me driving? A piece of junk." As they were about to go back in, Hank asked, "Did you really have to deal with this?"

"Yeah," said Aaron. "But my scenario didn't turn out as good as yours." Aaron then mimed a person diving. His shoulders slumped; he sighed and gave Hank a totally blank stare. Hank's jaw dropped.

Oh my God, he actually saw someone kill himself! Aaron's eyes widened and he broke into a huge grin.

"Just kidding!" He laughed and then went quickly through the door and back into the conference room, leaving Hank standing there.

"Okay," Aaron said to the assembled staff as he strode in, "who can tell me what's the first thing to do with a crisis intervention?" Hank watched from the doorway as Aaron once again had everyone's undivided attention. Although he was a little embarrassed that this guy had fooled him so easily, he was intrigued that Aaron could go so quickly from fooling around to so amazingly serious.

"Henry?" Aaron was summoning him. "You want to come back in here for a minute?" Hank started to walk back in. "Henry Longo ladies and gentlemen," Aaron announced. "Let's thank him for his fine effort." And with that Aaron began clapping and encouraged the audience. The enthusiastic response from everyone made Hank grin. He felt good, especially when he looked at his own staff that were clapping, whistling and stamping their feet. He walked over to where Aaron was and they shook hands.

"Now what Henry did right," Aaron said to the admiring audience, "was he listened and he used words, not action, to talk the distressed student down from the ledge. When in crisis, people are overwhelmed by the things they can't control. They need a shoulder to cry on so they can find a way to process what's going on. As difficult as it seems to envision, Hank controlled the situation by letting me be in control. He talked to me, but he also let me talk. And, he listened. Most people who become depressed have no one to talk too. So being a good listener is especially important." Aaron turned to him. "Thank you Hank. You can have a seat."

*   *   *

"We've got a pretty diverse staff," Hank said to Ira as he passed the maintenance reports they were filing at their dormitory's front desk.

"I think bizarre is more accurate." Hank had gotten to know Ira, the junior from Boston, during training week. He was a bit odd looking, but a real brainiac.

"My point is," Ira continued, "if you embrace the philosophy of the residential life programs, dorm staff should be composed of various students with different backgrounds." Ira took a long pull from his beer. "But there are a lot of things about many of us here that are under the radar, so to speak. Put it all together and it certainly makes us at the very least unique."

"Okay," said Hank. "Who do you think on our staff is odd?"

"Well, we all are really. I mean where should I start?" Ira reached into the Doritos bag to grab another handful.

"What about the girls on the staff? Are they all weird?"

"Well not weird per se," Ira said as he munched. "But certainly not normal."

"What about Lauren and Tracy?" Ira looked sideways at Hank and allowed his eyebrows to furrow.

"Well they are definitely of the West Nashville grand ballroom gown characterization, don't you think?" Hank nodded his agreement, before asking, "So what's strange about me?" Ira gave Hank a quizzical look.

"You're weird because you get along with everyone. You're like one of those guys where half a dozen cliques could develop on this staff and you'd be welcome in every one of them." Ira had an afterthought.

"Hell you're Italian, I'm a Kike, and you're even friends with me!"

"What are you saying? You're easy to get along with?"

"No. I'm a Jew from Boston. And I'm a Yankee fan as well. I mean come on! What the hell am I doing at the University of Miami, in Coral Gables no less? You want to know something? I am the only member of the Berkow family in the sunshine state. I don't have a single relative who is retired or lives down here. Now that's odd, don't you think? You know I got into Brown? And Dartmouth."

"So what are you doing here? Those are great schools."

"Because of the women, Hank! Do you think for one moment that the girls at an Ivy League school even compare with the girls here at UM?" Hank looked at Ira and realized that he was dead serious. He would have followed up on that thought but Al Sampson, the advisor from the seventh floor, came out from the elevator with a large duffel bag.

"See you guys Monday. I've got R.O.T.C. all weekend."

The 12th floor resident advisors Tracy Bishop and Dave Horton entered through the lobby's main doors while Al exited. They had been out jogging.

"How's the desk clean up going?" Tracy asked Hank.

"Pretty good."

"Great. I'll change and be right back."

"Can I watch?" Dave asked lasciviously. Tracy gave a short sarcastic laugh and walked away. Aaron came into the lobby from the hallway that led down to his apartment. Hank watched as Aaron chugged a beer and walked over to the trash can that was by the entrance. He tossed the can and then pushed the crash bar to the middle door and stepped out onto the concrete deck that overlooked the lake and the north campus. Hank followed him outside.

By the time he got there, Aaron had lit a cigarette and was sitting on the steps that led down to the concrete walkway. He was gazing at the evening sky.

"Hey," Hank said casually. He sat down next to Aaron. "I didn't know you smoked."

"Yeah well, not that often. Takes me a month to smoke a pack. You want one?"

"No, thanks." Hank shook his head and waved off the red-topped box Aaron was offering.

"I tried once and almost choked to death." Aaron withdrew the pack and continued to stare out at the lake.

"It's pretty dumb. Actually, I really don't smoke all that much, but after drinking I get a hankering for one." He took another drag and then dropped the butt between his feet, stamping out the burning end. "Man, it's so beautiful here." Hank looked out as well.

"Yeah it's a great campus."

"No, I mean the whole place," Aaron said. "Florida. I never knew it was like this." Hank looked around. The Brazilian palms swayed in the breeze as their leafy branches rustled in the wind.

"Feels like rain again," said Hank. He noticed that the sidewalks were still wet from the last downpour.

"That's what amazes me," said Aaron. "The rain here comes fast and the squalls are so powerful." He waved his hand at the sky. "Up where I'm from in Connecticut, it doesn't rain like this. When it rains, it rains! A front comes in and it rains all day. Sometimes it'll rain for a couple of days. Here it just comes and goes."

"Tryin' to reason with the hurricane season," Hank said smiling. "I've lived here my whole life, so I'm used to it."

"Well, I'm already loving it," Aaron finished off by standing up and brushing off his backside. He offered Hank a hand up. "Hey, you did a nice job handling that suicide workshop."

As he took Aaron's hand to help him up, he gave him a caustic look. "Yeah, thanks for picking me out of the crowd."

"For some reason you stood out," Aaron said good-naturedly. "You looked like a guy that could be a bit of a trouble maker, so I figured I'd take care of you right away." Hank was incredulous.

"A trouble maker? Me? That's ridiculous!" Aaron turned back to Hank and laughed.

"Hank. I'm just kidding. But really, you did a good job."

"Thanks." Hank was happy about Aaron's compliment. He wanted to add his own. "I have to say, you made it very believable."

"Yeah, well. I guess that's the actor in me."

"You were pretty convincing. So, you really dealt with that, huh?" Aaron stuck his hands in his pockets and gave Hank a pained look.

"Similar."

"What happened?"

"It wasn't on a roof," Aaron began, "it was a window. And it was only on the third floor of the building, so if he had jumped, chances are he would have only broken an arm or leg." Aaron paused to reflect. "He was a freshman on my floor. He got caught by other floor members jerking off in the shower." Hank grimaced. "They ridiculed him unmercifully. He was a fat kid and he just had a lot of shit he was trying to deal with."

"So he wanted to commit suicide because he was humiliated?"

"Actually," said Aaron, "I found out after talking to him that he wanted to fall out the window and hope that the floor members would get blamed for it. He was very immature."

"So what happened?" Hank found the story fascinating.

"I was alerted about what was happening, I got to his room, there were seven guys there, including his roommate. They were egging him on. He's crying hysterically, and they're shouting 'Jump! Jump Diddler, JUMP!!'"

Hank put his hands up to his mouth and groaned. He had heard of nightmare situations resident advisors had to deal with. This was definitely one of them.

"I got everyone out of the room and closed the door. I talked him off the window sill and then listened while he talked for close to four hours! He had a lot of problems: sex, broken family, money for school. In the end I got him out of there. Student Life got him housing off campus."

"Phew," said Hank. "Close one."

"Yeah, and you know what? In spite of all that bullshit, he ended up graduating. We've even kept in touch."

"Nice."

"Speaking of nice." Aaron waved Hank over to the door. Peering in they had a perfect view of Tracy's posterior bent over.

"You know . . ." they said simultaneously. Hank and Aaron looked at each other and broke out laughing. They both knew they had been thinking the same thing.

"Tracy's pretty awesome to look at."

"Yeah," said Hank.

"Is she seeing anyone?" Aaron's question had a degree of hope in it.

"I don't think so," Hank said casually. "Last year she had some guy back in Tennessee, but I think it ended over the summer."

"Mmm," Aaron said in contemplation.

"Tracy's a campus queen. I know that Dave's had a hard-on for her since they were freshmen. I doubt she'd go out with him though." Hank reached for the door. As he opened it, he could feel a cool air-conditioned breeze envelope him. "Ahh! That's better. You coming back in here nature boy?"

"Lead on MacDuff!" Hank pushed the door hard enough so that Aaron could catch it on his way in. Hank liked this guy. He hoped the new found friendship that had started would continue.

Chapter 6

Getting to Connecticut

TEN DAYS HAD passed since the dreadful news. Hank took the first morning non-stop to New York for Aaron's memorial service. Despite the early departure, the plane was packed, but he still managed to grab a window seat. All he wanted to do was sit with his thoughts, and avoid the typical in-flight conversations.

As the plane lifted off, his attention drifted back to Linda and the day she brought the news.

"They've made a mistake," he told her. "Aaron wouldn't let it happen." When he managed to track down Aaron's cousin, Hank learned Outdoor Magazine, who Aaron was employed by, had called with the news. Initially, what was posted on the website was accurate, but after the team's successful arrival on the summit, an unexpected storm struck high on the mountain. The story that followed was that communication was cut off, but fortunately many of the climbers were able to descend to a lower camp and wait out the storm. When it ended and communication was re-established, three people were reported missing. Miraculously, two men walked into the camp the next day. One was an expert climber who knew how to get out of the wind and freezing cold; they dug a snow cave and spent the night huddled together.

"Did you get the name of the person at the magazine?" Hank asked.

"It was the wife of the owner of the parent publishing company," the cousin replied. "Her husband was on the expedition and he was one of the men who survived the night in the snow cave."

Why wasn't Aaron in that snow cave, too? Hank wondered, as soon as he'd hung up. He leafed through the pages of his address book and noticed some names from college days. Correspondence with many of them had whittled down to the annual Christmas greeting. Quite a few jutted out as friends who also knew Aaron. *I guess I'll have to tell them?* Anxious to make a call, he opened to Dave and Tracy Horton's number in D.C. *Tracy would know for sure.* That was his thought, and then he dreaded having to make the call.

The phone rang four times before the answering machine kicked in. As he started to talk, there was a click, and then Tracy's voice came on the line.

"Hank? It's me."

"Tracy?" Hank stood as he listened to the tearful account of what had happened. Tracy had said that Aaron had been lost very high up, close to the top. She'd spoken to Dave from the hospital in Katmandu, where he was recovering from severe frostbite in his extremities.

"Dave told me he was dead when he found him. He had to leave him there." Tracy gulped for air as she broke off. He was well aware of the history she had with both men, the one she had been in love with many years ago and the one she was with today.

"Tracy?"

"I'm sorry, Hank. It's just that . . ."

"You don't have to apologize," Hank said reassuringly. As Tracy brought life to the painful story, it slowly sank in. His buddy for over twenty years, his partner in crime, godfather to Elisabeth; his lifesaving, soul bearing, hell-raising brother-friend, had perished up on Mount Everest.

After the calls, Linda tried her best to comfort him, but her own sadness prevented it. There were hugs and words of solace, but it was Linda who did all the crying.

Linda recounted the story of Aaron dating one of her college friends.

"It was because of Aaron we met." He had set them up on a blind date. Hank and Linda talked quietly about it. Then, spent, Linda finally fell asleep. Hank gently covered her with the extra blanket and headed back to the computer. He wondered why he wasn't crying too.

The internet information Hank pursued most of the night was vague and incomplete. As his fingers tapped the keyboard and his right hand pointed and clicked through the maze of pop up windows and web portals, his anger festered. *How could Aaron . . .* Hank couldn't finish the first thought before the next popped in.

WHY?

As Hank stared out from the window of the plane, he thought about how he would spend the day going from plane to train to whatever transportation he needed to get to Holy Trinity Church in Westport, Connecticut. The home of Aaron's boyhood ties.

"Something to drink?" Hank turned his head from the window. He had absentmindedly lowered his chair tray and now the flight attendant had thrown down a napkin and waited for a response.

"Thank you. Tomato juice, please." Hank accepted the plastic cup and acknowledged the attendant with a polite nod. As he sipped the juice, he replayed the frail voice of Aaron's mother over the phone.

"Henry?"

"Yes. Eileen? Oh my God, are you okay?"

"Yes dear. It's just that they gave me a lot of pills and told me to take it nice and slow."

"Eileen, I can't believe what's happened. I'm so sorry for your loss." There was a pause on the line.

"Henry? There's going to be a service for Aaron this weekend. Saturday I believe. I hope you can come." Hank was stunned. *She had just found out Aaron had been killed and she was already putting together the funeral?*

"Yes, yes of course. Are you sure you've given yourself enough time? I can imagine there's a lot to do."

"I have plenty of help dear. No need to worry. It will be at three o'clock," she said. "I do hope you can be here, Henry, I'd love to see you. You know you were Aaron's best friend."

"Of course I'll be there." There was a pause on the line, then another voice.

"Mister Longo? This is Emily Peterson. Mrs. Temple is getting along fine. I'm helping her with all the arrangements so there's no need to worry about a thing. You have my sincerest regrets for your loss." Hank could imagine that Emily was a young, entry-level office wonk Dave's company sent to handle Eileen's needs.

"Yes," Hank said. "We're all stunned. As a matter of fact, it seems that things are moving *very* quickly, Miss Peterson."

"Please, call me Emily."

"Yes well, I'm concerned that many of Aaron's friends and associates won't have enough time to make it to the service."

"Ibis Publishing is indebted to the Temple family for the great work Aaron has done." There was a change in Emily's voice. She spoke in a quieter, lower tone. "Although a tragic loss, of which the publisher cannot be held responsible, we none the less want to do our part in helping the family transition through this difficult time."

Oh my God, she's a lawyer. The image of a young staff member trying to help Eileen organize everything was now replaced by the corporation's desire to send in personnel to expeditiously wrap things up. Its demonstration of "helping" could be a hedge bet to evade the possibility of future litigation.

"What about the body? Are you going to retrieve it in time?"

"There won't be a body."

"What?" Hank suddenly recalled Aaron's profound thoughts on dying and spiritual transcendence. Personally, Hank hadn't given any thought about dying, but Aaron obviously had.

"No we only have a memorial planned," she said calmly. "There is absolutely no hope of recovering Aaron Temple's remains."

"That's unacceptable Emily! My friend needs to be brought home. Regardless of how costly it is, Ibis should pay the expense to have . . ."

"It's not about money," she said interrupting. "It's logistics. Your friend's remains are too high up for anyone to retrieve. Mount Everest is the final resting place for over a hundred people Mister Longo." Hank heard her pause and then she said with finality, "Everyone who climbs that mountain knows that if you die up there, you stay up there."

*　*　*

The plane landed at La Guardia on time. After retrieving his overnight bag, Hank followed the signs for ground transportation. Passing through the sliding doors to the outside waiting area, Hank breathed deeply and quickly noticed the change in the weather. It was a late spring in New York. The air's warmth blew in a mild breeze. Hank looked at the sun. It lacked the intensity he had come to know from all the years he had lived in Florida. Here it was springtime. *It's so gentle*, Hank thought.

He boarded a bus to Grand Central Station. As he stepped off and grabbed his bag, he looked up at the towering buildings that rose up around the train station. New York City was a sea of taxi-cabs, granite buildings, barricaded sidewalks and steel bar construction staging. Advertising was plastered everywhere.

As Hank entered Grand Central Station, he marveled at the vast dimensions of the place. It was loud and cacophonous, but the noise dissipated as he looked up at the sky blue ceiling with its zodiac drawn constellations. The egg shaped chandeliers complimented the streaming sunlight that poured through the huge ornate windows at both ends. Hank looked around at everyone hustling to different tracks. *We're all going somewhere.* He bought a Metro North ticket and made his way through the masses toward track 23.

The taxi pulled away from the station and headed for the bridge which took him across the Saugatuck River. *Man that's a lot of yellow,* he thought to himself as he noticed the abundance of Forsythia.

"It's a bedroom town. Everyone's dad worked in the city. We all graduated and went off to college. I didn't want to go back," he remembered Aaron stating.

"My home town's become a mall without a roof." Hank looked out from the taxi window and counted the number of boutique type retail stores.

"Amazing," he said quietly. Hank was dropped off on Myrtle Avenue across from the Episcopal Church. He watched as people walked along the sidewalk and up the granite steps to the church's main entrance. The house of worship was a large smooth-walled stone building. Its steeple stretched along the left hand side of the three-story Rectory. Swallowing hard, Hank crossed the street and approached the steps to the church, where he didn't recognize a single face.

Hank looked over the sparse crowd spread wide throughout the large seating area. It was depressing to see so few people. *There are probably a hundred people here, but it looks so empty because the place looks like it could hold a thousand.* Hank walked down the center aisle and decided to go to the left, down a long unoccupied pew. His church upbringing had him bow and quickly genuflect before turning and finding a place to sit down on the crimson velvet cushioned bench. Once seated, he looked around. Holy Trinity had huge stained glass windows on both sides of the great hall. A tall, lit candle was prominently located at the end of the center aisle, down in front of the choir area between the lectern and pulpit. Fresnel lighting from high in the roof gave the sanctuary bright illumination. Flowers and candles adorned the Alter. Hank spotted Aaron's mom, Eileen down in front, just to the right of the center aisle. Hank had no doubt that the young woman next to her was the lawyer, Peterson. Hank continued to scan the room until he spotted the two men wearing yarmulkes. The taller of the two, he knew was Ira Berkow, from college.

The service was about to begin. Hank looked back again at Ira, hoping that he would notice him. He had traveled thirteen hundred miles to get to this emotional event and he preferred not to be alone. Amazingly, his little prayer was answered. As Ira finished talking to his companion, he leaned back, and glanced straight at Hank. Even though they had not seen each other for many years, Ira quickly smiled and gave Hank a wave of his hand. He turned his head back to the pulpit to hear the minister's words. After a brief moment though, Hank saw Ira reach up and rub his eyes.

Hank dutifully listened to the minister's opening anthem. He had hoped that the start of the ceremony would generate an emotional outpouring he'd been waiting for. But it didn't come. A friend of Eileen's read from the Old Testament, Isaiah 25:7.

"He will destroy on this mountain the face of the covering cast over all people. He will swallow up death in victory . . ."

The congregation read Psalm 90 with the same relevance: " . . . before the mountains were brought forth, or ever the earth and the world were made, Thou art God from everlasting, and world without end." With the reading, Hank emotionally simmered down. He found comfort in the words from the Bible. Now, sitting again in a church sanctuary, like he had as a dutiful child with his family, his faith drew him close once more. *In the end there will be some answer to all of this. No matter what, I'll find it.*

The minister stepped up to read from the Gospel. He read from the Book of John.

"I am the resurrection and the life: he that believeth in me, though he were dead. Yet shall he live: And whosoever liveth and believeth in me shall never die."

Hank had remembered that passage. He also knew that there was one more line in chapter 11, verse 26: "Believest thou this?" *Did Aaron?* Hank became lost in thought as the sermon continued. He was quite aware that Aaron's spirituality was based more on Buddhist teachings than Christian to start off with. In fact, Hank recalled, Aaron had promoted many long-winded, one-sided conversations about his spiritual beliefs. He continually harped on the concept that life was ongoing, that he not only would live again, but had actually lived before as well. Unlike Hank, whose faith in everlasting life was tied into the understanding and acceptance of Christ's saving powers, Aaron believed he was in a state of constant spiritual transcendence that would one day lead him to something he called "complete awareness."

Hank recalled conversations where he and Aaron had discussed reincarnation.

"The man thought he was born before and would be born again," he said quietly to himself.

The minister delivered kind words to the small gathering of family members, friends and associates. The Reverend spoke about Aaron as if he knew him well.

Hank assumed that Eileen was an active participant in this church and therefore entitled to receive a kind and thoughtful pastoral service. The

Lord's Prayer was spoken. Hank knew that since there was no body, The Commendation and Committal would not be done. Hank picked up the Book of Common Prayer and read through the rite. He recited to himself the words he felt were significantly absent from today's program. When he replaced the book to the slotted space reserved for the hymnal and the Book of Common Prayer, the Reverend was giving The Dismissal:

"Almighty God, Father of mercies and giver of all comfort: Deal graciously, we pray thee, with all those who mourn, that casting every care on thee, they may know the consolation of thy love; through Jesus Christ our Lord. *Amen.*" Hank reached up and touched the cross that hung around his neck.

"Please help me." He closed his eyes wanting to pray, but was suddenly inspired in remembering Aaron's enthusiasm for meditation.

"Just think of nothing," he'd said. "It's the best way to clear your mind and get your head on straight." Hank decided to do that and slowly managed to push away the depression that wanted to wrap its arms around him. After a while he opened his eyes and felt like he had successfully staved off the assaulting emptiness. Guests were still milling about at the entrance to the church. And Hank was now ready to move onto the reception at the Temple house.

Chapter 7

The Reception

THE TRIP FROM the church to the house was a short one. Hank shared a ride with Geoffrey Bradstock, an English gentleman Aaron had done civil war coverage with in Africa.

"We were in Namibia. Bloody awful uprising. A lot of tribal ethnic cleansing. Our man's photos were brilliant."

"When was the last time you saw him?" Hank asked.

"Quite a while ago. You see I rather enjoyed working with him. But when we were on assignment he would take risks that were, to say the least, unnerving. As I, shall we say, matured, I became much more risk adverse. Aaron was just the opposite. So naturally, over time, our paths crossed less and less. I do remember telling him, years ago, that I thought his 'damn the torpedoes' lifestyle would eventually do him in. Sadly, my prediction has become a reality."

Hank nodded in agreement. Aaron had lived his life with reckless abandon. But he also knew that before leaving for Nepal, Aaron was taking an account of his life. And for the first time ever, was looking at his future.

After parking the car they said their goodbyes and entered the house separately. As trays of food were laid out buffet style, Hank noticed Ira through the sliding glass door, just beyond the dining table. He stepped outside onto the redwood deck.

"Ira."

"Ah, there you are." There was a dramatic hug between them. When they let go, Ira stepped back and gave Hank a head-to-toe appraisal.

"You haven't changed a bit, you dog!"

Hank smiled. "Well you have." He thought, *Jesus, he's enormous! He's the nose guard the Dolphins are looking for.* But, "It's great to see you," was all he said.

"I'm sorry it's because of this that we're meeting again. You know I thought the world of Aaron. He was a great guy to work with when we were in the dorms."

"I know," Hank said. "We've been friends ever since."

"You were his best friend, Hank." Ira put his drink down. "He told me that at graduation."

Hank was puzzled at this bit of news. "Really? He said that way back then?" The truth was Aaron had actually said it many years later and under a different set of circumstances. Hank noticed the Asian woman next to Ira. She was the same one he saw at the service.

"Hello." Hank reached out to shake her hand.

"I'm sorry," Ira said. "This is my wife, Lin. Lin, this is Henry Longo. We worked together in the dorms at Miami."

"It's a pleasure to meet you. I'm very sorry for your loss, Henry. Aaron was a wonderful person. I loved him very much." Hank's mind reached for a connection between her and Aaron.

"Oh, so you knew him, too?"

"Only briefly. I uh . . ." Ira finished for her.

"Aaron introduced us. We met in California years ago. If it hadn't been for him I'd never have found this beautiful woman." Ira gazed admiringly at Lin. "I owe him so much. I never thought I'd be able to love anyone. He went out of his way . . ." And then Hank watched as tears squeezed from the sides of his eyes. Lin gave Ira a hug as he reached into a coat pocket to pull out a handkerchief. He dabbed his eyes and blew his nose.

"So how long have you been married?" Hank broke the awkwardness of the moment.

"Eighteen years," said Ira.

"And you? You're married?"

"Yes. Thirteen years in September."

Lin asked, "Is your wife here?"

"No, she couldn't come. We have two girls, and they all have activities. It would have been difficult to tear them away from everything."

"Do you have children?"

"Six," Ira beamed. "Five boys and a girl."

"I finally got a girl!" Lin said happily.

"Six kids. That's unbelievable!" Hank envisioned Eva and Elisabeth plus four more running around the house. It was an unfathomable thought.

"Hey, what can I say? She wanted a daughter."

"Where are you living?" Hank asked.

"We came down from Boston. We've got an import-export business there. We deal mostly with China, but we're beginning to break into some other markets as well. And you?"

"I'm a comptroller for a hotel resort group in Orlando."

"Sounds like that keeps you pretty busy."

"Yes, it does." Hank wanted to change the subject again. "Ira, I'm really glad you came."

"Lin? Would you excuse me for a moment."

"Of course," his wife replied, followed by a moment of eye contact. "I'll see to Mrs. Temple." Ira and Hank watched her go.

"Okay, tell me how your wife can have six children and still look like that?"

"She looks even better than when I first met her." Hank thought of the extra twenty-five pounds the girls had added to Linda; childbirth had been disastrous for her figure. *It's a good thing I didn't bring her,* he concluded with a slight chuckle. Ira looked around the crowded deck.

"Let's take a walk." They moved from the house, across the yard. For a quiet moment they both feigned interest in the tall budding maple trees scattered around the property. Hank broke the silence first.

"This is fucked up."

"I couldn't agree more."

"You know, I just saw him a short time ago."

"I'm still in the dark as to what happened?" Ira said. "Do you know anything else?"

"Just that it was an expedition to celebrate the fiftieth anniversary climb of Everest. They invited Hillary and Norgay's sons to repeat the climb their fathers had done. Dave Horton hired Aaron to shoot the event. No doubt for the outdoor magazines he publishes."

"Yes," Ira said firmly. "I knew that jackass was behind all of this. What happened to him?"

"He almost didn't make it. Frostbite. Tracy told me he's going to need some facial reconstruction."

"Too bad his head didn't freeze off." Hank was amused that after twenty years Ira still loathed him.

A question popped into his head. "Whatever happened to Al?"

"Sampson? He's a full-bird colonel in the Army. Commands one of those attack and support helicopter squadrons."

"You're kidding?"

"Nope. Al's had a great career. Brave man, done combat in Iraq and Somalia. He practically ran the whole air to ground support show in Afghanistan. Getting ready to retire soon. We talk all the time. He's pretty much the only one I've held onto from UM days."

Hank looked at his watch. Although he'd enjoyed spending time with Ira, there were other people to talk to.

"Let's go back inside. I still haven't paid my respects to Eileen."

"Ira," Hank said as they walked, "I didn't get anything from that service today. Did you?"

"The world keeps spinning my friend. The service was set up for those who are ready to process the loss. It does feel rushed though. I mean we only found out about this ten days ago."

"Well, I'm confused." The two of them walked slowly. They admired the sunshine and warmth of the New England spring day. "It feels like he's still out there. I'm waiting for him to come back."

"But he's not, Hank. You know that."

Hank paused to reflect. "You know, he was always pulling my leg. He'd tell me something outrageous, and then work on me until I believed it. I was always a sucker to his strange sense of humor. Even now, I half expect him to pull up to the house in that old convertible of his, laughing at all of us, and shouting 'just kidding!'" Ira listened. He looked across the road at neighborhood children playing in their yard. Excited voices and laughter resonated across the street.

With a softer tone, Ira declared, "He's still with us, but he's not coming back."

"But he should be." Hank's response was barely above a whisper.

Ira pulled out his wallet and fished for a business card. He pressed the card into Hank's right hand with both of his.

"If there's anything I can do to help, call me. It was good to see you, Henry Longo." Ira pulled Hank toward him for another bear hug. He spoke quietly in Hank's ear as they embraced. "I'm sorry it had to be because of this."

Eileen Temple was sitting in her living room. Many people were gathered around her. Hank stood back and observed, waiting for the right moment to approach her. It had been years since he had seen Aaron's mother. She was old and very frail now. He remembered Mrs. Temple as being such a dynamic person. *God,* he thought. *Now she looks like she could hardly get out of bed.*

"Hello Eileen." Hank sat down on the sofa. At first she didn't know him, but then, her face lit up and tears of recognition flowed.

"Henry," she said crying. "You're here."

"Yes, I'm here. Are you okay?"

"It's all so confusing, you know. So many things just don't make any sense." Eileen leaned in to whisper. "Who are all these people?"

Hank looked around the room, but couldn't identify many of the faces. When he turned back, her look of confusion alarmed him.

"I guess they're friends and colleagues of Aaron's," Hank said. "People he's met over the years."

"Were you there as well?"

"Where?"

"Wherever Aaron went? To the place where he can't come back from?"

"Oh, you mean the Himalayas? No, I wasn't."

"That's right. What's it called?"

"Mt. Everest?"

"Yes. That's it." She closed her eyes and let out a frustrating sigh. "Why can't I remember that name?" Hank frowned. Besides her frailty, something else was amiss.

"I came up from Orlando, Eileen. I wanted to let you know how sorry I am about Aaron."

"Thank you Henry. You've been very kind, very helpful with the theater, too. We had a great time putting on those productions, didn't we?"

"Yes, we did. That summer doing theater at Martha's Vineyard was a wonderful experience for me, one I'll never forget. My daughter, Elisabeth is involved in a community theater project back home."

"I didn't know you had a little girl."

"Two, Elisabeth and . . ." Once again Hank could see utter confusion in Eileen's eyes. "You've been getting the Christmas cards I've been sending every year haven't you?"

"Oh, yes. It's wonderful to hear from you each year. I'm sorry Henry, my mind's not what it used to be."

"That's all right, 'Eye-*Lee*-in'." She smiled; it worked. The accented pronunciation of her name had started when they had been on the island years ago. Hank had never missed an opportunity to tease her like that. The young woman who had sat next to Eileen at the service came over to the sofa.

"Mrs. Temple? You have a phone call."

"Will you excuse me?"

"Certainly." Hank helped Eileen up. Both Hank and the young woman watched her go.

"Emily Peterson, I presume," said Hank.

"Yes," she responded. She reached to shake hands. "And you are?"

"Henry Longo, from Orlando."

"Oh, yes. I'm so glad you could make it." Emily gestured for them to sit. Hank looked to see who was in earshot and then sat down again.

"How well do you know Eileen? Is she okay?"

"She's suffering from dementia." Hank's eyes widened in shock and a curtain of sadness descended over him. "I've been told she's in the first stage of cognitive decline and the medication she's taking can only slow the process; it's not a cure. She also suffered a heart attack last year. It's been tough on her. I'm surprised she's doing this well."

All Hank heard were the buzz words. *'Dementia!' 'Heart Attack!'* Hank had always thought of Eileen as a second mom. Why didn't he know about her condition? Aaron had a history of being tight lipped about things, but he wished he'd told him about his mom's health.

"It explains a lot," he finally said. "Is she okay by herself?"

"She has a home health aide, and the visiting nurse comes regularly. There's also a group of neighbors who look in on her."

"She's so thin."

"Yes, forgetting to eat is part of the memory loss affliction."

"So there's no chance of getting Aaron back," Hank tried to change the subject. He already knew the answer.

"No, I'm afraid not. The body'll have to stay where it is. Everest is a graveyard for about a hundred people I'm afraid. He's too high up to attempt a recovery."

"Has anyone ever tried?"

"I don't think so," came her guarded response. "But I'm not an expert on mountain climbing. You'd have to talk to someone else about that."

"Did you even know Aaron at all?"

"No, I've never had the pleasure. Ibis Publishing retains my firm for a variety of legal contracts and obligations."

"Did you come up from DC?" Hank knew that Dave's publishing empire was headquartered in Washington.

"No, I work in New York City. The DC office called us in to put all this together. I would've asked one of our associates to handle this, but since I know Mr. Horton, Dave that is, and he's been one of my firm's long established clients, well . . . Are you flying back to Florida today, Mr. Longo?"

"Please call me Hank. I go by Hank."

"Thank you, Hank. Did you fly into New York?"

"Yes, I'm staying at the Fairfield Inn tonight and I fly out of La Guardia tomorrow afternoon."

"That's where I'm staying. Perhaps we could meet later on? I know you were one of Mr. Temple's closest friends. I'd like to hear more about him." She reached for her small pocket book, fished around for her business card and a pen to write her room number. "I'm staying in room 123. Call me . . ."

Hank glanced around. He spotted a gentleman who had been sitting next to Ira. It looked like he was leaving. There was something odd about this man, yet familiar, too.

"Excuse me a minute." Hank didn't wait for a reply, just hurried to the door.

"Wait! Please?" Hank shouted. The man stopped and looked at him.

"Yes?" Hank now had a chance to really see him. He was smaller than him, and thin. He had short wiry hair with touches of gray that emanated out from the yarmulke he wore. Although about the same age as Hank, the clothing he wore caused him to look older. It reminded Hank of how his grandfather used to dress.

"I'm sorry," said Hank. "We didn't get a chance to talk. I should know you, shouldn't I?"

"My name is Wayne," he said slowly. "Wayne Fishman." Hank snapped his fingers. "Wayne, Wayne."

"And you are?"

"I'm sorry," Hank said. "I'm Henry Longo, a friend of Aaron's . . ."

"Yes. I know the name well." Wayne closed the door to his car. With tears in his eyes he embraced Hank and said into his ear, "You're Aaron's *best* friend." Wayne then kissed him on both cheeks, pulled a handkerchief out of his pocket and wiped the moisture from his eyes.

"You were Aaron's roommate in college, in Washington." Hank stared at the friend Aaron had talked about frequently. They had met their freshman year at American University. "Complete opposites," Aaron had said. They roomed together for two years and probably would have all four if Aaron hadn't gotten the resident advisor position.

"Yes, I was," came the solemn reply. "This is a terrible day." The two of them looked around. The sun was shining, birds were singing and the breeze tingled with warmth. "God has made a beautiful day today," Wayne said as he gazed upward. He looked back at Hank, tapped his own chest and finished, "But it's a terrible day here in my heart."

"I'm really lost right now," Hank said. "It's like today's been a day for everyone but me. I'm not ready to say goodbye!" How easy it was for him to confess his feelings to Wayne. He had just met the guy and already he was spilling his guts. "I'm sorry," he said.

"I'm not ready either. I'm not ready because, like you, I feel Aaron is not ready." The two men stared at each other. And right then and there the connection was established.

From the corner of his eye, Hank saw something across the street. It was only for a second, but it was a figure of a man in a snowsuit, with ropes and climbing gear draped over him. As he tried to focus better, the apparition disappeared. Hank shook his head in disbelief and Wayne, who'd been looking at his watch, hadn't seen a thing.

"I'm sorry," Wayne said, "I must go. I have to get home and there is usually a lot of traffic."

"Where is home for you?"

"Long Island, West Hempstead to be exact." Wayne took a paper from his pocket and wrote. "Here is my number, in case you should want to call."

The hotel was by the interstate, conveniently close to exit eighteen. Emily had driven Hank, and as they passed the Sherwood Diner, which was just across from the hotel, they agreed to meet there for dinner.

Since he'd brought his running shoes and there was plenty of time, he decided to burn off some of the day's tension. Just a short distance down the road, he'd noticed a large lake, with a lighted walkway around it. If he ran the circumference four or five times, the distance should be equivalent to what he ran back home. And just what he needed right now.

Chapter 8

Visiting Wayne

DINNER WITH EMILY turned out to be quite nice. She was polished, intelligent and kind.

"I'm going back to the city in the morning, I'd be happy to drop you off at La Guardia." Hank accepted Emily's gracious offer, but asked if she would drop him at Wayne's house instead. Since his flight wasn't until evening, he was grateful to have the time to visit Wayne.

Sunday morning traffic was light as they crossed the Whitestone Bridge. It wasn't long before Emily's Mustang pulled up to the Fishman house and Hank grabbed his luggage and thanked Emily for the ride. A quick look around told him it was a modest neighborhood, with Tudor style homes on small lots. Wayne's home was pleasant to look at from the street but as he approached the front steps he could see paint peeling from a window frame and a rusted rain gutter by the left corner of the roof. There was a gated yard just beyond the detached single car garage whose doors looked like they hadn't been open in twenty years

Hank rang the bell. Looking up to his right, he noticed a mezuzah. He'd seen the same ornament once before. It was on the apartment door of an elderly couple, the grandparents of a Jewish girl he'd dated. Hank remembered the girl kissing her hand and then touching it. "It's for luck," she explained.

He reached up and pressed his finger to the raised Hebrew letters. That's when Wayne's door opened.

"You must be Henry?" said the tall, thin woman with the raven black hair and tortoise shell glasses.

"Yes. I'm Hank Longo."

"Please, come in. I'm Lori, welcome to our home." Hank noticed the worn wooden floors, mismatched furniture and cast iron radiators that had been painted over.

"Ah, there you are," Wayne said as he entered the room. He was dressed in warm-up pants, a t-shirt, and a pair of sneakers.

"You'll have to excuse me Henry, I just got back from the tennis center."

"Please, call me Hank. You play tennis?"

"I teach. Come," he motioned with his hand, "let's go in the kitchen. Would you like a drink?"

Hank sat at the small formica table and sipped from a tall glass of lemonade. On the floor next to him was a waist high pile of newspapers and along side of that, a paper bag filled with empty soda cans.

"So you've come up from Florida?"

"Yes, I have a flight back tonight."

"I'm glad you managed to stop by before you went back. Aaron would have liked that we met. It's just so terrible."

"I still can't believe it myself," Hank said.

"His body, it stays on the mountain?"

"That's what I'm told."

"Terrible Hank, just terrible. They should have brought the body back, don't you think?" Wayne's eyes watered. He blinked back the tears and looked away. Lori put a comforting hand on his shoulder. Her soft voice murmured, "They should bring back the body."

"I have a few more people to talk to, but it seems impossible."

Wayne looked at Hank. "Is Tracy one of those people?" Hank's eyebrows rose. "He spoke to me about a Tracy he knew."

"She's the wife of the man who organized the expedition. We all went to school together at Miami." Hank smiled at Wayne.

"Tell me more about you and Aaron, at American."

"It's kind of funny," Wayne responded. "We didn't grow up very far from each other in Connecticut. I was from Stamford and he was from Westport. But we were quite different. To start with, I'm Jewish as you know. I don't think Aaron had too many Jewish friends."

"He always referred to you as the only friend he had at American. Is that true?"

"No, it's not." Wayne chuckled.

"Well, I never heard him talk about anyone except you."

"That's because . . ." Wayne paused. "Some people go through a lot their freshman year. Aaron had it pretty rough those first couple of months we were together. I think a lot of other people would have bailed on him with all the problems he had. I almost did." Wayne looked up at the ceiling and shook his head. "Tsk, Tsk, Tsk. He was so troubled."

"Aaron told me what a rotten first semester he had."

"Well, you know about the father committing suicide." Hank nodded. Wayne leaned forward and counted with his fingers: "his grandfather died, and then the fraternity he'd joined black balled him. And just before Thanksgiving, his girlfriend ended their relationship in a letter."

"Jesus Christ! I'm sorry." Hank recanted. "I didn't mean to offend . . ." Wayne waved off the apology.

"It was a nightmare. When I first moved into the room, he already had pictures of her everywhere. He called her all the time. A dyed in the wool romantic, that's what he was. I've never seen anyone wear his heart on his sleeve like that. Her name was Marian."

Hank's ears pinned back and his head tilted upward, as he recalled the story of Aaron's first girlfriend and the long distance relationship that didn't last.

Wayne inhaled with exaggerated expression and then exhaled the same way, slow and deliberate. "You can imagine what a mess he was."

Hank just nodded up and down. "When I first met him it was very different. We were in residential life training together and there was this program about crises intervention. He and I did this scenario about a depressed student wanting to kill himself. He had a 'Dear John' letter . . ."

"It was the same letter. Did this scene take place on a roof?" Hank didn't have to answer. The look on his face was enough. The two sat silent for a few moments.

"What was most difficult for me," Wayne said, "was that Aaron didn't want help. All he wanted was to forget and the quickest way to do that was to drink, which he did, a lot."

"I partied with Aaron at Miami. It was hard to keep up with him; he'd want to keep going, and I'd already be blotto."

"That was my problem too," Wayne confessed. "We'd go to floor parties. I tried to get him to meet some new people, maybe find another girl and forget about the high school sweetheart. But the trouble was, while I'm getting a good buzz on from a couple of cups of Purple Jesus, he's doing beer bongs! And when he got drunk, he got crazy. He'd be out of control, shove someone, and start a fight. He was very angry. And he had a right to be. But I got tired of it." Wayne pointed a finger in the air. "I told him he needed help. I wasn't going to baby-sit him anymore. The next thing I knew, I was on the roof of Letts Hall getting him off the ledge."

"You saved his life?"

"No, he saved himself. Everyone was up there pleading with him, talking to him about how wonderful life was and not to throw it away, and all the stuff you're supposed to say. But I knew his life wasn't okay. It sucked, and I told him so. And I don't know why, except I knew he wasn't suicidal." Wayne paused. "So I told him to stop wasting everyone's time and go ahead and jump."

"What?"

"It wasn't even a gamble. We had gotten past being roommates; we'd become friends. As a friend, I told him if he really thought his life was shit and was never going to get better, he might as well get it over with."

"That's how you talked him down?"

"Sort of. He got so mad he jumped off the wall and went after me! It took three guys to hold him back." In spite of his sadness, Hank laughed. "Later on he thanked me. He said it was the best thing I could have done."

"And you ended up rooming together for two years?"

"It could have been four, but when he got the resident advisor position our junior year . . ."

"And it was because of that job, he came to Miami."

"Yes."

Hank looked at the man that had known Aaron as well as he did.

"We hung out a lot, but after that night on the roof, he lost something within him. It was like he began a quest to find the meaning of true happiness and forget about women; it was a radical change."

"Wait a minute," Hank objected, "what are you talking about?"

"He vowed never to allow any girl to hurt him like that again. Aaron was embarrassed that anyone could've had that much emotional control over him. The frat was one thing and his grandparent's death was another, but he couldn't get over thinking that the only way to punish that old girlfriend of his was to kill himself. He promised me, and in tears I might add, he would never let it happen again."

Hank processed Wayne's comments as his head bobbed in unconscious agreement. It was a lot to think about, but at the same time it explained a lot.

The walk to the synagogue was not a far one. Wayne asked Hank to accompany him to the Temple. "There is something we can do there that may help us find some peace."

The residential neighborhood soon gave way to the more settled village. Wayne pointed to the building where he worked. His office was only a few blocks from his home. As they passed it, Wayne explained the nature of his business, supplemental insurance policies for large corporations in the metropolitan area.

"It's wonderful you can walk to both work and worship." Even the stores were all within the Fishmans' fingertips.

"It's convenient," said Wayne.

"It's not like Florida. I'm always a car ride from everything."

"Yes, but I'll take your weather over any winter day here." When they came to the intersection they waited for the light to change. Traffic whizzed past them in both directions.

"I met with Aaron right before he left for Nepal." Wayne looked at the light.

"I spoke with him too. He called, said he was in LA, but coming east and hoped to see me."

"I met him at a sports bar where we've gone to in the past to . . ."

"He told me he bought a place in Florida," Wayne interrupted.

"That's right. He told me that night, he had bought a home not far from where I live. We played air hockey, shot some pool, and drank a few pitchers. Ended up having a long conversation about the things we'd done over the years."

"Anything else?"

"Well, we got pretty buzzed, and we ran the gamut of personal feelings that night. In the middle of it all he tore up an envelope and tossed it into the trash, like a piece of junk mail you don't even want to look at. It was that letter I knew he had hung onto for years."

"He threw it away?" Hank and Wayne passed in front of the open firehouse door. Wayne stopped and grabbed onto Hank's arm.

"Tore it up right in front of me and tossed it." Wayne stared at the ground.

"Aaron was in love again," Wayne mumbled. "He'd found someone Hank. After all these years, he'd finally found someone."

"I don't understand." Wayne took a moment to gather his thoughts.

"He told me years ago, he would always keep that note to remind him how rotten it is to have your heart broken. Don't you see?"

"Oh, I don't know about that," Hank said shaking his head and looking down at the cracks in the sidewalk. "Aaron had a lot of hot and heavy romances over the years."

"Hot and heavy for whom?" The light changed and Hank thought about some of Aaron's prior girlfriends as they crossed the wide avenue. His thinking was cut off when Wayne asked, "Hank, what can you tell me about Tracy?"

Talk about hot and heavy. He was about to begin the story when a voice from the fire station interrupted.

"Hey, Rabbi! Fishmaninsky, watcha doin'?" Hank and Wayne turned to look into the building.

"Is that you Pete?" Out from the shadows of the garage came a tall young man wearing fireman's boots and pants, and a black t-shirt. He looked to be in his early twenties. His hands held a hose nozzle, and a grimy cloth. He continued to clean the tool as he walked.

"Watcha doin? You goin' to Temple again?"

"After burnin' you last week with that baseline reverse dribble," Wayne said proudly, "I figured I'd better go pray for you." Pete snickered. "Never again in a thousand years my friend. Never again." Wayne turned to Hank.

"This is Pete Saltus, Hank. I play basketball with him and the other men every Tuesday."

"Nice to meet you," Hank said. "Any news yet?" Wayne asked Pete.

"Nah, not yet." He motioned for Hank and Wayne to follow him into the station. "It doesn't look too good Wayne." He looked around to see if anyone was within earshot. "Between you and me?" he said to Wayne. "I think Engine Company 256 is done." Wayne shook his head.

"I'm sorry to hear that."

"So am I." Hank looked around the station. It was an old building, well worn with age and obviously small for the two pumper trucks housed there. Once upon a time it must have been the centerpiece building in the neighborhood. Now it was a relic to a time gone past.

"What'll happen to you and the guys?" Wayne asked.

"Furloughs and retirement for some. Captain says we'll have to sit back and wait for the reassignment."

"Any idea how long?"

"Nope." Pete finished cleaning the nozzle and brought it over to the pumper. He reattached it to one of the curled up hoses in the back of the truck. "Couple of months. A year. Maybe longer. So where you off to?"

"Synagogue; Hank's up from Orlando. He and I have a mutual friend. Had a mutual friend." Wayne sighed. "Mountain climbing accident. We're going over to the Temple to have a special version of The Kaddish."

"I'm sorry to hear that guys," Pete said. "Tell you what, when you're done, come back to the station. We've got a big lunch planned." Pete smiled at Hank. "Wayne can introduce you to some of the guys he plays basketball with, and you can tell us about your friend." Hank looked at his watch, and did a quick calculation. There was plenty of time before his flight, so he nodded to Wayne; it was a go.

"Excellent," said Wayne. "We'll do that."

* * *

Colored light filtered through the large mosaic window on the side of the schul. Almost to the ceiling against the far wall Hank noticed an electronic display of numbers. He lightly grabbed Wayne's arm and pointed to them.

"They are dates to remember the passing of loved ones within our congregation." Wayne motioned for Hank to follow him to a small room just off the left side of the altar. Red velvet curtains lined three walls and a stand of candles stood next to the heavy wooden door on the fourth wall.

"If you'll sit there," Wayne pointed to a row of high back chairs. He walked over to a glass paneled cabinet and picked out a small gold leaf covered book. He wrapped a prayer shawl over his shoulders and brought out an ornamental candle and placed it on a small table. He then opened the book and turned to Hank.

"Now, I'm going to wish Aaron peace and thank him for the love he gave me." Hank silently acknowledged Wayne's words. Wayne rocked back and forth on his heels as he prayed aloud in Hebrew. Even though the scripture sounded foreign, the melodic tone of Wayne's voice filled the room with a soft winded splendor and somehow, it did give Hank a small amount of calming peace.

When Wayne had finished, he turned to Hank and waved for him to join him at the small altar.

"The candle is symbolic of the body and its flame is a guiding light for Aaron's soul. It is my hope that Aaron sees the light and follows it to the world beyond." Wayne lit the match and together they lit the candle. After another prayer, the short service was concluded.

"Thank you," Hank said. "That was nice. Maybe the candle will show me the way as well. Right now, I'm still searching for answers."

"And you might never find them." Wayne's words weighed heavily.

"That's exactly what I'm afraid of."

*   *   *

Upstairs at the fire station, Hank, Wayne, and eight firemen passed around large platters piled high with food. The second floor was furnished as a lounge, and a dining area. There was also a kitchen, bathroom and sleeping cots for six.

"Are any of the guys here Jewish?" Hank whispered.

"No. But they all have souls." Wayne helped himself to the potatoes. "I think the men would rather run into a burning building knowing God is with them instead of leaving it up to fate whether they come back out. Wouldn't you want God with you when you run into a burning building?"

"I think I'd prefer experience, training, and teamwork. So what's your unofficial position here?"

"I'm an ear to listen, a voice to say things that others can't. Sometimes it's a prayer or a blessing they need, and I'm the one they count on for that."

During the meal, Hank got to know the crew. Captain Jim Allston sat at the head of the table. He'd been with the department for twenty years. Premature gray betrayed his age and Hank attributed it to the stress of command. At the other end of the table was Lieutenant Ed Casey, another veteran with the department. Ed was a short, bull of a man who looked more like a linebacker than a firefighter. To Wayne's right was Pete, a rookie to the force. So was Rick Catano, who sat on Hank's left. Across the table were more veteran members of the crew. Larry Fusca, an ex-cop; Colin Webber, a part time jazz musician; and Rusty Taylor, who followed in his brother's footsteps and become a fireman seven years ago, after high school. Last but not least was the other lieutenant, Tom Beckett, who had joined ten years ago because his military career wasn't exciting enough.

"So Jim," Wayne asked, "what do you think will happen if they close the firehouse?"

"It's tough to say." The captain was slow to choose his words. "When they opened the new station last month, I was told we'd stay on as an auxiliary. The big problem is, since the town's grown so much, our response time is off. We should be at a fire in six minutes; truth is, it's closer to ten."

"That's why they built the new station."

"Plus, we don't even have a full crew."

"How many men is a full crew here?" Hank asked.

"Eighteen to twenty. We have eight. The new station not only has a full crew, but overlaps almost our entire coverage area."

"There's no way to merge the two of you together?" Wayne asked.

"They're fully staffed," Rusty chimed in. "And they're all veteran."

"You know I got a family to feed," said Tom. "They talk about giving us furloughs, which is one thing, but I don't like not knowing when or if I'll have a job again."

"I'll have to do something else," Rick said. "Pete and I are on the low rung."

"Tell us about your friend, Hank." Colin switched subjects. "Wayne mentioned you lost a mutual friend."

"He was mountain climbing on Mount Everest," Hank said.

"That's the world's tallest mountain, isn't it?"

"It's over 29,000 feet," Rick announced.

"Bullshit," Rusty spat. "How do you know that rookie?"

"I looked it up."

"Forgive me," Rusty said. "But don't you think it's stupid to climb up that high? I mean why would anyone . . ."

"As stupid as it is to run into a burning building?" said Larry.

"That's different," said Rusty. "That's my job."

"It was his job too," said Wayne. "Aaron was a photographer. He was on assignment."

"Well that's different."

"Was he killed in an avalanche?" Pete asked.

"I'm not sure exactly what happened. I'm still trying to get all the facts."

"Gentlemen," Captain Jim called out as he stood up from his chair. "A toast." The men stood with raised glasses. "A salute, to the heroes we have known, and to the brave men who carry on in their name."

The lunch had lasted longer than both Hank and Wayne had expected. After a quick good-bye to Lori, back at the house, Hank jumped into Wayne's old Chevy Caprice, for a ride to the airport. Wayne apologized for the muffler he had been meaning to get fixed. In spite of the noise, the windows needed to be down, the sun had made the interior hot and stuffy, and the car was without a/c.

"Thanks again for everything you did today."

"Thanks for coming out," Wayne said as he exited the expressway. Signs for La Guardia passed above them as they made their way to the main terminal. "I'd like for us to keep in touch." Wayne drove the car into the departure lane of Terminal B.

"I want you to know," Hank said with trepidation, "Aaron and I go too far back for me to let go of him just yet."

"Aaron lived recklessly. He always took risks. Mountain climbing is dangerous. It's sad to think, but the law of averages caught up with him." Wayne put on his turn signal and eased into the next lane. "Go get yourself checked in. I'm going to park and see you off."

Hank used the automated kiosk and walked over to the security area. Wayne caught up with him a few minutes later.

"When I spoke to Aaron, before he left, he said a lot about being a changed man." Wayne looked down at the floor, away from Hank, to remember the conversation. "He was happy."

Hank enthusiastically responded. "He said the same to me. And that's what's bugging me. He was scared. Not scared-scared. Happy-scared. About his future."

"Now, is that him?"

"I've never known Aaron to be nervous about anything." Hank stood up and checked his watch. It was time to go.

"Hank, don't forget to talk to that Tracy person. Aaron mentioned her. She may have some of the answers you're looking for." Hank put his backpack on the conveyor belt. He shook Wayne's hand. Wayne pulled him into an embrace. Stunned by the affection, Hank responded with a double pat to Wayne's back.

"Thanks for all your help."

"You have a wounded heart my friend. Call me if you need anything else; we're friends now." He smiled, grateful for the sentiment and the offer.

Hank's forehead pressed against the hard plastic window cover as the DC 9 banked to the left and vectored down the Hudson River, revealing the light of the Manhattan skyline. He could see the familiar Empire State Building. He looked to the area where the towers had been. He thought about all the people who never came home that day. Went off to work and disappeared.

"Like Aaron," Hank said softly. In his thoughts he knew that wasn't totally true. He hadn't vanished like the others lost in the two towers, his remains were still out there but Hank had no idea how to claim them. As the plane gained altitude, he looked forward to his own homecoming.

Chapter 9

Back in Orlando

THE LONG WEEKEND was finally over, but by the time Hank walked through the door, Linda was already fast asleep and the girls were tucked in beside her. Hank crashed on the living room couch.

Before long, Hank's sleep became restless. He dreamed he and Aaron were at a tiki bar in the Florida Keys, listening to Jimmy Buffet music. As they sipped rum runners, Hank was momentarily distracted by a couple of beauties in skimpy swimsuits. When he turned back around to share his carnal thoughts, he was shocked to discover Aaron dressed head-to-toe in a mountain climbing suit. And although it was eighty-five degrees by the bar, he was covered with snow and violently shivering. As Aaron looked up from beneath the fur-lined hood of his parka, Hank glimpsed the frozen disfigured face.

"I'm so cold," he moaned, "I'm so cooooold!"

Only an hour shy of the alarm, Hank woke, drenched in sweat and gasping for air. It took a minute or two before he realized it was a dream. He shook it off and decided to go for an early run. "Might as well get a head start at work while I'm at it."

*　　*　　*

"Listen," Charo began, "it's pretty slow right now; I can handle things. Why don't you take the week off?" Hank could see the concerned look on her face.

"That's very thoughtful," Hank replied, "but I don't think I can take a whole week off."

"I spoke with Palm Beach and they said given the circumstances, it was fine for you to take the time. Hank, go home," she ordered.

Although he was concerned that things would get fouled up in his absence, he listened to Charo and left the office.

Nagging curiosity led him straight to the interstate. The address Aaron had given him was still tucked away in the glove compartment; it was time to conduct his own little investigation. As he drove, he wondered why Aaron had chosen a home in this little village twenty-two miles north of the city.

Once past the urban sprawl, the state road opened to a four lane divided highway. The one sign for Mount Dora and Route 52 was so tiny, if Hank hadn't paid attention, he would have missed it.

The town of Mount Dora was nothing like Florida's typical flat topography. It rose and fell, and created a ripple effect that elevated the outskirts of town.

"It's beautiful," Hank said as he turned the corner onto Donnelly and gazed at a group of beautifully restored Victorian homes. As he crossed over Third Avenue, he could see the town's center had many two and three story red brick buildings. The town bore a striking resemblance to Westport, Connecticut where Aaron grew up. Having also spent time with him and his mother at their summer home on Martha's Vineyard, he could see that the homes had an architectural style that blended the Victorian and Greek revival elements of residences he knew from the island.

After a quick stop for lunch at the local eatery, Hank walked back to his car. A little more searching and he was able to find the street and house. It was the brand new home centered on a simple, but beautifully landscaped lot. The concrete stucco bungalow had a red tile roof that stuck out against many of the other homes in the area. Hank turned into the stone gravel driveway.

Cozy.

"Whatever Aaron planned to do, it was going to start here," he observed. "It's a place to come home to." *Or a place to come home to someone?* Just as Hank noticed the dark clouds gathering, a sudden strong gust of wind swirled around him causing the trees to thrash back and forth in the humid breeze.

Yesterday's conversation with Wayne had him wondering about Tracy. *Was she a part of this?* She and Dave lived a good life. They had money, and played a big part in the DC social and political scene. But he wondered if they were happy together. Aaron and Tracy had hooked up years ago; could it have happened again? He took one last look at the house from the road before he drove away. *What did he say before he left the bar that night about knowing who she was right away?* Wayne had suggested he get in touch with her. He said it was important.

Hank checked in with Charo.

"Your wife called. She wants you to call her." Hank's mood changed.

"Whatcha' tell her?"

"I just said you were out of the office. She wants you to call when you get the message." And then the phrase that always made his blood pressure rise. "She said it wasn't important." Hank had tried not to be petty. It was common for Linda to call and leave him a message to call her back about something that wasn't important. At first it was amusing and he would tease her about it. "If it wasn't important, then why did you bother calling?" But the happiness of their couplehood slowly gave way to the familiarities of married and family life. *Today it should have been a call to see how I was doing.*

"Yellen & Yellen called, too. They asked you to call back when you have a moment." Hank switched lanes. He'd be getting off the thruway soon, so he decided to go back to the office. Jan Yellen's number was in his card file.

So is Tracy's, he mulled. He also wanted to check a few things on his computer. He'd been in touch with Jan Yellen often in the past few weeks. His Uncle Gino's estate had been a complicated matter. Although Gino's life partner, Sebastian had been designated executor, he didn't have a shred of organization in him, and was too emotional to handle all of Gino's affairs. Hank acted as primary back up in most of the probate matters, and also resolved any disputed bills.

Uncle Gino had been the guiding voice in Hank's life. The doctors had done everything they could, but the vivid picture of the seventy-four-year-old lying there on his back, with eyes half open pointed at the ceiling tortured Hank. After a vigil that lasted weeks, he took a night off to see a movie and get some sleep. Uncle Gino died that night.

It took almost a year, but the estate was finally wrapping up.

A series of turns brought Hank back to the Ramada. On the way he passed Benny's; the sports bar for wings, beer and gorgeous servers. That's where he and Aaron had spent their last visit. He decided to stop there later to have a beer and sit where he and Aaron had sat.

Once again, Hank sat in his office with the door closed. He typed: Mt. Everest, Everest speakers, 50th anniversary climb and Edmund Hillary into his computer. Then decided to add one more, one letter at a time: m-o-u-n-t-a-i-n c-l-i-m-b-i-n-g e-x-p-e-d-i-t-i-o-n-s.

*   *   *

"So, I'm going to fax you these last two requests for payments," Jan Yellen said over the speakerphone. She had a nice voice, was very professional, and genuinely sincere. Hank knew that his Uncle Gino had been a good judge of people. He'd picked the right legal counsel to handle his business and affairs over the years.

"Okay Jan. I'll take a quick look, and fax it back."

"We can probably execute the will by the end of the month." Hank could hear her thumbing through paperwork. "Checking the calendar, I could do it the twenty-ninth."

"Okay. That works for me. You do want me there, right?"

"Yes please. Sebastian instructed me to ask you to be there . . . for the dispersal." Hank closed his eyes in dismay. His thoughts turned to images of him once again having to comfort his uncle's partner. Another episode of hand holding, tear flowing melodrama that he had endured several times before and had enough of. Hank liked Sebastian, and he appreciated the affection he had given his beloved uncle, but he acted so helpless it annoyed him. There was also something about Sebastian's demeanor that made Hank uncomfortable.

"Uh, you know what? On second thought, I've got month end reports due. Can we make it the following week?"

"How's Friday, June 5th? Late afternoon?"

"That's fine." One of the good things was the estate paid for the trip. Uncle G had been a father to him since his own dad died many years ago. He thought it would be a good thing to bring closure to this chapter in his life. With Aaron's death appearing so open ended, he was glad to be finishing the book on another person he had cared for.

"I'll be there."

"Great, I'll look forward to seeing you." Hank pushed the orange speakerphone button and stared at the phone for a while. He pushed the button again and pressed speed dial for his home number. When the phone rang, he lifted up the receiver.

"Hi honey." Linda knew Hank was calling from caller ID. "How's work?"

"Slow."

"I didn't hear you come in last night."

"It was late. Real late. You and the girls were already asleep and I didn't want to wake you up."

"I didn't even hear you get up this morning. Did you go running?"

"Yeah, real early," Hank said flatly. The conversation was not going the way he had hoped.

"Boy, it must have been. I never even heard the shower."

"Yeah well, like I said, it was early." There was a pause between the two of them.

"Linda, I had a bad dream last night about Aaron."

"Oh." There was another pause.

"I had one the other day," she said casually.

"What was it about?" Hank hoped a discussion about her dream would be the back door he needed to talk about his.

"Oh, it was nothing. Never mind."

"Come on," Hank pleaded, "tell me."

"It was a few days ago," she said with some irritation. "I can't even remember half of it." Hank knew it was pointless to keep prodding.

"I went up to Mount Dora this morning."

"What? When?"

"I just got back. I went to see the house Aaron bought."

"Why on earth would you do something like that?"

"Because it's important Linda. He was going to live there and I wanted to see what the attraction was."

"I don't understand?"

"Look," he pleaded, "I'm just trying to deal with this, okay?"

"Okay," she said.

But it's not okay, he thought.

"I just hope that it won't affect your job too much."

"As a matter of fact, I'm getting the week off."

"You are? How?"

"The corporates at West Palm said I'm entitled to it."

"Good for them. 'Bout time they showed you how much you're worth."

"It helps that it's slow right now. Charo can handle it."

"And what are you going to do with all this time off? You're not going to go psycho on me are you?" Hank smiled. It was the first endearing thing she had said. Their courtship had been a whirlwind romance. On a road trip to meet his parents, she had admitted that although she was madly in love with him, she barely knew him. She confessed that he was a sweet and adorable man, but realized he could be an ax wielding, homicidal serial killer as well. And she had asked him if he was, which to Hank, was so ludicrous a question that he couldn't stop laughing. But she was serious and in the end he had to swear that he wasn't "psycho". In their years together they used that little story whenever things got off kilter.

"No," he chuckled, "I won't do that. I'm probably going to do some more stuff about Aaron which could include . . ."

She cut him off right there. "Do you think you'll have time to clean out the garage?" Hank pulled the receiver away from his ear and looked at it. He had been trying to say something important, but she wasn't listening.

"You called me earlier," he said curtly. "Did you need something?"

"Elisabeth has a play date tomorrow with Tessa Cummings. Will you be able to go pick her up around five? I don't have the time, Eva's troop is having a cookie sale at the Millennium Mall Saturday and I need to plan for it."

He closed his eyes and pinched the bridge of his nose. "Sure, I can do that."

"Good. Thanks." Hank waited for another request, but none came.

"I'm going to leave the office soon, but I may be a little late getting home for dinner."

"Oh okay. And that's because . . ." Hank knew she had a right to ask. He just wished that for once she could find a way to give it a rest.

"Linda, I need some time alone. I just got back from his funeral, went to see the house he wanted to live in, it's a lot. Can you understand?" There was silence at the other end of the line. While he waited, he hoped for a little compassion. He didn't get it.

"Should I keep something warm, or do you want to make your own when you get home?"

"I miss him Linda!" Hank wondered if Linda could tell that his voice expressed the sense of frustration aimed at her for not grasping how he felt.

"Oh okay. You go ahead and do whatever you need to do, all right?"

"Thank you," Hank said, with his voice cracking.

"I miss him too, you know." Her tone was condescending. "Don't be too late."

"All right. Bye." And just like that there was a click.

As he drove out of the parking lot and headed over to Benny's he wondered if their love, which had taken off and soared for so long, was off autopilot and losing altitude.

* * *

Hank had always liked Benny's because it was a game playing, sports bar. He arrived around three o'clock, and just as he expected, the place was quiet. A few people stood around, but the bigger crowd would come later with the free food and discounted drinks. Hank bought a long neck beer and carried it over to the pool table. After shooting several rounds, Hank sat at the bar. The bartender bought him his fourth beer and he was feeling a little fuzzy so he decided to call Tracy before he got too inebriated. At the office he programmed her number into his cell phone, so all he had to do was pull her up from his contact list and press send.

As the phone rang, he grabbed his beer for a long swig.

"Hello?"

"Tracy, hi! It's Hank."

"Hank! Hello."

"How are you?" She had done a lot of crying the last time they spoke.

"I'm coping."

"How's Dave?"

"Good. He's back here at the G.W. Hospital. He'll be there a few more days. They're doing hydration therapy for his feet and hands. He's lost two toes and they're hoping they won't have to amputate any more." Hank cringed at the thought of having anything cut off. He wiggled his own toes to remind him how wonderful they all felt snuggled close together inside his shoes.

"Did you go to the service?"

"Yes, I went to Connecticut for the memorial."

"How was it? I wanted to come, but I had to fly to Katmandu to get Dave home."

"Things like that are meant for people to 'turn the page', so to speak." Hank paused for a moment. "Frankly that wasn't happening for me."

"I had a long talk with Dave. He's convinced that Aaron had suffered some kind of stroke up on the mountain."

"A stroke? How could that be?"

"It's a medical condition. Cerebral something-or-other. You can get it in your lungs or in your head."

"Amazing."

"Hank, you throw out the rule book when you get above 20,000 feet. Dave didn't know anything was wrong until he reached him. By that time, there was nothing he could do."

"I see."

"And there was no way anyone could pull him off the mountain. The storm was so bad it was every man for himself." Hank listened to Tracy's words. It was obvious she was repeating what Dave had told her.

"Well, maybe I'll have to pull him off."

"What? Hank, that's impossible. You can't get him, no one can."

"Maybe not in the physical sense . . ."

"What are you going to do?"

"I don't know yet. But I think he's waiting for me to do something."

"Hank? He's dead." Her cynicism came right through the line.

"How was Katmandu?"

"Hot, smelly, and crowded."

"Too bad. I always imagine places like that to be exotic."

There was a tap on Hank's shoulder. He swung himself around to see a mountain of a man standing in front of him. He was caught so off guard that all he could visually take in was a bald head, flaming red goatee and biceps that bulged through a black t-shirt.

"Excuse me," the man said politely. "Is this seat taken?" Hank lowered the phone from his ear as Tracy talked.

"No, by all means." He gestured with his hand for Goliath to take the chair before he swiveled back around to continue his conversation.

"Are you there?"

"I'm sorry. Someone was talking to me."

"Where are you?"

"In a bar."

"What are you doing there?"

"I don't know. Hanging out, thinking." He looked back at his beer sitting on the bar getting warm.

"Having a few.

I went out to Mount Dora today. It's where Aaron bought a house." Tracy paused long enough for Hank to know she knew what he was talking about.

"I knew about the house, not the name of the town."

"And did you know what Aaron intended to do with it?"

"Live in it?" He deserved the sarcasm for the stupid question.

"I've seen the place. It's not a bachelor's pad, if you know what I mean. Neither is the neighborhood."

"Tell me what you're saying Hank?"

"Aaron was moving there to settle down. Was someone going to settle down with him?" It seemed like forever for her to answer.

"Yes."

There was a long pause. "Is it you?"

"I have to go now!"

"No, wait. I'm sorry, I didn't mean . . ."

"Don't judge me right away Hank, and I won't judge you." She could barely finish before she stifled a sob. The line went dead. He pushed redial. When it connected to voice mail, he hung up. She had paraphrased a quote Aaron had always said from the bible. It was his mantra for liking so many people. "Judge not," he said aloud as he picked up his long neck, "that ye be not judged." He took a swig.

"What'd you say?" Sitting next to Hank was the big guy, chomping on a plate of chicken wings.

"I'm sorry," Hank said. "I was talking to myself."

"I know the quote; it's from Matthew, chapter seven."

"Really? And you know it?"

"Yeah. Let me see." Hank watched as the man tapped his right hand fingers against his forehead. He had the body of a world federation wrestler, but spoke with a gentle voice.

"The actual verse is: 'Judge not, that ye be judged. For with what judgment ye judge, ye shall be judged'." He smiled again. "Jesus said it in his sermon on the mount."

"That's pretty good. You're not a man of the cloth, are you?"

"Nah. But my name *is* Matthew; Matt Haskins." He and Hank shook hands.

"Henry Longo."

"Nice to meet you. When I was young, my folks gave me a bible and when I found the chapter with my name it was kinda neat, so I kept reading it until one day, I had the whole thing memorized."

"That's quite an accomplishment." Hank looked at the plate of wings. His stomach grumbled from all the beer and it wanted food.

Matt slid his plate toward Hank. "Here man, help yourself." Hank picked up a Tabasco drenched piece. He dipped it in the bowl of bleu cheese and took a bite. "Mmm, spicy."

"Why were you reciting Matthew," Matt asked.

"It was something a good friend of mine used to say. My best friend." He drained the last of his beer and put the bottle down, then flicked his fingers to push it away.

"Hey, you want another? Come on I'll buy. Hey Jenna!" Matt waved his hand to get the bartender's attention.

"You know I think I've had enough. I've been here for awhile and . . ."

"Oh okay," Matt responded. "No pressure Henry, believe me. I'm drinking cranberry and soda. You want one of those? You gotta have something if you're going to eat these wings."

"That sounds good. In fact, I'll get some more." Hank got up and made his way to the food. He hadn't realized how crowded it had gotten. By the time he returned with the plates, the drinks had arrived.

"There ya go now, so shut your yap," the bartender blasted Matt with her thick accent. Hank guessed Texas. She looked at Matt with scorn. "Hollerin' and wavin' at me like I'm ya personal servant."

"But you're the love of my life, Jenna. Marry me!"

"Phht," she said as she walked away. Over her shoulder she added, "Been there, done that, won't do it again."

Matt turned to Hank and said, "I really do love that woman."

"What do you do for a living?"

"I'm a blacksmith."

"Excuse me?"

"I shoe horses."

"Really? How'd you get into something like that?"

"After the service I was kinda lost. That's why I don't drink anymore. Did way too much of it after leaving Special Forces."

"You were in Special Forces?"

"I was a S.E.A.L."

"Holy shit!" Hank blurted. "Did you see action?"

"My team secured the desalination plant in Al Shareed during Gulf War One. We were also part of a covert landing in Kuwait City. Got behind the lines and blew up a communication tower."

"But you decided not to stay in?" Matt looked down at the wings on his plate.

"Without being too melodramatic, I killed a few people." He paused. "Some were civilians." Matt looked at Hank. "And I lost one of my own."

"Oh man," Hank said.

"It was rough to deal with. I tried to put it behind me, but couldn't. So I opted out. I thought if I got home I'd be able to work it out. I'd see my Mom and Dad; catch up with friends, just do something else."

"And it appears you've succeeded."

"Yeah, but it's been a long road Henry. For about a year all I did was drink. I couldn't come to grips with a lot of things. It's one thing to train to kill; it's another to do it."

Matt took a sip of his soda.

"After about a year at home, it was coming up on Memorial Day. I had been asked to march in the town parade. I politely declined. But on the day of the parade I decided to stand on the sidewalk and cheer, to show a little patriotism. I'd worn my dress hat along with a couple of service medals." Hank listened with interest.

"The parade went by and everyone had a good time. As the crowd thinned out this little boy, not much older than four or five, walked up to me and asked, 'Are you a soldier?' I bent down and said, 'Yes'. Right behind him, his father came running. The little guy had gotten away from his dad when the crowd dispersed, and he'd been frantic trying to find him. He thanked me for helping him find his son. The little boy said to his dad, 'Daddy, this man's a soldier!' As he picked up his kid, the father asked me, 'Are you a veteran?' I told him I was, and that I'd been in Kuwait during GW 1. He put the boy back down and then shook my hand with both of his. And all he said was, 'Thank you.' I looked back down at the boy, and he gave me a salute. When I snapped him one back, I realized I didn't need to hide anymore. You got kids, Henry?"

"Yes, two girls."

"There's something so amazing about children. I'll never forget that little boy. That happy smile as he saluted me. His innocence. And a week later at my uncle's horse ranch I found out the blacksmith, who'd been working the area for years, wanted to retire. A short apprenticeship later, and here I am today."

"That's some story," Hank said. "I'm glad everything worked out."

"Now, if I can only convince that beautiful bartender over there that I would be the best thing to ever happen to her, my life will be complete."

"You're really into her, huh?"

"She's the real deal. Beautiful, mature. Problem is she's been married before so she's not kidding when she says 'been there, done that'." Matt pointed to one of the cocktail waitresses working. "And since I've already gone out with Karen she thinks I'm only interested in younger women. So I'm kind of in double jeopardy don't you think?"

"I guess." Hank didn't know what to say.

"How long you been married Henry?"

"Eleven years this September."

"Congrats, my man! And what do you do?"

"I'm an accountant. I work for some of the hotels here in Orlando."

"And you've come here to unwind?"

"Whenever my best friend from college would come into town, we'd always meet here. Play some pool, drink a few beers." Matt just listened. "He was killed in a mountain climbing accident, recently." Matt's eyes reflected the sadness he knew all too well.

"Aw, Henry I'm sorry," he said. "It's God awful to lose a friend." They both sat in the quiet of their thoughts.

"I should go." Hank glanced at his watch, and then looked at the money Matt left on the bar. "Hey, I should help with that."

"Forget it. My treat."

"You sure?"

"No doubt." Matt shot him a definite grin. "It's been great to meet you." Matt draped his arm over Hank's shoulders. "Come on Henry, I'll walk you to your car."

It had rained just before they came out of the bar. The sun was finally setting and a humid dampness filled the air.

"You sure you're okay?" Matt said as he reached for his keys.

"Yeah, I'll be fine," Hank responded. "I ate a lot of wings. I think there's more Tabasco in me than beer. Besides, I didn't have that many."

"You have far to go?"

"Nah. I live less than a mile away. Where are you headed?"

"Ocala," Matt said. "That's mine." He pointed to a sleek, black Ford F-350. Hank was impressed with the customization Matt had given the truck.

"Nice rig."

"It suits me. I'm on the road a lot. Between here and some other farms I handle up at Gainesville and in the Panhandle, I do a lot of driving."

"Do you do a lot of work here, in Orlando?"

"I've got a few places. Next week I've got to come down and do some stuff for a place out in Clermont." Matt pulled out his wallet and extracted a business card. "You said you had two girls?"

"Elisabeth and Eva."

"Well tell you what, I'm going to be at that farm. Give me a call and we'll set it up so that when I'm there, you'll come visit with your girls? The owners let me have complete run of the place, so I can show you what I do, and maybe get your daughters up on some of the ponies. You can even take a ride yourself." Hank looked at the card and then waved it at Matt.

"Great. I'll call you."

"Hey, listen. Once again, I'm sorry about your friend. Believe me when I tell you, it takes time."

"You're right about that."

"Do what you need to do, but do productive things. Drinking is not productive. Take it from someone who drank himself into a stupor every day for a year. That wasn't a good way for me to spend time remembering the buddy I lost in Kuwait."

Hank watched as Matt climbed into his truck. A deep throaty rumble emanated from the exhaust. He backed out, gave Hank a quick salute, and then torque jumped the truck forward and drove away. Hank watched him go.

Later that night, after the kids and Linda went to bed, Hank sat at his computer and checked some postings. Most of them were useless, all except one. The Senior Center in Sebring was sponsoring a free lecture given by a former Sherpa guide, Umesh Bhuju, who had climbed Everest ten years ago. Hank pulled out his organizer and wrote down the date, time and number. A strange sense of purpose washed over him. It was as if some force had compelled him to set up the search just so he could find this event. He knew he would go.

Chapter 10

Meeting Umesh

THE DRIVE TO Sebring two days later had been a quiet one, the argument with Linda the day before was not.

"Look, it's a great opportunity for me to learn more about what happened with Aaron."

"Didn't you talk with Tracy? And didn't she tell you what happened?" Linda asked as she folded laundry on the living room floor.

"Yes, but this guy's been there."

"So you think this Sherpa guide from Nepal can help you understand how Aaron died or why? He's going to help you figure out what happened?"

"No, I just think he might give me a better understanding."

"Hank." Linda got up with the full basket of folded clothing.

"Linda. I made the reservation." His shoulders slumped. "I need to go. Please?" Hank despised looking pathetic, but he knew from experience it was his best weapon. And once again, it worked.

"All right, go. But answer this . . ." She put the basket down and counted off with her fingers, "You've been to Connecticut for the funeral; you needed to go out to Long Island; you needed to take time off from work; you needed to go to Mount Dora and now it's Sebring. How much more do you need?"

Hank looked up at her from his chair. His eyes went moist as he said, "Enough to really know."

Linda took the basket and walked out of the room.

The next morning, Hank went for an early run. While he jogged, he thought about how his love affair with Linda had changed over the years.

"We never used to argue," *until the babies*. Hank felt a stretching of their bond like a rubber band with the two of them at either end.

Hank found his rhythm and now ran effortlessly around the recreation center. Linda was already up and making breakfast by the time he had finished showering. Her mood had improved considerably with the night's rest.

The conference room was large and the presentation well attended. "Umesh . . . Bhuju," introduced himself, and began with the visual presentation.

"This is Lukla, a small airstrip built to accommodate groups who choose to climb the Himalayas. It is the closest point for supply drops," Umesh said as he clicked off different shots of the high plateau airfield and the aircraft. "From there it's still a two week trek to the base camp of Mount Everest."

Subsequent slides showed narrow river gorges, terraced farming fields, and long rope suspension bridges. There were pictures of Umesh along side a climbing team. The slides continued with images of wooly Dzopkyos; a crossbreed of yak and cattle they use as pack animals.

"Each of these 'Naks' is capable of carrying between two hundred and three hundred and fifty pounds of mountain climbing equipment."

Western doctors smiled for the camera at a hospital built in the little village of Kunde, by Sir Edmund Hillary. Umesh told about how much the famed climber had done for people in the region, building schools and providing educational and medical supplies. He continued the narrative, as he pointed a small red beam of light at each slide that clicked off the carousal and onto the screen.

"This is a Buddhist monastery where prayer flags are blessed and divinations are requested to ensure a successful climb. The mountain is revered as a female deity, who must be appeased in order to climb her safely, and respected when her anger warns not to go.

And here you can see the sign for the entrance to Sagarmatha National Park. The name Mount Everest was chosen by the British for George Everest, surveyor general for the Royal Geographical Society in India.

I was the climbing sirdar, or head Sherpa. Sherpas," Umesh explained, "established a series of four camps above base camp. Each one was approximately 2,000 feet higher than the last. Food, cooking fuel, and oxygen were shuttled from encampment to encampment until all supplies had been distributed and stocked, all the way up to 26,000 feet." Hank and the audience were stunned to learn the amount of time needed to properly acclimatize was almost a month. "It was from camp four we began our one day assault to the summit. It would take almost eight hours to cover the remaining 3,000 feet."

The presentation concluded with pictures of the team having reached the top, and Umesh attaching multi colored banners to a battered aluminum survey pole. Behind the Sherpa guide was another team member holding up the old confederate flag of the South. Hank laughed.

When the lights went back on, Hank was glad he'd come. The room emptied within minutes, while the man who had kept everyone entertained was now by himself as he packed up the equipment.

"Excuse me, Mr. Bhuju?" Hank felt odd not knowing how to pronounce the name. Umesh looked up from the carousel he was trying to put into a travel box, smiled, and reached out to shake hands.

"I am Umesh Bhuju. And you are?"

"Henry Longo, from Orlando."

"Thank you for coming, Mr. Longo." Hank found Umesh's sincerity ingratiating.

"I wanted to thank you for the slide show. I really got a lot out of it."

"Well, I wish I had more time because there is so much more to tell." Umesh's face changed from exuberance to puzzlement. "I noticed you taking notes. Are you doing research?" Umesh wrapped an extension cord around his arm.

"Uh, no," was the guarded response.

"Are you planning a trip there? You should go," Umesh said as he threw the extension cord into a milk crate. "It will do you good."

"What do you mean? I'm a hotel accountant." It was the only excuse he could think of.

"Last time I checked," Umesh replied, his smile returning, "accountants are allowed to travel to Nepal."

Hank laughed. "Not this accountant."

"Is there something you would like to talk about?"

"My friend, he was climbing Everest . . . He didn't make it back down. I wanted to find out more about the Himalayas, about climbing, what it's like in Nepal."

"It's a mystical place." Umesh looked at his watch. "I'm sorry," he said, "but I have to get back to my store." He turned to gather up his equipment. Hank could see he had more than he was able to carry.

"Can I help you with that?"

"Yes, thank you. If you can carry the boxes of slides I'll be able to make it in one trip." Hank nodded and picked up the boxes. "Why don't you come with me to my store. It's close by. We can have tea." Umesh paused to say what Hank wanted to hear.

"And then I can tell you more."

The "store" was a restaurant with an old-fashioned ice cream parlor. It was just like the one he'd go to with his grandparents on Sunday's after church.

Umesh had a pressing meeting in his office, so Hank was given a booth and offered lunch while he waited for Umesh to join him.

As he sat, Hank studied the place. It was mainstream America with a dollop of Asia mixed in. A nice mix. There was a separate area to the right of the soda fountain bar with sofas and small tables. Beyond a beaded doorway entrance Hank could hear a sitar playing. He recognized the song; it was the Beatles' "Within Without You". He smiled.

His eyes widened when his sandwich was delivered, big and meaty with homemade fries. Hank dug in. As he finished his sandwich and cleaned the rest of the ketchup off of his plate with several fries, Umesh joined him.

Hank wiped his mouth with a napkin. "This is great," he proclaimed. "Best turkey club I've ever had."

"We put a little sage in the mayonnaise and always use hickory smoked bacon. It's the little things that make a difference."

"Nothing wrong with paying attention to the details."

"I am so sorry. I had a meeting with my lawyer about the possible purchase of the building next door."

"Wow. So you're looking to expand?" Hank smiled and watched as Umesh looked around for the server. Spotting Luja, his niece, he summoned her with a wave of his hand. She came and cleared away Hank's plate and empty glass of iced tea.

"Luja? Would you bring us some tea please?" She nodded and bowed. Umesh chastised, "Slow down," as she hurried away.

"How old is she?"

"Sixteen. She's only been here six months."

"It looks like quite the family operation here."

"I don't run the business much anymore. My sister's son just got his business degree from Gainesville. He's in charge of the day to day operation."

"It looks like most of the help is from your country," Hank said.

"Yes, and from India, too. We have tried to help as many as we can who have sought a better life. For themselves and their families."

"What brought you here?"

"It's a long story," Umesh said while slightly laughing. "Are you sure you want to hear it?" Hank nodded silently.

"I came to this country," he began, "because of climbing. I grew up in a village called Khumjung. It is in the Khumbu valley, at the base of the Himalayas, not far from Mount Everest. I am a Sherpa. Sherpas are one of many ethnic tribes who live in Nepal. Because we live in the northeastern part of the country and are adept at climbing and working in thin air, and also because of Tenzing Norgay, who climbed with Hillary, we are famously known for being the porters and guides for those who want to climb above 25,000 feet."

Luja returned with a tea service. In silence, she put the tray down and placed the china cups and saucers in front of Hank and her uncle. With a small towel that had been tucked into her apron, she picked up a beautifully engraved teapot and poured the steamy liquid. Hank tried the brew before adding a generous amount of milk and sugar. "Thank you Luja," Umesh said. Hank watched as Umesh said a few words in their language before she departed.

"So I trained for a number of years," Umesh continued. "At first, I was a base camp Sherpa, then a porter; each time getting the opportunity to carry the expedition's supplies higher up the mountain. When Jack Dawson came along with his quest to climb the last of the seven summits, I was ready. He hired me as his climbing Sherpa and on May 22nd, 1990, we reached the top of Everest together."

"That must have been an amazing moment."

"It was an event I look back on with difficult memories. Happy to reach the top and to have followed in the footsteps of my father who had climbed with the American group back in 1963, but my younger brother was killed during Jack's expedition. He was swept away in an avalanche." Hank stared at the man in disbelief. He watched as Umesh first shifted in his seat and then looked up at the ceiling.

"So you see Henry, I too have lost a loved one on Everest."

Their conversation continued and Hank learned that after the '90 climb, Dawson and Umesh went into business together. They started a climbing consulting group. "High Mountain Adventures" planned out climbs to the different highest points on the Earth and clients paid exorbitant sums to be taken there.

"But you haven't answered my question," Hank said, pouring himself more tea. "How on earth did you end up here in Sebring?"

"I was almost killed during our last expedition and . . ."

"Really? You didn't mention that in your slide show."

"No, I didn't want to upset anyone."

"What happened?"

"We had summited and were descending on the Lhotse face when a rock about the size of a television broke loose and came hurtling down. Someone shouted and I was lucky enough to see it coming. But all I could do was press myself flat against the fifty-degree slope and pray. It bounced right over me; just nicked the top of my head."

"God, you were lucky!"

"A member of the expedition," Umesh said, thinking back, "had seen where the rock broke off. Later on when we descended we found the boulder and he had calculated that based on its weight and rate of fall it was traveling at ninety-three miles an hour when it went by me. I was more than lucky. And that was it for me. Many in my family had made a good living by taking the risk involved in climbing the mountains. But after my brush with death, I decided to choose a healthier way to live my life."

"My friend had just gotten around to realizing that it wasn't for him anymore either. He had planned a change, but . . ." Umesh allowed a moment for Hank to reflect. The noise in the restaurant seemed to disappear for Hank. He could only hear the voice of the man sitting across from him. The pain of his loss stirred deep within him.

"Buddha," Umesh said with compassion, "once said that the law of death is that among all living creatures, there is no permanence. No one lives free from suffering and loss my friend. Just as your friend had put off changing his life, I sense you are putting off expressing your grief." Hank could feel the tears well up in his eyes. He swallowed hard and instead asked, "So. You gave up climbing and moved here?"

"Yes, one of the clients I had from the expedition business is a dermatologist who lives here. We became close friends and he helped me to emigrate here and sponsored me for citizenship. Through him I was able to secure the loans I needed to start this business and bring other family members over. And here I am today."

"So, what's it really like to climb that mountain, to climb any mountain?"

"It takes skill," Umesh began, his arms around his teacup and his fingers interlocked. "And patience." Hank frowned in confusion. He was a numbers man who relied on linear thinking.

"In Buddhist traditions Henry, mountains like Everest are sacred. Mountains and other holy places are circumambulated, not climbed. When you enter into hallowed ground, it is best to seek benediction from the unseen spirits of earth and air. One must acknowledge their presence or disaster is bound to happen." Umesh pointed to a scroll painting that hung on a far wall. Hank could see the beautiful figure of a woman, her radiant hair studded with gems.

"Miyolangsangma," Umesh said the name slower so that Hank could pronounce it. "She is the protector goddess who resides on Everest. She is a Buddhist deity, who along with her four other "long life" sisters, provide protection and spiritual nourishment to Khumbu and the nearby valleys."

"I see," Hank said. "Miyolang-sangma."

"Yes, that's it. If you go to Nepal and wish to climb Everest, you must first visit the temples and ask for blessings, and make offerings to Miyolangsangma for her protection and care. You must also ask the temple Lama's for a divination before you climb. A journey out to climb Everest is both physical and spiritual. If you want to know the more technical aspects of the climb, my partner, Jack is the one to ask. Since he has organized climbs from start to finish, he would be your best resource. Here," Umesh reached for his wallet and pulled out a business card. "He is an amazing fellow." He handed the card to Hank.

"Thank you Umesh, I'll give him a call."

"Call me Umi. All my friends do."

"If you'll call me Hank. All my friends do as well."

At that moment, Luja approached the two of them with dessert. A small glass dish of ice cream was placed in front of Umesh and another, twice the size, was put in front of Hank.

"It's a banana split!"

"Yes," Umesh said with pride. "The house specialty! And it's on the house."

"Thank you." He picked up the extra long metal spoon. "I don't know where to begin, but I'm sure it's too big to finish."

"Start on the right," Umesh pointed. "There are three syrups and the butterscotch is especially delicious."

"I haven't had a banana split since . . . well I can't even remember the last time I had one." Hank took a bite and while enjoying the treat asked, "Are you Buddhist?"

"I try to follow the Buddha's path," Umesh smiled.

"My friend Aaron was very spiritual. He meditated a lot. Talked to me about kindness and compassion."

"It sounds like he was a practicing Buddhist. The Buddhist path is one to enlightenment, happiness, and compassion for all living things. These are experiences one tries to achieve in each life on a road to total consciousness." Hank noticed Umesh's face change. His questioning became serious.

"Henry, how did your friend die?"

"I was told he succumbed to the elements. There was a storm, he got sick, some kind of altitude illness. I find it hard to believe though. The guy was as tough as nails."

"HAPE or HACE, conditions that affect either the brain or lungs. They do happen and if you can't get off the mountain quick enough well . . ."

"So, he could've had a stroke?"

"Yes, cerebral edema. Can you tell me, what condition was he in before he left for the climb?"

"He was in good shape; always been strong ever since I've known him."

"No, I mean was his mind clear?"

"Well, he was nervous, which was unusual for Aaron."

"Nervous? Was he afraid of the danger involved?"

"It wasn't anything like that. He liked to climb. As a matter of fact, he once had a photo shoot in Africa. After finishing up, on a whim, he signed himself up to climb Kilimanjaro. He told me that it was one of the greatest experiences of his life."

"Wait a minute," Umesh said, "I'm a little confused. Was your friend part of the fiftieth anniversary team?"

"Yes, he was the still photographer hired to photograph the event."

Hank could see that this new information changed Umesh's perspective and his thinking. "So he was working?"

"Yes, does that change things?"

"Perhaps. My belief is that when you are climbing the mountain to reach its summit, your journey is both physical and spiritual. You must," Umesh emphasized, "ask the deities there for their blessings. You must seek out guidance from the monks and lamas that live by the mountain. Since he was only hired to photograph the climb, maybe he did not feel it necessary to ask Miyolangsangma for her help." Hank scoffed at the idea.

"I'm going to have a tough time with that one. Forgive me for being skeptical, but I don't think Aaron died because he didn't ask a Goddess permission to climb up her backside."

"Fair enough." Umesh put his hands up in a gesture of surrender.

"As a matter of fact," Hank recalled, "he was looking forward to visiting the Buddhist temples and participating in their rituals. Aaron would've been first in line to seek out divine counsel." Umesh reached for the teapot and refilled first Hank's cup and then his own. "This assignment was going to be his last, and then he was going to finally settle down."

"I see."

"In fact he was pretty emotional about it. A big change in the way he saw things, about how his life was going to be different." Hank scooped out the last of the ice cream and let the spoon fall with a clang, into the dish. "Boy, that was great."

"Inner contentment?" Umesh was puzzled.

"I'm not sure of his exact words. We were at a bar when he started spewing all this stuff about mistakes he had made. Man, he cried that night. He was so happy, and so afraid."

Luja came to take the dishes. When she was out of earshot Umesh asked, "Have you seen him again?"

"What?"

"In your dreams, does he come to you?"

"What? How do you . . ." Looking at the man across the booth, Hank could tell he already had his answer.

"Why are you here today? What do you think brought you here? To me?"

"Google?" Umesh closed his eyes and shook his head.

"I set up an internet search," Hank explained, "about Everest. It let me know that you were giving a lecture. I thought I might learn something so here I am."

"And what prompted you to set up this search?"

"Uh, let's see; I had come back from Mt. Dora where I had just seen the house that Aaron had planned to . . ." Hank remembered the wind. It wasn't like the sun soaked humid kind before the approach of a typical Florida squall. It was cold, and made Hank shiver.

"Is Aaron trying to communicate with me? I can't even begin . . ." Umesh held up his hands.

"Wait, let me explain. What we may be dealing with is an unsettled consciousness. Buddhist tradition maintains that those who perish must pass through the bardo; an interim place one spends time in before passing from one life to the next. In the case of an untimely death, their ghost can wander. They are called shrindi. They are lost, and unaware they have died."

"Wow," Hank said. "So I've had these dreams . . ."

"Tell me about that."

"When I saw him, he was calling to me, telling me how cold he was; he needed my help." Hank paused, reliving the nightmare. "But he was so far away, I couldn't reach him."

"I'm afraid his consciousness will continue to haunt you until you direct it to move on."

Hank went numb. A part of him wanted to conclude the whole thing was complete nonsense. It was all too fantastic to believe. But at the same time he also knew that Aaron believed in this. They had many talks about life and death. He had witnessed Aaron's spiritual outlook and rugged determination to control his life.

"Damn, Umi," Hank said in a whisper. "What am I going to do?"

"I don't know Hank," Umesh whispered back. "But when you do, I will help."

*   *   *

That night Hank couldn't sleep. He got up early and went to the makeshift den. After signing in his personal Yahoo website, he typed Aaron's Hotmail address and began to compose.

<Hey, where are you buddy? Are you close, or far away? It's Hank!
<I thought I'd drop you a note.
<Listen! I know this is crazy, but I think you've been trying to get in
<touch with me. I'm sorry that I haven't been able to get back to you,
<but frankly I don't know how. It's like I don't have the right calling
<card or something! So, are you okay? I'm kind of worried. It's like
<you're such a long way away, I don't know how to fucking reach
<you!! Hey listen, I've got to ask; was that you out at Mt. Dora the other
<day? Nice place buddy, I checked it out. You did well my friend.
<Hey, it's getting late, Linda's probably wondering where I am.
<So I was hoping, if you can, get in touch, okay? I miss you, Bud.
<Tell me what to do.
<Hank.

Hank stared at the message. He was writing to a dead person, but the ethereal Internet seemed like a place where spirits and ghosts could congregate. It may not be heaven, but it was a place that had Aaron's name on it. Hank clicked to send off his message. As the computer acknowledged that the message had been sent, he hoped it would not be the last.

Chapter 11

Arrowhead Farm

"I don't know Hank," Linda said. "You really don't know this guy from Adam and you want to go clear out to Clermont?" Hank called Matt using the speakerphone so that Linda could listen in. His politeness and assurances that the girls would have a lot to do out at the farm besides riding had won her over. And having a Saturday without the girls would give Linda a chance to take her mom to a matinee movie; something she had wanted to do for weeks.

The directions Matt had given took them south of the lakeside town. They came upon a long stretch of curving white fence that separated the farm's pasture fields from the road. The entrance to Arrowhead Farm was impressive with a large Neolithic stone atop the columned gateway. The long canopy of trees that bowed over the road had Hank thinking the owners of this place had serious money. Just past the main house was the barn and paddocks. Matt's gargantuan truck was parked in front. Hank pulled along side and helped Eva and Elisabeth out. Matt was a sight, as he headed over to greet them, wearing a baseball cap and stripped to the waist except for a large black leather apron.

"Henry, I'm glad you could make it." *God, he's a big man.*

Both Elisabeth and Eva grabbed Dad's hands.

"So, let me guess." Matt squatted down. "You're the oldest so you must be Eva, right?" Eva smiled and nodded. "And I've heard that you can ride, is that true?" Eva nodded again and this time let go of Hank's hand. In spite of his massive appearance, Matt's disarming smile had won her over.

"Well," Matt continued, "there's a chestnut mare in the stable called Wisteria. She needs a rider for her morning workout. Do you think you're up for that?"

"Sure," gushed Eva. Matt stood back up.

"How tall are you?" Elisabeth asked. Matt turned to her. "Well, I'm six foot four little Elisabeth. How tall are you?"

"Daddy?" Hank looked down at his puzzled daughter. "You're three feet, seven inches," he said.

"Daddy says three feet, seven inches."

"That's just perfect, Elisabeth. You're one inch taller than the minimum required to ride the ponies here at Arrowhead."

"Really?" Elisabeth beamed with delight.

"Yes, and I've got several that are eager to make a new friend. Would you like to meet them?" Elisabeth nodded with enthusiasm.

"And Hank," Matt said with a crooked grin, "I have something for you to do as well."

"Uh oh," he said, as his smile faded.

Matt had the whole morning planned out with Hank's girls working with the farm hands giving out feed to the different animals on the farm and having Hank muck out several of the horses' stalls. When every one had done their "chores", a morning ride was arranged for everyone on a trail that ran around the back half of the breeder farm.

"Look at me daddy!" Eva happily exclaimed as she took up the lead on the trail.

"Don't get too far ahead," Hank called back. "Stay with the rest of us, okay?"

"I knew the girls would get a kick out of this," Matt said as his legs gently tapped his horse's side urging him forward.

"Oh, the two of them probably think they've died and gone to heaven. Who owns this place?"

"A couple from New York own it. They're originally from Kentucky, grew up in horse farm country and plan to retire in another five years or so from the family brokerage business. Then they'll be here to run the place full time."

"Nice," Hank said.

"The guy's not much older than me."

"It must be great to have a plan," Hank said, shaking his head.

After the ride, Matt arranged for one of the farm hands, a young girl named Becky, to take the girls while he and Hank went off and do other business. Hank watched as Elisabeth and Eva waved good-bye and walked off with the teenager.

"That's it Tri Star," Matt encouraged the large black horse out of his paddock. "Come on, it's new shoes for you." With his tongue, Matt made a series of clicking sounds. As he and the horse made their way slowly out the back door of the barn he called over his shoulder to Hank.

"Follow me Henry. My office is out here."

"Whoa. Easy there Tri Star, easy." The horse's head jerked up and down as Hank tried to hold his bridle steady.

"I just want to check his coronet before I put the new shoes on. Give him some more of those treats I put in that pail." Hank reached down with his free hand for the oats Matt had put out on a small knee high table. Glancing down the side of the animal, he could see Matt seated on a small tripod stool. At his side was a metal toolbox and several tools were laid out on a strip of worn cowhide. He had the horse's right rear hoof in one hand and a large metal file in the other.

"Is this a crucial moment?" Hank asked. He watched Matt scrape the hoof and wondered if it was painful.

"Naw naw, he's fine," Matt replied. "Just talk to him and give him those oats. They're special made from California, from Sacramento Valley. He loves 'em." Hank lifted up the handful of meal he had grabbed and then grimaced as the horse slurped up the treat. "Talk to him, Henry," Matt repeated. Hank could see Matt was just about to hammer on a new shoe.

"Atta boy Tri Star! You like those oats don't you. Good boy." Hank could see calmness in the horse's dark brown eyes. After finishing the oats, Hank gently stroked the animal's long snout.

"Okay," Matt shouted, "you can let him go." Hank released the straps around Tri Star's head. He let out a loud whinny as he galloped off into the adjoining pasture.

"That's a happy animal," Hank said as he watched Tri Star gallop around the pasture with the other horses. Matt wiped his hands with a rag and then passed it to Hank.

"New shoes are about all the happiness that one's ever going to get."

"What do you mean?"

"That horse, my friend," Matt pointed, "is what they call a 'teaser stallion'. They're deployed to arouse the mares and test their readiness for breeding. But at the moment when their foreplay has gotten the girls all hot and bothered, they're replaced with a breeding stallion and sent to the bench."

"Ooof," Hank grimaced. "That's painful."

"Boy I tell ya, sometimes life's not fair."

"No," Hank said, still laughing, "it sure isn't."

Hank watched the horse run through the open field. His legs kicked out awkwardly as he tested his new shoes.

"So," Hank asked, "you enjoy doing this?"

"I am." Matt walked back into the stable. Hank followed from behind. "There's an amazing harmony," Matt continued, "with these beautiful creatures. To know horses is to love them and I do." Hank followed Matt back into the barn.

"Ajax! Come here bud." Matt said as he reached into his pocket for a treat. "You ready for some new stylin', huh?" Matt opened the bottom part of the paddock door and led the horse over to Hank. "Look at him," he said, bringing Ajax's head close enough for Hank to pet. "Calm, noble. A bit of a prima donna this one is, but still, I can see the steel in his eyes. He's a determined beast when he wants to be. You know in war the horse fought and died in battle alongside the men who rode them." Matt pulled on the horse's reigns and walked Ajax outside. Hank followed.

Hank leaned against the barn's wall and watched as Matt worked on Ajax's front hooves.

"You know the job itself has many plusses." Matt concentrated on the horse's hoof as he talked. "I get to work outside, which was a big factor in my decision to do this. I get to work independently, which has helped me a lot."

"So what else appeals to you about being a blacksmith?"

"Uh, let's see," Matt said as he wiped sweat from his eyebrows with his massive forearm. "The people I work for are all very nice. The pay's good and I get my expenses covered on top of it." Matt became quiet and focused on tapping in the nails to the shoe. After securing the fourth one he reached for a small metal file and began scraping around the shoe's edge.

"Anything else?" Hank said.

"It's peaceful," Matt said. "There are some real nice quiet times where it's just me and the horse. Beautiful beast." Matt reached up and patted the side of Ajax's long neck. "Both huge and quick, a paradox of mass and speed. One of the three things I have gotten from the horses is a simple way to think clearly. My head is no longer a cluster fuck of tasks that have to be constantly sorted out."

"Man I know what that's like," Hank said. "It's what I do."

"The second thing about horses is when you're with them, you understand how they take in everything around them."

"And now you do?"

"Yeah, I do. I've retrained myself to stop and appreciate the world." Matt turned back to Hank and said, "The Buddhists believe that the less you have to think about things, the more aware you are."

I knew that, Hank thought to himself. *Aaron reminded me of that all the time.* "What's the third thing?"

"There's just a great fellowship in hanging around with the beasties. The downside of course is, the conversations are pretty much one sided."

They both chuckled.

*　　*　　*

Lunch had taken place in the cool, air-conditioned kitchen. The house cook had prepared a delicious seafood gumbo and salad that had both Matt and Hank going back for seconds. The girls had eaten the sandwiches they'd brought, along with the carrot sticks Linda had provided. As soon as they were done, they headed right back outside to play fetch with the farm's two dogs. From the window, Hank watched as they threw sticks from under an enormous elm that stood next to the main house.

"Are they okay?" Matt asked. Hank watched his girls enjoying the company of the two black Labradors, "Buddy" and "Boo".

"Yeah," Hank said, still looking out. "Actually, I'm more concerned about the dogs."

"Ah, you don't have to worry about those two. Farm dogs've got lots of energy." Matt walked across the room and deposited the dishes into the sink. "Henry, I want what you've got," Matt declared as he picked up the sponge.

"You mean the kids?"

"Yeah, the kids, family, everything. I'm more than ready to have that in my life."

"Be careful what you ask for," Hank said.

"Yes, I know. Want some coffee? I'll make a pot."

"Sure, if it's not a bother."

"Nope." Matt placed the last of the washed dishes into the drain board before he wiped his hands with the dish rag. "Believe me," picking up from where he left off, "I've had enough friends tell me all about the pitfalls of parenthood."

"And there are many," Hank confirmed.

"Yeah, but I also know that I've gotten to that point in my life where I'm going to need something more." Matt returned from the pantry with a coffee can and brown paper filter. Back over at the counter, he pulled a coffee maker from the cabinet.

"You know, as much as I love my job and the people I've met, I'm beginning to realize that this may be all there is." He plugged the unit in and pulled the glass pot out for inspection. A quick sniff confirmed it was clean. Matt poured the water into the back of the machine.

"If I'm going to be shoeing and working over a hot fire and anvil the rest of my life; which has been great but is getting a little redundant, I want a family to come home to." Matt put in the filter and then scooped four times from the can with a measured tablespoon. "At first," he went on, "I thought having a wife and family really wasn't meant for me." He closed up the can and flipped the lighted switch to start the brewing. "Not with my background," Matt confessed. "I worried about the violence instilled in me. You know what I'm talking about?" Hank nodded. Today's media had done a great job singling out the troubled returning veterans and the tragedies that unfolded because of their inability to reinsert themselves into society.

"I despised the idea of passing myself off to another generation. I asked myself what good works have I done that entitles me to a legacy? But I've gotten over my past. So I kind of like the idea of being someone's soul mate. And to have the opportunity one day to look into someone's eyes and really know." Matt stared straight at Hank. "Really know what love is all about."

Hank was dumbfounded. He took a deep breath and pulled his hands up to cover his face.

"What?" Matt said, confused. "Did I say something wrong?" Hank pulled his hands away and looked at Matt.

"No. It's just that this is almost the exact same conversation my friend Aaron and I had before he left on the climbing expedition. And I'm having a hell of a time trying to figure out what he meant."

"How do you take your coffee?" Matt took two mugs from an upper windowed cabinet.

"Black," Hank said. He watched Matt pour and place the steaming coffee mug in front of him before he sat down again.

"How did you get to be friends with Aaron," Matt asked with genuine interest.

"College buddies, Miami, twenty years ago. He was actually my boss working in the dorms. We hit it off almost from the very first day we met. Did a lot of things together. In school, after school. Road trips to the Keys.

We even worked together one summer up on Cape Cod. Aaron actually introduced me to my wife. He was best man at my wedding. He's Elisabeth's godfather."

"Incredible," Matt said as he sipped. "A true friend."

"None better," Hank said reflectively.

"Tell me about your friend who died," Hank said.

"Rick was a great guy. I didn't know him as long as you knew Aaron, but still, we enjoyed doing a lot of things together. He was my second at both Al-Shareed and in Kuwait City. He saved my life at the desalination plant."

"Wow."

"Yeah. He picked off a guy who had a bead on me. If it hadn't been for him, I wouldn't be standing in front of you today."

"What happened to him," Hank asked.

"Later on, we did a covert beach landing to blow a communications tower in the city. We accomplished the mission, but heading back a sniper pinned us down. We couldn't move and we had to get out of there. Rick ran into the street to draw him out. He just made it to the other sidewalk. The sniper got him in the head. It was awful, Hank. It was like watching the Magruder film all over again." Matt dropped his head down and exhaled.

"And then we got the sniper." Hank felt as if someone had punched him in the stomach. Matt's story was worse than he expected.

"I can't tell you what it's like," Matt said, looking up at the kitchen ceiling, "to watch someone go from being a husband to his high school sweetheart, a Michigan State varsity defensive back and father of three, become a corpse in a fraction of a second."

"He was a hero," was all Hank could think of to say.

"Yes. He was." Matt and Hank stared into their coffee mugs.

"We hauled him out of there, which we always do, no matter what."

Matt's words struck deep inside Hank. *No one gets left behind.*

"For a long time, I carried the weight of his death on my shoulders and drank because of it. I couldn't forgive myself.

About a year after I quit drinking, Rick came to me in a dream. Told me he was okay, said everything was all right and not to worry. Four months ago, I went back to Kuwait, back to the street where he had fallen. I laid a wreath down, along with some pictures of his wife and kids, on the spot where he had died. Said a few prayers. It wasn't much, but it was enough."

Hank looked at his watch and realized it was time to go. They finished their coffee and then walked outside to get the girls. When he reappeared from the back of the house, he had his elbows up and both of them sitting comfortably on each side of his massive shoulders. All three of them had an ear-to-ear grin.

"Look what I found!" Matt lowered each of them to the ground.

"What do you say, girls?" Hank cued.

"Thank you Matt," they said in unison.

"It was my pleasure, Elisabeth, Eva. I hope to see you again." The girls climbed into the car. When Hank turned around, Matt already had his hand out.

"Thank you," Hank said as he shook Matt's hand. "We had a great time."

"Thanks for coming out. Jobs like this go a lot quicker when there's someone you can hang with."

"Thanks for telling me about your friend Rick," Hank said. "It made me think about things."

"You've got a lot more to think about than I did, I'm afraid."

"I'm thinking now I should try to do something similar to what you did going to Kuwait."

"Good for you. I don't know what I'd be able to do, but if you need help, I'm here for you."

"I'll keep that in mind, thanks," Hank said.

"Okay Amigo, I gotta run. Jenna's working today and I don't want to miss her."

"How's that going by the way?"

"We're going out on our first date this Friday."

"Congratulations!"

"I'm nervous as hell," Matt admitted.

"Are you kidding?" Hank was incredulous. "A guy like you, nervous around women?"

"Not just any woman, Henry. We're talking about the future Mrs. Haskins."

"Well don't have too many expectations okay? Just enjoy the evening and take it from there."

"Good advice." They shook hands again and climbed into their vehicles. Matt backed out first.

That evening, after the girls were in bed, Hank parked himself in the bedroom den and paid some bills. Linda was glued to the couch and a favorite TV show. Knowing that she would stay put, he called down to Sebring.

"Umesh? It's Hank Longo."

"Hello Hank, how are you?"

"Fine thank you. I wanted to ask you about those monuments in the slide show, the ones at the base of the glacier."

"The Chortens?"

"Yes, that's it." He spun the executive chair around so that his back was to the door. "Tell me about them."

"They're religious monuments."

"Do you think one should be erected for Aaron?"

"Based on what you've told me," Umesh paused to consider his words, "I believe that your friend has had an untimely death and his spirit is in fact wandering aimlessly about the mountain. His consciousness seeks its path to enlightenment, but is either lost or something is blocking its way."

"I understand."

"I hear you say you understand, but do you believe." Hank had to pause. He understood what Umesh was getting at; there was no point in going on if he couldn't accept the concept.

"I grew up with a faith that believes in Heaven and Hell, but you're right. Aaron can't move on." Hank thought for a moment.

"I think I have to go help him. If anyone could seek out a way to guide Aaron's spirit, it would have to be me."

"Yes, I agree."

"Do you think erecting a chorten will be enough? Or do I have to do something more?"

Umesh paused to think of the right words. "You see there is a road before you. It may be the only one. It may be one of many. But it is there, isn't it? You need to get on it and find out where it goes."

"I don't know the first thing about how to do this," Hank complained. "How do I get there? Who do I ask for help?"

"It's okay Hank, I can help you. There are many people in Nepal that I know. Just let me know how you want to proceed and we will make it happen."

"I don't know what to say, Umi. Thank you."

"It is fine my friend." They exchanged a few more pleasantries before Hank hung up the phone.

Swiveling around in his chair he was startled to see Linda leaning against the door frame with her arms folded across her chest.

"That was an interesting conversation," she said.

"How much of it did you hear?"

"Enough."

"That was Umesh, the man who gave the slide show down in Sebring."

"Yes, I remembered who he is," she said. Linda moved into the room and sat down on the small convertible sofa they kept in the room.

"I didn't mean to eavesdrop, I was just coming to tell you that Christian was voted off." Hank and Linda enjoyed watching the reality show together.

"No, not Christian. What happened?"

"He tried to form an allegiance with Julia and Brock. They gave him up to keep Jesse."

"Great," Hank said, pretending to be disgusted.

"You and Umesh were talking a lot about spirits. I take it your conversation was about Aaron?"

"Yes it was."

"So what do you think, Hank? Do you think Aaron's ghost is haunting you?" She half smiled at him. Hank could see that she was concerned.

"Let's put it this way, I've had some pretty bad dreams about him. He's frozen, calling out to me, begging for help." Linda stayed quiet. Hank decided to add some more.

"At the memorial, up in Connecticut? I was talking to Wayne, his roommate from DC." Hank didn't want to go on. He didn't think Linda would believe him.

"And?" she said.

"Out of the corner of my eye, just on the edge of my view, I saw him."

"You saw Aaron?"

"Yeah." Hank was encouraged. Her gaze was one of intrigue and not contempt. "Or his image. Or something. He was in his padded climbing suit. Snow was swirling around him. His arms were outstretched."

"Really?" Linda smiled. "You saw his ghost?" Hank leaned forward in his chair.

"I don't know. It wasn't even two seconds. But I have this image of him and I can't get it out of my mind. You know Aaron really believed that there were these places . . ." Linda cut him off with a wave of her hand.

"Yes, I know, gaps in the time continuum. I remember the argument I had with him about it. He tried to convince me that there were these special places; blank open voids where consciousness and thought could go. Mind portals."

"You didn't think it was possible?"

"I don't know Hank, that was a long time ago. I'm pretty sure we were all stoned at the time. I know he was."

"And what," Linda inquired, "does the Sherpa man say?"

"He says my dreams are true." Once again, Hank chose his words carefully. "Aaron's death is untimely. He is in a wandering state and calling out to me to help him find his way." Linda exhaled and looked away. He could tell she wasn't buying it.

"Look," he said defensively, "you know how spiritual Aaron was. He believed in past lives. He was constantly seeking that inner self thing."

"Yes," she reluctantly admitted.

"All Umi's done is point out to me that Nepal and the mountains are very spiritual places. There are lots of temples and Goddesses that rule and live in the mountains." Hank watched as Linda rolled her eyes in disbelief.

"Hey!" he said sternly. "Don't be so narrow minded, okay?"

Linda gave him a cold hard stare. "Go on."

"So it just may be that what's going on here is the collision of two spiritual worlds. Aaron's gone but his spirit does not have the ability to move on. And Umesh believes the message I'm getting is that Aaron needs help, he's in some kind of purgatory and somehow, I've got to help him."

Linda opened her mouth but didn't speak. He knew she wanted to argue the point, but couldn't.

"So what is the Sebring man's solution?"

Hank wanted to come up with a nice diplomatic answer. "He thinks a stone monument and a prayer service; maybe some readings from the Tibetan Book of the Dead."

"Where?" Linda said. Hank didn't want to answer her.

"Over there."

"In Nepal? You want to go to Nepal? Oh honey no, come on! You're not being sensible."

"It's not about being sensible Linda, it's what I need to do."

"Look, you're the most logical person I know. Why can't you do something like that here? You could do it up in Mount Dora. By Aaron's house."

"I have to get as close to Everest as I can."

"Says who? This total stranger you just met?"

"Umi is from a village in the Khumbu region . . . He knows a lot about this."

"I don't care if he's the king of Siam, Henry. You are not doing this! Let's reason it out.

First of all, how much do you think this is going to cost? It can't be cheap. Thousands, right? We don't have thousands to spend right now."

"I have the deposit money for the new car," Hank answered.

"Hank, you've been wanting a new car for two years now. And you need a new car." He had already been to three dealerships and had his eye on a sleek red Toyota Camry.

"It will just have to wait."

"Secondly, if you did go, how long do you think it would take? Last time I checked, Mount Everest wasn't exactly off of I-4."

"Spare me the sarcasm."

"So how long? Three weeks? Two?"

"To get out there and back would be somewhere around eighteen to twenty days."

"You see?" Linda emphasized. "Where do you have twenty days in your schedule?" Hank knew she was right. The girls would be out of school soon and the hotel was just about to get into the busy season.

"I guess I'd have to quit my job."

"And you don't want to do that, right? Hank, do you? You've come so far with this company and you like your work. And what if you can't find another job, the way the market is."

Everything she said was true and he hated her for being so sensible.

"I've got to do something!" Hank put his head into his hands. "I don't know what to do." She came around the desk and hugged him.

"It's going to be okay. C'mon," she said, "let's go to bed." She led him out of their converted den. As she headed for the bathroom and he made his way to turn off the TV and lights, his thoughts still nagged him. "It'll be okay for who Linda?" he mumbled.

"For me? Or for you?"

Chapter 12

The Inheritance

AS THE PLANE lifted off the rain soaked runway, Hank pulled out the gold cross from under his shirt. Caressing the crucifix, he prayed, just in case.

A week had passed since Hank and Linda had their argument. The school year was ending and adjustments had to be made as the Longo family shifted into their summer routine. Hank's work schedule also had to be altered. His absence had created a back-log of work, which had to be addressed and it was during those late night catch-up sessions he tooled around the Internet. There was always more information to uncover about Everest's history, and mountain climbing in general. He found out that attempts to reach the summit began back in the 1920's, and over one hundred and sixty people have died trying.

Other than research, the only other bright spot in the last week was a surprise message from Umesh. He had gone ahead and contacted Jack Dawson, the climber, on Hank's behalf. Dawson agreed to talk with Hank and suggested he call to set up a time.

In the midst of his search, Hank discovered Dawson's presentation on high altitude climbing, scheduled for Georgetown University, in mid June. *It had to be fate.* The opportunity to see Dave and Tracy and then meet with the famed climber was too compelling. A quick call to Dawson's secretary confirmed that he would meet with Jack after the lecture.

*　　*　　*

"Thank you," he said to the attendant as he accepted a diet soda. Here he was, on his way to Miami to meet with Uncle Gino's attorneys, and settle the estate, and all he could think about was how miserable he had been since May. The only exception being that one day with Matt.

The view of Florida's farmlands and the expansive Everglade swamp reminded him of Aaron's constant testimonials about the beauty of Florida. Hank smiled as the plane began to descend through the cloud cover and lower its gear for the final approach.

Yellen & Yellen's office was several miles south of the city. Hank got in his rented car and headed toward the Dolphin Expressway. The meeting was not for another hour so he decided to drive a bit first. He made a left and found a metered parking space on the street that led to the building where Uncle Gino had lived. It had been built in the seventies and was small compared to the giant residences that made up Brickell's condo row. "G's" ninth floor corner apartment had a spectacular view of the Rickenbacker Causeway that connected Key Biscayne. Hank thought about the many times he visited, the parties Gino and Sebastian had invited him to, and the haven Uncle Gino's apartment had become when he needed a place to cram for exams. He had stayed here during his Uncle's final days, the familiarity of the place and its surroundings helped ease Hank's conscience while dealing with "G's" journey from life to death. *This place was home.*

St. Jude's, a small Catholic church, sat on the corner of Brickell and Fifteenth. A wedding rehearsal had just finished and the large group had forgotten to shut the varnished oak doors. From where he stood, Hank could see the stained glass windows behind the altar. He walked up the granite steps and onto the burgundy carpet that lay across the aisles. Three pews from the front, on bended knee, he genuflected and moved in to sit for a few moments. Alone in the silence, he debated whether to stay. As he put a hand on the top of the bench in front of him, ready to get up, the statue of the Virgin Mary caught his attention. Without thought, he sat back down.

Hank closed his eyes and focused on the darkness. His shoulders and head relaxed as he brought his hands together. The ball of confusion evaporated.

Once before Hank had tried this, on a beach with Aaron. What started out as an attempt to meditate ended up as a sand throwing, body shoving, and fist swinging argument. The incident was soon forgotten and Hank never again tried to find his inner self—until now.

The tomblike stillness was working. There was a circle of calmness around him. Further and further away were the responsibilities, problems and personalities that collared him daily. As the circle expanded, there were images of his dad reading a bedtime story, a baseball game with hot dogs and an autographed ball. These were the unburdened days, before homework, facial acne or girls. It was a wonderful sensation that bewildered him.

From a distance he heard a faint voice. He opened his eyes, and once again, there he was.

"Aaron?"

"Hey, Henry. Do you feel the peace man?"

And right then, Hank was transported back to reality. A robed clergy member stood in the church's trancept and smiled at Hank.

"That was quite a long prayer," he said.

Hank looked at his watch. "Oh my! I can't believe . . ." He stood up quickly. He had been sitting there for forty-five minutes and was now going to be late for the dispersal.

Not good keeping lawyers waiting, he thought as he made his way out of the pew.

"Is everything all right?" Hank and the priest came together in the middle of the aisle.

"Yes, thank you," Hank replied. Once more his eyes gravitated to the Holy Mother. The smile was still there, only it appeared bigger now.

"Everything is just fine."

*   *   *

Yellen & Yellen's offices were at the far end of the hall. The receptionist escorted Hank to a conference room with a large mahogany table and eight leather chairs. Three of the walls were lined with bookcases, which were filled with volumes of Florida's statutes and laws. On the other wall was a portrait. "The brothers' Yellen," Jan explained; her husband's grandfather and great uncle. They had started the firm fifty years ago.

"Henry, it's good to see you." Sebastian hugged Hank and kissed his cheek, then stepped back to appraise him. "You've lost weight, haven't you?"

"Yes, I run a lot; twenty to thirty miles a week."

"Fabulous!" Sebastian replied. "I'll bet you've lost at least fifteen pounds."

"Actually, twenty five."

"Wow," Jan said. "I wish I could do that."

"What are you talking about?" Hank said as he moved into one of the chairs. "Look how thin you are already."

"Not the weight, just the commitment to exercise." She sat at the head of the table, while Sebastian chose the chair next to Hank.

"Oh I know what you mean," Sebastian said. "It's so hard to be consistent in anything these days." Hank looked at Sebastian and saw that he had a very big smile on his face. *What's up with him?*

"How are the girls Hank?"

"They're fine Jan; happy about summer vacation."

"And your lovely bride?" Sebastian chimed in. Hank had to smile. His Uncle's lover was never at a loss for a romantic term.

"She's fine as well." Hank decided for Sebastian's benefit to add, "Linda sends her love and best wishes to you." Sebastian sighed in appreciation.

"Shall we get on with the settlement?" Jan asked. She pulled a rubber band off of several long file folders.

"First of all," she began, "I'd like to thank Henry for all the work he's done. There were a lot of issues in probate and a lot of bills that had to be paid."

"Well, I earn a living getting bills paid on time so . . ."

"Yes thank you, Henry," Sebastian added. "I'm just useless when it comes to things like that. Besides, some of those things . . ." Sebastian's eyes welled up. He put his hand up to his mouth. Hank gently patted his forearm.

"Hey, it's okay. I was glad to do it."

"I'm so glad you were there for Gino in the end. It meant a lot to him that you were. He loved you very much."

To get their attention, Jan cleared her throat. "I want to let you know that Mr. Cole and I have already executed the part of the estate that specifically deals with him. It was your uncle's wish that the value of Sebastian's inheritance remain a private matter. As the additional, and only other beneficiary in Mr. Longo's will, the balance of the estate has been left to you." Sebastian had a huge grin. His pleasure was apparent.

She pulled out a sheet of paper. "Your uncle asked me to read this."

"Dear Henry, I'll start by thanking you for the acceptance you have always shown me in spite of the lifestyle I'd chosen. As you know, being queer didn't endear me to many members of the family, but you took the time to keep me informed as to what was going on with each and every one. When my brother, your father, died, I grieved considerably. However, the time I spent with you was a great comfort. I wanted you to know I considered it a great honor to mentor your education and share in the special moments of your life. Your marriage to Linda has not only given me great joy, but the chance to see Francis's spirit live on in your daughters, Elisabeth and Eva." Jan paused for moment. Hank could hear Sebastian sniffle. He reached for the Kleenex box, took a wad of tissues out and blew.

Jan continued. "By the time this is read, I will be on my way. My life has been quite successful, but as everyone knows, 'you can't take it with you.' So I am leaving a large percentage of my estate to you. Please promise to invest a portion of it for your daughters' college education. The rest, you can do with as you please. I will also ask you to check in on my beloved, Sebastian, from time to time. He is also very fond of you and adores your children.

A final note: take time to enjoy each day, Henry. Have faith in who you are and don't compromise in what you believe. Remember, you are a Longo; success is imminent."

Hank was stunned by his uncle's powerful words. Jan put the letter down. She picked up another document and continued.

"I, Eugene Longo, being of sound mind and body, do hereby order the liquidation of my investment portfolio, including stocks from Beckwith Industries, Instat Communications, LLC, and Inca Consolidated Mining. The proceeds, I bequeath to my nephew, Henry Longo . . ." Jan paused as she flipped to the second page. "To be paid in one lump sum, by cashier's check, in the amount of 4.5 million dollars."

Hank watched in disbelief as Jan handed him an envelope. He opened it and stared, first at his name and then the string of zeroes.

"Congratulations Henry," Jan said. Hank felt Sebastian's arms drape around him and then the familiar sound of sniffling.

"I'm sorry I didn't tell you Henry," he said. "'G' wanted it to be a surprise."

Hank had never been so shocked in his life.

"Oh, Uncle G," he muttered.

After the meeting, Hank drove around the lavish residences and expensive landscapes of Coral Gables. He realized he was now in a position to purchase one, if he chose. Hank drove until he realized that he was headed for the backside of UM's campus. The four dorm towers were soon within view as well as the intramural fields. The campus was quiet; the spring semester had finished a month ago. Hank pulled into a spot under the banyan trees, next to the residence halls and the lake. The engine idled as the memories flooded. Before they could grip him, he picked up his cell and pressed the speed dial.

"Hello?" Linda said.

"Hi honey, what are you doing?"

"Laundry; you still in Miami?"

"Yeah. Wrapped things up with the lawyers about an hour ago."

"And how did that go?"

"Are you sitting down?"

"I'm sitting on the floor sorting underwear. Why?"

"Because I need to tell you something, and I don't think you should be standing when I tell you."

"Okay, I'm on the floor with my back up against the couch and a wicker basket full of whites in front of me. Give it to me."

"Gino left me an inheritance Linda."

"How much?"

"Would you believe, 4.5 million?"

"Come on, quit kidding."

"What if I told you I wasn't kidding?"

"Oh, my God. You're not kidding are you?"

Hank listened to the celebratory eruption with great amusement as Linda ran around the house, into the yard, the garage, and then went next door to tell the neighbor.

"Think of all the things we can finally do, Hank. Hank? Are you there?"

"Yes. You know what? Let's *really* think of all the things we can do, okay?"

"There are so many things."

"Can you, off the top of your head, think of what some of those things might be?" Hank closed his eyes and rubbed his forehead as he listened.

"Well gosh," Linda said, "where do I begin?"

How about with me wanting to go to Nepal? Hank thought.

"We're definitely going to have to put some of it toward the girls' college fund," she said without much thought.

"That's a given." *And Hank, you can go to Nepal now.*

"We can probably plan for a really neat trip somewhere this summer with the girls," Linda said.

"Okay."

"We need to replace the dishwasher."

Come on Linda! We talked about it. You know it's been on my mind. Money is not a factor anymore. Tell me I can go.

"You know," Hank began, "that's all good stuff. We can replace the dishwasher. But my point is we now have *a lot* of money. If we've had dreams, now we can live them. So, what've you dreamed of, Linda?"

"Oh, I don't really think about those kinds of things. I've always been content with what we have."

"There must be something? Anything at all." But the conversational drought continued. He shook his head in amazement that Linda couldn't think of a single thing.

"Well I have to admit," she said, "I always thought it would be nice to go back to school and get my masters degree. So I think I'd probably do that."

"Really?" In all the years they had been together, she had never once mentioned the idea of going back to school. Maybe he didn't know her as well as he thought.

"I know what it is you want to do."

So, she has listened.

"You want your new car, don't you? You've got the money to buy it outright now." The line went dead. He looked at the screen: "No Service." Good thing the call dropped at that moment because he was just about to lose it.

"God, she doesn't know what I'm all about, does she?" He opened his door and got out to stretch.

He checked the phone again; the signal was back. Hank hit redial.

"Sorry about that," he said when Linda answered. "For some odd reason, my phone just went dead."

"Yeah, I wondered what happened."

"Listen, there's a lot more I need to do here. I'm going to have to stay overnight."

"Okay." Her response didn't indicate concern.

"I also think," Hank added, "that Sebastian needs me to be around for another day, maybe two."

"Did he inherit a lot, too?" Linda inquired.

"I'm sure he did, but they didn't disclose the amount to me. I just want to be sure he's okay. It was kind of a final day for him."

"Don't worry 'bout me, I understand. The girls and I are fine. Just keep me posted."

"I will." As he put his phone away and walked back to the car, he made a promise to himself. He would never lie to Linda again.

After a stop at the mall for clothes, toiletries and something to eat, Hank continued down the Dixie Highway. Signs appeared for the spur that would put him on to the Turnpike. He was headed first to the Keys, where he and Aaron had gone together on road trips during their UM days, and then, with a voice of determination he declared, "I'm going to Nepal."

Chapter 13

Holiday Isle

HOW DIFFERENT THE drive was this time; twenty years ago he and Aaron had gone to the Keys in a beat up old van. This time, Hank went in a rented Escalade.

It was late afternoon when he turned into Holiday Isle Resort in Islamorada. Not much had changed.

He walked over to the open-air tiki bar, but was uneasy about going in. The nightmarish image of Aaron's ghastly apparition still haunted him and he wondered if he'd have to face his ghost, again. Hunger won out. *And a rum runner wouldn't hurt either.* After he ate, Hank lingered at the bar with a cup of coffee and his cell phone.

"Umesh? It's Hank Longo."

"Henry, it's always a pleasure to hear from you."

"I'm down in the Keys."

"On that road we talked about?"

"I think so."

"Good," Umesh said. "Very good."

"I've decided to go to Nepal."

"A wise choice. I had a dream you and your friend were at the base camp on Mt. Everest. You asked me to take a picture of the two of you, together. Aaron gave me his camera. The two of you were shoulder to shoulder and you had big smiles."

"That's amazing Umi. How did you know it was him?"

"Aaron is tall, taller than you or I, right? He has light brown hair with a little gray in it . . ." And in unison, " . . . he has blue eyes." Hank searched his mind. Had he described Aaron to Umesh or perhaps shown him a picture? No, he didn't think so.

"It was him, I'm sure of it."

"Listen, Umi. I'm going to Nepal, but not for the reasons we discussed."

"Oh?"

"I'm going to climb the mountain and bring Aaron *home*."

There was a significant pause before Umesh finally spoke. "That would be an amazing thing for you to do, Henry."

Thank you for not saying it was impossible.

"There are a number of things you must first consider before you attempt this." Hank wanted to walk off the meal. He talked while he exited the bar.

"Now, I must tell you," Umesh began, "there are steps that have to be accommodated in order for you to do this."

"Okay, hit me with those."

"First of all, it's going to take money to do this, a lot of money. You are going to need a big support network to be able to have a shot at climbing that high. He is so close to the summit, what you are talking about is putting together an expedition to go all the way to the top." In his mind, Hank agreed. The task would be huge.

"How much?"

"Hundreds of thousands of dollars, probably a half-a-million. Maybe more."

"I've got the money. Next."

"Good," Umesh said. Hank was a little surprised that Umesh didn't ask how he had so much money.

"The next hurdle is, when."

"The sooner the better," Hank replied.

"Well there are two favorable windows for climbing. If you want to do it soon, then it would be early October, after monsoon season. Otherwise you will have to wait until next May."

"Is there enough time to do it in October?"

"Barely. You have paperwork that needs to get done. Permits, visas. You have to line up a big group of people. You'll need porters to get your supplies there and Sherpas to guide you up the mountain." Hank listened and thought his idea was all but dead. Then Umesh said, "I can help with all of that."

"That would be great, Umi. Thank you."

"Do you have an idea who would be climbing with you?"

"Well, I thought perhaps you would." Hank winced as he listened to Umesh guffaw. It took a while for the Nepalese store owner to regain his composure.

"Oh no my friend, my climbing days are long past. But I'll tell you what? You're going to need someone to get everything to base camp. I could do that for you?"

Hank could not believe his good fortune. "You would do that?"

"Yes, but only if you pay me a lot of money!" Umesh laughed. Hank knew he meant it. He knew he'd have to pay through the nose for doing this, if he was going to have a chance to succeed.

"I'll pay you whatever you want," Hank said with confidence.

"Here is your first rule: always negotiate with the people you hire from Nepal. We pride ourselves on being able to bargain."

"Deal."

"And after you've negotiated everything, you will probably have to negotiate some more."

"I'll remember that."

"You will need to train for the climb," Umesh began. "You will need special equipment and you'll need help if you want to bring your friend off Everest." Hank listened while Umesh paused to think. "Jack Dawson, you must talk to him."

"I'm going to a lecture he's giving up in DC. I've already made an appointment to meet with him afterward."

"Do not wait. Call him today and convince him that you are going to do this and he'll come around and tell you the 'how' of climbing Everest."

"Alright," Hank said. "I'll call him today."

Hank paused to listen to the water lapping against the shore. He looked at the expansive view of the open Atlantic and the patchwork of fluffy white clouds twisted around rays of settling sunshine.

"Henry?" Umesh said. "Are you sure you want to do this?" Hank's reply was firm and assured.

"Yes, Umi. Yes I am."

Chapter 14

Calling Jack

HANK THOUGHT ABOUT how youth was an excuse for impulsive behavior. He considered how he had climbed the old Flagler Bridge for the sake of loyalty; put himself in harm's way. Now, twenty-two years later, he planned to risk his life once again, for the same reason. Only this time he would be smarter.

Looking at the beautiful view of the Atlantic, he flipped open his phone and dialed the number Umesh had given him. After a few rings a voice said, "Hello?"

"Jack Dawson? Hello, this is Henry Longo."

"Oh yes, Bhuju said you would ring." Hank was impressed with the clipped British accent.

"So you understand what I want to do?"

"I do."

"And your thoughts?"

"Other than which sanatorium you should be sent to?" Hank closed his eyes. He stayed calm. Umesh had warned him about Dawson, and perhaps Dawson was right, maybe he should be committed.

"Look, I don't mean to be curt, but I don't think you have the slightest idea how difficult it is to climb 29,000 feet."

"I've never done it, if that's what you mean."

"But I suppose you want to do it anyway, right? Where are you?" Dawson asked.

"Right now, I'm in the Florida Keys."

"Wonderful!" Dawson proclaimed. "Perfect example. So right now you're at sea level?"

"Yes," Hank said. "I'm overlooking the Atlantic Ocean."

"Right then. First thing you've got to realize is the air up on Everest is only one third of what you're breathing now. At the moment, your heart's pumping out blood to you at sixty-four beats per minute. Above 25,000 feet your heart rate will double to try and provide your body the same amount of oxygen you are breathing now. Do you know what it's called above 25,000 feet?"

"The Death Zone," Hank said.

"Correct, The Death Zone. Your heart pounds, you hallucinate, you can hardly function. That's where you want to go?"

"That's where my friend is," Hank said.

"He's on the moon, Mr. Longo. Do you realize that? He's as far away as anyone could possibly be from the living world."

Hank thought the analogy was appropriate, a frigid, isolated alien part of the planet. But like the moon, it was proven to be reachable.

"Please, call me Hank."

"You know there are many people who have never left that mountain."

"Yes, I'm aware of that. I know it's over a hundred."

"Oh, so you've done a little homework," Dawson was impressed. "And so you know there's good reason for that."

"Yes," Hank said. "They died while attempting to reach the summit."

"Or trying to get down once they had reached it. Or from a fall, or being buried in an avalanche."

"Yes, that too," Hank said. He knew where Jack was going with this and he wanted to argue his own point. "But the people who are still up on Everest are there because their expeditions were about getting to the top. They weren't set up for people who fell into trouble or needed assistance to get down."

"And what you propose is?"

"Different. My expedition is not about getting to the top. My goal is to get my friend off."

"Well, it's an extraordinary idea. And one I doubt you can accomplish, but you might as well plan for the summit; from what I read, your man's almost at the bloody top anyway."

"That's not my objective. I plan to build this expedition around getting Aaron off the mountain. Nothing more, nothing less."

"Do you have any experience climbing?" Hank shifted his gaze away from the open sea to a dried leaf being blown across the old bridge's road.

"None."

"Good start then. Are you fit?"

"Excuse me?"

"Are you fit? Are you in good shape? Do you think you're up to the challenge?"

"I run every day," Hank said. "Almost thirty miles a week. As a matter of fact, I've lost twenty five pounds in the last six months."

"By the time you finish climbing the Himalayas, you'll lose at least twenty more." There was a pause.

"Look," Jack began, "although climbing experience is preferable, it's not essential. You're going to need some, but Everest is not that difficult. On my last climb I guided a group of people that had very little experience. I took them because they paid me a king's ransom, but they didn't know the Queen's name about climbing."

"So it can be done," Hank was encouraged.

"Yes, but you have to be in incredibly good physical shape. And keep in mind that the less experienced you are, the more people you'll need to support you. For every climber, you'll need three to four people to assist." Jack paused to give Hank a chance to soak in the information. "And many people don't even get there. Many have to turn back due to weather, lack of supplies, illness, or not enough time. You have to remember one thing if you plan to go, getting to your friend is optional, getting off the mountain is mandatory."

"What are the Himalayas like in October?"

"A little warmer than climbing in May, but there's a lot more snow on the ground and a greater risk of avalanches than in the spring. On the brighter side the wind may not blow as hard. The wind is your greatest enemy. It penetrates through your clothing and screams in your ears like the engines of a jumbo jet. There's a stark beauty to the place, but at the same time it can be bloody awful." Hank turned to look at the amazing vista all around him. The elevated view of the water, dark green islands, and warm air were so sharp a contrast to the setting Jack had just described. His skin crawled at the thought of being so cold.

"Do you know exactly where the body is?" Jack asked.

"My friend, Dave Horton knows. I plan to attend your lecture, and visit with him. He lives in the area."

"It's extremely important to know that Mr. Longo," Jack said. "By October he could be well buried in snow. You won't have time to get all the way up there, and 'have a little look around', if you get my meaning."

"I understand."

"It's a very small window for each expedition to attempt to summit."

"Dave has the exact position, so I'll have it before I go."

"Good. Very good." Hank was encouraged. He thought he would ask now the question for which he had called.

"I'm going to be well supplied and have people working to line up the help I'll need. What I lack are people to climb. Any suggestions?"

"Not off the top of my head."

"How about you? Umesh speaks volumes of your experience."

"No," Jack said flatly, "I'm retired."

"If it's a question of money . . ."

"I'm sorry, I just can't. I've climbed Everest for the last time, I'm done with that mountain." The distress in Jack's voice was unmistakable. "Umesh knows people in Nepal; he'll assemble a team of porters and Sherpas to support the climb. Do you have corporate sponsorship for the financing arranged?"

"I'm paying personally."

"Hmm. That's rather good because it will release you from additional concerns. Since the weight of financing has already been resolved, what you need to do next is delegate all other responsibilities and leave yourself the task of physically and mentally preparing for the climb. Don't waste an ounce of energy worrying about your expedition. Stay focused on your goal: getting to your friend and bringing him home."

"I think that's what I'm doing."

"So the first thing you'll need is someone in charge of getting your expedition from Katmandu to base camp. That person is critical not only for the logistical concerns, but to lead your team and everyone else on the trek out."

"Do you know of someone?"

"I can't recommend someone who'll be a stranger to you. This part of the mission is vitally important. It'll have to be someone you know and trust."

Hank drew a blank until Dawson said the word, mission. *I'll ask Matt. He would be ideal.*

"There is someone," Hank said. "Someone well qualified."

"Very well then. Now, the greater concern is the team that climbs. There is someone I can recommend. Her name is Sara Hobson. She's finishing a Ph.D. in human physiology and she's an experienced climber. Once you get to base camp, she'll be instrumental in getting the team up the mountain."

In spite of his mainstream attitude toward equality, he couldn't imagine a woman leading his expedition up Everest.

"A woman?"

"She's out at Cal Tech. I'll give you her number when you come up." Hank was borderline flabbergasted, but Jack hadn't even bothered to go on the defensive with his suggestion. His confidence was so apparent that Hank had to assume, in the world of climbing, she was superior.

"Here's the dilemma," Jack said. "Assuming you, she, and your other leader ascend well, it's still not enough."

"Not enough?"

"To carry the body. It will be tricky to descend with that kind of weight. Parts of the descent will require six or maybe even eight people to negotiate the mountain. The team will need to take turns carrying or sliding, or however you plan on getting your friend's remains down."

"I see."

"On a good note, you'll have a lot of the spring expeditions' gear left behind to help."

"What do you mean?" Hank asked.

"There were fourteen expeditions out to Everest this past May. Quite a lot of them made it past the Hillary Step. So for you and your climb, there's already a lot of fixed rope up there. It'll help."

"But I still need manpower, the muscle, so to speak."

"Yes," Jack said. "And I'm afraid I draw a blank on who would be right for your trip."

"But Umesh said that you knew a lot of people? A lot of climbers."

"I know a lot of climbers who would go for the glory of a summit attempt, but that's the selfish aspect of mountain climbing. In the end, it's a battle between you and the mountain. So the concept of climbing that far without going to the top would be bloody ridiculous to anyone I know."

"You mean not worth it?" Hank's focus zeroed in on a brush fire that was raising black smoke in the distance. "If you're telling me mountain climbers are out, who's left?"

"Let's think creatively. Like yourself, you're going to need people in good shape. It'll take a month of back and forth climbing to get acclimatized. It would also be preferable to have a group who has worked together before. The task you face, Hank, will require a great amount of coordination; the more your team knows each other, the better."

"What else?" Hank asked as he stared off at the smoke rising into the sky. "They'll also need training, like you. You'll all be climbing ladders through the Ice Fall and have to get used to masked oxygen above 20,000 feet." *Ladders, oxygen . . . That's it!*

"And I guess above all Hank, you're going to need people who are brave enough to go in, knowing they may not make it back out."

"And I know just where to find them," Hank nodded in confirmation to his own realization.

Chapter 15

Off to DC

AFTER THE CALL to Dawson, Hank headed back to Miami International. He was fortunate, no traffic and after returning the car, he hopped on his flight and was in his driveway by midnight.

Once again, Linda and the girls were fast asleep; at least in their own beds, this time.

After his morning run, Hank got on the phone.

"Hello Wayne? It's Hank Longo."

"Hank, it's good to hear from you. I was just thinking of calling you. The last time we spoke, you were looking for answers. Have you had any success?"

"Yes I have, but they aren't answers, they're decisions."

"Decisions?"

"I can't go into the details right now, but I need your help."

"What do you need?"

"Are the men still at the fire station?"

"No. They shut it down two weeks ago." Hank slumped in his chair.

"Jim, the Captain, he's still there. I saw him yesterday. He has to stay another week to oversee the dispersal of the equipment."

Hank brightened. "Wayne, how can I reach him? I really need to talk to him."

"Well, I guess I could walk over there and tell him you're trying to reach him."

"Would you do that for me? It's very important. Please, go find the captain and tell him I have to talk to him, right away. If he asks why, tell him I'm planning a trip to Nepal in three months. I'm going to get Aaron; I need him and his men to go with me, help me recover Aaron and bring

him home. I'm going to bring him back Wayne. I want to bring him home."
Hank's voice cracked.

After a long pause Wayne spoke. It was simple and to the point. "I'll go right now and get back to you in twenty minutes."

The next call was to Matt. He answered on the third ring.

"Well, I gotta tell you," he said, already knowing who the caller was, "I wouldn't stop working on a draft horse for just anyone. How's it going buddy? You back from your trip?"

"Yeah, got in last night."

"How'd it go?"

"Great, I'm a millionaire."

"Oh really?" Hank could tell Matt didn't believe him. "And how much did you inherit there, Diamond Jim?"

"Four-point-five," Hank fired back. "Listen, I don't want to keep you from your horses, but I need to know if you can get some time off. Say, a couple of months in September and October."

"What? C'mon, be serious. Did you really . . ."

" . . . Really."

"Since I have the money, I've decided to launch an expedition to bring Aaron off Everest. We leave at the beginning of September and won't be back until somewhere middle of October. I need someone to lead the expedition from Katmandu to the base camp. I want that to be you. I'll pay you for your time and expertise."

"Are you serious? Holy shit!" Matt exclaimed.

"Honey?" Linda called from the laundry room.

"I have to go. Linda's calling me. Think it over and get back to me."

"Decision's made, I'm in." Hank's fist shook with a mix of relief and determination. "Excellent. We'll talk more later."

Linda smiled when she saw him. "There you are," she said, arms outstretched. "Home at last." Hank hugged her and then looked down at all the bags she had stacked in the laundry area.

"Where'd all that come from?"

"All over. Mostly the mall," she gushed. "I'm sorry, but with what you told me, we went out and splurged."

"Hey, great!" Hank said.

"Daddy, look at this." Elisabeth had reached down and pulled out a flowered summer dress.

"It's beautiful Elisabeth. Did you pick it out?" Hank's youngest nodded.

Eva tugged on Linda's arm. "Mom? Can we go over to Christian's now?"

"Sure."

Hank watched as his daughters ran across the street to the neighbor's house.

"So," she said, "where's the money?"

"Inside." Linda followed as Hank headed to the office and searched his coat for the envelope. "Here it is. Want to see it?"

Linda grabbed the check right out of Hank's hand. "Wow. Look at all those zeros. Good thing we've got it, 'cause I think I maxed out my credit card again."

"You won't have to worry about that anymore. But there are a few other things you and I have to talk about."

Hank watched as Linda sat down. She sensed his concerns and prepared herself for the discussion to come.

"What are you going to do about work?" Linda asked.

"I've given that some thought. I'm going to leave the hotel and start my own office."

"Really?" She rolled her lips inward against each other and nodded. "Hmmm."

"There's plenty of business out there. I can make a living on municipal audits alone. In the long run, we'll build equity and make more money."

"Can you do that all by yourself?"

"I'm going to ask Charo to come with me. She'll make more money and enjoy the added responsibility."

"Okay, sounds good. What the heck, go for it."

"Before I set it up, there's something I need to do first."

"What?"

"Go to Nepal." Hank braced himself for her reaction.

"I knew you were going to say that."

"You talked me out of it for a lot of practical reasons."

"Yes, and a lot of it had to do with time and money."

"Neither of which is a factor anymore."

"Yes, but it's still not practical," Linda said firmly.

"Maybe not practical to you, but it is with me."

"Hank, what are you talking about."

"I don't expect you to understand Linda, but I'm going to Everest to get Aaron's body off that mountain. I'm gonna bring him home and put him to rest right here in Florida."

Linda listened. "Oh Hank, you can't possibly be serious?"

"I'm afraid I am. I'm leaving in September. If everything goes well, I'll be back with Aaron's body by the middle of October."

"But you don't know the first thing about climbing. Why on Earth . . ."

"Because he was my best friend, Linda, for twenty years. And because I loved him."

The phone rang. Hank waited several rings before he answered.

"Hello?" It was Wayne. "Wayne, hello. Did you find the captain? . . . Great put him on . . . Jim? Hello, it's Henry Longo . . . Yes, from back in May . . . That's right. Listen, I've heard from Wayne that the fire station is closed? Are you still in touch with the men?" As he listened, Linda got up from the couch. Her expression was one of total shock as she moved toward the door.

"I need your crew for a recovery mission. I'm putting together a team of people . . ." Hank spelled out his plan. As he spoke, he knew his journey had begun.

*   *   *

The plane touched down at Ronald Reagan Airport and within a short time Hank had found a cab, and was headed for Tracy and Dave's Georgetown home.

He rang the bell of the two-story townhouse, which sat behind a wrought iron gated fence.

"Henry Longo," Tracy said. "Oh, my goodness, you haven't changed a bit!" Hank smiled and took a good look at her. She had the look of high society. Everything about her reeked of money; she still had her figure, and she was as beautiful as ever.

"Tracy. It's been way too long."

"Yes it has." Tracy swung the door wide and motioned for Hank to come in. As he stepped into the foyer, Hank noticed the magnificent selection of paintings, all encased in gold leaf frames.

"This is a lovely house, Tracy."

"It's pre-civil war," she said as she closed the door.

"I'm glad you're here," she said, her voice laced with sadness. "Dave's upstairs. He asked to talk with you privately. I wondered if you had plans for this evening?"

"Yes, a lecture at Georgetown. The presenter is a Himalayan climber, someone I've gotten to know through acquaintances. I'm invited to his house afterward."

"So, you're going to Nepal? To get Aaron's remains?"

"I'm going to try."

She put her hand on Hank's forearm and said, "There's an event at the D.A.R. I have to attend tonight. We can meet later on . . . at J. Paul's on M street. I'll be there about eleven. If you want to have a drink, we can talk."

"I don't know how long I'll be . . ."

"I'll wait for you." Tracy leaned in and kissed Hank on the cheek, then turned, picked up a small purse from a chair and headed out the door.

"Dave?" he yelled out.

"Up here," came the voice from the ceiling above. Hank took the steps two at a time.

Dave was behind a desk filled with papers and reference books. "There you are," he said. "Looking the same you dog!" Hank noticed the paisley pajamas. One of Dave's feet was wrapped in an ace bandage with cotton wedged in between his toes. His right leg had a Velcro strap cast. Hank figured it was because of the amputated toes. Dave tried to get up from the chair.

"Hey, don't get up." Dave slumped back in his chair and waited for Hank to reach him to shake hands.

"It's good to see you," Dave said. A close look at Dave's face almost made Hank recoil. The lower end of his nose had undergone some kind of reconstructive surgery and his face was puffed out with black and blue marks around his eyes. Hank took hold of Dave's right hand, which looked fine, but then he noticed the other hand was bandaged. The handshake became a brotherly like pull toward each other.

"I hear you're going to Everest?"

"Well, maybe not, if the end result is looking like you."

They both laughed. And then Hank came right to the point. "What happened to Aaron, Dave?"

"To be honest, I'm not a hundred percent sure. He was dead by the time I reached him."

"He was dead? How did you know?"

"We had just reached the summit. I got a radio report that bad weather was headed our way. It was some kind of rogue storm; I could see it coming right up the mountain. I ordered everyone off the top. It took a while 'cause there were so many people up there and you just don't move that fast at 29,000 feet. I was the last to leave."

"Where was Aaron?"

"As I started down, I saw him about a hundred feet off to my right, off the ridge trail. He had squatted down against a rock and wasn't moving. I gestured to him to get up and head down, but nothing, no response. I waved at him with both arms. He faced me, but didn't move. So I went to him."

"He didn't move, at all?"

"No. I came off the line and went to him. Not the easiest thing to do on a thirty degree downhill slope with the wind blowing and snow swirling all around you. When I got to him, he was unresponsive. I yelled, and I shook him; I even grabbed him by the front of his wind jacket and tried to haul him up. I yelled right into his face: "Get up or you're going to die!""

"And he didn't respond?" Dave shook his head.

"I want you to understand that I held myself responsible for everyone at the summit. If I had seen any sign that he was alive, I would've stayed with him. When I leaned in close there wasn't any breath." Dave paused. "There was no hope."

"What do you think happened?"

"Altitude sickness. Blood seeps into your brain and you stroke out. I'm not an expert, but I can tell you that a huge part of climbing is acclimatizing. You go up a little, and you come back down. You go a little further, and you come back down, again. It gets pretty tedious and you have to be patient as hell, but it's the only way to get to the top."

"And you're saying Aaron didn't do that?"

"Oh, he did it," Dave said. "But he didn't do it enough."

"I don't understand."

"He took shortcuts. He never went lower than base camp, so for a month he never went below 17-5. Then there were times when he was supposed to rest at camp for three days, but he wouldn't. He'd go on a day hike to take pictures or climb back up through the Ice Fall, just for the hell of it. One time, he and I climbed all the way to camp three. From there the orders were to go all the way back to 'BC'. But Aaron decided to stay at camp two because he wanted to photograph the Sherpa porters carrying equipment through the Coom and up Lhotse's face. That's when a storm hit and there were fierce winds; he ended up stuck there for two days."

"Sounds like he was doing his job."

"Yes," Dave admitted, "he was. But he had terrible headaches the whole time. I told him he wasn't resting enough. He had to spend more time at lower elevations."

"He didn't listen?"

"He did, but . . ." Dave paused to find the right words. "It was like he couldn't get in enough shots. I told him that Telstar was paying for photos of Hillary's son on the phone, talking to his dad. They didn't give a crap about anything else."

"He was always like that," Hank said. "Searching for mystical places. He'd quote Thomas: 'The Kingdom of God is spread across the earth, but men do not see it.' Aaron never stopped looking."

"I hired him because he was the best, but I thought since he had climbed Kilimanjaro he had an understanding of high altitude climbing. Either he didn't, and never let me know, or he did and wouldn't let on how it was affecting him."

"Knowing Aaron, it was probably the latter."

"I had a lot of people to take care of up there. There was a helluva lot to deal with. I don't think I neglected the condition he was in, and I didn't ignore it either." Hank heard the defensive strain in Dave's voice.

"How did Linda take the news about Aaron?"

"She was upset. Aaron was godfather to our daughter Elisabeth."

"I'm sorry I couldn't bring Aaron back."

"That's what I intend to do."

"You're crazy! It's impossible."

"I have a plan."

"Everest is too dangerous a place."

"I'm putting together a crew. We can handle it."

"Hank look, why do you . . ."

"Because I loved the guy Dave, and we've been through a lot together." Hank swallowed his emotions. "I've read the dispatches from last month's summit attempts; almost all of them mentioned passing Aaron's body. It's like he's by the side of some road and I can't just leave him there."

Dave pushed himself up and out of his chair. He limped his way over to the nightstand where a small metal box lay next to a lamp. From it, he pulled a folded piece of paper and made his way back to Hank.

"That's where he is. I used the GPS." Hank looked at the latitude and longitudes' degrees, minutes and seconds. "It's a weird thing," Dave said as an afterthought, "having nothing else to think about except those coordinates saved my life. I should have been terrified. I was frostbitten, vomiting, and descending in a whiteout; I couldn't see. But I just repeated Aaron's position, over and over again, so I wouldn't forget."

Hank folded the piece of paper. "Thank you for this." And he tucked it into his pocket. He checked his watch. "I have to go. The lecture starts soon and I want to get a good seat."

"You're seeing Jack Dawson?" Dave asked. "He's a good man. He'll give you a lot of good ideas. He's very experienced. Come on, I'll walk you to the door." Hank protested as Dave got up again. "I'm all right. The doctors told me I have to keep moving around. I've got to get used to walking again, without the digits." As they descended the stairs, Hank saw that old stubborn determination in Dave. When they got to the foyer, Dave smiled in triumph.

"A few more weeks of hydra therapy and I'll be good as new . . . Hank, when you leave in September, I'd like to go with you."

"What?"

"I'd like to help."

"Dave, you're not in any condition to climb again. How could you possibly . . ."

"I don't want to climb. I'll never climb another mountain again as long as I live. But I know the place. And you're going to need a base camp manager. I could handle that for you."

"You want to go back? To Nepal?"

What he said made sense. He did need someone to supervise his base of operations; it was on Umesh's list. Dave's knowledge would be useful.

"It's my expedition, Dave. Understand? I'm running the show, not you."

Dave nodded in acceptance of the terms.

"And you'll be fit enough to go?"

"Yes. I'll have something to work for."

"I'll give it some thought." Dave said nothing more about it.

"It's good to see you again, Bro," Dave said. "You're not far from Georgetown. Just stay on this street about five blocks and you'll run right into the university."

*   *   *

The lecture had Hank mesmerized. Jack Dawson's bio said he was seventy, but he sure didn't look it. The man was tall, thin, had a handsome face, and black hair that streamed back from his forehead. The only sign of age was some gray around the temples.

Jack spoke with the fluidity of an educated English mind. His long fingers added great expression to each picture projected onto the huge drop screen. As Dawson put it, he had "conquered" Everest four times. In the hour that had been allotted, the views he'd shown examined climbs from both the Nepalese and Tibetan sides of the mountain. The question and answer period ran past the scheduled half hour and when the lecture ended, dozens of hands were still up.

Hank hung back during the reception while Jack took the time to drink wine with the faculty and talk more with the students. When the crowd thinned, Hank made his way toward Jack.

"Henry Longo? At last we meet."

"May I call you, Jack?"

"By all means. Listen, I've ordered a car to take you to the house. After I tie up a few things here, I'll be along. Would you mind? I have a lot to tell you, and this really isn't the place."

"That's fine," replied Hank.

*   *   *

The driver informed Hank they would be going across the river to Virginia; the residence was in McClean. Although it was dark, Hank could see the gated driveways and finely landscaped property as they drove through the wealthy community to Dawson's house. Just off the winding road, the driver pulled up to a call box by an elegant wrought iron gate. He tapped in the code and the private gate slid open.

Up and over a hill was an enormous contemporary ranch. An elderly Asian woman was already at the door waiting to greet Hank. She escorted him to a large, airy living room, and offered him a seat on the couch. The full wall of windows displayed an exquisite view of a gently lit garden. He sat there, absorbed, as the secretary crossed the room to the bar. Hank could see the finest details of a rock garden and a small pond with a waterfall.

Exquisite. As he accepted, then sipped his drink, the secretary bowed slightly and left the room. It was an awkward surprise when he realized he'd been given straight scotch on the rocks.

"Oh my God," he said aloud and brought the full glass to his eyes for inspection. As he carefully took another sip he wondered how many more surprises were in store for him this evening.

Jack walked in twenty minutes later.

"Good God, Hank, I hope I haven't kept you waiting too long."

"Not at all. I've been admiring your home."

"You've met Keiko, my secretary and personal bodyguard? KEIKO! Where are you?" Hank watched as the secretary reemerged and moved quickly to take his hat and coat.

"Keiko, no more student lectures, okay? Me no want to chit-chat with twenty-year-olds." Hank watched with great amusement as the secretary first pondered Jack's request, and then whacked his arm with the hat she'd been handed. She bowed and exited once more.

"Sorry about that," Jack said. "It's a game we play. She books me around the world to speak at various functions and I always have to complain about it. So, you're going to Nepal to recover your friend, right?"

"That's what I hope to do."

"Right then. Let's go to my den and see what I can do for you and your cause." Jack headed for his bar. "You have a drink already?"

"Yeah," Hank said with a slight grunt.

"I apologize," Jack said over his shoulder, "if all you got was my Glenfiddich. Keiko assumes everyone who knows me drinks single malt and nothing else." Hank waited while Jack fixed himself something neat. He took a sip and said, "There, that's better. Right, let's go see what this lot's all about then."

The den was a significant walk from the living room area.

"So what did you think of the lecture?"

"Eye opening. The mountains, the valleys, the people . . . it's a whole other world."

Jack sat behind his desk. He motioned Hank to pull over a chair and sit with him.

"I'm terribly concerned about the inexperience of you and your climbing team, but if we can encircle you with some expertise, your devotion to your friend should carry the day."

Hank watched as Jack pulled a sliding panel from the interior of the cabinet. He stepped away and invited Hank to take a look at a three-dimensional replica of Everest and the surrounding area. A brass plaque was affixed; the inscription read: "Sagarmatha National Park".

"This is amazing." Hank leaned in for an eye level view of the three peaks. "What direction am I looking at?"

"North." Jack used both hands to point. "Your expedition will trek up from Dingboche, along the Khumbu Glacier. You'll set up your base camp somewhere around here, below the Ice Fall." Jack pointed with his index finger to an area below the terraced, snow covered steps in front of a long glacial plain. "As you can see," Jack continued, "there are three ridges in which to climb. You'll be taking the most traveled route along the Southeast Ridge. The porters will establish a camp at the other end of the Ice Fall. That will be camp one. Camp two, or what is also known as advanced base camp, will be at the base of Lhotse. From there, you have a sixty-degree climb up to camp three, which will put you at 24,000 feet. Camp four will be just below the ridge in the 'South Col.'. Now, you're 26,000 feet up, and from there you should have enough of a window to get to the body and haul it back to camp four. After that, it's whatever good days are left to get the rest of the way down." Hank studied the model.

"I know it'll be difficult," Hank said, after he examined the route. "Are there parts of the climb that are worse than others?"

"The Ice Fall is a nasty bit of business," Jack took another swallow of his drink. "You'll have to navigate over huge ice splinters and large crevasses to get through. You'll use narrow aluminum ladders and be in constant fear of the ice walls shifting and falling on you. And worse still, you'll have to pass through it eight to ten times."

"Eight to ten times?"

"Yes, back and forth, back and forth. It's to get acclimatized."

"What else?" Jack stroked his chin and then said, "I don't know how you're going to get the body through the Ice Fall."

"Umesh explained that scenario to the head of the team that's going. They're seasoned firefighters. They've got some special equipment they've used for different types of extractions, and they're confident it can be adapted."

"I hope that's the case because the other difficult part will be getting off the Hillary Step, here." Jack pointed to an area on the ridgeline, close to the summit. "It's a rock step, about forty feet high and near vertical. Your group will have to climb up over it with equipment, and then somehow manage to get back down with your friend's remains." Hank watched as Jack stepped back from the model. He picked up his drink and took a long swallow. Hank glanced at the model once again.

"Well, when we climb through it, we'll just have to figure out how to get back down." Jack turned away from his trophy exhibit and sat back at his desk. He rummaged through his desk drawers.

"Jack? What's this x-mark for off the North Ridge?" Jack stopped his search and looked back toward Hank and the reproduction.

"That's where Peter Hightower is."

"Who's Peter Hightower?" Hank already had his answer by the look in the retired climbing man's eyes.

"A colleague. We shared many climbs. He was a friend."

"What happened?"

"We attempted to retrace an expedition climb from the twenties. The weather and the wind were awful. On the way down, Peter forgot to hook on to the next set of fixed ropes. He fell 3,000 feet into the Great Coulier."

"When did it happen?"

"Almost twenty years ago." He got up from his desk and went back to the model.

"I never knew where his body was until recently. An expedition went out to search for George Mallory and Sandy Irvine's remains. While they searched, quite by accident, they found Peter."

"I'm sorry." Hank now understood why Jack acquiesced so easily when he learned the climb was to retrieve his friend's remains.

"This is what they brought back to me, from Peter." It was an old, rusted, broken watch. "This is all I have."

"Jack, do you think I really have a chance?"

"The odds aren't in your favor. But that doesn't mean you shouldn't try. I left Petey on that mountain. I shouldn't have. He doesn't belong there. He belongs back at Clyde Next-The-Sea, where he grew up. I'm too old now to go get him." Hank watched as a smile broke through Jack's melancholy face. "But I can help you." Jack walked back to his desk, opened a drawer, and pulled out a folder with dozens of 8 x 10 photos.

"Come," he said as he motioned with his arm, "pull up a chair. I have photos of every step you'll take to go up the Southeast Ridge. Let me show you." Hank looked at his watch and realized he might be late to meet Tracy, but this was important. He pulled his chair around and dropped his sport coat over the back. Jack shuffled through the pictures until he came to the first one he wanted to show. "Here it is," he said. "The Hillary Step."

Hank had a surge of energy as another relative stranger decided to join him in his quest. Jack talked about the mountain and Hank listened to every expert word. And for the first time he really believed he had a chance.

*   *   *

The saloon's entrance was open when the town car pulled up. Hank took the steps two-at-a-time, and ran right past the doorman, into the bar.

I'm late, he thought as he approached the hostess. He worried that Tracy had already left.

"Hello," he said to the college-aged hostess. "I'm looking for a friend I was supposed to meet here."

"Are you Mr. Longo?"

"Yes, I am." The hostess took Hank's arm and guided him through an open area to another seating area in the back of the big room.

"We opened up the back dining area for cocktails a half hour ago. Tracy's back there on the right." With one hand on Hank's back, she used the other to point the way.

"Thank you." Hank squeezed through the crowd and made his way to Tracy who waved when she saw him coming. As Hank slid into the booth, Tracy leaned over to offer her cheek.

"Sorry I'm late."

"It's all right. I thought you'd be." Hank looked at her as she smiled at him. There was a subtle elegance about her. She had a look that turned heads.

"You're on a first name basis with the hostess?"

"Dave and I are regulars. We eat here and bring friends when we want to socialize." Hank sensed an ever so slight slur in her speech.

"Are you smashed?" Hank asked.

"Let's say, I've been here a while. Don't you remember? I've always been able to hold my liquor? As a matter of fact . . ." Tracy shot her arm up to get the attention of a passing waiter. He stopped and pulled out a notepad from his backside.

"Derrick? I'll have another one of these," she said, raising her Grand Marnier snifter glass. Hank watched as she drank again.

"I'll have coffee," he said to the waiter.

"Coffee? I don't think so. I'm here with you for a drink, remember?"

"I'm sorry Tracy, but I've been drinking scotch. I really don't feel like having anything more."

"We have a lot to talk about," she said. "I can assure you that by the time we've caught up on the last twenty years, you're going to need something strong." Hank wanted to be adamant, but Tracy quickly told the waiter, "Bring him his coffee and put a little Irish in it." She waived him away and then turned to Hank and smiled.

"So, how long has it been?" Hank asked. "Twenty years?"

"That's right, twenty years ago; at graduation, right?"

"I guess you're right. But you and Aaron have seen each other over the years, isn't that true?"

"Yes," she said. "But not too often, just enough to keep a friendship going." She took a sip of her orange liqueur. "Sometimes it was just for lunch when he had a layover at Dulles. Once I had a meeting in San Francisco and he flew up from LA . . ." Hank sensed that she didn't like the way that came out. "He stayed with us before he and Dave went to Nepal." Hank frowned in puzzlement. The subject of Tracy never came up when he and Aaron got together.

"I shouldn't admit this, Hank, but back at UM I had hoped there would be a future with him." After a short lull, Tracy asked, "How was your talk with Dave?"

"Fine, I guess, considering what he's been through. He looks pretty beat up, but he says he's mending well."

"Yes, he is. Believe me, he's a hundred percent better from when he first got back. He's always been very determined in whatever he does, whatever he pursues."

"Is that why he got you?"

"Got me?" Tracy looked at Hank. "Why on earth would you think he got me?"

"I knew that Dave had always liked you when we were all together. My impression was that after Aaron broke up with you, Dave made his move."

"Is that your impression?" Tracy took another swallow. Hank could see the lecture coming. "Well that's not the case. First of all, Aaron did not break up with me. We realized that being on staff and seeing each other was not working so we decided to just stay friends."

"I always wondered how you and Dave managed to hit it off so well."

"Look, I admit that Dave was a bit of a rebound for me. He was very kind and treated me well. It was flattering to have someone tell you you're special. And you know what else? Whenever we were together, his eyes never wandered. I was his; there was no one else." Tracy looked toward the bar. Hank could feel her sadness. The love for her husband had become a past tense.

"Dave told me he wants to come on my expedition. He wants to be my base camp manager."

"What? That's news to me. He told me it was the most hellish experience he's ever had. He still has nightmares about it. I can't imagine why . . ."

"Do you blame him for Aaron's death?" Hank was blunt.

"Of course not." He suspected Tracy wasn't being truthful. "He told me there was nothing he could do. By the time he got to Aaron, he was already gone. I believe him, Hank. Did you take a good look at him? It's a miracle he even survived."

"You know, I had a hard time with that irony."

"That Aaron was the only one?" Tracy asked. "So did I. For all the risks, and near death misses . . ."

"That's one of the big problems I'm having. Aaron was never concerned about danger. He always said, 'if it's my turn, I'll be ready'. But when I saw him before he left, things were different. He was edgy about going. His mind was on something else, and he couldn't wait to finish this. But he wouldn't tell me what."

"So you're going to climb Everest? You're going to put together this massive undertaking, spend a fortune in men and supplies to get his body off the mountain?"

"Yes. I'm in a position to try," Hank said. "I owe it to him and believe it or not, I think he's been asking me to come get him."

"What does Linda think?"

"She's opposed to the idea."

"Really? I'm surprised." Hank heard the sarcasm but chose to ignore it.

"It would make things a lot easier if she was supportive, but . . ."

"But you're going to do it anyway?"

"Yes."

"And what'll you do when you bring his remains back here?"

"What do you mean?"

"Are you going to have him cremated? Are you going to bury him? Where are you going to put him?"

"I'm going to bury him back where I live. He told me at one point that Florida was home for him."

"Does he have a will? Does he have last wishes?"

"No. I don't know. He never said anything to me about stuff like that. All I know is he loved Florida. He wanted to live there."

"Traci knows."

"You know?"

"No, Hank. Not Tracy with a 'y', Traci with an 'i'. Traci Simmons. Aaron's long time girlfriend." She paused for a moment and then said, "The mother of his child."

"What did you just say?"

"There's another Traci, Hank. I don't know why Aaron never told you, but he said he didn't want you to know, not yet."

"A child?"

"Yes, Hannah. His daughter." Tracy leaned toward Hank and put her hand on his forearm. With a sad smile she said, "Hannah is Traci and Aaron's daughter. She's five years old."

"Aaron has a daughter? Why on earth didn't he tell me?"

"I don't know. Perhaps Traci has that answer too. You'll have to ask her."

"Where are they? Where do they live?"

"In Southern California, Huntington Beach." Hank was dizzy. The effects of the alcohol as well as the day's revelations from Dave, Jack, and now Tracy had him reeling. The name 'Traci Simmons' was charging to the front of his head like a runaway locomotive. He tried to grasp a memory of Aaron perhaps mentioning her. He had an unusual feeling that he knew or should know who this woman was.

"Wait a minute," Hank said, and then put his hands over his face. "Why do I know that name?"

"Perhaps you're more familiar with her screen name, 'Trace Element'." Hank's hands fell away from his face. He looked at Tracy with complete exasperation.

"Trace Element? The PORN STAR?"

Chapter 16

The Argument

HANK FLEW BACK to Orlando the next day. He had a lot to think about. What a preposterous idea, Aaron involved with a porn star, much less had a child with her. And then Tracy filled in the blanks.

Aaron had met Traci when he first moved to LA, right after he finished a full year of photography with the Vineyard Gazette. To make rent, he shot stills for pornographic magazines. That's where he met Traci, on the set of one of her first films. A relationship ensued and for a number of years they shared a place together. As his career soared, so did hers.

It did clear up the mystery of Aaron's emotional state. His admission of mistakes and decision to reform his life . . . It all made a lot more sense now.

As the plane began its descent, Hank ran through a mental checklist. He had to contact a mountain climbing school in New Hampshire. Jack Dawson had recommended the four-day intensive training program for him and the team. Clothing, gear and supplies had to be gathered and shipped within the next three weeks. Government agencies needed to be contacted, flights booked and documents all had to be in order. And on top of everything else, he had to maintain his running to stay in shape. Jack put into perspective the physical drain every climber would face trying to scale this mountain. There was even more to do now, Hank realized. First, he had to see to Aaron, then he would see to his legacy.

Linda surprised Hank at the greeting area. They hadn't spoken much. Between finishing work and planning the trip, he'd been on the go a lot, but he knew they would be talking now.

"Hi," he kissed her cheek. "Where are the kids?"

"They're with Mom. How was your trip?"

"Eye opening, that's for sure." Linda wasn't interested until Hank's announcement.

"Aaron has a daughter."

"What?"

"Hannah. Aaron has a five-year-old named, Hannah. Let's go get some lunch and I'll fill you in."

The restaurant was crowded in the busy terminal and the noise level was such that they had to sit side-by-side to hear each other. Hank was grateful for that, it was more intimate and preferable to across-the-table conversation.

When Hank's rack of ribs came, he dove right in. Linda only picked at her Caesar salad.

"Hank look," Linda began, "I'm as surprised as you are about Aaron's secret closet. But I still don't want you going to Nepal."

"The news about Hannah has given me even more reason to go, don't you see?"

"No, I don't see."

"If I need closure, how do you think his little girl feels?"

"What about your own little girls? How are they going to feel when they find out their daddy is leaving for two months and might not come back?"

"I've already talked to them."

"When?"

"The day after I told you."

"That's something we should've done together."

"Maybe." Hank put the pork down and wiped his mouth. "But since you're not behind me on this, why would we talk to them together?"

"What did they say when you told them?"

"Eva asked me if you thought it was okay."

"And what did you tell her?"

"That you weren't happy about it, and you'd let her know why. They were sad that I'd be gone so long. I explained to them that just like the way they've buried their pets in the backyard, I have to do the same thing for Aaron. Elisabeth did say she was glad I was going to bring Uncle Aaron back. She wants to be able to say goodbye to him."

"Don't you realize what you're doing to them? What if it ends up they have to say goodbye to the both of you?"

"It's because of them this expedition is only going to be an attempt." Hank hoped this concession would lessen the tension. "I know it's risky, and the odds of success are only fifty-fifty. If it gets too dicey, we'll bug out and come home. I promise." Hank forked up some coleslaw and then pulled off another rib. He was just about to bite into it when Linda asked, "Are you mad at me?" The question took Hank by surprise.

"Mad at you? No."

"This whole thing is the result of something I've been doing for years, and now you're punishing me."

"That's ridiculous."

"You're unhappy with our marriage." Hank chuckled.

"If that were the case, I'd choose counseling instead of climbing Mount Everest." He took another bite of gooey rib.

"I've been too demanding, I haven't paid enough attention to your needs. I've put too much of myself into the girls and not enough into us. I've been a bitch . . ."

"Whoa!" Hank said. "Linda, stop. It's not about us, okay? Look," he began, "I'll admit that we're probably long overdue for a talk about how we feel and where we're going in our marriage, but what I'm dealing with right now is about me and Aaron."

"What you're doing right now Hank, is screwing up your life." Linda took another sip of iced tea.

"He was my best friend Linda. I'm sorry if it sounds selfish, but it's the way I feel."

"Are you having a mid-life crisis?"

"I'm not having a mid-life crisis."

"This is some kind of low esteem thing isn't it? You haven't had enough adventure in your life and now, all of a sudden you want to be a hero. You want to be extraordinary."

"No," Hank said, shaking his head, "that's not it."

"Well, then what is it?"

"If anyone is extraordinary, it was Aaron. I've always considered myself to be an ordinary guy, but for his sake, I have to try and do this one extraordinary thing."

When the waitress came for the plates, Linda asked for her salad to be wrapped.

"So you're going to climb . . ."

"Attempt to climb," Hank corrected.

"Who's the expert that's going to lead you up there? It's not Matt is it?"

"No. He's in charge of getting us from Katmandu to the airstrip in Lukla, and then the trek out to base camp."

"And from there?"

"Dave's the expert on running the base camp. Umesh will handle the supply porters and climbing Sherpas. I'll climb with the crew of firemen and possibly Matt, along with an expert guide who has been referred by Jack. He said she's climbed Everest before."

"A woman?" Linda was not happy.

"She's amazingly qualified. I plan to fly out to California to meet her Thursday."

"You are?"

"And while I'm out there, I figured I'd look in on Aaron's daughter, too." Linda's shoulders slumped. A moment later, without another word, she got up and left. Hank watched her go. She didn't look back. The waitress came and put down a container for the remains of her lunch.

"Will there be anything else?" Hank turned to look at the server.

"No, just the check please."

Hank grabbed a cab home. He checked the machine for messages. "Beep."

"Hank, it's Ira Berkow. Please call me, right away. 617 . . ." Hank wrote down the number. He walked to the office den and sat at his desk to call back.

"Hank Longo. You dog. How the heck are you?"

"I'm okay, thanks. How are things in Boston?"

"Just great. Listen, I've been on the phone with your wife and . . . are you really planning a trip to Nepal to get Aaron?"

"Yes I am."

"That's unbelievable. I didn't think anyone was capable of such a thing."

"Well, I may be the first. Linda called you?"

"Yeah. It was a little odd talking to her since I hardly know her. She wanted me to try and talk you out of going."

"Really?"

"When are you leaving?"

"September."

"How many in the expedition?"

"There are three of us here in Florida. One out in California and eight from Long Island."

"Phew. Big expedition. How long you gonna be there?"

"Two months." Hank could hear the soft whistle. "That's awhile. What's your supply tonnage?"

"I don't know."

"Do you have a point of departure yet?"

"What do you mean?"

"Do you have anyone working on getting everything over there?"

Ira's questions shed light on a logistical concern: how to get everyone *and* everything to Nepal.

"Not really; I hadn't even thought about it."

"Look," Ira said with a firm voice, "I want to do this for you, okay? It's what I do and I'm good at it. Just give me a name and number." Hank gave Ira Umesh's info, and added, "Dave Horton's going to run the base camp for me. I should give you his number too, so he can tell you what he'll need."

"Dave?"

"He's been there already Ira. He knows the lay of the land."

"It's just a little too weird, you asking him to . . ."

"He asked me if he could."

"Okay, you know what you're doing I hope. E-mail me all the information; names and contact numbers for everyone. Also, make a list of supplies you'll need, so I can cross-reference everything. We'll deal with perishables later."

"We're going to need a lot of lightweight aluminum ladders, tents, oxygen bottles . . . Hey, Ira? I thought you were calling to talk me out of this?"

"Oh, yeah, that's right. Hey Hank? I don't think you should do this." Hank smiled at Ira's less than compelling plea. "There, I tried. Still going?"

"Yup."

"Okay then."

"Why are you helping me?"

"Tell you what, when you bring him back, I'll be there to really say goodbye, and I'll tell you then." Ira's voice cracked with emotion. "I also wanted to let you know I spoke to Al Sampson. He knew about Aaron and he's been pretty hammered by it. He may call you; he wants to be a player. He's got a lot of connections and the hardware as well."

"What do you mean?"

"When I told him about the expedition, he got all excited and started talking about people he knew in the Indian Air Force and some liaison work he once did. Don't be surprised when you get off the plane at Tribhuven, if he's there waiting for you."

"Okay," Hank said. "That would be great." They talked awhile longer, caught up on other stuff and when Hank finally hung up, he realized the irony. In the year they had all worked as a staff in the dorms, it was Aaron who had brought them all together. And now, he was doing it again.

Chapter 17

Benny's

April 1st, 2003

HANK WALKED THROUGH the double doors to Benny's Sports Bar & Grille, and scanned the room for Aaron. Aaron saw Hank right away and threw his arms around him in a back slapping bear hug.

"You look great," Aaron said. "You've lost weight."

"A lot of running buddy," Hank replied. "Watching what I eat a little better, and good old fashioned exercise."

"I hope a few beers and some games of pool won't ruin your regimen."

"Nah, shall we?"

Aaron thrust out an arm. "Lead on MacDuff!" He called out.

Their initial conversation was small talk. Aaron asked the usual questions about the family. He rendered his apologies for not being able to see the girls, but explained he only had a few hours in Orlando before flying to Washington to meet up with the expedition.

"So you're going to Nepal," Hank said. "And with all people, Dave Horton."

"Yeah," Aaron said, taking another sip of his beer. "I've worked with him before. His publishing empire has some magazines that are right up my alley. It's fun charging him more and more each time he calls."

"Have you seen him much?"

"Once in a while, most of the time he calls to ask me for something. It's strange too, how he always knows where I am."

"How do you mean?"

"Well, back when I was in Spain covering the Olympics, out of the blue he called me wanting to know how quick I could get over to some village in the Pyrenees for a bicycle race. When I told him I was already in Barcelona, he got all psyched to set me up. And I was happy cause I got another job that paid well, and I didn't have to go far."

"Weird," Hank said.

"And you know what? Over the years that's happened a few times." Aaron drained his glass and signaled the bartender for a pitcher. "I can't figure it out," he continued. "Dumb luck I guess."

"Have you seen Tracy?"

"Yeah." Aaron hesitated and then added, "I mean you do things for Dave, well . . . she's part of the package."

"How's that been?"

"Interesting. Hey I want to introduce you to someone." Aaron reached into his jacket and set out a long-haired little doll.

"This is my newest friend, Satchmo. He's going with me to the top of Everest."

"That's one odd looking doll. Where'd you find it?"

"He was given to me by someone very special." Aaron looked reflectively at the doll and smiled.

"Really?"

"Yep. By a lady I've known for a while. Satchmo here is supposed to keep me company." Aaron put the doll back in his coat pocket.

"Or keep an eye on you I should think, knowing your rep with the ladies. So who is this mystery woman?" Hank asked.

"You'll know her right away when you see her."

"Is she going to be like all the rest and let you run around loose all the time?"

"Not if this whole thing works out." The bartender brought the pitcher. Aaron reached for his wallet. Hank noticed Aaron's demeanor change when he asked, "You're my friend, right?"

"Of course," Hank said. "Last time I checked I was first on the list." Aaron pulled a twenty out and put it on the bar.

"The only one on the list. So if in the end I turned out to be the biggest hypocrite of all time, you'd find a way for us to still be friends."

Hank frowned. "I guess. Being a hypocrite is more forgivable than being a liar, or a thief, or a murderer."

"Well, that's good."

"Why?" Hank asked.

"No big deal. It was something I said a long while back that turns out won't be the case." Aaron smiled and changed the subject. "Hey, I wanted to tell you that I bought a place in Mount Dora."

"What?" Hank said, flummoxed. "You're shitin' me!" Aaron took his change and left a five for the tip. He picked up the pitcher and his glass.

"C'mon Henry, grab your glass and some wings. We'll shoot some pool, talk about the good 'ol days at Miami and I'll tell you all about the move to Central Florida."

Another pitcher of beer replaced the one they had and the quarters were slotted into the side of the table.

"So that's it in a nutshell," Aaron said. "I figured out that Florida is where I should be and I'd rather be here than anywhere else." Aaron took careful aim with his shot. Banking the cue ball, he narrowly missed the scratch.

"That's great news. It'll be fun having you around more." Hank looked at the position of the three striped balls he had left. "And I guess from here you can get anywhere right? Every airline in the world flies in and out of Orlando." Hank lined up his shot and sunk the four in the side pocket.

"I don't think you understand Henry. I'm not planning on going out much more." That statement stopped Hank from looking for his next shot. He picked up the square chalk and rubbed the tip of his cue stick.

"You putting down roots?"

"In a way, I guess. It's time."

As Hank lined up his next shot, he noticed Aaron pull from his back pocket an envelope which he quickly tore in half and then threw away in one of the sports bar's trash receptacles.

"Hey what's that?"

"Nothin'. Come on, take your shot." Hank missed and scratched the cue ball. Taking a stripe ball out, he put it back on the table and rolled the cue ball toward Aaron.

"Just wish it hadn't taken this long to realize everything."

"What about your search?" Hank said. "Your journey to whatever place it was you were looking for? You're telling me Mount Dora's 'Nirvana'?" Aaron laughed in spite of Hank's sarcasm.

"It's no longer about finding someplace, it's about finding someone." Aaron lined up the cue ball. Aiming for the eight, he pulled the stick back through his fingers.

"Really? So it's someone in Mount Dora?"

"Eight ball, corner pocket." Aaron tapped the cue ball. It rolled across the table and kissed the eight, which dropped right into the pocket he had called.

Hank slotted another set of quarters into the table's dispensary and pushed the metal tab. The balls rolled heavily into the open receptacle.

"I finally saw the place I was looking for reflected in someone's eyes. It was that special place I've been looking for. But it's not a physical place that was in those eyes."

"And what you saw was . . ."

"True love."

"And this was reflected to you by someone?" Hank said as he racked the balls. "This really must be a special someone."

"She is, and I should've known it from the get-go."

"You know," Hank stated as he lifted the rack, "I've never been able to understand your, what shall we call it, quest for the meaning of everything? Maybe I didn't try hard enough to believe all the stuff you've said over the years. But I knew you believed it, and I guess that was good enough for me."

"Do you remember when I told you about my dad?" Aaron asked.

"Yes."

"And do you remember when I told you that there was a strange moment I witnessed just before he killed himself? He had the gun pointed at my mother. The two of them were fighting in the bedroom, and when I came in, the gun was pointed at her." Hank struggled to remember the conversation.

"I remember you saying he almost shot you before he shot himself."

"That's right," Aaron said as he moved to the head of the table and placed the cue ball on the other break spot. "He was pointing the pistol at my Mom and I got in front of her."

"You wanted him to kill you instead?"

"At the time I didn't think, I just reacted." Aaron bent over and took a couple of practice strokes. "When I put myself between my mother and my father, he stared at me for a brief moment. Then he lowered the gun, pulled up a chair and sat down. What I thought, until recently, was that my Dad sat there and went to some kind of magical place. He stared off into the distance and began smiling. He smiled for a long time."

"This was when you got the idea that there was such a place?" In spite of the beer, the conversation had become so intense it sobered Hank.

"Eventually, yes." Aaron said with enthusiasm. "At the time I didn't know what to think. Even though he calmed down, in the end, he still shot himself."

"So that's what you've been seeking? That fraction of a second, corner of the eye place, you thought your dad achieved?" *And then he killed himself.*

"As I grew up," Aaron began, "I became convinced that my dad's suicide was a singular moment when he overcame all the demons that plagued him. For an instant, he discovered a place that had peace, happiness, and perfection. And I thought that when it started to slip away, he didn't want to lose it. So he put the gun to his temple and shot himself."

"And," Hank added, "you've been searching ever since."

"Not at first, but when I began to understand Buddhist teachings and intertwined it with my own experience, I was convinced that some kind of state of perfect enlightenment existed. I needed to find what I thought my dad saw."

"And now you've discovered it, but it's something different."

"Yeah, but don't you see?" Aaron said as anger rose within him. "I was wrong. I've spent all this time looking and it . . ." Hank stared in disbelief as Aaron lined up his break, tears dripping. *He's angry and he's crying.*

Aaron yelled, "IT'S NEVER BEEN OUT THERE!" The cue ball shot off the end of the stick and rifled toward the top of the triangle. Balls exploded in a chaotic fashion. Several dropped into pockets. Hank looked at his friend. He held the cue stick close, but his head was down and his shoulders were heaving.

"What my dad saw was me, Hank. In my eyes he saw that no matter how mean and nasty he was, I still loved him." From that, Aaron concluded, "There's no special place out there where you can find perfection. It comes from within. Just as my Dad knew what true love is, I know it now too. The difference is, he didn't want to stick around because he knew his drinking would've killed it. And I hated him for that."

"Hey," Hank said, "you okay?"

"Yeah." Aaron looked up and gazed around the room. "Just angry I guess. Angry and at the same time happy." Aaron squeezed his eyes shut and allowed more tears to fall.

"You're not acting this time are you?" Aaron managed a slight grin. "So what are you going to do?"

"I've still got assignments up the ying-yang, but after this expedition I'm just going to finish up the commitments I have. That'll keep me going for about another year. But that's it, I'm not taking on anymore. I'm going to work on staying put."

"What'll you do?"

"Who knows, maybe I'll hook up with the Sentinel. Maybe open a store. I could sell cameras, or develop pictures. I'll shoot weddings."

"You'll get bored," Hank said. "I know you too well."

"You're wrong about that."

"You know," as he put down his stick, Hank said, "it's too bad you couldn't have figured this out years ago."

Aaron took a card from his wallet. He summoned the bartender and borrowed her pen. He jotted down an address and handed it to Hank.

"When I get back, I expect you, Linda, and the kids." Hank looked at the address.

"You're serious about this?"

"Yes, and I need you to be my anchor."

"Okay, but don't stretch the chain too long," Hank smiled.

Aaron looked at his watch. "Hey, I gotta go catch a flight." Aaron pulled out his wallet again, but Hank protested, "Put your money away. I got this one."

"Thanks buddy."

"Thanks for coming in," Hank said. "Great news about you coming here. I know the girls'll be psyched."

"It's gonna be great."

"Hey, well, you know the usual litany of cautions." Aaron gave Hank a quick across-the-shoulder hug and a slap on the back and then watched him go out the door. He shook his head and smiled. Curious, he went back over to the trash can and pulled out the torn-in-two envelope. He put together the letter that had been in it and read the faded cursive writing. After the first few sentences he stopped in amazement.

I read this—twenty years ago!

Chapter 18

California

8:30, HANK OVERSLEPT. THE curt note was taped to the empty coffee pot. Linda and the girls had decided to go to Sea World; he'd have to drive himself to the airport.

His flight at the end of June to California was scheduled for eleven thirty; that didn't leave much time. With a small suitcase open on his bed, he loaded his clothes, showered, shaved and then added the toiletries.

Seated in first class, he reflected on how his life was changing. *In a man's heart, there is no better understanding of one's self than responding to the call of duty.* The quote was from a book on English explorers and their expeditions to the Himalayas. Hank closed his eyes comforted that this was Aaron's final gift to him; a journey that would take him around the world and make him whole.

"Henry Longo? Hi, I'm Sara Hobson; nice to meet you." Hank was startled to find his expedition-climbing leader at the gate to meet him.

"I thought we were meeting at the university?"

"Dawson told me this was your first visit to California. So, I thought I'd meet you here and have you follow me with your car. It's a little tricky to get from here to the campus." There was a pause as the two of them looked at each other. Hank smiled. In front of him was the woman who, in the next few months, would guide him and his team up the tallest mountain in the world. And she was no more than five-and-a-half feet tall. Her complexion was fair, her strawberry blonde hair pulled back into a tight ponytail.

"I'm sorry," Hank said, snapping out of his stare. "It's just that . . ."

"You were expecting more?" Sara put her hands into her pant's pockets and laughed. "Boy that Jack, I tell ya. Every time he gets me involved in a climb, he always makes me out to be some kind of Amazonian warrior queen."

"You're right. My impression . . ."

"Oh, it was written all over your face," Sara said. "I don't know what it is with that man."

"He speaks very highly of you. Said you're more than capable of leading this expedition."

"It's a great opportunity for my thesis. I don't know if Jack told you, but he must have, knowing Jack. I'm working on my Ph.D. My research is on high altitude edema. I've read the physical profiles on the crew and they'll provide an excellent range for my study."

"I read that you've climbed Everest before?"

"Well, if you've read up on me, you know I was part of a group that Dawson brought to the Himalayas a few years ago. You'd also know that I've climbed a lot of other mountains, too. And if you have any doubt about my abilities, I could easily haul you up on my shoulders and 'dead man' carry you out of this terminal."

Hank saw the determined look in her eyes. He had no doubt she could do it.

"That won't be necessary," he said smiling.

"How 'bout lunch? There's a place close to campus. It's Italian."

"Sounds great," Hank said.

*   *   *

"So what are your concerns?" Sara said as Hank reached for another slice of pizza from the elevated serving platter.

"Concerns?"

"Yes, concerns, worries. Is there anything you're really worried about that I can help you with?"

"The whole trip worries me." Hank took a bite from his slice and reached for the bottle of red wine they ordered. He poured the last of the wine into their two glasses. "And I don't want to freeze to death," Hank said flatly. He was surprised to see Sara laugh.

"Don't worry, you won't," she said. "Here are the rules: Dress in layers; drink lots of water; don't push yourself too hard or you'll overexert and freeze to death in your own sweat; keep your body's core warm with calories; and protect your eyes and ears so you can see or hear danger coming."

"I don't know anything about climbing. I don't want to be a liability."

"The training you'll get in New Hampshire should take care of that. I know it's only a week, but you'll learn a lot. After that, you'd be more than ready to climb Denali or Hood, or even the mountains down in South America."

"Yeah, but they're not Everest."

"But technically to climb, they're the same. Everest is just higher."

"Much higher," Hank said.

"The difficulty with climbing so high in the Himalayas is that you expose yourself to the law of probabilities. I hate to say this, but your friend Aaron dying of altitude sickness is rare for those who have been killed on Everest. The weather and avalanches and shifting seracs in the Khumbu Ice Fall have ended more peoples' lives on the mountain than pulmonary or cerebral edema."

"Tell me more about that. It's never been explained to me *how* Aaron died."

Sara wiped her mouth with a napkin. She looked first at her lap, and then looked at him.

"Edema is the accumulation of excess fluid in the body. Cerebral edema occurs when plasma leaks through capillary walls, driving up pressure inside the skull. We don't understand the cellular and chemical reasons why brain capillaries leak."

"Is that what you're studying?"

"I'm doing research on a chemical called vascular endothelial growth factor. It stimulates new capillary growth in low-oxygen conditions. It's another suspected cause of CE." Hank shook his head, impressed with her knowledge on the subject.

"This may be a hard question to answer," Hank began. "I kind of want to know if it was bad for Aaron in the end."

"I don't think so," Sara said with compassion. "If it was CE, it would have been disabling and there might have been some discomfort, but ultimately it was hypothermia that killed your friend. I think you can take comfort in the fact that he fell asleep. And of course, he never woke up."

"Okay," Sara said, wanting to move on. "Let's say we beat the odds and manage to get to him. How do you plan to get the body off the mountain?"

"The firemen that are acting as my crew have a special gurney. It's lightweight aluminum and comes in sections. Each of them will carry pieces of it, and put it together when we reach Aaron." Hank paused for a moment.

"Tell me about Aaron. What was he like?"

"He was my one best friend. Sometimes he was like a big brother. A lot of times he was just a pal. When there were big moments in our lives, we were always together."

"Hank, you're about to go on the most grueling journey of your life. You're not going to get Aaron's remains off of Mount Everest, you're going to get Aaron off of Mount Everest." She said exactly what he needed to hear. Before he could express his thanks, she blurted out, "How's the pizza? Can I try a slice?"

"That depends, do you like sausage and pineapple?"

"Sure do, it's very California." Hank watched as she picked up a wedge and bit in. She chewed and nodded in approval as she ate.

"There is one thing you and the boys should know before we get into this." Hank waited as she focused on the slice and decided where to take the next bite next. "I won't take any guff about me being a woman and the whole sexist bullshit thing."

"I don't have any doubts about your abilities." Sara put her slice down and leaned toward Hank.

"I'm not worried about you, but Hank, eight firemen and a former Navy S.E.A.L? You don't think they're going to have a tough time with me being in charge?"

"The Navy guy I'm not worried about. I'll make sure the other guys stay in line."

"Yes Hank, you will. When we start climbing, my word is gospel. Peoples' lives depend on my decisions. You, the porters, and everyone else that is climbing has to do what I say. I need to hear you swear to it. If it gets to the point where I think we can't continue and have to turn around, you won't argue with me. You'll accept my decision as final, regardless of how close we are to Aaron." Hank looked at Sara and could see how serious she was about this.

"Agreed."

"So convince me. Look me straight in the eye and swear it. You have to promise that you will defer to my decisions about the climb."

"I promise."

"I'll do my best to get you to Aaron. After that, it's up to all of us to get him, and us back down."

"Yes," Hank said with finality. Sara leaned back and then picked up her plate. "Would you like to try some of my anti pasta? The provolone and olives are excellent!"

*   *   *

Hank woke the next morning in his room at the Hilton Garden Inn in Garden Grove. In spite of his tiredness, he was up by 4:30. Since his internal clock was on East Coast time he was rising as he usually did, for work. After another thirty minutes of tossing and turning, he resigned himself to the fact it was time to start his day. He showered and dressed and went to experience the Pacific.

Hank was in awe, watching teenagers in wet suits carry surfboards to the beach. He parked in the lot and sauntered down the pier. With his forearms against the safety rail, he watched as each of the surfers bided their time looking for the right wave. This was Surf City, the mind's picture of Southern California.

Knowing that he was supposed to meet Traci at a restaurant by the pier, Hank walked over to check out the facility.

There it was, at the far end of the pier, Ruby's Surf City Cafe. Although it wasn't open yet, a bride and groom were posing for pictures. The couple reminded Hank of his own wedding, and the eight by ten photo that still sat on the bedroom dresser. It was his favorite picture. Aaron had captured the bounce in Hank's walk and Linda's joy as she lifted her bouquet of white Calla Lillies in the air.

Hank studied the surf again. Watching the water rear up and crash down brought his thoughts back to Aaron. "I have to get to you," he said aloud as he watched the waves roll by. He closed his eyes and envisioned Aaron buried in the snow, an arm reaching with fingers wide and grasping in the air, waiting for another hand to pull him out.

Chapter 19

Traci

HANK WATCHED AS the former porn star made her way over to him. She looked every bit as good as he recalled. Then she got closer and he could see that she was not exactly the same as he had remembered.

She was shorter in height than he had imagined. She wore pleated pants and a cream colored frilly blouse. Her hair was shoulder length and had a nice salon look.

"Hello Hank," Traci said as she extended her hand to greet him. "I can't believe I finally get to meet you."

"I'm pretty amazed to be meeting you." Hank took her hand and held it lightly in his. He looked down to where their hands met and felt soft warmth in her palm that carried his eyes back up her arm to her shoulder, past the coifed hair that fell around her face and to her eyes. Her chin quivered. Without hesitation he pulled her close for an embrace.

"I'm sorry," she whispered. "I didn't want to act like this; I wanted to be stronger." Hank heard a sniffle.

"It's okay," was all he could think to say.

"Aaron would be so mad at me for acting this way." She sighed and paused for a long moment, "I miss him so much."

"Me too Traci." She looked back at him and smiled.

"Well, you look exactly as Aaron described you."

"You're my biggest puzzle," he admitted.

"Yes, I know. I don't know why he never told you about me or Hannah."

"I think he was just about to." Hank hoped that would make her feel better.

The waitress came. Traci ordered a Virgin Bloody Mary and Hank decided to have one as well.

Traci pulled a photo from her bag and handed it to Hank.

"Hannah?"

"Yes. She's five."

"She's in kindergarten?" Traci nodded her head and looked away. "How's she taking it?"

"I haven't told her yet, about Aaron. I haven't had the courage."

"You haven't?"

"No. I haven't. For now he's just away. Like always."

Hank thought about the many occasions when Aaron had been out of the country on assignment; some quite lengthy. He had a vague memory of him being in Europe one time, for a year, covering the fall of the Berlin Wall.

"Yes," he finally said, "I suppose he is."

"For now, it's really all I want her to deal with," Traci said. "She's used to it and it gives me time to figure out what to do next." Traci looked out at the surf. Hank followed her gaze. The heat from the mid day sun made the water shimmer. When Traci looked back to Hank, her expression was calm.

"You know I have to ask," she said, "how on Earth do you plan on bringing Aaron back?" Hank was relieved to talk about something he had more confidence in. His emotions had been on the verge of unraveling.

"I tell you what, let's order some lunch and I'll tell you all about it."

After lunch, they drove to Traci's apartment. The drive from the café wasn't far. Traci directed Hank to a spot on Warner Avenue.

"My place is just a few blocks. Hannah's at camp over at the playground," Traci said, pointing to an area that appeared to Hank as being opposite of where she lived. "We can walk over and get her." The two crossed the busy road and turned down a quiet side street away from the traffic.

"I have to warn you, Hannah can be a bit on the shy side."

"Okay," Hank responded.

"There've been a lot of men," Traci said in a tone of admission, "including Aaron. They come in and out of our lives. Some have been kinda nice, but by the time she gets used to them, they're gone."

"And that includes Aaron?" Traci looked at Hank, but didn't respond. They just walked for a while, in silence.

"Hannah was almost two when she met her dad."

"And how did that go?"

"I had been with so many men at the time, Aaron wanted to be sure she was his." Hank looked at her and was surprised that there wasn't even a hint of embarrassment in what she'd said.

"But as soon as he saw her, he knew right away. She looks so much like him."

"Yes," Hank added, "I have two daughters. I've had the same feeling." They crossed another street. Up ahead, Hank could see a large fenced playground sandwiched between several large community buildings.

"But even though Aaron knew then that he had a daughter, he was miles away from becoming a dad."

"So he didn't see her much?" Hank asked.

"He took care of her, financially. He was paying into a college fund, sent me money for clothes. As a matter of fact I just found out he left a house in Florida for her."

"In Mount Dora! I've seen it. It's not far from where I live."

"But you see," Traci said as she stopped walking, "until recently he hadn't spent much time with either one of us."

"I'm pretty sure that was going to change."

"You think he was going to try and take Hannah to Orlando?" Hank could see her anger swelling. She didn't realize what Aaron had intended the house for.

"It's a home, Traci. The house is meant for a family. Dad, daughter, and mom." Traci didn't say anything, but looked down at the pavement and walked back and forth in front of him.

God she is confused. Hank had taken a liking to her and thought she deserved better from Aaron.

Hank spoke again. "I'm pretty sure Traci, what he was hoping for was that the three of you could be a family. It was buddy talk over a few pitchers of beer and a few games of pool, but that was the impression I got before he left for Nepal." Nothing more was said as the two of them walked on.

"That's Hannah." Hank strained his eyes to see a child waving in the distance. At the end of the street the fence ended and there was a gate, which opened to the playground.

Hank watched as Traci waved and then moved ahead of him to meet the little girl that was now running toward them. She bent down to receive Hannah in a motherly embrace. Traci led the little girl back to Hank.

"Hannah," Traci said, "this is Mr. Longo. You can call him Hank."

"Hullo," Hannah said with a small voice. She gave a half-hearted wave and moved closer to Traci. Hank bent into a catcher's position and smiled at the little girl.

"Hello Hannah, I'm very happy to meet you." Hank looked at the shy child. Right away he could see the resemblance to Aaron. She looked more like her mom, but she had his blue eyes and thicker eyebrows. In that instant, he realized what Aaron had said about the ending of his search had everything to do with Hannah; his little girl. Just as Aaron's father had seen the reflection of himself in Aaron, he too had seen it in his daughter. This was the person he was bringing back to Florida. Traci was a part of it, but it was in Hannah that Aaron had found his true path.

"Hank went to school with daddy, many years ago. He's your father's best friend, just like Samantha's your best friend." Hannah thought about that and then smiled.

The apartment complex on Warner Avenue was a series of two story buildings clustered together with narrow walkways between them. The place looked outdated, run down and in desperate need of renovation. Traci's small two-bedroom walk up was well kept, but Hank could see the carpeting should have been replaced ten years ago, and the furniture five. Traci went to make iced tea in the kitchen and Hannah played on the floor with her collection of pony dolls.

"Do you know where my Daddy is?"

"Yes I do. He's a long way from here, climbing a very tall mountain." Hank felt relief when Traci came into the room carrying a tray with three drinks.

"Hannah, here's your lemonade. Hurry up and drink it before Samantha's mom gets here. You're going over to her house this evening."

"Night time play date?" Hank asked.

"I have to go to work tonight," Traci said flatly.

"You work at night?"

"Not usually, tonight's an exception. They're doing a night club scene and the place they've rented is only available tonight." Hank had a dozen questions, but Hannah blurted out, "Do you know when my Dad is coming back?" Hank turned to her. He got up from the couch and walked around the coffee table to where Hannah was and sat down next to her.

"I just wanted to know about my Dad, that's all." She continued to comb the mane of one of her plastic ponies.

"I want to know if Satchmo's okay, too," she added.

"Satchmo?" Hank looked to Traci for help, before he remembered.

"You know what Hannah? I've met Satchmo."

"You have?" Hannah gave a big smile. "When?"

"Right before your dad left for the mountain. He introduced us. He told me his name was Satchmo."

"Satchmo," Traci said, "is one of Hannah's best friends."

"I let Satchmo go with Daddy," Hannah chimed in, "to keep him company and to see what's on the other side."

"I see." Hank said. "And what," he said back to Hannah, "did you mean by the other side?"

"Daddy said he was climbing the highest mountain in the world. So when he gets to the top he'll see what the other side of the world looks like. So I wanted Satchmo to go with him, so when he gets to the top of the world, he'll be able to see everything as well."

"What do you think is on the other side?" Hank asked.

"Daddy said Neverland, Wonderland and the Emerald City all wrapped in one. I think he was joking, but Satchmo will know for sure." Hank smiled at the little girl's mature thinking.

Hannah put down her pony doll and brought her knees up to her chin. While hugging her legs with her arms, she looked at Hank and asked, "Are you going to the mountain where Daddy is?"

Hank was surprised by the question, but knew just how perceptive children could be.

"Yes, Hannah. Yes I am."

"Do you think you will see him there?"

"That's the reason I'm going. To see your dad."

"Is he having a hard time finding his way to the top?" Hank could only shrug his shoulders. He knew he needed to hedge the truth.

"I think he needs my help, Hannah. I'm going to Nepal to help your dad."

"Will you say hello to Satchmo for me and tell him to hurry back?"

"I will," Hank pledged, as a lump formed in his throat. Just then, the doorbell rang. Traci left the room and returned with a backpack, and a small blue denim coat.

"Here you go honey. Your pajamas are in here, as well as your toothbrush." Hannah slung the backpack over one shoulder and grabbed the coat with her other hand. With her head down, she marched to the door. Halfway to the door, Traci intercepted her and whispered into her ear. Hannah turned around and walked back to Hank.

"It was nice to meet you, Mr. Longo."

"It was *my* pleasure to meet you, Ms. Temple." Hannah smiled before she turned again to leave.

After Traci escorted Hannah she returned to Hank in the living room. She took a seat next to him on the sofa, but appeared even more nervous and agitated than before.

"I have to tell her," she said, as she brought her hands up and over her face. "She needs to know. Oh my God, my little girl, my little girl." Traci's cries turned to sobs. Hank tried to comfort her as the meltdown launched into total despair. Right there and then, everything Traci had been holding back let loose in a torrent.

"It's all right, it's all right, it's all right," he repeated. As Traci continued to cry, Hank felt an exuberant pride swell within him; the feeling of being strong during someone's moment of weakness.

I've missed this. He flashed back to the comfort he often gave Linda when she was plagued with worry or doubt. But somewhere along the way, Linda had evolved into a person that no longer needed him as an emotional outlet. Hank was elated to once again be strong for someone.

"I need a tissue," Traci said. Hank stepped back to see that she was in dire need. She held the back of her hand to her nose and sniffed hard to prevent anything from dripping down.

"Oh, yes you do," Hank said. "Where are they?"

"The kitchen, by the fridge." Hank moved fast to bring the box to her. First she wiped and then she blew, hard. She took more tissues and dabbed her eyes. She exhaled deeply and took a moment to regain her composure. After another deep breath, she got up and went to her bedroom. From the narrow hallway, he heard her say, "Oh, my God! Look at me, I'm a fucking mess!" When she returned she had a zippered tote.

"I can't go to work looking like this. God, I don't want to be late."

"Are you all right?"

"No, I'm not." Traci wiped the mascara that ran from her eyes. "Years ago, when Aaron and I were living together, things were great. I was getting famous in porn and making lots of money and he was getting assignments and shooting for the local papers. It never seemed to bother him that I was fucking people for a living, and I was happy to have a boyfriend that wasn't in the industry. The shit started happening when he got work that would send him out of town. Often it was for weeks at a time." Traci began applying new makeup. "I was lonely when he wasn't around. I was in love with him and didn't want to hurt him by shacking up with someone else." Traci stopped applying and looked directly at Hank. "So I started using."

Traci looked into her compact. "At first it wasn't much. And I would stay away from it whenever he came back. But slowly I got hooked, and one day he noticed."

"Aaron would have been a hypocrite if he told you he had never used drugs himself. I can tell you that."

"Yes," Traci said while once again working on her application. "But smoking the occasional joint is nothing compared to the shit I was doing." Traci mimicked a needle being injected into her arm.

"Oh," Hank said, "that."

"So we fought. He yelled and yelled and yelled at me. He said he'd leave and never come back." Traci paused as she repacked her bag. "So I stopped. It was an easy choice, him or the drugs. I didn't want to live without him. As corny as it sounds, I loved him; more than anyone I've ever known. And the only way to stop was to get out of the industry."

"So, you got pregnant."

"Yes, with Hannah. She was my ticket out."

"But you're still in, aren't you? I mean you're going to work, right?"

"I'm not on screen anymore Hank. I'm a 'Set Mom'. I'm behind the scenes making sure the girls in the film stay within the guidelines of their contracts."

Hank nodded his head.

"So you just make sure the scenes stay true to what's written in the script."

"If there's a script," Traci said while she laughed. "After a scene I'll escort them to the showers, make sure they're okay, stuff like that."

"I see, but it's not what you want?"

"Oh God no. I'd give anything to get Hannah and I away from all this. I am so done with LA. You know I've tried to do other things. I can type, answer phones, file. At one point, I had a great job as an executive secretary; good pay, benefits, nice boss."

"What happened?"

"Wife found out who I was and had me fired. So back I went 'cause the studio always needs someone to do something." Traci looked at her watch. "I've got to get going," she said, getting up.

"I'll walk you to your car. I've got to get back to the airport as well."

"So does your wife know about me?" Traci asked as they walked along the sidewalk. "Does she know you came out to see me?"

"You're one of a few people I needed to meet with before going. Yeah, she knows."

"And?"

"She really didn't say much." Hank recounted how little had been said between him and Linda since he decided to go find Aaron.

"There isn't a wife on this planet who likes the idea of their husband meeting up with a porn star, active or retired." He had remembered she said that, but he wasn't about to share it.

Under the streetlight of a residential alley sat a solitary Honda Civic.

"This is mine." Based on the faded blue paint and numerous dents and scrapes Hank guessed that it had to be at least ten years old. He imagined the speedometer showing two hundred or more thousand miles on it. "Not much to look at, but it runs." Hank had been so absorbed in conversation with Traci that he had lost his bearings on where he was.

"Now where am I parked?"

"Go back out this side street and cross back over Warner. Your car will be two blocks down on the left."

"Great." Hank put his hands into his pockets and fidgeted. He didn't know what to say next.

"I'll tell Hannah. I have to," Traci said as she exhaled.

"Tell her again that I was her father's best friend. Tell her I'm going to Nepal because I have to climb the same mountain her daddy climbed and bring him back so we can all say good-bye."

"Bury him in Florida, Hank. He loved his time there with you the most."

"And when you come for the funeral, plan on staying."

"Sorry?"

"You and Hannah, in Mount Dora, it's your house and your ticket out of here Traci."

"I can't leave," she said, totally confused.

"Yes you can. You're done with LA, remember?"

"But I don't know anyone there. I'll have no job."

"You'll know me. I'll be there, and I'll help you."

Hank watched as tears of hope spilled down the woman's cheeks. To Hank it was simple. The greatest gift he could give to his friend was to take care of the family he left behind.

"Without a doubt."

"Thank you," Traci said with a quiet voice, "for everything." Hank just nodded.

"Be careful," Traci ordered and then gave him a tight hug. "I couldn't deal with another loss." He stepped back from the embrace to look at her.

"I will Traci. Believe me when I tell you I've had to make that promise to a lot of people."

"You'll stay in touch?"

"Of course, I'll keep you posted. There's a Mount Everest website. I'll be sending dispatches." Hank reached for his wallet and pulled out one of his business cards. "Do you have something to write with?" Traci unlocked her car and dove head first into the console area between the seats. She came out with a pen.

"This is the web address," Hank said as he wrote on the back of his card. "Log onto the page and then go to the mail. You'll find me there." As Hank handed Traci the card she read what he had written.

It was time for her to go to work and for Hank to go home. He had accomplished everything he set out to do in California. There were no more bases to cover or loose ends to wrap up.

"It was great to meet you, Trace Element."

Hank watched as she climbed into her car and started the engine. She waved as she pulled away from the curb. He stood motionless as the Civic disappeared around the corner. Hank looked up at the high trunk palm trees that dotted the residential area, and then headed back to his rental.

Chapter 20

Linda's Problem

THE FOUR DAYS of training at the North Conway climbing school had gone well for both Hank and the fire crew. As he settled into his seat on the flight back to Orlando, he was optimistic. Just a few days ago he was apprehensive about his stamina, whether he could keep up with the team, not hold them back or trip them up. But the school's program revealed he was more than capable. Not only did he keep in step with the other rescuers, he was often chosen to lead.

As the plane lifted off, he thought about the camaraderie that had developed. The men were professional, paid attention, and after a couple of days when it started to make sense, they relaxed.

When the session ended, most headed back to New York, where they would assemble their gear and in three days board an Air India flight that would take them first to England, and then on to Katmandu. Hank's plan was to fly back to Orlando, gather up some last minute items and fly with Matt and Umesh to pick up Sara in Los Angeles. The four would then cross the Pacific to Nepal from the Asian side of the globe. It would be a three-day trip. Hank had never flown so far in his life or had been so far from home.

*   *   *

Here he was, lifting off from Orlando again. Matt and Umesh were seated on each side of him. He was headed for Nepal but his thoughts were on Linda.

"Did I hear that right?" she asked. Hank had been on the phone to Dave dealing with costs and logistics.

"Remind me to keep the door closed so you won't have to listen," he had said over his shoulder. When he got to the refrigerator, she was in front of it. He wanted a cranberry juice.

"I'm trying to find a sane reason why you're doing this, listening may give me a clue?" As soon as she moved, Hank pulled out the juice container and walked to the cabinet for a glass. He moved back to the fridge and depressed the ice dispenser. "Plunk, plunk," the ice dropped into his glass. He went back to the counter and poured some juice.

"Does Sebastian know what you're doing?"

Hank frowned. Another broadside.

"What?"

"I just wondered if he was aware of what you're doing and how you're squandering all this money Gino left you?" Linda cornered him. The word "squandering" was a direct hit to his anger button.

"Yes, he's aware of my plan, and he doesn't have a problem with it."

"Well, I have a problem with it. I have a problem with everything you've been doing since Aaron died."

"I'm going to Nepal Linda. I'm going to climb that mountain and find him. And when I do, I'm going to take him off Everest and bring him home."

"At the risk of losing everything you have?"

Three days later, they were still at it. The only difference was, Hank was about to leave for Nepal.

"How on Earth are you going to be able to keep in touch with us?"

"There's a web site dedicated to Everest climbers and expeditions. I'll be posting a blog on how we're doing. We can e-mail through that."

"You can e-mail all you want, Hank. I'm going to be too busy trying to be both mother and father to our children."

"When I can, I'll call." Linda folded her arms across her chest.

"Don't bother," she said in a whisper.

"When I get back," Linda finished the sentence.

"There may not be anything for you to come back to . . . If you love me you won't do this Hank." He looked at her.

"If you love me Linda, you'll let me do this."

The muted sound of a car horn came through the bedroom wall. Hank looked at Linda and for one fleeting moment it appeared to him that she might cry.

"That's my ride," he said. Gathering up the rest of his things, Hank zipped up his backpack and headed for the door.

"Come on girls," Linda called out. "It's time to hit the road."

The car horn blew again.

"I don't think I can do it Hank." Hank could see Linda standing in the hallway.

"What can't you do?" Hank grabbed his suitcase in one hand and slung the backpack over his shoulder. He walked toward her.

"Sit in this house and not feel like I've been abandoned."

"I'm not abandoning you."

"You're not the one being left behind."

Eva and Elisabeth came out from their rooms. They ran to Hank who dropped to one knee and received hugs and kisses.

"All right you two," Linda said as she stepped forward to take each of the girls' hands. "We're off to visit Aunt Lucy."

The four of them walked out of the house together. Eva and Elisabeth veered off to the right, pulled open the minivan door and climbed in. Hank looked across the lawn to where Umesh was parked. He was pointing to his watch and waving for Hank to hurry.

"So you'll be here when I get back?" Hank's heart was hopeful. But it sank fast when she didn't respond. She just turned and climbed into the van.

Chapter 21

Katmandu

ONCE AGAIN HE rubbed the thin cross and thanked his Maker's son. The plane touched down onto the runway at Katmandu. After going through both customs and immigration, Hank, Matt, Sara and Umesh walked to the central terminal. At the end of the long, narrow walkway, the four strolled into a loud, cavernous structure supported by high arched steel trusses. From behind security roped sections came the cries of reunited families and men in fierce competition hawking taxi fares. Then there was the military presence that Hank noticed, and the assault rifle each soldier held.

"Man will you look at that," Matt said as they continued to walk toward the center of the building. Hank looked at Matt and followed his gaze to a corner of the terminal where two soldiers stood over the transient crowd.

"Those are Belgium FAL submachine guns," Matt said. "They must be on alert 'cause they're locked and loaded."

"It looks like a lot of military here," Sara added. "Is there a problem?"

"Depends on who you talk to," Matt replied. "There are rebels fighting the monarchy. The government calls it an insurgency. Others think it's a civil war."

"Great," Sara mocked.

"Most of the troops are just for show," Matt added as the four reached the center of the open hall. "If there was trouble, most would run with us to escape. But those guys there," Matt pointed, "and there, and there. Those guys mean business."

"Henry," the voice shouted. Hank and the others turned to see Dave cut through the crowd. Next to him was a man Hank didn't recognize. He wore a military outfit, distinctively different from the military personnel in the terminal, and aviator sunglasses.

With a hand out for a shake Hank said, "Wow, Dave, you're looking a whole lot better."

"Thanks," Dave said as he gripped Hank's hand. He paused for a moment. "You gave me something to get better for." Hank realized it was true, for Dave at least, and maybe for him as well. Turns out, this journey meant different things to a lot of people.

As soon as Hank let go, both Matt and Sara stepped up to introduce themselves to Dave.

"I have a surprise for you," Dave announced. The military man stepped forward into the circle of introductions. Hank watched as he took off his sunglasses and smiled. Immediate recognition incited a wave of memories.

"Al Sampson."

"Colonel Sampson, at your service."

"What the heck are you doing here?"

"Word's out, you're going to go get Aaron Temple. I'm here to help."

Where would I be in my life without my friends?

"Thank you," came Hank's choked reply.

"Come on everyone, follow me. I'll show you one way I can help." Hank, Matt, Sara and Umesh picked up their luggage and hurried to catch up with Dave who was already in hot pursuit. At a heavily guarded door, Al pulled out his ID. The officer in charge looked it over and stepped back to salute Al. Two soldiers held the door for them.

"Right this way," Al said, waving them through. The exit took them out onto the airport's tarmac.

The faded markings on the enormous helicopters indicated they were once part of the Soviet military. Sara took a slow walk around the tail while Matt climbed in and made his way to the cockpit.

"They're Mi-17's. It'll get you, your supplies, and crew up to Lukla."

"Is that why you're here?" Hank asked.

"In part," Al said. Dave walked over from where he had been examining one of the copter's enormous rotor blades. He explained.

"Al got in touch with me once Ira had told him we were coming. Ira knew the time frame was critical." Dave looked at Al. "When I explained the shuttle jump system I used last time, and how long it had taken the airline to get everything to Everest, Al said he had a better plan." Al continued the conversation.

"Instead of using just one STOL aircraft for that short landing strip up at Lukla, we'll use two choppers." Al pointed to two other sleek new helicopters that were in a hanger building. "Those copters are for training maneuvers with the Nepalese army. They're capable of high altitude reconnaissance." Al paused for a moment. "If it becomes necessary, as a back up plan, I can get even further up the mountain."

Hank looked at Al standing next to him. He noticed some gray in his short cut hair, but other than that he was still as slim as ever, and he was still R.O.T.C. Al, in all his glory. Hank shook his head slightly and gave a large bemused smile.

"Al. I can't believe you're here," Hank said.

"What's more unbelievable," Al replied, "is that you're here."

Hank and his group left the airport in route to the Yak & Yeti Hotel, where the rest of the expedition was waiting. From the taxi they got a healthy sample of the traffic, noise and stench of the exotic, but ancient metropolis of Katmandu. Hank noticed the mix of old and new; square and rectangular two story buildings combined residential and commercial life together with power lines running helter skelter over the freshly paved black asphalt street. People moved in and out along the sidewalk less roads buying goods from street vendors or waiting for a ride among the packed jitney vans that plowed along the main thoroughfares. They passed temples of worship and ancient landmarks, also overcrowded and polluted with auto exhaust.

Three of the firemen were in the lobby when they arrived.

"Hank! You've made it," boasted Captain Jim.

"Yes," Hank said as he shook hands. Behind Jim he could see Lieutenant Ed Casey and one of the younger fireman, Pete Saltus. The two grabbed the luggage from the taxi.

"Is everyone here?" Hank asked.

"Yes. We got in yesterday. Some of the guys are out exploring, but I expect them back soon. The hotel planned a tea reception for us in a few minutes, and then dinner will be at five."

"Is the place okay?" Hank's words spoke of apology.

"Well," Jim chuckled, "from a Fire Inspector's perspective, a little short of code. But if you look around the neighborhood, what isn't?"

Sara had unzipped her backpack and was looking through it when Pete asked, "Is this your first time here?"

"No," she said as she stood up with the camera she had been looking for. "Hey Matt? Can you take a picture of me in front of the hotel?"

"Give it here." Matt, whose head was in his own gear took the camera from Sara.

"Your name?" Sara asked.

"Peter Saltus."

"Wanna be in the picture with me?"

"Sure." Pete's face brightened and he followed like an excited puppy.

"Hey! I'm in the picture too," Ed yelled. "No way a rookie gets solo photo op with the chic climber."

"Hey whad' you call me?"

"Aw. I was only kiddin'. Can I stand on this side of you? This is my best side."

The rest of the crew had returned to the hotel just in time to jump into the picture. They crowded together on the front steps of the hotel as Matt immortalized the first leg of their journey.

"It's a good sign, I think," Umesh said from behind Hank. "They like her."

"It's all fine n' dandy now," Dave said as he watched them together. "I just hope it's the same when they're in a blizzard at 26,000 feet." Hank nodded because he knew Dave was right.

"Come on," Umesh said to Dave, Hank and Jim. "First social lesson here, never be late for tea."

The Yak and Yeti turned out to be more than enough for the group's needs. The staff could not have been more helpful. During dinner Hank noticed with satisfaction how everyone was eagerly getting to know one another. Matt and Tom spent the entire dinner discussing their military careers, Colin Webber talked with Umesh on the music of the region, and the others listened as Sara regaled them with stories of her last expedition.

After dinner, they adjourned to a large conference room which had been set up for a power point presentation.

"I'd like to start by thanking everyone for helping me in the recovery of my friend, Aaron Temple. We have a long journey ahead and besides the risks you're aware of, there are others we may face along the way." Hank smiled at Al, who had slipped in and took a seat beside Dave.

"Everest can be a hostile place. I've been told, we must seek spiritual advice and ask permission to complete our mission." Hank smiled at the quiet laughter around the room. "Miyolangsangma will surely see our request as just. I'm sure of it. Our goal, as you know, is to get Aaron Temple off the mountain. Al has offered to get us up there by copter, and then assist in getting Aaron home."

"At your service," Al stood up and saluted.

"Dave Horton is our mission manager," Hank continued. "Having already put together a successful climb, he's well suited to oversee this one. Dave would you like to explain some things?"

Dave walked over to the podium, which stood adjacent to the screen.

"The expedition will be divided into several phases. A leader will be assigned for each part. It's my responsibility to be the base camp manager. Umesh Buju is in charge of resources while we're here in Katmandu. Matt Haskins will take charge when we leave here and lead us to the base camp. From there, Sara Hobson will take charge of the group for the climb. Now, if I may have the lights . . ." The room went dark and the visual presentation began.

"We have another two days in the city before we head back to the airport for the trip to Lukla, which is in the Khumbu Valley." A map of Nepal appeared on the screen. "Thanks to our flying friend here, we'll be together for the first part of the journey. Most of the supplies will be flown to this area here at Namche." Dave used a laser pen to indicate on the map where the supplies will go. "Umesh will go with the supplies and secure the animal transportation needed to bring the supplies to base camp, as well as some additional manpower to get us up the mountain."

"What animals are we using to carry the supplies?" Ed asked.

"Dzopkyos, a crossbreed between yak and some cattle they have up there. They're well suited for hauling heavy loads at high altitudes. We're fortunate the supplies can be airlifted ahead, it'll give us more time to get to Namche Bazaar and acclimatize."

The group watched with great interest as Dave went on to point out the other stops planned before reaching base camp. He emphasized the need for short trips, plenty of rest and the necessity to adapt to the altitude.

"When we reach base camp," Dave said in his final remarks, "we'll be 17,500 feet above sea level. We'll remain there until we accomplish our goal; probably three weeks, but more likely a month." Dave shuffled his papers into a neat pile.

"Thanks to Hank," Dave continued, "the base will be well equipped and have a lot of amenities to make everyone as comfortable as possible. Now, I'll turn over the presentation to Sara Hobson. She'll tell you about the ascent up the mountain."

Hank watched as Sara pulled down a topographical map of the mountain from behind the podium.

"We will ascend the mountain along the most traveled route, following along the same path that Hillary and Norgay used to first climb to the top in 1953. We'll leave base camp and establish our first camp above the Khumbu Ice Fall. Getting through the Ice Fall will be the most dangerous part of our climb. The enormous seracs and crevasses are in a constant state of motion. We'll use ladders and ropes to get through this part of the mountain. I should point out that we'll be traveling through this section a number of times as we acclimatize." Sara picked up the laser pen Dave had used. She pointed on the screen. Hank and the others watched as the projection changed and several dramatic photos were shown of the ice walls and men attempting to cross open gorges on narrow, roped together aluminum ladders.

"Our Sherpa guides," Sara continued, "will determine the path for us. They'll do most of the work fixing ropes and setting up ladders."

"How dangerous is it?" Captain Jim asked, and Sara thought for a moment before she answered. She looked at the group, gave a partial smile and said, "Probably as dangerous as running into a burning building, knowing it could collapse at any moment."

"Right up your alley," Rusty said to Ed. While Sara continued, Hank looked over to see the lieutenant staring at the image of an extremely long ladder up against the side of a bouldered ice ridge.

"I'm no stranger to it," came Ed's casual reply.

Rick Catano shot his arm up for a question to Sara.

"Are those ladders strong enough to support us?"

"Oh, they're quite strong," Sara replied. "They'll bend, but they won't break. We take turns and go one at a time. A key ingredient in the success of all this is you have to trust the equipment. Everything has been time tested by many climbers before us. What you need to do is know and understand what each piece of equipment is used for, and how. That way you can depend on it to do what it's been designed for." Everyone acknowledged her advice.

"Okay," Sara said as the screen changed images, "ABC's at 19,500 feet. We'll establish camp two at the base of Lhotse after traversing the glacial Western Cwm. 'Coom' is a Welch term for a valley. It's a four-and-a-half-mile walk and 1,700 vertical feet higher. From there, we go up. Literally. The expedition will climb the Lhotse Face and establish camp three about half way up, at 24,000 feet." Sara paused to allow several shots of the mountain to hit the screen. "The climb will be done in phases with objectives, which will include planned retreats. There'll be limited time at each camp before descending back to base camp. Number one goal is to acclimatize." Hank and Matt had been thoroughly educated by Sara during the plane ride on the potential problems with high altitude. Her knowledge of human physiology at heights above 25,000 feet was extensive. Her Ph.D. work had made the "Death Zone" her own back yard of study. Hank felt stress by the scale of the whole expedition, but was at ease with Sara's capabilities.

"From camp three we push on to this 26,000 foot plateau here." She pointed to an area just below the Southeast Ridge of the mountain that looked to be just below the summit. "This is known as the South Col," she said. "Our goal is to get there, rest as much as we can and then push to the objective here." The image changed. Pictures of another expedition climbing the sloped ridge appeared on the screen. Hank had learned enough to know that the roped climbers in the photo were climbing the Hillary Step.

How are we ever going to get above that, he worried.

"Three thousand feet more gentlemen, just above an area known as the Hillary Step, that's our objective. That's where Aaron Temple is."

The lights came back on and the screened image disappeared. Dave came back up to the podium.

"This is a global positioning device. Each of you will have one. Programmed into it will be the key areas on the mountain and also Aaron's position, not more than a hundred yards from the summit."

Captain Jim and three other members of the fire team got up and went over to a large canvas equipment bag where they extracted what looked like large metal serving trays. Once each man had one, they followed the Captain to the front of the room.

"This is what we'll be using to transport the body," Jim began. "It's one of the basic types of rescue sleds that's been customized to suit our needs to recover the body. It's been sectioned into two foot parts, so it can be carried by six members of the team." Jim showed everyone the top part of the sled as it slotted into two tubes of the next section that ran parallel down the sides. Within moments the entire sled had been assembled and stood upright in front of a fascinated audience.

"It's made of lightweight aluminum, real easy to carry," Jim went on. "Once we reach the body we'll get it immobilized with these straps to the sled and then either carry or toboggan him, depending on what part of the mountain we descend through. As you can see, there are pulleys and rope tie downs on either end for when we have to lower the body through steeper parts of the descent." When Jim was through, Dave reclaimed the podium.

"You're going to see a lot of death up there, not just Aaron Temple's. Many people have barely enough stamina to get themselves off the mountain, regardless of whether they made it to the top or not. You're going to try and get off the mountain carrying two hundred *extra* pounds." Dave looked down at his hands. Somberly he added, "The odds aren't good you'll succeed. You need to understand that." Dave looked at Hank.

"I know," Hank admitted. "But we're here to try."

"Please don't die trying," Dave said. For a moment the room went silent, and then Umesh, in a more cheerful voice said, "Listen to the Sherpa guides. They spend their lives hauling heavy loads up and down the mountain. Watch how they do it; it will be the key to your success."

From across the room Al announced, "If you can get Aaron to base camp, I can get him back to Katmandu."

"Seriously?" Matt asked.

"Seventeen-thousand-five-hundred, that's why I'm here, that and to teach high altitude flying. When you're ready, just give me the word."

Later that night, Hank sat outside to look at the moon. Matt strolled out and spotted Hank seated on the wooden bench.

"Hey man, don't want to bother you if you're enjoying a little peace and quiet."

"Does the night feel familiar to you?" Hank asked.

"Well," he said as he took a seat, "we're actually on the same latitude as Tampa. So that's probably why it's familiar."

"Are we really? I had no idea."

"'Course when we get ourselves up on the mountain . . ."

"You glad you came?" Hank asked. Matt snorted.

"Hell yes; you kidding? How long did it take me to make up my mind when you called?" Matt paused. "I asked Jenna to marry me." Hank sat up in surprise. His eyes went wide.

"Walked right into Benny's day before we left. Pulled her right out from behind the bar, went down on one knee and proposed. Had a ring and everything."

"She said yes?"

"No."

"She said no?"

"She didn't say anything. She tried to shoo me away. Said I was being ridiculous, but she knew I wasn't."

"So what happened?"

"I put the ring on her finger and told her I was going away. Told her if she needed time to think about it she could give me her answer when I got back from the expedition."

"And, what do you think?"

Matt shrugged his shoulders. "I don't know, but I love her; I can tell you that." The two sat in silence after that.

Hank walked through the lobby to the elevator. As he pushed the button for the fifth floor he thought about Linda and the girls. He loved them, but in a snow drift somewhere on Mount Everest lay the body of his best friend, frozen in death, with the full moon hovering over him. Hank could still hear Aaron's voice calling out to him. He squeezed his eyes shut.

I'm coming man, I'll be there soon.

Chapter 22

Flying to Lukla

www.everestjourneyblog.com
September 3rd, 2003

Greetings to family and friends from Nepal!

After a very long flight, we spent a few days in Katmandu before taking a helicopter to Lukla. It was an amazing ride through a mountain thunderstorm. Our goal, for the next few days, is to hike up to Sagarmatha National Park and get to Namche Bazaar.

Other members of our group have flown ahead to line up the Sherpa porters, and the pack animals to carry our supplies. We've planned a few stops along the way to visit monasteries and receive blessings for our mission. Everyone is in good spirits and looking forward to the climb. The trek to base camp will take about 10 days, so I plan to dispatch another post then.

Love to all,
Hank

*   *   *

THE GIANT HELICOPTER touched down at the end of the Lukla airstrip. Hank opened his eyes and tucked the cross back under his shirt. He had never held on more tightly to that cross than he did today. Looking around at the faces of the others he wondered if he had the same look—scared shitless. The ride had taken them one-hundred-and-forty miles up into the

Khumbu region in a roller coaster fashion, unlike anything Hank had ever experienced.

"It's going to be a little bumpy," Al had warned. He'd already brought a load of supplies to Namche and there was a lot of weather to deal with. "But don't worry," he said with a smile, "I'll get you there." Al then turned to Hank and bent down low so no one would hear. His smile disappeared. "Hang on," he said. And then he left for the cockpit.

The vibration on liftoff was so strong it made Hank's vision blur. The roar of the engine was head splitting. After a minute of ascent, Hank could feel the helicopter dip its nose down and hurtle forward. Booms of thunder were heard over the drone of the engines. The helicopter banked left and then right, up and then down as if being slapped back and forth by two hands playing with a slinky toy. He could lip read the repeated profanity coming from the mouths of his fellow passengers as they hung on for dear life.

When the rotors slowed to a windmill's pace and the cloud of dust and fuel exhaust settled from the landing some forty minutes later, the helicopter door opened and everyone scrambled out into the bright sunshine of the mountain day.

Colin and Matt walked up to Hank.

"That was some ride, huh?" Matt said.

"I'm thankful my feet are back on the ground," Hank replied.

"Come with me!" Umesh yelled. Hank and the others followed him along a stone covered path that took them away from the solitary airstrip, into a little village.

Lukla's streets were narrow and crowded with people, cows, and donkeys. Many of the town's residents had blankets set out on the side of the road where they sold trinkets, food, and colorful articles of clothing. The crew, distracted by the wares, drifted apart.

Umesh looked at his watch, tapped it twice and said, "We really don't have time for this, we're already behind schedule."

"Alright Umi. Come on everyone," Hank called out in hopes of reunifying everyone. "We're on a mission, remember?"

They soon approached a long, rectangular two-story building, which Hank assumed was the hotel. As they walked through a vine-covered arbor they noticed exquisitely carved stones on the ground, each with a Sanskrit inscription. Umesh had explained they would pass many of these stones along the way. The writings were Buddhist prayers, and the flat stones were placed on the middle mountains and high plateaus of the Himalayas. Although he didn't understand the language, Hank was mesmerized by the magical quality of the stones with the white painted lettering.

The hotel was modest, but Hank was told the overnight accommodations would include a meal, comfortable beds, and hot showers. Dave reminded everyone to enjoy the amenities because the further they trekked, the less civilized things were.

"I am sorry," Umesh began, "but I must make my way back to the airport and fly onto Namche before it gets too dark."

"Yes Umi, I know," Hank said.

"I will get the rest of our gear transported and then make the arrangements for the help we will need to bring everything up to the base camp. My brother has told me he has lined up excellent help for the journey."

"That's great. I can't thank you enough for all your help." Umesh pulled a folded paper out of his pocket and spread it out onto the bed in Hank and Matt's room.

"We are here," he pointed. He looked to Matt. "You will lead the expedition up the gorge following the Dudh Kosi River. I have hired several porters and a special man from the village here to be your guide. The trail leads first to Monju where you will spend one night and then you will continue onto Namche. Your journey will take you 2,000 feet higher into the Khumbu. You can take a second day at Monju, if you need more time to acclimatize, but I will need you to be in Namche by day three."

"Understood," Matt said.

"Let the porters carry your gear, please," Umesh said. "They will be offended if you offer your help. They are getting paid to do the job, so let them."

"That's important," Dave added.

"Okay, got it."

"Your guide has taken the route many times," Umesh said. "In fact, he will be your personal climbing Sherpa, Henry. His name is Lopsang Norbu." Hank could sense a change in Umesh's voice. In a hushed tone, Dave added, "He was Aaron's personal climbing Sherpa during my expedition."

"I don't understand," Hank said. "He was with him when . . ."

"Lopsang got hurt," Dave began, "carrying supplies between camps three and four. He sprained his knee falling on some rocks while crossing the Geneva Spur. Aaron saw that he wasn't capable of continuing and convinced him he needed to descend for medical help. Lopsang was reluctant, but agreed. These Sherpas take great pride in making sure their clients are taken care of. Aaron had assured him that he would be okay, so he went back down. I was the one who had to tell him that Aaron didn't make it off the mountain. He took it hard."

"I see," Hank said. Umesh spoke next.

"When it was learned that an expedition was coming to retrieve the body, my brother contacted Lopsang first, to see if he would want to go back and find Aaron. He knew that the chance to bring Aaron back from the mountain would help to ease his guilt."

"Which is misplaced," Dave interjected. "It wasn't his fault."

"Of course not," Hank said. "When can I meet him?"

"He is in the lobby," Umesh said. "I will take you to him and then Dave and I will head back to the airport and fly on to Namche."

The small lounge was adjacent to the front desk. When Hank, Matt, Dave, and Umesh entered, two Nepalese men approached them. The man on the left moved ahead to embrace Umesh.

"This is my brother, Nadra," Umesh introduced him to the other members of the expedition. Nadra brought his hands together and bowed slightly, "Namaste." Hank could see the family resemblance.

"Namaste," Hank replied with the same gesture.

"And this," Umesh said, allowing his brother to step aside, "is Lopsang Norbu Sherpa." Hank repeated his little bow, and once again uttered the Nepalese greeting. Lopsang bowed in return.

"Lopsang, this is Henry Longo."

"Mr. Henry," Lopsang repeated. "We get Mr. Aaron?"

"Yes, Lopsang. We get Aaron; you and I."

"So sorry," Lopsang began, tears welled in his eyes. "My fault Mr. Aaron still there. I make Miyolangsangma angry. My fault."

"No, Lopsang," Hank said. "It's not your fault."

"My fault. Must go back. Must go." Lopsang's small voice choked off as he covered his face and cried. Without hesitation, Hank pulled the smaller man into his arms to comfort him. In between sobs came the repeated cries, "my fault, all my fault," to which Hank could not respond. Instead he just held the diminutive man until he had calmed himself and regained his composure.

"It will be okay, Lopsang. Aaron's calling out to both of us. We will find him together."

"Yes, yes," Lopsang said as he nodded his head. "I will help." Lopsang smiled. "We will ask Miyolangsangma for this one wish. I will pray she say yes."

"If that's what it takes," Hank said, "I will pray, too."

Chapter 23

Monju Monastery

HANK WOKE WITH the light. He had the leftovers of a headache he had gone to bed with the night before. Matt was still asleep in the next bed, so Hank went to search for breakfast. A buffet was being assembled in the main dining room. Outside the sunlight was streaming through the hotel's lobby entrance. He stepped outside to take in the view.

Terraced steps led him down toward the road that traced back a short distance to where he had seen the Buddhist prayer stones. Hank spied a narrow trail that led to an open field with a large stone structure in the middle. The monument was made of assembled rocks and stood about ten feet high at its pointed top. Fluttering from strings attached to it where flags of different sizes and colors. Upon closer inspection, the structure had a multitude of items placed on it: coins, photos, hair combs, and empty wallets; even old watches and letters with faded writing, and they were held down, safe from the wind, by small rocks.

As Hank walked clockwise around the circular structure, he was surprised to find Lopsang on the other side. He watched in silence as Lopsang finished his prayer before he put his hands together, palm-to-palm, with fingers matched and erect.

"Namaste."

"Namaste," Hank replied with more confidence now, as he tucked his chin into his chest and lowered his hands in the traditional greeting.

"Today we go. We journey to get Mr. Aaron," Lopsang said with calm authority.

"Yes, Lopsang. Right after breakfast." Lopsang acknowledged the news with a determined nod and a small smile.

"This monument here?" Hank asked while pointing at the stone structure. "What is it?"

"A Stupa, built for protection of Khumbu valley and mountains. There are many here in land of Sherpa." Lopsang reached inside the woolen vest he was wearing and pulled out a Polaroid photograph. It was one of Aaron and Lopsang together, arms wrapped around shoulders with beaming smiles. The Nepalese man stepped toward the monument and placed the photo on a shelf with some other artifacts and used a stone to hold the picture in place. After he stepped back again, he put his hands together in prayer.

Hank closed his eyes and listened. The sun had now lifted high enough around the surrounding peaks to take away the morning chill. When Hank opened his eyes again after several minutes, Lopsang had already rolled up his mat and was patiently waiting for Hank to come out of his private moment.

"He knows you here,"

"Who?"

"Mr. Aaron. He thanks you for coming."

"What?"

"I heard him." Hank could only stare at the man. *Is it true? It can't be.* But at the same time he could see the calm, compassionate look on Lopsang's face.

"I'm sorry Lopsang, I didn't hear him."

"Oh, message not for you. Mr. Aaron already talk to you. It is why you here huh?"

"Well, ah, yes," Hank sputtered. "I guess he has spoken to me." *Jesus, how does Lopsang know that?*

"He not belong with Miyolangsangma. We must help now so he go to better place."

"I see," Hank began. He wanted to discuss the matter more, but the Sherpa guide had already started walking. "Hey," Hank shouted, "where are you going?"

"Hotel," Lopsang shouted over his shoulder. "Time to eat." Hank broke into a jog.

"Hey! Wait for me!"

Hank filled his plate with cooked eggs and peasant bread, and helped himself to a cup of Nepalese tea.

"Do you live far from here Lopsang?"

"My village is days walk from here."

"Is climbing your profession?"

"I farm most of year. I have terraced fields at home for wheat and barley. I grow potatoes, have large apple orchard."

"I see. But you climb as well."

"Climbing is short time each year. Money very good."

"You've climbed Everest before?"

"Eleven times. Been to summit twice."

"Wow," Hank said, impressed. This man sitting opposite him didn't have the look of a veteran climber. His soft-spoken words and shy personality were a contradiction to his apparent skill.

"I didn't know you had so much experience."

"Climbing sirdar very important. Takes much experience. Could have still helped Mr. Aaron, keep him safe. My job to keep him safe."

"But he didn't want you to stay, right?" Hank said. "He knew you were hurt and he wanted you to get medical help. That's the way Aaron was with all his friends. He cared more about them than himself."

"He not one to send Lopsang away." Lopsang looked beyond Hank's shoulder toward the buffet where the others were moving through the line. Dave was among them.

"Horton told you to go down?"

"Ordered down."

"And what did Aaron say?"

"He agree. Insist I listen to leader."

"Good morning." Dave called out as he approached the table. "Mind if I join you?" Dave took a seat next to Lopsang. Hank watched as Dave removed two of the five tall glasses of water he had on his tray and passed them over.

"Now, the first order of business as we begin our climb is you have to drink plenty of water."

"Please excuse me?" Lopsang stood, "I have to get porters ready for Monju."

"That's an amazing man you've got there, Hank. We're lucky to have him. Do you know how many times he's climbed Everest?"

"Eleven. But he got hurt on your expedition and was sent down, forced to leave Aaron on his own." Dave heard the accusation in Hank's voice.

"Listen," Dave said as he put his napkin into his lap, "Aaron didn't rely on Lopsang the way you will. Aaron had climbing experience, remember? He was mine and Aaron's guide, together. We shared him. His job was to lead the team of Sherpas who hauled the supplies up the mountain. When he hurt his knee he couldn't continue to lead, and had to descend to get medical help."

"I see."

"There was no question," Dave continued, "of him staying on the mountain. He was useless to do anymore hauling and *both* Aaron and I told him we could finish on our own."

Hank decided to let it go for the time being. He picked up one of the water glasses. "So what's the deal about drinking all this water?"

"No matter what, you've got to stay hydrated. Altitude sucks the water right out of you." Dave stopped eating to emphasize his point. "Your blood becomes sludgy, your intestines dry up. It's God-awful; Sara can tell you. I heard her saying the exact same thing to the guys last night. It's imperative to drink four to five liters of water each day if you want to get through this. So drink up."

"Thanks," Hank said, tipped the glass and drained its contents.

$$* \quad * \quad *$$

The expedition moved out right after breakfast. Hank and the crew had gathered in the lobby for the briefing. Matt produced a map, which he had Ed and Tom hold up for everyone to see.

"We're here, in Lukla," he began, "and our goal is to follow along the trail that runs along the river gorge and get ourselves to Monju by late afternoon. The porters will carry most of our gear so the plan is to travel light and make good time to the village." Hank looked at the group of Nepalese, hired from the village to carry supplies to Namche. Already they had mounted enormous wicker baskets to their backs, stuffed with supplies and supported by a leather strap across their foreheads.

"Listen up," Matt commanded. "Pair up and keep a good pace. We've got several hundred feet to climb each day so we've got to pace ourselves. There'll be a lot of great scenery, so let's stay together and enjoy it." As they exited the hotel, Matt grabbed a large stick from the ground. "All of you should find a good walking stick to use." Matt took the bark less tree branch and turned it around in his hands a few times and then bounced the end of it on the ground.

"If the trail gets narrow. A walking stick will help with balance. It's like an extension of yourself. It can push things out of the way without you having to use your own hands or you can use it for leverage and, if necessary, a weapon, just in case you have to defend yourself." Matt took his stick and swung it like a baseball bat.

"So find one and treat it like you would your favorite girl," Matt said as he twirled the stick he had in the air.

"Or boy," Sara added with a grin. Matt smiled back and presented his stick to her.

"My lady . . ."

"Thank you, kind sir."

"Hey, is that what you learned in the S.E.A.L.S.?" Ed remarked.

"No, the Boy Scouts." Matt's grin spread wide. "All right everyone, let's move out." Matt walked over to Hank. "You stay with Lopsang toward the back so he can communicate with the porters. I'm going to put Sara and Pete in front, and Dave and Jim in the middle. I'll be up and down the line so you'll see me every now and then."

"Alright," Hank said.

"Oh by the way," Matt shouted, "keep an eye out for leeches." The group stopped.

"LEECHES?" they shouted in unison. Hank looked to Lopsang, who smiled and nodded in confirmation. Hank made a gap between his thumb and index finger to gauge the size of the bloodsuckers. Lopsang used two hands to indicate the actual size; Hank was flabbergasted.

After everyone shared their thoughts, Matt continued. "They're in the grass and they fall out of the trees, so keep an eye out for them. Let's move."

The heat of the day took its toll as the expedition walked downhill into the Dudh Kosi Valley. They shed some outer layers of clothing in an attempt to cool off. Hank was used to the heat and enjoyed the warmth and humidity as they journeyed up through the heartland of the Sola Khumbu. The steep hillsides were carved into terraces filled with thick green carpets of rice shoots. There were wild flowers everywhere, little jewels of red and pink, blue and purple. They passed clusters of houses with brown earthen walls, wooden slatted windows, and roofs made from weathered thatch.

After forty-five minutes they reached a churning, boulder-strewn river and followed it north, staying on the east bank in order to get to the village of Phakding.

"All stop," Matt commanded from the front of the group.

"Look at that bridge," Ed said. The group watched as the porters passed them and walked onto the wood slatted walkway, almost a hundred yards high. Five-foot planks had been laid out six across to accommodate two people side by side. The planks were bolted on both sides and then attached to eye rods, which were tied on to two steel cables that ran the length of the bridge. Nylon fish netting hung from the cables down to the boards and on one side of the bridge, hundreds of colorful scarves and prayer flags were strung the length of the bridge. They flew horizontal in the stiff breeze that channeled through the Kosi Gorge below.

After watching the porters cross, Matt signaled with one hand above his head.

"All right, two at a time; spread out and wait until the two in front are two-thirds across before you step on." At that moment a group of monks appeared at the other end of the bridge and began to cross. "If you're on the bridge," Matt continued, "and there's traffic coming the other way, stand still and wait for them to pass. Hold onto the cable if you have to." There was a moment of hesitation, as no one wanted to volunteer to go first. Matt looked at Hank. "Henry. You and Lopsang show everyone how it's done." Hank turned back to see the monks carefully negotiating the swaying bridge; their robes billowing in the wind as they walked across.

"Okay," he said. "Let's go Lopsang." Hank moved through the group and took a few careful steps onto the bridge. He stayed to the right just in case he had to grab onto the cable. As the monks were about to pass him, he brought his hands together and recited, "Namaste."

"Lopsang? What are all these banners flying?"

"They are Katas, pieces of cloth given to pilgrims on spiritual journeys. They be attached to bridges, stupas and chortens for luck and best wishes."

Elated that they had reached the other side, Hank waved his arm.

"Come on," he shouted. Pete and Sara were already halfway across when Hank felt Lopsang's hands on his shoulders.

"Tell them go back, fast. Yaks about to cross!"

"What?" And then he saw the small herd of woolly cows.

"Yaks not like bridges. Cross very fast!" Before Hank could say anything more the first of the farm animals gave in to the pressure of being squeezed forward toward the bridge's narrow entrance and started a fast trot toward Pete and Sara.

"Lookout!" Hank yelled. He watched in shock as both of them first saw the cows coming and then froze in place, each one grabbing the cable on opposite sides of the bridge. Hank realized at that moment that the two of them thought if they stayed to the sides the herd could pass. Hank turned to Lopsang and saw his arms frantically waving as he shouted something at Pete and Sara.

"Go Back!" Hank shouted as hard as he could. The Yaks were now trotting faster and making considerable noise. "RUN FOR GOD'S SAKE RUN!"

Pete and Sara turned and bolted. Hank watched in horror as the lead animal ran faster as well. With twenty yards to go, the first Yak was right behind Sara, lowering his head and horns in preparation to butt her. As Pete came off, Matt pushed him to the side, grabbed for Sara and jumped out of the way.

"Jesus that was close," Hank said out loud. Lopsang nodded in agreement. The group reorganized and when the bridge was clear they started again. This time Matt was first, and Pete and Sara were last.

"Everyone okay?" Hank asked.

"Oh, yeah; they're laughing about it now, but that was close."

"You know," Matt began, "when the farmer came off the bridge he didn't even acknowledge that his Yaks almost killed two of us. He just waved his stick and kept on going."

"He didn't even apologize?" Hank said exasperated.

"He is Arhata," Lopsang said. "His path does not include forgiveness."

"That's awfully selfish."

"Forgiveness makes for attachments. He does not desire it; interferes with life and destiny." Lopsang looked at the crew as they filed off the bridge, then the ground and sky. "To show remorse beautiful, yes?" He finally said after listening to the rush of the water through the boulder-strewn riverbed. "But beautiful just word for desiring mind. His herd needed to cross, they crossed. To him, it all very simple."

When Ed walked off the bridge with Pete and Sara, Hank was glad they were smiling.

"That was exciting," Sara said.

"Hey rookie," Ed said to Pete, "I'd like to see you run that fast next time we retreat from a burning building."

"I think I'm ready for Pamplona," Pete joked.

"All right then," Matt said. "Enough with the bulls. Let's move on."

They reached the village of Monju by late afternoon. Now they had several hours to wait at the first checkpoint, the entrance to Sagarmatha National Park. Dave and Hank, with Lopsang as translator, argued with officials over paperwork. It was a definite glitch in the plan not to have Umesh on this part of the trek. Although Umesh had made the arrangements with the ministry officials, it soon became obvious that they were looking to extort money from the team before stamping the permits. He was just about to reach into his knapsack where he kept a wad of cash when Matt decided to bring his six foot five inch frame and menacing demeanor into the room. The diminutive Nepalese civil servant took one look at Matt, conferred with his cronies, and stamped the paperwork.

The village was small and the team had to be divided among several small inns. Hank and Dave went around checking on everyone's rooms while Lopsang made sure the porters were taken care of.

The group ate dinner and drank barley brewed "chang."

When all was quiet, Lopsang made a proposal.

"The Lama at monastery here; he known for divinations. He great uncle to one of porter's daughters. She visits him tonight. She invites you come see. He give favorable prediction."

"Really?" Hank said. "He can see the future?"

"Geshe Rimpoche at Monju well known for predictions."

"Glorified fortune telling if you ask me," Dave interjected.

"Sounds great," Hank said. "Matt, you want to come?"

"Thanks, but I'm heading to the cafe. I heard they have Internet there, and I wanted to see if Jenna gave any thought to my proposal."

"Sounds great. You want to come Dave?"

"No thanks. Excuse me." Hank saw how bitter Dave was toward the idea of going to see the Lama.

"Mr. Dave upset because he did go see Geshe Rimpoche last time," Lopsang began. "Divination from Lama said climbing not favorable then, told no go."

"Well, I'd like to go."

"You hope Lama finds climb favorable for us," Lopsang stated.

Outside the inn, Hank was introduced to the Lama's niece, Saraswati. Hank put his hands together and gave a slight bow. The young woman responded in kind before she turned to lead the way.

What if I'm told that I shouldn't climb the mountain? As they walked along the path to the brightly lit temple, Hank realized he would face the same dilemma that Dave had encountered; half-a-million-dollars invested for an expedition that could be forecasted to fail before it began. All of a sudden he wanted to turn around, but instead he pressed on.

As they entered the courtyard garden, they were received by one of the monks who asked that they wait to be admitted to the Lama's chambers. Saraswati handed Hank some fruit and several Kata scarves.

"You should present as gift," Lopsang said. Hank thanked the young girl and asked Lopsang to tell her he was grateful for the opportunity to meet her uncle and for being so thoughtful as to bring something for him to give to the Lama. As Lopsang spoke, Saraswati smiled at Hank. She didn't say anything but Lopsang did for her. "She thanks you for hiring to carry supplies to Namche." Hank was surprised to find out that the young girl in front of him was also one of the expedition's porters. She was only a teenager and although tall, didn't appear to have enough on her to carry such heavy loads. The monk returned holding a long lit candle and motioned the three of them to follow.

The corridor that led to the Lama's quarters was dimly lit with small butter lamps. The stone and earthen walls gave a strange aura to the place, like the set of an English manor horror film of the thirties or forties.

Behind the curtain door sat Rimpoche. He was old and thin and covered in a maroon robe. After a warm greeting for his niece, he extended himself to both Hank and Lopsang. Lopsang spoke of Hank's quest, and then Hank presented the kata blessing scarves and some rupee notes that Lopsang had added to the array of gifts. In silence, the Lama placed the rupees on his prayer table and draped the scarves over the necks of his visitors, as a blessing in return. Everyone was invited to sit as the attending monk left for a brief moment to go and get the tea service. The lama then sat cross-legged on his bed and waited for the tea to be poured.

For a short time the uncle spoke directly to his niece. As Hank drank his tea, he assumed that the two of them were catching up on family matters. But it was more like a lecture being given from an elder to an inexperienced family member. When Rimpoche was done, he turned to Lopsang and in their native tongue, asked a series of questions. Hank wondered why his responses to the Lama's questions were long and animated. Then the aged monk looked at him.

"So why is it," he spoke in perfect English, "that you want to do this?" Hank was on the spot.

"Because I *need* to. My friend calls out to me to bring him away from here."

"You seek the truth?" the Lama asked.

"I seek my friend."

"He was your nedrog?" the Rimpoche asked. After Lopsang had spoken in their tongue, giving what Hank could only assume were further details. Lopsang spoke.

"Those who are companions in pilgrimage are what Himalayan Buddhists call, nedrogs."

"Karmically linked on a spiritual quest together," The Rimpoche added. Hank looked back to the Lama and nodded.

"Yes," he whispered.

"This is good," the old man sat back on his bed. He mouthed a prayer before he pulled a string-tightened pouch from the folds of his robe. Inside were three dice. He placed them in his cupped hands, concentrated and then blew hard into his hands. One by one, he rolled them onto a small table. The process was repeated three times, but with the third throw he looked directly at Hank as the dice landed. "Ah yes, he is there," Rimpoche said. "This friend that you seek." He paused for a moment, "but there are obstacles in the way. The season does not look right, but Miyolangsangma is not entirely unfavorable if you choose the right time."

"And that time is now, I hope," Hank said. The Lama didn't answer.

"What about obstacles?" Lopsang asked.

"Make many offerings and rituals. And prayers," the Lama said. "You should have some obstacle-removal rituals done, and make offerings at the other monasteries along the way." He turned back to Hank.

"You must have patience." The Lama's attendant handed him an urn and both Lopsang and Saraswati came forward and cupped their hands. Hank watched as water was poured into their hands. They sipped half of it and rubbed the remainder into their hair.

Geshe Rimpoche smiled politely as the three of them stood to leave. "Thank you," Hank said. Before they left, the Lama added, "I can also see that you will give up a part of you. Prepare for that."

In the courtyard once again he drew a deep breath and looked at the other two.

"So what do you think?" Hank asked.

"Rimpoche divination," Lopsang began, "not good, but not bad. We not tell other Sherpas. Very superstitious." Seeming to know what Lopsang had said, Saraswati vigorously nodded in approval.

"We must make many offerings and many rituals. Please, you should tell Umesh about visit," Lopsang said. "He will know what to do."

The three walked back and said goodnight. Hank climbed into bed and thought about what the lama had said, *lose a part of you.* Linda? His family? He tried to clear his mind of all concerns. Thinking of nothing was the way to meditate and find inner peace. And so he focused on the nothingness around him, and fell asleep.

Chapter 24

Namche Bazaar

www.everestjourney.com
September 5th, 2003

Namaste from Namche! After a two-day hike through the valley and terraced villages of the Khumbu, we've finally reached Namche Bazaar. It's the last stop for supplies before the long trek to Everest's Base Camp. Already we've had a few adventures and everyone's looking forward to spending a few days here. Many of us have already begun to feel the effects of the altitude, but we're going at a slow pace so our bodies can get used to it. We've visited one monastery and plan to see a few more. There is much to do to prepare, time is limited, but the process cannot be hurried. Please keep sending us your e-mails and keep us in your prayers as we journey to recover Aaron.

Hank

Hank looked at the typed message. It didn't even begin to describe his thoughts and feelings. The team had been reunited with Umesh and all the supplies had been transported to this village over eleven thousand feet above sea level. Hank absorbed the enormity of what he was trying to do and fought the doubts of whether he could accomplish it. Sitting in the small lounge of the lodge, Hank knew that from here on in, he would have to be led. As more and more events occurred, he would defer to those with the expertise of mountain climbing.

As Hank finished the necessary keystrokes to attach it to the expedition's website, he sighed deeply for the daughters and wife he missed. There had not been a single communication between them since he left. He had sent numerous e-mails and called several times from Lukla, but nothing. The closest he got was the family answering machine, "we'll call you back." But they never did. Hank even tried Linda's mom, but got no answer.

Hank privately thanked God for the friendship Matt had openly offered him. Matt had done an excellent job leading everyone out of Lukla and Hank was confident that he would get everyone the rest of the way to base camp. And then there was the linking of Hank to Aaron through Lopsang. The trek up from Lukla had given Hank the opportunity to know more about Aaron's journey into the Himalayas. Lopsang recounted the many stories Aaron had told him about his life, and his friends. He had confided in his climbing partner about a new life he would soon have.

As Hank closed up the laptop he remembered that his anniversary was getting close. It surprised him that the expedition and all the planning had completely obscured the fact he would be in Nepal on the celebratory 27th of September. *First time we're not together*, he reminded himself sadly.

When he looked up, there was Sara. "Hi," she said. "I'm going into the village to do some shopping. Want to come?"

"Sure, why not?"

Life in the village was very much twenty-first century. Sara and Hank passed enough pizza parlors, pool halls and cybercafés to see how western tourism had changed the livelihood of residents here.

"Hungry? Care to try some local fare?" Sara asked. Hank saw that they had come to an area where merchants had set up a number of stalls to sell varieties of different dishes. Sara led Hank over to one of the stalls that had a large metal cauldron over a fire.

"Well, it's not exactly the food court at the mall, but . . ." Hank's voice trailed off as he watched Sara order two steaming bowls of what looked like gray sludgy porridge.

Sara handed him a bowl and paid the vendor. "This is *shakpa*, potato stew." Hank caught a whiff and turned his face away.

"Oooof—It smells awful!"

"It's a bit pungent, but if you can get past the smell it's pretty good." Hank watched as Sara ate. He sampled a few of the chunky morsels and then gave the bowl back to the vendor.

"I don't taste much of anything. Everything seems pretty bland."

"That's one of the effects of altitude," Sara replied. "You don't eat much because you're taste buds sort of shut down. How are you feeling by the way?"

"Okay, I guess," Hank said with reluctance. "I've got this headache I can't seem to get rid of."

"Yeah, that's common too." Sara took another spoonful before continuing. "Headaches, intestinal bugs, respiratory infections. All the things you can come down with when you're in the Khumbu."

As they continued to walk through the open market, they came upon another small plaza where they found Lopsang and Saraswati.

"Hello Lopsang."

"Ah, Mr. Henry. Saraswati and I look for you. We sent by Umesh to come back. He has news."

"Good news, I hope," Hank replied. Saraswati came forward and presented Hank with several braided strings.

"They called *sungdis*," Lopsang said. Hank looked down at the colored strings that had been draped across his open palms. "You wear around neck or tie to most important climbing equipment."

"They are meant for protection," Sara added.

"Thank you Saraswati," Hank said. She smiled as Hank tied the strings around his neck.

"We head back," Lopsang said. "We meet them at bar not far from lodge." The four of them walked down the narrow street. Sara took hold of Hank's arm and held him back slightly, allowing the other two to get several paces ahead.

"Be careful," Sara said. "I think the young lady has quite the crush on you."

"Huh? What are you talking about?"

"Saraswati is what I'm talking about. I think that whole gift giving thing had more meaning to it than you realize."

"Oh, come on. Me? Now why on earth . . ."

"It's not that extraordinary, Hank. She's a young woman; you've provided her with money for her family. You've given her an opportunity in a society that looks down on people like her."

"I don't follow," Hank said.

"Many people here follow Buddhist teachings and are very compassionate. But she's not a Buddhist, and she's not Sherpa. She's Tamang. Tamang's have caste distinctions that are pretty rigid. And then there's the fact that . . . being from the lowlands and then when you factor in her age and sex . . ."

"How could a young girl like that be interested in me? She's a teenager."

"So?" Sara said.

"I'd be surprised if she's even seventeen."

"So?"

"I'm over forty and married."

"You're not in America, Hank. You're in Nepal. It's a different society." The two started walking again. Lopsang and Saraswati were now out of sight. "Are you aware of the fact she's impaired," Sara said. "Teenage boys would have no interest in her."

"What?"

"She's mute. She has no vocal chords. That's why."

"I didn't realize," Hank admitted.

"No one's ever shown her any kindness the way you have." Sara put her hands through the straps of her backpack and quickened the pace.

Up ahead, Lopsang and Saraswati waved to them from in front of a basement entrance to a four story hotel. Umesh, Dave, Matt and Captain Jim were also there. Their concerned looks gave Hank a reason to worry. Through a heavy blanket, Hank wandered in to the dark, low ceiling room. Tables and chairs were nestled between wood beam footings that held up the building. Christmas lights were strung around the room and disco music played from somewhere by the bar. Everyone grabbed a chair and sat.

"There is some information that I wanted to share with everyone." Umesh handed out sheets of paper.

"Okay the first piece of news is very good," Umesh began. "I have just found out that there is only one other expedition group currently on the mountain. There were three groups on the schedule to be there at the same time as us but one has given up because of lack of supplies and the other has withdrawn because the group leader was killed by a serac in the Ice Fall."

Hank frowned, *Jesus Christ, that's good news?*

"The remaining group is a team from Sweden. They should be in position for their summit attempt when we arrive at base camp." Umesh flipped a page from his spiral bound notepad and read for a moment. "Henry it is very good that we came here in the fall. There are seventeen groups scheduled to come here next spring. It is important not to have so much traffic on Everest."

Hank felt good about the fact that they would have room to maneuver on the upper part of the mountain. He knew the account of the '96 climb and one of the key components of that disaster was there were too many people vying to get to the top at the same time.

"The weather report," Umesh announced, "shows that it is still warm and the monsoon season has not ended. There is a lot of snow on the lower half of the mountain, but the high winds have kept the upper half clear."

Umesh passed out copies of a meteorological survey. "Now the second item is of great concern to all of us," Umesh began. "The doctor I had lined up for the base camp has gone home because of a death in the family."

"Shit," Dave said plainly.

"We have to have a doctor," Sara said.

"Some of the guys have certified EMT training," Captain Jim proposed. "Will that be good enough?"

"No," Dave said. "Not even close. What about Sara?"

"My research is in high altitude physiology," Sara stated. "I can diagnose certain things, but I would be in over my head in terms of treating anyone."

"I have one idea that might work," Umesh said. "I have contacted the Swedish group and their doctor would consider staying on to support our expedition."

"Start to finish?" Matt asked.

"Yes," Umesh said. "But she has a list of supplies we must bring, which is quite lengthy and she's asking for twice the money we were going to pay the other doctor."

"She!" Dave cried out in chauvinistic alarm.

"Can I see that list?" Sara asked. As Umesh handed the request for items he told everyone, "The Swedish team is all women. They are being sponsored by some cable channel in Stockholm."

"They're Swedish, all women, and what else?" Dave demanded.

"What do you mean?" Umesh asked.

"Well, they're obviously some sort of feminist group and I'm assuming they have an angle. Any idea on what that may be?"

"I'm sorry," Umesh said. "I don't understand."

"They're a group of women, Umesh. And their climb is being documented for television," Dave said now to everyone in the group. "So what are they? Over fifty? Are they climbing for a cause? What's the issue with them? Are they all from the same sorority and this is some kind of reality TV show?"

"Perhaps they're lesbians," Hank said.

"Oh, come on!" Sara shouted at Hank. "Honestly you men, it's all you think about isn't it? A bunch of women get together to do something without having men involved and right off the bat you think they must be gay."

"It says here," Umesh began reading from his notes, "that they're members of a climbing society in Stockholm and that a majority of them belong to a Hellenic Order that is based in Rome."

"Oh my God, they are lesbians!" Dave shouted.

"No they're not," Matt said calmly. "They're nuns."

Silence engulfed the group as Matt's statement hit home. Jim said, "So God will truly be with us, huh?" After a long pause, Hank turned to Sara.

"We need a doctor right?"

"We need a doctor," she responded. Seeing the truth in Sara's eyes, Hank turned to Umesh.

"Can you get back to the doctor and tell her we are in great need of her services and that whatever she wants, she's got."

"Yes Henry, thank you. Now the next issue we need to discuss is that we have additional supplies I was not aware of that have been delivered here to Namche. They belong to Captain Jim's crew. He has told me that we need to bring this equipment, but I have no one to carry them."

"We'll carry them," Jim said. "I'm not asking this expedition to do any more than it has to. My crew will carry the stuff."

"Yes, but your loads are supposed to be very limited to get to base camp," Umesh said. "You have to reserve as much strength as possible for the descent with the body."

"I'm well aware of that Mr. Bhuju," Jim replied. Hank could tell the fire captain was steeling himself for a fight on this issue. "But we're a ladder company. We're used to carrying a lot of weight and we don't ever go into a rescue or recovery action without *our* equipment."

"Yes, but what you have brought is not needed for this expedition. I don't see how you could possibly use it."

"That's because you're not a fireman!" Jim said with authority. "When a fireman is on the job, no matter what it is, his equipment comes with him."

Trying to diffuse the argument Hank asked, "What equipment did you bring?"

"Standard bunker gear," Jim replied. "Stuff we're no doubt going to end up using." Hank watched Jim pause for a moment and then added, "And of course our jackets and helmets."

"Now you see," Umesh protested, "that is exactly what I am talking about, Henry. We don't have any room for this stuff." Hank realized there was a much more involved idea here than the crew needing their rescue clothing and tools. The gear was symbolic of a team going out together, one last time. Hank thought highly of Jim and the honor of his fireman he was trying to preserve.

"Okay," Hank said, "bring the equipment. But find the porters to carry it for you. I can't have the additional weight jeopardize the final part of this mission."

"But there are no other porters!" Umesh said with exasperation. "I have hired everyone available. There is no one left."

"Wait a minute," Sara said. "What about the low level porters? I'll bet they'll do it."

"No, you can't," Umesh said. "We only paid them to get to Namche. They are not allowed to carry any further."

"What are you talking about Umi?" Hank asked.

"It's tradition. Different groups of people for different parts of the trek." Matt chimed in. "But if there's no one left to carry and you have this group of people willing to go, why not let them?"

"I'll be happy to pay for their services," Jim added.

"You don't need to do that Jim," Hank said.

"Listen," he replied, "you've already paid a half a million dollars for this mission. I got no problem getting the guys to pick up the tab for hauling our stuff up to base camp."

"And besides," Dave added, "you should have told us you were going to do this in the first place." Hank listened but didn't like Dave's scolding tone. At that moment he found his purpose for the group he had put together. Dynamic individuals with strong personalities and even stronger egos, he would have to be the mediator.

"I am telling you," Umesh began, "if the high level porters find out that the low levels are also participating, they will strike."

"Umi?" Hank said, "we leave tomorrow with our supplies and all the people you've hired out of Namche, okay? Now we have Jim and the crew make arrangements for the other porters to bring their equipment."

"It won't work. It will be a disaster."

"No it won't," Hank counseled, "because the other porters will schedule themselves to leave here three days after we do." Hank turned to the Captain. "Jim, you don't need that equipment right away, right?"

"No."

"Umesh? What do you think?" Hank could see the light bulb go off on top of his head. "You know? That could do it."

"Jim," Hank began, "go and get Lopsang and tell him what we want to do. The girl with him is one of those porters. Between the two of them I'm sure they'll be able to recruit enough people to get the job done. Whatever you pay them, I'm sure they'll be very happy to make the extra income."

"I'm sure Saraswati will be happy to see more of you," Sara teased.

"Okay," Jim said as he got up. He leaned in to Hank and said in a quiet voice, "Thank you."

Matt and Hank just sat there while the group dispersed. Matt ordered them a round of beers. Dave sat back down and ordered a beer himself.

"What's the matter Dave?"

He shook his head in disbelief. "Nuns on Everest," was all he could say.

Chapter 25

Tengboche

CONSIDERABLE EFFORT WAS necessary for the group to prepare themselves for travel. Early morning, predawn hours turned out to be the best time for them.

It was agreed that the expedition's next leg would be divided into four sections, each with its own leader and pace, as they would head for base camp. Matt would be in charge of the recovery team, have all the firemen plus Sara, Dave and Hank. They would set off first and would be the slowest to travel, climbing only a thousand feet a day in order to properly acclimatize. Lopsang would stay with the climbing Sherpa team and attempt to make it all the way to base camp, with the essential tents and equipment. Once there, they would clear an area on the glacier that would become the expedition's home for the next four weeks. Umesh had given himself the dubious task of staying with the other porters and the two-dozen yaks used to haul the bulk of supplies. The hope was that when Hank and the crew arrived, base camp would be waiting for them.

The fourth element would be the small group of porters from the lowlands that would leave well after Hank's "armada," as he liked to call it. They would carry the firemen's gear. Although he had not seen Saraswati again, he found out she had been put in charge.

"That's Ama Dablam," Dave called out to Hank's group, which had just pulled up. They looked at the spike of the mountain, thousands of feet above them, like a cartoon monster whose shadow hovered, waiting to pounce. But what really caught Hank's eye was the peak that dwarfed Ama Dablam, the one in the distance. Hank recognized it from the many pictures he had seen, with its horizontal plume of condensation rocketing away from the summit.

The group crossed the Dudh Kosi one last time at Phunki Tenga. From there, they left the river they'd followed since Lukla, and taken up a new one, the Imja Khol.

As Hank and his crew descended in to the Khola Gorge, and went uphill through a fir forest, Hank saw the mountain "tar" goats he had been told the region was famous for.

"Amazing," Hank said.

"Keep your eyes peeled," Matt added, "this is Yeti country. You look hard enough and maybe you'll spot the Abominable Snowman." Hank chuckled. Although he had remembered stories about the famed creature, as well as "Big Foot," his present image had been jaded by the success of Pixar animation. No longer could he think of the Yeti as being the fearsome creature legend had created him to be. Thanks to "Monsters Inc," the Abominable Snowman was a snow cone eating, happy go lucky guy, with the voice of Cliff Klavin.

They reached the small village adjacent to the monastery, just as the sun started to set. The plan was to spend several days in the village to properly acclimate and at the same time, visit the monastery and receive a blessing for the climb.

"Not only us, Henry," Umesh had informed him, "but the Sherpa climbing crew will be visiting this monastery, too. It is the most prominent monastery in Khumbu."

"The whole area considered sacred," Lopsang had said of their planned visit. "It became the first celibate gompa in the Khumbu. Today they have over forty monks there."

Tents were pitched on the margin of a yak pasture, close to the monastery. Hank sat that evening, after dinner, with Sara, Matt and Dave around a small fire and watched as a procession of porters and Sherpa guides carried small butter lamps in single file as they walked to the monastery. One by one the lights disappeared as they entered.

"Did you have any of this done before your climb?" Sara asked Dave.

"Oh yeah. You have to, at least for the locals."

"I think it's kind of neat getting caught up in the religion in this part of the world," Sara said.

"It's more superstition than religion," Dave replied. "Those people aren't going in there to worship, it's just one big blessing ceremony."

"We're not seeing the head Lama," Hank said. "He's been in a meditative retreat for several months and I was told that no one knows when he plans on ending it."

"Well, from what I heard," Matt began, "the monastery's *Lopon* is giving us a protection ceremony. And we didn't have to ask for it."

"Yes," Hank confirmed. "Lopsang told me that Aaron was well received when he was here. The monks saw the Buddhist awareness in Aaron. They know of our mission. We're being seen because of it."

"My expedition almost failed because of those monks," Dave spat on the ground and walked off into the darkness.

"Whoa, touched a nerve?" Matt said. Hank got up and brushed himself off. "I guess I'll go find out."

Hank jogged until he could see Dave in the distance. He was watching the ceremonial march as he leaned against a large boulder.

"Hey, you okay?" Hank asked when he found him.

"Look at them, walking in like that. Doesn't it amaze you?"

"It's an awesome sight, like something out of a movie." The two of them sat and watched the procession. "So what was it that tied Aaron to this place?"

"No idea," Dave began. "We were here for three days. The whole time, Aaron never left the monastery. When it was time to push on, I had to go find him. He told me he wanted to stay a few extra days and he would catch up with me at base camp. I wasn't happy about it, but there wasn't much I could do to change his mind. Too much 'voyage of discovery' swimming around in his head, and mystical Buddha awareness crap; not enough common sense, that's what I had to deal with."

Hank couldn't quite figure out from the tone of Dave's voice if he resented or envied Aaron for what he believed.

"I told him he could do whatever he damned well pleased after the climb, but don't you see, Hank? He skipped days that were necessary to acclimatize. It's just another example . . . I think it was his undoing."

"You think so?"

"I know so!" Dave barked. "When he got to base camp, I could tell he wasn't the same."

"What do you mean?"

"He was acting strange, disconnected from the rest of us. He stayed in his tent a lot." Dave looked down at the ground as he recalled the events. "I could tell he wasn't sleeping, and when we got back from an acclimatization climb, he came down with a bad stomach virus. It waylaid him for five days."

"Are you saying he shouldn't have climbed?"

"Are you blaming me Hank? My judgement? My leadership?"

"No, but I'm not sure I understand the whole story, or if I've even heard it yet."

"I watched Aaron one day, by the glacier stream we used for water. He was seated on some rocks and staring at a doll. When I asked him about it, he said it belonged to a daughter he had out in California."

"He told you?"

"I was surprised," Dave said.

"I met her," Hank said. "Her name's Hannah."

"Look Hank, you may have a ton of reasons for going after Aaron, maybe it's because of Hannah, who knows? It doesn't have to make sense, a lot of things in my life don't; the fact that I'm even here makes no sense at all. I'm damaged goods because of that mountain. But I came back to help you because it takes a lot of manpower to get yourself setup just so you can have a shot at it, and I want to make sure no one else gets hurt, or killed trying to climb that mountain."

Dave was right, but his help in this expedition wasn't completely magnanimous. Hank felt he had another reason.

"Okay," Hank said. "I'm going to depend on you. You're right, I can't afford to lose anyone on this journey." Hank headed back to the campfire. He got about six steps before he heard, "I want to get him out of there as much as you do." Hank looked back at Dave. "So let's go get him."

Dave took his time, but followed Hank back to the group.

It was the next day when Hank's wristwatch alarm beeped him awake. Many of the others were already prepping themselves for the visit to the monastery when Hank emerged from his tent. Umesh and his team had arrived late the previous evening and were resting as Lopsang and his group left for base camp.

"Do not expect your meeting at the monastery to be brief," Umesh announced to Hank, Sara, Matt, and the fire crew who were all headed there together. "They like having company."

Other than its larger size, this monastery was similar to the last one. Different buildings made up the campus, some of which were old and not in use. Other buildings were either new or renovated. Hank noticed the prayer flags strung out to each corner of the compound from a may pole stationed in the center of the courtyard.

The group entered the main assembly hall just as the sound of horns blared somewhere on the outer fringe of the monastery. Hank and the crew halted in front of two immense, colorfully painted wooden doors. Umesh took off his shoes and the others followed suit.

Over the threshold they stepped, into the massive interior where a Buddha sat fifteen feet high.

"That is the Buddha Sakyanuni," Umesh whispered. "He is the 'Buddha of the Present.'" Hank looked at the gilded statue in amazement as he noticed that the shoulders and head extended through an opening in the second floor, as if the building had been altered to accommodate his growth.

"What are the other figures standing in the front and the back of the Buddha?" Matt asked Umesh, as he pointed to the smaller gilded figures behind the great Buddha. Umesh said, "They are the bodhisattvas Chenrezig and Jambayang, and the disciples, Shariputra and Mangalputra. All of them possess miraculous powers as enlightened Buddhas."

More than a dozen monks sat in rows and recited from long texts opened on low prayer tables. Some read aloud while others chanted along. The team watched in silence as Umesh lowered himself to the floor, touched his forehead to the ground and then got up. He repeated the process twice. Matt tapped Hank on the shoulder.

"Hey, when in Rome, right?" The fire crew hit the floor; Sara and Hank smiled, shrugged and joined in. When Hank touched the ground with his forehead, he breathed in deeply and exhaled, then put his hands together, closed his eyes and focused on the darkness.

"Come," Umesh said, breaking Hank's train of thought. "Did you bring your Kata?" Hank pulled from his pocket the long white scarf Umesh had given him. Umesh signaled to Matt and had him take a roll of prayer flags from Pete. With Umesh leading, the group proceeded to the throne like platform. Hank could only assume it was for the Lopon. Perpendicular to the row of monks was an altar surrounded by small butter lamps and draped in burgundy cloth with gold knitted symbols. Umesh whispered in his ear.

"Present the scarf and flags first to the altar and then hand them to the Lopon." Hank nodded and turned to the altar. After presenting the scarves there, he turned and presented them to the head monk.

As he continued his chant, the Lopon reached into an urn and grabbed a handful of grain. He dribbled the grains into the folds of the material. He paused to meditate, and as he did, his face grimaced with intense thought.

"What's he doing?" Hank heard Sara whisper.

"Communicating," Umesh replied. "Lamas can visualize the deities as objects of meditation."

"I have no doubt," Umesh added, "that the Lopon is speaking directly to Miyolangsangma on our behalf, asking for her to bless our mission."

Hank fingered the Sungdi strings Saraswati had given him, the ones that now mingled with the gold cross around his neck. He wore both as a source of strength. When the Lopon finished his meditation, a horn blew, and the room full of monks immediately stood at attention.

An elderly man in a crimson robe, accompanied by two young attendants, appeared at the far end of the room. With his walking stick he crossed to join those already gathered.

"It's the Rimpoche," Umesh said with excitement. "Looks like he has come out of his meditative retreat to be with us." The Lopon greeted the aging priest with a polite bow. The Lopon spoke for a brief moment and listened as he received instructions from the master. The other monks departed the room. The older man took what had been the Lopon's seat and waited as his attendants brought him a gold embroidered vestment, which was carefully lowered over his head and onto his shoulders.

"Welcome. Please, come sit," he said in perfect English. The Rimpoche gestured with his arms the large area in front of him. Hank sat first in front and closest to the wizened man. The others joined him on the floor in a semicircle around a low table that separated the group from the throne chair.

"Why do you choose this journey?"

"I seek my friend who died on . . ." Hank had almost said Everest, but then changed to "Sagarmatha." Hank debated revealing to the elderly man the ghost like encounters he had experienced but thought if he revealed it now, the crew might think he was nuts.

"He is calling to you," the Rimpoche announced. "Aaron Temple has made you aware of his predicament and asks for your help."

"You know my friend?" Hank asked.

"You have seen him, yes?" The Rimpoche asked. "In his journey through the spiritual world?" Hank closed his eyes and recounted the moments he had seen Aaron. More than ever now, he believed it happened and here he was, in front of this holy man because of it.

"Yes," Hank nodded in agreement. "I have seen him." The crew whispered utterances, which didn't surprise Hank.

"Yes, so have I, many times." He turned to the others. "This disturbs you? The spirits of all those you have loved and lost still swirl around us. Almost all choose to observe from a distance, but some do have the need to reach out on occasion. Come, let us close our eyes and meditate." The Rimpoche clapped his hands twice to gain silence in the room. His interlocked fingers rested in his lap. He closed his eyes.

By the time Hank's eyes opened, his crew had departed; only the Rimpoche and his two young orderlies remained. The elderly man soon opened his eyes and smiled at Hank.

"You have come a very long way," he said to Hank.

"Yes."

"And you still have a long way to go."

"I am prepared."

"He no longer calls to you, your friend Aaron," the Rimpoche said.

"He did, I saw him cry out for my help."

"But he no longer asks, does he?"

"That's because he knows I'm on my way."

"What if I was to tell you that he has accepted Miyolangsangma's offer to stay with her? Your journey to Sagarmatha would be fruitless, and would only endanger those you have brought."

"If this is what Miyolangsangma is saying, it isn't true. If Aaron is telling you, he's being forced."

"Come," the Rimpoche said as he stood. "I wish to show you something." Hank followed the robed monk down a long hallway to a door decorated in gold leaf and encrusted with jewels. The Rimpoche knocked three times, lowered himself face down onto the floor, then stood and knocked again. After the ritual, he stepped back and put his hands together in prayer before he pulled a large key from the folds of his robe.

The heavy doors opened with loud, timeworn *krrrrriks* denoting decades of use. Shafts of light streamed from a small skylight falling against a large painting, which dominated the chapel. Miyolangsangma came to life on the walls of this room.

"Miyolansangma," the Rimpoche began, "Sagarmatha's protector goddess is one of the five sisters who reside on our Himalayan peaks. She was a demoness who converted to Buddhism centuries ago." Hank focused on the women's face that was turned toward him. He remembered a similar picture at Umesh's restaurant back in Sebring.

"She rides comfortably on top of a lactating female tiger," said the old man. "Her hair is studded with wish-fulfilling gems. The fruit in her left hand represents an offering of good fortune, wealth, and abundance, including supernatural powers, while her right hand holds a flower. This gesture is meant to be one of inexhaustible giving." Hank realized the reason for this visit.

"She's not capable of deception is she?"

"She favors those that believe in her and her powers."

"Miyolangsangma doesn't want me to climb the mountain?"

"Perhaps it is your friend who does not want you to climb, perhaps Aaron Temple is saying that he is fine where he is." Hank looked once more at the painting. He closed his eyes to think. *Could that be? Wherever he is, has he found the peace that he wants? Or is it something else?* Hank opened his eyes again and turned to look at the Rimpoche.

"If my friend tells me not to come, it is only because he is afraid of the danger I will face trying to reach him. He would rather sacrifice himself to this place than see me hurt in an attempt to rescue him."

"Let Miyolangsangma be the one to guide you and grant safe passage up the mountain," he said. "Talk to her often and perform rituals asking for her blessings and permission to climb. Seek out her protection from the peril you will face." Hank turned to face the smiling goddess. He brought his hands up, opened to one another, duplicating the motion of the devoted monk.

"She has extended her loving kindness to our friend who fears for your safety. Let her now step down from her tiger mount and put out her hand to you for the powerful protection she can provide for your journey."

With his eyes closed, Hank heard the creak of the door. He was now alone with his thoughts, doubts and fears. He felt compelled to lower his body to the floor, in front of the altar. After a time, he lifted himself into a crouched position, like that of a baseball catcher. He stared up at the painting.

I believe in Jesus, don't I? Hank reached into his shirt collar and pulled out the cross he wore. This simple piece of jewelry was a reminder of his faith; that Jesus would save him. And because of that, Hank had never had the need to ask for any other protection.

"For us and for our salvation," he said as he stood up. Faith in the Lord isn't preventative, he reasoned. He could never have asked for things not to happen, only for His strength and kindness when they did. "But you're different, aren't you?" He said to the image on the wall. "I have to ask you to protect me and my crew from the dangers of Sagarmatha." *And in order to do that, I have to believe in you as well.* Hank struggled with the concept of a separate belief.

"Is there such a thing as a Catholic Buddhist?" He fingered the Sungdi strings. *Are these strings to be my other cross?* If he believed that the threaded multicolored strings had the same qualities as his cross, then they too would remind him of the faith he had in what he was doing.

Hank looked up at the painting. *I can believe in you.*

Hank dropped to his knees. He brought both hands up with the Sungdi still weaved in between his fingers. Closing his eyes tight, he allowed the silence and darkness of the praying chamber to quiet his mind and bring him into a complete stillness. When he finally heard nothing more than his own breath, he prayed.

"Miyolangsangma, pure and wonderful Goddess of Sagarmatha, grant your protection to me. Hand me the flower that signifies your inexhaustible giving . . ."

Chapter 26

Base Camp

www.everestjourney.com

Hello from the Khumbu Glacier! It's late September and we've finally made it to base camp. Today is a day to rest and catch up on business. It was a difficult journey from Namche Bazaar, but we made it and are now setting up for the weeks we'll spend here acclimatizing and training for the climb. By all accounts, this place that serves as Everest's Base Camp is a barren wasteland. We're at 17,500 feet and the terrain is capable of sustaining little except for a few single-cell creatures and lichens that live on the million-year-old granite. There is no view of the upper section of the mountain that weighs so heavily on our minds. Tomorrow we'll climb Kala Pattar, which towers up to 18,550 feet. Our hope is to be rewarded with a complete view of Mount Everest. Standing on the summit of Kala Pattar, we will be above base camp and about as high as the first camp we hope to establish on Everest.

I'll report again in a few days, after we've set up our gear and trained some more.

Hank signed off and transmitted the post, but the pain in his gut was worse, so he left the expedition's main tent and walked back over the rocks to his own small quarters in the compound.

After a swig from a plastic water bottle, he dropped his body onto the makeshift bed and closed his eyes. The nonstop diarrhea had left him nearly incapacitated. As he lay there, he thought about all they had gone through just to make it to base camp.

They had moved from Tengboche and continued to trek along the Imja Khola River toward Periche where they turned again, heading for the Khumbu Glacier and base camp.

All had agreed that the visit to the monastery had been a fascinating experience.

"I still can't get over the fact that I was in that hall with those monks," Colin said to Hank while they stopped at the health post in Debuche. "For the life of me, I didn't think I could sit in one place for so long."

"I fell asleep," Ed added. "Took a nice long nap."

Matt walked over to Hank.

"By the way," he asked, "where'd you go?"

"Separate mission," Hank replied. "Spoke to the powers that be."

"So you've had the chance to make your case? And the verdict is?"

"We talked. I think the lady upstairs is pretty cool with it."

"Good," Matt said, pumping his fist. "Keep me posted." Hank appreciated that Matt believed that their expedition needed mystical admittance.

The week-long journey and overnight visits to the little villages of Shomare, Orsho and Zambur, had revealed how rugged the region was. Accommodations became sparse and while meals could be had, the crew for the first time had to break out the cold weather gear for sleeping arrangements. They also had to scramble for the use of makeshift sanitation. Body odor was a constant reminder that the journey would be difficult and would stretch everyone's level of endurance. The crew made the best of it, poking fun at several pungent members.

Hank came back to the present when he realized there was a shadow looming over his tent.

"Knock, knock, Hellooo," came the unfamiliar female voice. Hank unzipped the front of his tent before he slumped back down. His visitor wore a bright blue parka with the Swedish flag embroidered on the left sleeve. When the woman took off her woolen cap, her auburn hair fell to her shoulders. Hank noticed the weathered lines around her eyes.

"I am Dr. Lindros, Melissa Lindros. I was told you might be in need of medical attention?" She was the doctor Umesh had talked about back in Namche.

"Yes, thank you," Hank began, "I'm Henry Longo, the organizer of the expedition. I've come down with something I . . ." Hank stopped as the woman put her hand on his forehead and then his wrist to check his pulse. There was concern in her beautiful blue eyes.

"Henry? Are you strong enough to walk to the infirmary?" Although weak, Hank nodded in agreement. He followed the doctor out of his tent. From a distance, Matt spotted Hank and gave a look of concern when he saw the doctor with him. Hank flashed him a quick thumbs up, sort of a nothing to worry about gesture.

The tents the Swedish team had set up were just across some rocks with the medical tent in the middle of the compound. Hank was impressed by how well laid out the facility was, ready to handle any kind of medical need.

"So, Henry? How long have you been sick?" she asked.

"A few days. It started after we left Gorak Shep."

"Are you coughing much?"

"No, not really."

"What exactly are your symptoms?"

"Weak, a lot of headaches, and I'm going to the bathroom a lot."

"Urine?"

"Diarrhea, I can't seem to hold anything in." The doctor grabbed a clipboard and led him over to a scale. Pulling a pen out from beneath her parka, she began to write.

"Do you think your intestinal problems began after eating a meal or did they come on over a period of time?" The doctor looked at the scale and recorded the weight.

"Well," Hank began, "I've been dealing with headaches since we left Tengboche, but I've been pretty regular. As a matter of fact I haven't even needed to go much at all." The doctor handed him the clipboard.

"Here," she said, "I need you to fill in the background information." As Hank took the clipboard he watched as the doctor put her hand to her chin and looked at him. After thinking for a moment she said, "Constipated?"

"No, just didn't feel like it." He finished the forms and handed her back the clipboard. "Now that I think about it, it was after dinner at that God awful lodge we stayed at. They served a Nepalese version of shepard's pie." Hank broke off as he saw the doctor break into a large smile.

"Ahh, now I see." She went to the cabinet, pulled out a bottle of pills, and handed him two small tablets along with a bottle of water.

"This is Imodium. It should help."

"Shepard's pie, not a good choice I take it?"

"I'm sure the potatoes were fine, but who knows what constitutes 'meat' in this part of the world." She smiled. "Several of our expedition was at that same lodge and came down with the same problem." Hank finished the water bottle and looked at the doctor who was now scanning the information he'd written.

"Where are you from?" Despite the bulkiness of the alpine gear she was wearing, Hank noticed she was quite attractive.

"I live and work in Malmo. It's along the coast of southern Sweden, across from Denmark, near Copenhagen."

"Are you a nun? I mean are you a member of this expedition's Pan Hellenic . . ."

"My sister is. She and a few others from the order have been with a climbing club for years. They've trained for a long time, and now they're finally climbing Everest."

"Is she on the mountain now?" Hank asked.

"Elke's at camp four right now. They're going to push for the summit tonight."

"Wow, that's great!" The doctor reached for a blood pressure cuff. She motioned for Hank to sit.

"We need to keep our fingers crossed that the weather holds," she said as Hank took off his coat and rolled up his sleeve. "They've been delayed because of high winds on the summit."

"How long?"

"A little over twenty four hours." Hank felt himself cringe. As she began pumping he thought about the danger involved staying up so high. Most expeditions use camp four as a way station, picking up oxygen bottles and resting briefly before moving to the top.

"I hope they make it." She responded with a shrug of her shoulders as she took off the wrap.

"One-ten-over-seventy. That's very good."

"You don't seem very enthusiastic about your sister's goal."

"Elke and I have never been on the same page about a lot of things. She's my sister and I love her, but this whole thing about climbing, about having to prove something . . ."

"You don't approve of her climbing?"

"I don't approve of her risking her life. It's just that I cannot understand why people risk their lives to accomplish this goal. I mean, look at your chart . . . You are from Orlando, Florida; married with children, and yet you are here."

"My best friend died on Everest six months ago. I'm here to find him and take him home." The doctor just stared, then reached for a chair to sit down.

"I was not told that when I was asked to stay on with your group. My God," she said to him in a quiet voice. "I never knew that loyalty could be such a powerful thing."

"We've been friends for twenty years," Hank added. "Please don't get me wrong doctor . . . Melissa; everyday I find myself in a quandary as to why I'm here. There's so much that's been put on hold just so I can be here." Hank stood and took three steps to reach where she was sitting. He leaned down to her until they were face to face. "But I'm here. There's a force that's led me here. I can't explain it except to say that I've heard from my friend; I've heard his voice cry out for deliverance. And that's the *only* reason I'm here."

"The wind seems to be calming down a bit," Melissa said. Hank looked to see that the tent was no longer flapping against its aluminum frame. "Did you bring the additional supplies I requested?"

"We're unpacking supplies now. We were able to get everything in Namche. I'll send someone over this afternoon . . ."

"I'll come up," she said. "I'll want to meet everyone." Hank watched as his doctor got up from her chair and put the clipboard back. "The other two expeditions that were here brought us nothing but bad luck. Perhaps your energy will bring us some good fortune."

"Nothing would make me happier, Doc."

"Please," she said, "call me Mel."

A steady stream of yaks brought in extra gear, bottled oxygen, food, and fuel throughout the day. Hank, Dave and Umesh watched as piles of materials were unloaded in front of the kitchen and communication tent and then sorted and stored by the Sherpa guides.

"We have sixteen thousand liters of fuel and fifteen hundred meters of rope," Umesh reported. "There's enough fuel to last two weeks beyond our schedule."

"I don't want to spend one more minute here than necessary," Dave said as he looked through the lists of supplies being brought into camp. Hank looked at the various tents scattered among the rocks that littered the lower end of the Khumbu Glacier. The Sherpas and porters had begun to hang strings of flags between the larger kitchen, communication and the command central tents. The bright colors were a welcome sight in an otherwise bleak area.

"Do you see where they are building the stone *chorten,* Henry?" Umesh pointed to an altar of rocks and stones piled in the center of the emerging camp.

"Yes," Hank said. "I can see it. But why are they laying out all that equipment?"

"That," Dave chimed in, "is going to be the Base Camp's *lhap-so,* where all our gear is going to be blessed."

"The Sherpa's here," Umesh continued, "will want to perform a *puja,* a ceremony where a local Lama will be brought in to bless our expedition."

"All our equipment?" Hank asked. Umesh nodded. "Even the ropes?"

"Especially the ropes," Umesh added. Hank's gaze went beyond the emerging stone pillar to a sight of the firemen walking together with several of the climbing Sherpas. Leading all of them was Lopsang.

"Where are they going?" he asked Dave.

"There's a three meter serac on the other side of the glacier the Sherpas have used in the past for practice. They're going to practice crevasse extrication."

"I should be a part of that, shouldn't I?" Hank asked more to himself than to the two men standing with him.

"They asked not to include anyone else," Dave said. "They told me that they'd like to continue training as a team."

"Any news about Saraswati?"

"Nothing yet," Dave replied. "But they should be here in another day."

"Perhaps I will see them on my way back down," Umesh said. "If I do, I'll radio you from Namche before going on to Katmandu." It took Hank a moment to realize what had just been said. He turned to the man who had been so inspirational in creating the voyage he was now on.

"You're leaving?"

"Yes, that was the plan Henry, remember? My duty has been fulfilled. I must return."

"I can't even begin to tell you how much your help and guidance has meant to me I . . ." Hank voice was overcome with emotion.

"I have a lot of business to catch up on, but I will be back in Katmandu. By the time I return, if the deities are with you, you should be close to the summit." Umesh draped an arm over Hank's shoulder. He moved him a small distance from Dave's ear. "Is there a message you would like me to deliver to your family?"

"At the moment, I'm not even sure where they are."

"I will find them," Umesh said with determination.

"If you do, please tell them how far we've come. Tell them I think about them everyday. And tell them that I love them." Hank dropped his head and Umesh nodded in silent agreement.

"You still have a long way to go and I am not done helping you, my friend." At that moment a gust of wind blew past; the cold air made each of them shudder.

"I must be off." Umesh reached for Hank and embraced him in a hug.

"Keep talking to Miyolangsangma." Umesh stepped back. With a big smile on his face he said to Hank, "Listen to an old climbing Sherpa who knows. It really makes a difference."

"Don't worry," Hank returned the smile, "I will."

Hank felt the wind blow again. *Damn, it's getting cold!*

Chapter 27

Kala Pattar

AFTER A FITFUL night of sleep, Hank noticed his smoky breath cloud above him. His throat was so dry it pained him to swallow.

"Mr. Henry? Mr. Henry, good morning," Lopsang cried out.

"Is it morning Lopsang?" Hank turned on the battery-operated light beside his portable cot to check his watch; five-thirty a.m.

"I bring tea," Lopsang announced, "and cookies." As Hank moved out of his sleeping bag the intense cold sent shivers through him. He unzipped the nylon flap over the tent's screened window to reveal Lopsang's face tucked deep inside his hooded parka. In his hand was a ceramic mug and a napkin filled with shortbread cookies.

"Thank you Lopsang, I thought breakfast wasn't until eight?"

"Yes, but I bring news from doctor. The wind has died down. Their team attempts to summit. She wants you come to communication tent."

"Tell her I'll be right there."

"Also Mr. Henry? Please do not sleep with feet pointed to Sagarmatha. It is disrespectful and bad luck." He took the admonishment in stride.

"Okay Lopsang, I'll turn myself around."

The overnight snow accumulation during the night was significant. It took careful navigation through the slippery terrain to reach the large tent where Dr. Lindros sat with a Sherpa guide, who was talking in his native language, through a transmitter on top of a large battery pack.

"You look like hell," Hank announced.

"I've been up all night. The weather improved, so they left about ten last night." Hank could see she was drained. "The weather report came in showing favorable conditions for the next ten to twelve hours."

"The wind died down?" Hank asked.

"Yes, Elke has already radioed, it's completely stopped. She says it's very calm up there."

"Is there enough time?" Hank asked. The doctor could only reply with a shrug. Hank gazed at the radio as another burst of communication came through.

"This is Pharbat Sherpa," Mel explained. "His brother Nima is still at camp four. He's in contact with the climbers and is relaying their transmissions to us."

"Did you talk to your sister?"

"Yes briefly," Mel said. "She told me she slept with oxygen and that she was okay. She's exhausted, but she's going anyway. There is one problem; one of the cameramen has developed a severe case of retinal hemorrhaging in one of his eyes. His vision is so blurred that they've decided he needs to descend."

"Can he make it back down by himself?"

"No, but two others are also in poor shape and need to come down, too. Two of the climbing Sherpas are going with them to help. So it looks like almost a third of the expedition is descending."

"Is there enough support for those going for the top?" Hank asked.

"Barely, and in the meantime we've got an emergency medical situation to deal with."

"My crew is ready to help in any way we can," Hank offered.

"Thank you, but there won't be anything to do for quite some time. What do you have scheduled for today?"

"We're having a puja ceremony with a local Lama, and then we head out for a little climbing on Kala Pattar."

"Oh good," she said with reserved enthusiasm. "By the time you get back, I should have news for you."

"We'll be back by late afternoon."

"And I will be here with all the news." Hank took her hand and gave it a gentle squeeze. She looked at him kindly and then refocused on the transmissions.

In the meantime, the Sherpas had gathered stones and rocks to make an eight-foot high structure in between the mess tent and the communications center. In the middle of it was a flagpole with seven lengths of rope, each adorned with prayer flags and secured to the tops of the larger tents.

"That's called a *tharshing*," Matt explained as they walked toward the ceremonial site. "Attached to the top of the pole is a tree branch. If the tharshing breaks or is dismantled, this expedition is in trouble. On the other hand, if a bird lands on that branch, we're in."

Everyone put their hands together and bowed to the priest in greeting. The Lama from the small monastery in Pangbouche returned the gesture.

"*Qi namchee ves hara—cho?*" the Lama asked Hank.

"He asks if you climb for yourself," Lopsang translated.

"I don't understand?"

"The puja asks Gods for blessings and protection; he asks why you here. For glory of climb? What else do you seek on Sagarmatha?"

Lopsang translated as Hank spoke to the Lama. "I am here because my friend is up there." Hank pointed in the direction of Everest's peak. "His life was foreshortened and his consciousness still lingers within his body. I must give him a proper burial so that he may once again travel on his road to Nirvana."

"Peace?" the Lama repeated in English.

"Yes," Hank exhaled. "Peace."

The Lama nodded first, then smiled and commanded everyone who was not seated to do so. He placed three white stones on the stone altar and began chanting.

"Stones represent Miyolangsangma and two other Long-Life Sisters," Lopsang whispered in explanation. "Lama call on presence of eight different deities: the guru, the Dharma Protectors, country-gods, and angels called *Dakinis.*"

"So in other words," Hank responded, "we're going to be here awhile."

The chanting continued for an hour and then a cushion was brought for the Lama to sit while tea was poured. Hank noticed many of the Sherpas remained in intense prayer throughout the ceremony. After another hour of prayer and meditation, the Lama called for the climbing teams to come forward and make offerings. Hank and his team watched with interest as the Sherpas took grains, potatoes and some fancier items such as power bars and chocolate, and placed them on different parts of the *stupa*.

"Gifts to gods," Lopsang clarified to the onlookers. "We all make gift for Miyolangsangma to appreciate." When the Nepalese retreated from the altar, Hank, Matt, Sara and the firemen approached; it was their turn to deliver an offering as well, so they reached deep into their coat pockets and out came subway tokens, candy bars, a miniature statue of Lady Liberty, even a pint bottle of Jack Daniels, which were all laid on the altar.

A young monk brought juniper boughs to the base of the altar and with a lighter nursed them to flames. Incense was lit and the priest continued to chant as the chained urn swung back and forth, mixing the smoke from the two smoldering fires together. The Sherpa climbing crew returned with ropes, crampons, ice axes, and other equipment to be passed through the smoke, bathing each item in wafts of incense.

"I don't get it," Ed announced. "They want all our stuff to smell like crap?"

"The smoke expels spiritual pollution," Matt replied. "Clearing the way for favor from the deities." Hank and the others began picking up equipment to assist in the ceremony.

With all the climbing gear now blessed, Lopsang and several of the other Sherpas began distributing tsampa flour. Hank's team watched as the Lama demonstrated to them the final act of consecration. With everyone now standing, right hands were lifted while chanting in unison, in a long rising tone, "SwoooooOOO!" The gesture was repeated and on the third time the flour was launched skyward. The Sherpas shouted *"Lha Gyalo!"* And then ran around and through the American climbing team, smearing the remains of the flour into everyone's hair and on their unshaven cheeks.

When it was all over and the Sherpas had retreated, Rusty Barbeiro exclaimed, "Okay, what the heck was that all about?"

In broken English the Lama said, "Flour rubbed onto you signifies hope that you will all live until your hair and beards turn white." To complete the ceremony, water was poured as a communion. Hank accepted some of the holy water in his right hand, keeping his left hand respectfully beneath it. Then, as he was instructed, ran the rest of it through his hair so as to fully incorporate the blessing. Hank closed his eyes. *Now we can climb.*

*   *   *

The climbing team began the traverse down the Khumbu glacier toward Gorak Shep and up a well used path to the peak of Kala Pattar. When they passed Dried Lake, a cleared, flat area, a rumbling sound caught their attention.

"Look!" Everyone stopped and followed Sara's arm to the peak of Pumori where a massive snow avalanche hurtled down the mountain. The team stood motionless as the wave of snow and rock passed, less than two kilometers from where they stood, astounded by the strong gust of wind as it knocked them off their feet and raced on.

"The greatest tragedies on these mountains have been expeditions swept away by avalanches," Sara said. "If what hits you doesn't kill you, suffocating, buried in snow will."

Hank looked back again to where the avalanche had settled. There was silence among the crew.

"Hey," Sara announced, "I'm glad you saw that because it's one of the things you have to be aware of at all times. It's just as important to look up as well as down when you climb."

"Everyone got that?" Hank asked. "Okay then, let's move."

Sara led the way with Matt and Pete close behind. Hank stayed in the middle and worked his way along the sloping path that wove its way between the north and east faces of the mountain.

"Congratulations gentlemen," Sara announced when they'd made it, "you've just scaled your first eighteen thousand foot mountain. We're now higher than Kilimanjaro in Africa." The view of Mount Everest was extraordinary against a backdrop of a cloudless and bright blue sky.

"Guys, come over here a minute." With everyone assembled, Sara began the lecture. "There's a saying: 'When men and mountains come together, big things happen.' Right now we're as high as where we'll establish camp one, just above the Khumbu Ice Fall. Going back and forth between base camp and what you'll come to know as advanced base camp will be the most dangerous part of the climb."

"Doesn't look too bad," Pete said.

"Yeah," Sara said smiling, "but in order to properly acclimatize, we'll have to go through it probably eight times."

"How long do you think acclimatization will take?" Rick questioned.

"Several weeks. I don't see us making a summit attempt until the first week of October. Now the easiest part of the climb is going from "abc" to camp two, just below the Lhotse Face . . ."

Hank wandered off; he already knew the route so well he dreamed about it.

"Wonderful," Hank said out loud. He looked again toward Everest's summit and thought about his friend, lying in the snow and ice. *I'm coming.*

Chapter 28

The Ice Fall

SARASWATI AND THE caravan of porters had already arrived and were unpacking the gear by the time the crew returned to base camp.

"Saraswati!" Hank stepped away from the others and ran toward her. She looked up with a weary smile. "You made it." Sara and the firemen crew mixed themselves in with the other porters, shaking hands and slapping the Nepalese men on the shoulders for the good work they had done. Out of the huddle of men Lopsang emerged. He walked over to Hank and Saraswati with a toothy smile.

"Very good sign for group to make it, Mr. Henry."

"Yes Lopsang."

"Several porters tell me big delay caused by landslide near Tengeboche. She knew of path uncle used to escape Chinese; detour took extra days, but they make it."

"Now that girl," Matt said to Hank, "is a steely eyed expedition leader."

Hank checked back with Mel. "They made it to the summit," she said as she sat down with Hank, Matt, Dave and Sara at the large mess tent table. "I heard from Elke about an hour ago. She's at camp four safe and sound with everyone who went for the top."

"That's wonderful news Doc," Matt said. "Everyone okay?"

"Yes, the crew that descended earlier is at camp two. They will try to get all the way back to base camp tomorrow, or at least get to one and then try to get through the Ice Fall after that."

"We're making our first run up tomorrow," Sara said. "If we make good time we might get to them before they make their descent."

"How is Elke?" Hank asked.

"Tired, but happy. This was her dream, and now she has done it."

"Well, I'm very happy for her and everyone," Hank said. "I know how much you worried."

"Thank you." There was a pause in the conversation long enough so that everyone at the table could fork up their pasta and tomato sauce. Bread and salad were passed around. The doctor waited for everyone to have a few bites before speaking again.

"There is something else Elke told me."

"What's that?" Hank asked with his mouthful.

"She came upon your friend." The eating at the table stopped. Hank turned to Mel.

"Was she sure it was him?" The doctor took her time to respond. Hank could sense her apprehension and knew it came from the look on his face. The image of his best friend, dead and frozen in the snow was going to go from imagination to stark reality.

"Yes," Mel said quietly. "He is so close to the summit and . . ."

"Blue and red wind suit?" Dave interjected. "Black triangle patches on the shoulders?"

"Yes. He is a tall man right? Over six feet?" The doctor looked to Hank who, with a nod, confirmed Aaron's height.

"She logged his location into her GPS." Mel looked squarely at Hank. "You have to understand she didn't have time to do more than log in the coordinates."

"I understand. Thank you for the news."

"We're still a long way away from him, Hank," Sara said. "Right now we have to concentrate on getting through the Ice Fall and familiarizing ourselves with the route. We've got several stages of climbing to do before we even get close."

"Yes, I know." Hank looked at his dinner. "It's good news really. At least we know he's not buried in the snow."

"Hey," Matt chimed in, "he's not going anywhere." Matt leaned in and in a quieter voice said, "He knows you're coming."

"It's why we're here isn't it?" Hank said to Matt. His friend from Florida gave a reassuring nod.

For the first time Hank didn't feel a need to worry that he had put people in harm's way. Gazing out at the eating crowd he had the satisfying notion that everyone was meant to be here. With his mind at ease he looked at Matt and asked him to pass him the salad.

Early the next morning, Hank woke to another snow squall, but by the time he had dressed and went to the communications tent, the snow had stopped. Although only half of the climbing team was going and the other half waiting until tomorrow, everyone was up and busy with preparations. Hank first looked over the weather reports with Dave. He confirmed for Matt, Sara, Captain Jim, Pete Saltus and Larry Fusca that it would be a go for the climb through the Ice Fall. Lopsang, the appointed climbing sirdar, and several of his Sherpa team had gone on ahead to lay down guiding ropes and set up ladders. Others, who would be carrying supplies to the ascending camps, were busy assembling their loads. As Sara, Matt and the three firemen began attaching the ice crampons to their boots, Hank went to say good-bye to Saraswati. When the emotional sendoff took longer than anticipated, he had to rush to get his own crampons on and his gear together.

"Gentlemen," Sara began, "our climb today is to push ourselves as far as we can through the Ice Fall. As I've said before, this glacier has towers of ice that we'll scale and large crevasses to cross in order to get to camp one. If we succeed we'll have climbed over a thousand feet. Keep in mind that these ice towers can dislodge themselves and tumble down. Don't be underneath one when that happens. Climb at your own pace. If you have the strength to get to camp one, okay. But no matter where you are at 10 a.m., turn around and head back."

"Why so soon?" Larry asked.

"The midday sun makes the icefall even more unstable," Sara replied calmly. "The first time around I want everyone out of there before the possibility of any trouble. The goals are to learn the route and acclimatize. Some of you will get used to the altitude and some of you will need a longer period to adapt. That's all right; we have plenty of time. Please pay attention to your body." She stopped for a moment to look specifically at the firemen.

"Look, if you get cold or dizzy, or too fatigued, descend. No macho bullshit, got it?"

"Yes Ma'am," Matt said in a louder than usual voice. Hank greatly appreciated the way Matt handled himself. If anyone on the climb began to have doubts about Sara's ability to lead, the assumption would be to turn to Matt whose background in leading men would make him a preferred alternative. But Matt was quick to let everyone know that he would not abrogate Sara's authority.

"Be careful, and don't rope yourselves to each other," Sara continued. "For the sake of expediency the Sherpas have established a static line that extends itself from the bottom of the Ice Fall to the top. Take the safety tether attached to your waist and snap-link it onto the line. Make sure it's secure and slide it up the rope as you ascend." Hank pulled the three-foot cord from his side and checked the latch on the karabiner.

"All right, everyone ready?" Sara smiled. Hank looked at his watch. 4:45 a.m.

"Let's climb," Sara ordered.

Hank, his crew and several climbing porters loaded with supplies set out for camp one. It wasn't long before the ice under his feet began a series of loud cracking noises, like tree branches being split in two. Hank tried very hard not to think too much about the glacier's shifting depths beneath him.

"Sara?" Hank called. "You said the Ice Fall is a slow moving river?"

"Yes, I did. Experts think it travels about three to four feet a day." She pointed up ahead for Hank to see a crevasse with several aluminum ladders latched end-to-end extending over it.

"Because the glacier is moving," Sara remarked, "there'll always be a level of uncertainty with every ladder crossing."

As the other climbers arrived, they grouped themselves at one end while Sara inspected the ice screw anchors that secured the ladders and the lines to the glacier. Hank recalled when he and the firemen had practiced ladder crossings back in New Hampshire. The difference between then and now was those ladders were just on the ground, not over a crevasse that could shift at any moment. Hank felt his sphincter tighten.

"How far down you think it is?" Matt asked Sara, as he shot his helmet flashlight down into the void.

"Over a hundred feet, at least," she said. "The trick is not to look down as you cross. Who's first?"

After several climbing porters made it across with minimal effort, Hank volunteered. He latched himself to one of the guidelines and planted his right foot on the metal ladder. Relieved that the spikes of his crampon fit perfectly between the rungs and his boot, he began to cross, until somewhere mid-cross, the ladder developed an unnerving bounce. Panic welled as he dropped to his knees and went for a choke hold around the ladder's rungs. The Sherpas leaned out to him from the other side, yelling for Hank to continue. Just a few more steps, and then Hank grabbed for the waiting arms to pull him to the other side.

"Thank you," he said as he collapsed onto the ground.

"How is it?" Matt hollered from the other side.

"Piece of cake," Hank sarcastically answered.

Hank and the crew pressed on falling into a steady pace behind Sara with Matt bringing up the rear. As dawn broke, their pace had become slower than the firemen with them and soon Jim, Pete and Larry, along with the Sherpas, had forged on ahead and out of view.

"How you holding up?" Sara called out. It was almost rhetoric, what could he say?

"Just fine," Hank responded on cue, right before the ground quivered and the roar of a crashing serac reverberated around them. Hank, Sara and Matt crouched fast as they waited for the avalanche to overtake them, relieved when the wave of snow and crashing ice passed a mere fifty yards to the left. The three remained motionless.

"Well that was enough to loosen my bowels," Matt said between jagged breaths.

"Me too," Sara added.

"Jesus, I've never been so scared," Hank chimed in.

At 19,000 feet they had reached the base of a gargantuan serac.

"How high do you think this one is?" Hank asked Matt.

"About twelve stories." Hank had tilted his head back and saw the heads of two climbing porters bobbed out from above. After an exchange of smiles and waves, the three were directed to a rope next to a catwalk.

"Our road, I presume?" Hank mocked as he presented the line in his hands.

"Clip on your ascender," Sara instructed Matt. Hank watched as Matt took the oval device that was connected to his harness and attached it to the rope. "Slide it forward as you move upward," she continued, "it'll grip the rope if you lean back or fall."

"Okay, I'm off," Matt said.

"Wait Matt," Hank commanded. From a cotton drawstring pouch, Hank pulled out some blessed grains of barley that Saraswati had given him, a gift from her uncle.

"Use these to give thanks and praise to Miyolansangma for your journey," the note had instructed. Throwing the grains against the serac's wall he exclaimed, "Thank you, Miyolangsangma, for your kindness and accepting us into your lap as we continue to climb." After a moment of silence Hank said, "Okay Matt, you're good to go."

Hank went next and huffed his way toward the security of the serac's crest. His lack of expertise prevented him from going any faster than a crawl, managing only four or five steps before a needed break to suck hard at the thin, bitter air. At the flat summit, he flopped breathlessly to the ground as his heart pounded like a jackhammer. *I'm going to have to climb that seven more times?* He dreaded the thought.

At nine-thirty a.m. Hank and the others moved past the last of the seracs and arrived at camp one.

"I had missions behind enemy lines that weren't as scary as that maze," came Matt's declaration as they pulled into the safety of the camp.

"What took you so long?" Pete emerged from one of the tents. "We're just about to have some soup. Want some?"

"How was your trip through the Ice Fall?" Matt asked.

"I have to give the Sherpas a lot of credit," Pete replied, "they really helped us up here. The only scary moment was when one of the ice chunks broke off and fell. We'd just gotten past it when boom! Down it went."

"Yeah," Sara said, "it rumbled right by us. Scared the bejesus out of me."

"So, this is the Coom?" Hank asked Sara.

"Yep, it's the highest box canyon on the planet." Hank looked at the horseshoe shaped, valley floor of the canyon and the walls of the mountains that defined it.

"The plan," Sara added, "is to get both teams up here today and tomorrow and then go back to base camp. On the next trip we'll stay here at camp one for two nights and then trek up to camp two for a night before we head back down to base camp."

"How long is it from here to camp two?" Matt asked.

"Four miles and 1,700 vertical feet," Sara answered.

"And at that point we'll be how high?" Captain Jim asked.

"A little over 21,000 feet. Camp two will be our advanced base camp," Sara said. Lopsang, who had been laying out oxygen bottles, addressed the group.

"We have ABC ready for you, Mr. Henry. It right along glacier's edge."

"Hey look!" Pete shouted as he pointed up the snow-covered valley. "Do you see them?" The Swedish members that were forced to descend for medical reasons were headed straight for them.

"We should help them," Pete's voice boomed.

"Yes," Larry added.

The firemen team began to move until Sara yelled, "Stop right there! No one goes anywhere. Listen to me, you've already climbed over 1,500 vertical feet this morning; that's enough."

"Hey look," Larry announced, "I don't know about the rest of you, but I feel fine."

"We agreed at base camp that we'd turn around at 10 a.m. and head back." Hank looked at his watch. "It's 9:30 already and from the looks of it, those folks are more than an hour away."

"I know you want to help and it looks real easy out there, but there's a lot of hidden crevasses . . ." Sara's voice trailed off. Hank looked at her and then followed her eyes to the expeditionary group, which had stopped; one of them was lying on the ground.

"Does anyone have binoculars?" Jim asked before Lopsang disappeared inside a tent. He retrieved a large pair of binoculars, which he handed to the fire captain.

"There's five of them . . . Looks like one's down . . . Some are resting . . . Two are trying to lift the one who's down." Jim handed to Sara the binoculars.

"Don't see anyone else out there," she remarked.

"We've got the stretcher, might be a great opportunity to test it out," Matt suggested.

"Look, it's your call," Sara said to Hank. "But I've got to warn you, there're crevasses hidden by the snowfall, one wrong step and it's over." Hank nodded, as he stared through the binoculars.

"And if you're planning on going, you better strip off some of your layers." Hank pulled the binoculars down to look at his expedition leader.

"What do you mean?"

"It gets pretty hot out there, the sun's rays can turn this valley into an oven." Hank took one more look and thought about what she'd said and a moment later nodded to Matt.

"Alright," Matt barked. "Let's get the sled out." The tubular frame was slotted together by the firemen with Matt inserting the end piece last. The rescue board was passed around for everyone to inspect and then given to Hank. Matt called out to everyone.

"Okay, listen up. I know all of you want to go, but we don't need everyone. If we have to use the stretcher for transport we only need a couple of people; we can easily sled the guy in trouble out of there and if need be, carry him from here." Hank watched as Matt scanned the group.

"Lopsang, you know the way, you lead; Hank, you, me, Jim and Larry will go. That should be enough man power to get all of them back here."

"What about me?" Pete asked.

"You'll be in charge of getting us back down through the Ice Fall." Hank watched as the young man's eyes went wide. Pete looked to Sara whose concern gave way to a "thumbs up."

"Don't worry," she said. "I'll help you."

"Any questions?" Matt barked. "Okay then, let's move out!"

Hank estimated that the stranded group was four to six hundred yards away. Although the slope of the boxed canyon was only a slight incline, the team moved slowly as Lopsang carefully tested the footing along the way. They made good time reaching a stretch of open ground, but soon came upon a crevasse too wide to get across and had to walk parallel to its opening before it narrowed enough to safely cross.

As the rescue team approached the Swedish climbers, the sun's rays bathed the enormous valley in bright sunshine. The heat beat through the layers of clothing and wind suits were peeled off followed by sweaters.

When they had reached the distressed team, they realized the man down was the Swedish cameraman. A quick look confirmed he was in dire need of assistance.

"I'm Henry Longo. We're here to help you."

"Thank you."

"Let's get this man onto the stretcher and get the hell out of here. I don't know about you, but I'm sweating like a pig." After Matt's announcement, Larry was the first to dump the clothing that had been piled onto the sled. While he and the others eased the casualty onto the stretcher, he said,

"Anyone else got a headache the size of a mountain?" Hank didn't want to think about it, but his head did hurt, and the pain was approaching migraine status. His concern grew when the other rescue members complained of headaches, too.

It was afternoon by the time they made it back to base camp. The descent with the stretcher had been tricky and a lot of time was spent getting over the serac and across the roped ladders, but they made it through. The doctor was quick to check on the fallen cameraman's condition before she found Hank and hugged him fiercely.

"Thank God you're alright." She proclaimed.

"It was an amazing day," Hank replied. "I'm going to the mess tent to get a bite to eat."

"I'll meet you there when I'm done seeing to the team."

Matt was already seated at one of the long tables talking with the firemen and Sherpa porters that were scheduled to climb tomorrow. Everyone had large mugs filled with steaming soup. Hank walked over to the chef who was ladling out the tomato red liquid and asked for a mugful. With his mug in hand, he sat beside Matt.

"Hey, hey, what d'ya say?"

"I don't think I've ever been in a place that's as dangerous and beautiful as that Ice Fall."

"And the Coom," Hank added, "the Southwest face of Everest was right there, right next to us."

"That was a great test for us to haul that climber out of there. Nice teamwork and we gave that stretcher a chance to show its effectiveness. I think it passed with flying colors."

"Yes, it did," Hank said. He was about to say more, but after several sips he felt strangely funny.

"Of course," Matt said to everyone at the table, "the big test will come after we've climbed all the way up and we have to get the body all the way down. Today we didn't have far to go before turning around, but the next time . . ." Hank listened with his eyes closed. The headache had intensified, as if a steel rod was being pushed into the crown of his head. The pain was so bad a soft moan emitted from his mouth. Quick to follow was wave after wave of nausea; it was all Hank could do to mutter that he needed to lie down before he staggered away to his tent.

Chapter 29

A Conversation With Elke

AFTER HOURS OF horrific head pain, Hank dragged himself to the infirmary. "It's unbelievable," Hank muttered. "I've been in my tent unable to move for hours. I can't even . . ."

"Don't talk, okay?" Mel spoke in a comforting tone. "You were out in the sun three miles above sea level; acclimatization up here can be very painful. Anyone will tell you your body needs time to adjust." Hank watched as she reached into the dispensary and pulled out a bottle of pills. "Here," she said. "Take these with some water. They're an analgesic." Hank swallowed the pills and willed them to take effect without delay; and then he vomited, onto his shoes and the cuffs of his pants.

"Damn!" he said between gasping breaths. "Sorry."

"Well, that didn't work, did it?" The doctor reached for another bottle and gave Hank a very small pill.

"Don't swallow this one, just put it under your tongue and let it dissolve." Hank did as he was instructed. "This pill should keep you from vomiting. Too much sun will burn your retinas; it's a guaranteed migraine every time. You're not my first today."

Hank listened carefully as he allowed the bitter pill to melt under his tongue. Withering jolts of pain hit him every time his eyes moved, even with the lids shut.

"Okay, now I want to give you two of these," Mel said as she lifted his chin up with her hand. Hank kept his eyes shut, but opened his mouth, receiving two more tablets from the doctor. A small paper cup was put in his hand and he quickly swallowed the pills and the water together.

"It's codeine. Hopefully you'll keep them down and the pain'll subside."

"Thanks," Hank said with his eyes still closed. He sat with his head down and listened only to his breathing. When the tent flap opened, he heard Matt's voice.

"Hey, you okay?"

"Thank God for the Doc," Hank said.

"I know what you mean. A bunch of us were here earlier; almost everyone's got something, right Doc? Me, I've got blisters from new boots. Shoulda broke 'em in before we came."

At that moment, the tent flap opened and Dave walked in.

"There you are. I heard you weren't feeling well." Hank's eyes opened briefly to look at Dave and then closed again.

"I'm feeling a little better now. How're things going?" Hank's head still throbbed though relief was getting closer.

"I'm sorry to have to report this, but the Sherpas want to renegotiate their agreement."

"What do you mean?" Matt asked.

"It's routine for them; once an expedition group arrives and is set up, the Sherpas demand more money."

"So what we negotiated back at Namche is now unacceptable?" Matt was incredulous, the anger rose as he spoke the words.

"They claim conditions are worse this time of year," Dave said. "There's a lot more snow and the risk for avalanche is greater, so they want more money."

"But they knew that going in, right?" Matt asked.

"I heard there was a slide and an avalanche . . ."

"So?" The veins in Matt's neck swelled in response.

"They took it as a bad sign." Dave redirected himself toward Hank. "So, if we want their labor, it'll cost more."

"Hazard pay," Hank concluded.

Dave moved closer to Hank and explained. "It's not that much more, it's like a custom of theirs to make an adjustment so they can feel they're valued."

"Do we give them what they want or do we negotiate. In some cultures, if you don't bargain back and forth it's considered an insult."

"If that's the case," Matt said, "I want in on the negotiations." Hank smiled as he visualized Matt at the table, with arms folded, telling the Sherpas how much more they could ask for.

"Thanks Matt, but Dave can handle it."

"The other team's scheduled to leave bright and early tomorrow," Dave said. "And it's a good thing too, because the weather forecast in a few days isn't good."

"What's the call?"

"We've got a shift in the jet stream that's going to bring us high winds and they don't know when it's going to let up. We may be hunkering down for awhile."

"Any news about the other team?" Matt asked.

"They're in pretty good shape," Dave replied. "We got a report from the Sherpas at ABC; they're off the Lhotse Face and encamped for the night. If all goes well, they should be back down here by lunchtime tomorrow." Dave took a step toward the doctor and put his arm on her shoulder.

"Your sister radioed a few minutes ago. She said she's okay, and so are the four other sisters."

"Thank God," Mel said. "They made it to the summit and now they just have to get back safely."

"Why don't you go over to the command tent and see if you can get her on the radio," Hank suggested. "I'll go with you," Matt added.

"Are you sure? I don't want to leave you until there's some relief."

"There is," Hank said, opening his eyes and trying his best to smile, despite the lingering pain. "I think the codeine is taking effect. Go on. You've done more than enough for me." Hank watched as the Swedish doctor put on her parka and headed out with Matt. An awkward silence engulfed the triage tent. Hank knew it was because of the news about Aaron.

"So they found him," Dave broke the silence first.

"Yes, and you know what? I was surprised."

"In what way?"

"I look at how massive this place is," Hank said with his arms stretched wide, "I got to thinking that the mountain might've swallowed him up by now."

"I knew he was still up there," Dave said. "Six months or sixty years doesn't make much difference in the Himalayas."

"I know there are many dead up there," Hank said.

"Yeah, but it's a suspended kind of death. Not that any of this is easy, but you only have a corpse to deal with. I've got to live with the memory of him dying while I was up there with him."

"I remember you saying that he was already dead when the storm blew in." Hank watched as Dave only nodded in the affirmative. "How much time elapsed from when you saw him standing to when you found him dead?"

"It's hard to say; there were so many things going on at once." Dave's voice trailed off as he looked to the ceiling. Hank wondered if he was trying to remember or get his story straight.

"I saw him on the South Summit, moving slowly as others moved right past him."

"Did you pass him?" Hank asked.

"I was up ahead in the lead position, but I'd had concerns, which I voiced the night before, that he wasn't up for the remainder of the climb."

"He was sick and you let him go on?" Hank's head hurt again.

"Just a minute Hank," Dave said with his hand stretched out and up. "I didn't say he was sick. He looked tired. We all were; it had been a difficult climb with a lot of wind and freezing cold conditions."

"Go on."

"So I needed to know if he was going to make it. There were others that could take the camera if he wasn't up to it. But he said he was, and . . . I won't repeat what he said, okay?" Hank could only imagine the argument. "The last time I saw him alive was when I was at the summit and we were calling Hillary in New Zealand. Aaron was down below setting up his camera and I gestured to him to start shooting."

"Did he respond?"

"I think so. He waved back." Dave closed his eyes. "Then the storm hit and he was slumped over by the rock and . . ." Dave opened his eyes and stared straight ahead. For a moment he looked as though he was going to cry. He looked back at Hank and said, "I'm sorry, there was nothing I could do."

"No need to apologize." And then the conversation was over.

"I've got to get back, there's more work to do and I've got an early start tomorrow getting the crew out."

"Yeah," Hank said with a tired sigh, "I'm planning on being up as well." Hank watched as Dave exited the tent.

The pounding headache had all but disappeared. As he put on his wind parka and walked out of the medical tent, back into the frigid fall evening, he looked up at the twinkling stars in the night. It reminded him of Martha's Vineyard; the nights he and Aaron would sit on the deck of Aaron's mother's house and gaze at the stars. So far away from the haze of city lights, they'd light up the sky.

By the time Hank climbed into his sleeping bag and turned off his battery-operated light, his thoughts were on Aaron and Dave. It seemed there was unfinished business between the two. Dave had insisted on being here, maybe he shouldn't have come; he was battling some demons of his own, and Hank wasn't too sure if finding Aaron would help or hurt Dave's cause.

Maybe I'm here to save Aaron from the confines of Purgatory, and Dave from the gates of Hell.

Hank grabbed his pounding chest and gasped for breath; another night filled with fitful dreams. Hank turned on his Black Diamond halogen headlamp and looked at his watch, 4:30. From inside his sleeping bag, to preserve body warmth, he dressed himself and headed to the command tent, which was already abuzz with activity. Similar to his own start the day before, climbers assembled gear, checked radios and conferred on strategies in preparation to climb the Ice Fall.

"Good morning," Hank greeted the busy group. "Ready to head up?"

"I'll do anything to keep moving," Ed said. "It's so goddamn cold."

"My eyelashes are frozen," Colin added. Rick and Lieutenant Tom nodded their agreement, as Doctor Melissa brought in a tray of steaming mugs and a plate piled high with sandwiches.

"Breakfast for everyone," she announced. Hank waited for the climbing crew to grab theirs and then lifted a coffee mug for himself.

"How about a sandwich?" Mel asked.

"Maybe later, I'm not that hungry right now."

"You have to eat," she scolded. "Unless you'd like another headache. Food helps."

"Soon, I promise. I just want to enjoy the coffee first. I'm not going anywhere, I'll eat in a little while, when these guys get outta here." Hank turned back to the climbers and said, "So you guys ready? It's an amazing climb. You'll have plenty to talk about when you get back." Hank looked at his climbing sirdar. "Lopsang did an amazing job with us yesterday," he said to the group. "Listen to everything he tells you and you'll be fine."

"Dave? How's the weather?" Hank asked.

"Good for most of the day, until tonight, which may shut the climbing down for awhile." Hank tuned back to the doctor. "What about Elke?" He asked.

"They should be down by early afternoon. I'm going to radio her in an hour to make sure she's on her way. She already knows about the weather report."

"Let's be careful out there, okay?" As the team left the tent one by one, Hank watched them go and privately asked for a blessing.

Miyolangsangma, please allow these men safe passage into the body of your spirit. Their cause is noble. We depend on you for your kindness and grace in this difficult journey. Thank you.

Hank and Mel sat down at the radio table. She reached for the sandwiches.

"Now?"

"I'm really not a big fan of egg salad."

"Awe, come on. You need to eat." She pushed the tray closer to him. "Hey look, I made them myself. I'll be insulted if you don't have one." Hank knew he was cornered. Picking out one of the halves, he took a small bite and rinsed it down with coffee.

"Not bad," he said. Even though the sandwich was borderline tasteless, he realized his body would be grateful for the nourishment.

Until the sun came up, Hank monitored the radio. He enjoyed listening to the banter about the conditions and hurdles through the ice towers and over the crevasses, but he was still grateful to be relieved when Sara and a few of the other firemen showed up later in the morning. As he made his way through the compound, the Swedish crew sauntered into camp. Melissa and her sister shared a tearful hug. In spite of everything that made the mountain inhospitable, the Swedes proved dreams do come true. Hank hoped that the good karma the nuns had carried with them would rub off on his own crew and expedition.

Later that day, Hank met Elke.

"Henry Longo?"

"Yes," he said, and put down the cylinder of oxygen he'd been checking. He extended his hand, which she took in both of hers.

"Please, call me Hank." She was a taller and thinner version of her sister; stereotypically more like the Scandinavian woman he'd heard about, blonde with high cheekbones and a curvaceous figure. She was obviously tired and displayed the wear and tear of a 29,000 foot climb; a beaten look around the chin, nose and ears and a level of pain endured by merely standing.

"Peace be with you," she spoke with a soft voice.

"Thank you Sister," Hank said. "Do I call you that or . . ."

"Sister, Elke, it doesn't matter; whichever you're more comfortable with."

"Congratulations on your successful summit. It's an incredible accomplishment." Hank could see that she wasn't comfortable on her feet at all. He pointed to a couple of nearby boulders.

"Let's sit," he said. "I'm eager to hear all about it." Hank waited until he knew Elke was comfortable and then asked, "So was it everything you imagined?"

"It was nothing like I imagined," her effervescent smile and bright blue eyes captivated him as her tender voice continued. "I thought there would be a flood of emotions or some sort of epiphany about my beloved, maybe even a chance to see God himself."

"But it didn't happen."

"Far from it, in fact I was standing on top of Everest and I didn't have the energy to care. I hadn't slept in over two days, and with the lack of oxygen I couldn't even think straight. I was cold, tired and when I finally got to the top all I wanted to do was leave."

"But what about that view? It must've been spectacular."

"Of course, and we have pictures. It's something we have dreamed of and will always treasure, our journey to the top of this great mountain."

"And the great take away . . . I know there's something more . . . there has to be."

"You are right. How perceptive you are. A spiritual man perhaps?"

"In some ways. I'm still learning."

"And so am I. What I learned is that God was not up there waiting for me, which I thought might be the case. No, in fact, God was with me the whole time. It's the journey we take and the transformations we encounter along the way that brings us closer to Him."

"So yours is not a passive relationship with the Lord?"

"Jesus Christ was not a passive man. My savior did not say, 'blessed are the poor, for they will become rich' to mean that if you are poor, but believe in me, I will show you how to be wealthy."

"So what did he mean?"

"He meant that if you were poor, get up and do something about it. The process of finding your way out of poverty is what moves you closer to God. Jesus was a teacher. He came into the world to show us a new way to pray, build a stronger faith in a time of oppressive rule." Hank could hear the fire in Elke's spirit. He admired her conviction.

There was a pause in their conversation as the sun pushed through the cloud cover. Both Hank and Elke let the suns rays soak into their faces, a warm touch from the Father above, and a moment to reflect and give thanks.

When the moment had passed, Hank broke the silence with the questions he had waited to ask.

"Can you tell me about my friend Aaron? The condition his body was in?"

"When I saw the remains," she began, "he was face up and somewhat buried from the waist down in the snow and ice. Unlike the other contorted bodies I have seen on Everest, his is serenely laid out. And his clothing is pretty much intact."

"How much of him is frozen to the ground?" Hank asked.

"From the legs leading up to the waist area. I actually think he's been buried in snowfall for quite a period of time and only now has the body resurfaced."

"Why is that?" Hank asked.

"Because the clothing is pretty much intact," she answered. "And there is little wind burn to the exposed areas of the body."

"You said he was face up?"

"Yes, the hood of his parka protected his features quite well, considering he's been there for awhile. His eyes are open." Hank was inspired by what Elke had told him. "And that's what was so strange for me. When I came upon him," Elke continued, "his state of suspension was so complete, he looked as if he had just died. In fact, I thought about praying for him, but something stopped me." Hank was confused at what Elke was saying.

"Thank you, I'm sure he'd have appreciated it."

"I wanted to do more . . . Was he a Christian?"

"Aaron was raised in the Episcopal Church, but he had a great understanding of Buddhism."

"Tell me, what possesses you to take this kind of risk to retrieve your friend's body?" Elke asked with urgent need.

"I don't think his remains should stay on the mountain. It's hard to explain, but I believe there's a stream of consciousness that is waiting to move on and can't until he comes off of Everest."

"You believe that?"

Hank exhaled in admittance. "I do. He's come to me in my dreams and there've been occurrences where I've seen him."

"You've seen his ghost?"

"Yes, I have. You said you wanted to pray for him," Hank was reaching. "Tell me about that."

"I was kneeling by him and trying to think of a prayer, I know so many, but none seemed to come to mind. And then there was a sudden gust of wind; huge, it knocked me over."

"And that's when you decided not to do it?"

"I got back on my knees and looked at him again. I had a very odd sensation; what was it?" Elke got up from the large rock she had been sitting on. Hank watched as Elke attempted to work out the confusion in her mind. He waited patiently as she increased the speed of her back and forth movement, walking and turning, walking and turning. He picked up a few small stones and skipped them off the camp's glacial water stream until she was ready.

"What's the story behind the doll?"

"Satchmo? Satchmo is still with him?"

"I leaned over his body and saw a doll in his hand. It had long hair and a funny smile."

"Aaron's daughter gave it to him to keep him company on his way to the top."

"I'm not going to swear it because the wind was blowing and I was so oxygen deprived, but . . . I heard a voice."

"You heard a voice." Hank gave a reflexive nod.

"Yes. I thought it said to leave him alone." Hank's eyes went wide and Elke's body convulsed before she fell into Hank's arms and cried. "There are no other forces that guide my life except that of my savior," Elke said through a torrent of tears.

"So you don't believe there are other forces here on this mountain, here to guide us, or warn us?"

"I'm sorry but I can't. There is only one who is divine, and that is God." Elke slid her gloves off to wipe the tears from her cheeks.

"Perhaps then, Sister," Hank interjected, "it was Jesus that was talking to you." Hank watched as Elke looked down and put her gloves back on.

"No, it was not him. The voice was female."

Hank stared at her in disbelief.

"Here." Hank watched as she unzipped a pocket and extracted a folded sheet of paper, which she handed to him. "It is the coordinates from the GPS when I was with him; I took them from right over his body."

"Thank you, I do have them, but . . ."

"Hank, I would counsel you to put your faith in Christ and nothing else on this mission. He will be the one who will ultimately guide you."

"Thank you Elke. Hanging around my neck will always be my protector," Hank said. "As a matter of fact, I think he sent you to reinforce my faith in him."

"We are having a farewell dinner tonight in our camp," Elke said. "A celebration for our time and success here. When your men return from their trip through the Ice Fall, you are all to be our guests." Hank smiled.

"We'll be there." And with that she turned and left him. As he watched her go his thoughts centered on the fortitude the sister must have in order to have made such an arduous climb. He prayed for his own fortitude and determination.

As Hank made his way back to his camp, he opened the folded paper to look once again at the coordinates he had come to know by heart and stopped in shock as he realized they weren't the same.

The coordinates are different. How can that be? His mind raced to find a plausible excuse. Human error; Dave or Elke didn't use their positioning devices correctly? Operating a GPS was so simple . . . And then another scenario, and it was by far much worse. How was Aaron able to move around if Dave had left him for dead? *Yes Dave, how could that be?*

Chapter 30

The Lohtse Face

THE OTHER HALF of the expedition returned from the Ice Fall with less drama than the first crew encountered. As Dave had predicted, the weather deteriorated into a maelstrom of wind and snow that shut down the camp for several days. By the time it stopped, there was over two feet of snow to shovel so foot traffic could resume within the compound. As the climbers and porters worked to re-establish the camp's perimeter, the Swedish team packed itself up and moved out. Before they left, Hank thanked them for their hospitality during the weather lockdown. Now, they were the only ones left on the mountain.

After a lunch of meatball sandwiches, the crew sat together in the mess tent for the briefing Dave prepared.

"We've developed a route through the Ice Fall," he began, "and the next step is to spend a lot of time between camps one and two." Lopsang came forward with a map, which he placed on the table to show the next part of Dave's presentation. "Camp one, as you all know, is at the top of the Ice Fall and at 19,500 feet." Dave pointed to the area Hank and the others had briefly visited during their first climb. "Camp two," Dave said, as he moved his finger up the map, "has been established three quarters of the way up through the Western Coom by the Southwest Ridge of Everest, close to where the Lhotse face begins."

"Why there?" Sara asked.

"I thought we'd position the camp right at the base of Lhotse. The Sherpas and porters put the camp in a place least likely to be hit by an avalanche. There's a lot of unstable snow on the Lhotse Face and much less on Everest's southwest face, so that's why camp two is there." Sara nodded in acknowledgement of the strategy. Dave proceeded. "You'll spend time going back and forth between these two camps before returning here. Everyone can spend the night at camp one, followed by another night up at camp two. For those of you who are strong enough, you can spend the third day going half way toward camp three, which is at the top of the Lhotse Face, in an area known as the Yellow Band."

"And what if we're not strong enough?" Matt asked.

"Then, after a night at camp two, come back to base camp."

"Why only half way to three?" Lieutenant Ed asked.

"Three isn't set up yet; the porters are only now stocking the first two camps." Dave looked around the table and went on. "And camp three is for another day down the road toward acclimatizing. But climbing half way up will give everyone practice in crampon climbing."

"The face itself has a fifty degree slope," Sara added. "It's a huge accomplishment just to get up there. Then we can use the top camp as a jumping off point to go the rest of the way."

"How high are camps two and three?" Pete asked.

"Camp two is 21,300. Three is 23,400. Once back at base camp, everyone will have a turn going down to Namche for a little rest and relaxation, and also making the climb back up with the porters to bring supplies to the high camps." Hank, along with the others, expressed joyful surprise that they would have a chance to get back to the Nepalese version of civilization.

"Namche?" He questioned Dave. "That's incredible."

"We're going to be spending close to three weeks climbing up in the camp two area. Going back and forth between the lower elevations and the middle camps will give everyone's body time to acclimatize."

"When do you think we'll start the recovery?" Captain Jim asked.

"End of the first or beginning of the second week of October," Dave said. Already Hank's body felt as if it had been through four quarters of pad less tackle football; he didn't want to know what another three to four weeks would feel like.

"How's everyone holding up?" Dave asked the group, which set off a chorus of, "fine" and "no problem." Then Matt spoke.

"Well, I have to admit I haven't slept since we've been here and I've got this cough that just won't quit." A few of the other men murmured their mutual agreement with Matt's maladies. "I've also got these foot problems because of my new boots," Matt said, continuing, "and my tongue's swollen and my taste buds are shot."

After Matt's confession, everyone else fessed up.

"This is why it's so important to acclimatize," Dave explained. "And the timing, just after the retreat of the monsoon season, before the jet stream returns from Tibet."

"Is there a target date?" Sara asked.

"Somewhere around October 8th. It all depends on the weather." As Hank listened to Dave, uneasiness settled over him. He thought about the situation several weeks from now; waiting high up in camp four for the report from Dave, when to go for it. So much of what they hoped to accomplish depended on him. Was he sincere in wanting to help find Aaron or did he have a different agenda hidden beneath his troubled psyche?

"So tomorrow we wake up at 4:30 am." The team groaned at the thought of having to climb out of their sleeping bags and dress in the pre-dawn freezing temperatures, again.

They exited through the flaps of the large tent, but Hank stopped when he heard Sara call his name.

"I'll catch up with you later," he said to Dave who headed over to the operations tent.

"You want to tell me what the nun said about Aaron?"

"Let's sort out the ropes for tomorrow and I'll tell you all about it."

The next day, Hank stood in the middle of the highest valley on earth and took in the view of the majestic mountains around him. The sunshine had generated considerable heat; enough for the crew to shed their protective clothing once again as they walked up the gently sloping valley. Hank had just placed his second baseball cap full of snow on his head and enjoyed the cool melting water as it dripped down around his ears.

There was no wind this morning; the only audible sounds were his own breathing, the voices of his teammates, and the crunching of snow-shoes against compacted snow. He remembered reading the story Tenzing Norgay had written as the first humans to enter the Coom back in 1952. Because of the mountain walls, there was little wind. Norgay had referred to the area as the "Valley of Silence." Hank turned back to see how far they'd come and smiled when he saw Matt under an umbrella.

"Where on Earth did you get that?" he asked his climbing partner.

"In Periche. I ran into a guy who came to collect the used oxygen canisters. He recycles them."

"Really?"

"Yeah, makes them into musical bells. Anyway, he's been around the world and he told me the best piece of equipment he's ever used, no matter where he climbed, was an umbrella."

"Hmm, interesting, but you still look like Mary Poppins on steroids."

"Hey, the sun's off my head and I've got such a splitting headache that I'll take all the help I can get."

"I can't get over the fluctuations around here," Hank said as the two of them walked together. "In the morning it's below zero and a thousand feet later, I'm overheating."

"The firemen have adjusted well; they're tough sons of bitches."

"Them and the Sherpas," Hank replied. "It's amazing to watch them carry the loads up the mountain." There was a pause in the conversation. Just ahead, they watched five of the firemen march in a direct line behind Sara; although her steps were consistent, the rest of the team struggled to keep up. "Looks like little ducklings trying to keep up with their mama."

"You know," Matt said, "she's cut from strong stock. Everyone's had some complaint, but not a peep from her."

"She's a good leader," Hank confirmed. Just up ahead, Hank spotted a bundled plastic sheet on the ground; they realized it was a body. "Oh my God," Hank stood horrified as Matt bent down to get a closer look.

"Well, the sheet's fairly new." Matt examined the decimated mass beneath it. "Judging by the old clothing and the effects of decomposing, I'd say this guy's been here at least ten years."

"Or more," Hank added. The two of them walked on in silence until they reached the advanced base camp about an hour later. The dead man had triggered thoughts about Linda and the girls; Hank missed them and wondered where they were. His attempts to call were futile, and so he feared, just like the man under the tarp, his marriage too may be dead. *Maybe they're reading my dispatches . . . At least they know where I am.*

The boiled rice with olive oil and Sherpa tea was ready for them when they arrived at ABC. After they ate, the crew gathered around the telescope Sara had erected, and one by one, they took turns looking at the mountains' summits.

"At this camp," she began, "we're horizontally and vertically equal in distance from our objective.

"How far?" Hank heard Matt ask.

"About 1 1/3rd miles. We'll climb on the right side of the Lhotse Face; there's far less avalanche worry on that side as opposed to the gully area that lies between Lhotse and Everest. The climb goes up 4,000 feet to an area that's known as the Geneva Spur. That's where we'll make camp three. After that, we cross the rest of the slope including the Yellow Band. It's tricky, there's more rock to climb over there than snow and ice." Hank could see the protruding barren part of the mountain and the slatty rock that spread itself where the two mountains merged. "Once that's done," Sara continued, "we'll arrive at the South Col where we'll establish camp four; and gentlemen, the goal is not to stay there too long because at that point we're in The Death Zone." Through the viewfinder, Hank could see the small snow filled valley just beneath the two summits. And then, he angled the telescope further up the ridge where they would climb to find Aaron. "Do you see how hard the wind is blowing?" Sara waited while Hank absorbed the vision of the wind as it howled past the peak, pulling a plume of wispy snow out toward Tibet.

"The 'Train' is still running."

"The 'Train'?" Matt asked.

"The Lhasa Express, that's what the expeditions from the fifties ended up naming those fierce winds," Sara explained. "And we're going to climb right through the heart of it. They howl past your tent and can literally suck the air out of you as they gust." After giving the men a few minutes to absorb the information, Sara asked, "Anyone ready to do a little climbing?" Hank looked over at the shining polished slope of Lhotse's Face. Like everyone else, he remained quiet instead of responding to the question.

"C'mon, you see that gap in the ice by the base of the mountain?" Sara asked. "That's called the *bergshrund*. It's where the glacial Coom ends and Lhotse begins. We're gonna scale the face, about a thousand feet up, before we head back here for the night. All I need are five volunteers; who's comin' with me?"

"And the rest of us?" Matt asked.

"The rest of you can start back to camp one, and for those of you who can make it, keep going all the way back to base camp." Sara waited for hands. Hank raised his and was surprised that Matt didn't.

"Not up for the adventure?" he asked his friend.

"Not today," Matt said with a pained expression. "I had an awful night last night; couldn't stop coughing, and I've got a God awful pain in my left side here . . ." Matt patted an area around his rib cage.

"Will you be okay without me?"

"Yeah, I'll be fine. I've got the lads with me." Matt smiled at Hank's use of the nickname Matt used to collectively identify all the firemen.

"See you tomorrow then," Matt said.

Hank made his way over to the *bergshrund* and joined up with Sara and the four others who would scale the face of Lhotse. As he strapped the eight pointed spiked frames to his boots, he knew this climb wasn't about skill; it was to learn to trust the equipment.

"The fixed line is anchored in thousand-foot sections. We're only going to the end of the first section." Sara paused until everyone looked at her. "The rope is just a safety device; you'll clip on to it with your ascender, but don't use it to help you climb. Don't use the rope to haul you up!" Hank had a sudden vision of them using the rope exactly like Sara said not to and the collective weight ripping the rope from its anchors, causing them to all fall to their deaths.

"Use your legs and your arms," Sara continued. "Your ice axe and crampons are the only tools you'll need."

A few of the men went up before Hank clipped himself in. He kicked the two toe points of his crampons into the snow and ice; all he had to do was climb. Every step brought more confidence. *Breathe steady and climb that's all. It's that simple.*

Chapter 31

Dave and Aaron

www.everestjourney.com
October 7th

Hello from Base Camp,

It's been a month and the acclimatization process is now complete; the only thing left to do is wait for the favorable forecast before we attempt the actual recovery. There's a report we received this morning, which predicts a window of opportunity about to open.

This will be my last dispatch until our return, but we'll carry your prayers and good wishes every step of the way.

AFTER MULLING OVER the content, click, off it went to Umesh, who'd post the dispatch on their website and forward back any e-mail for the team. Usually, there was nothing for Hank, with the exception of a few messages from Traci, out in California, but it was Linda who he waited desperately to hear from.

Hank propped himself against some rolled up sleeping bags. He grabbed a small mirror from his bedside and looked at his face. The peeling skin and his sunburned nose didn't appear quite as cancerous as it had a week ago, but the puffiness in his cheeks and the raccoon-like rings around his eyes betrayed a face that'd been in the sun too long. He moved the mirror from one side of his face to the other.

God, you look like shit. He tilted the mirror up to his forehead and searched out the dull pain. He couldn't decide which hurt more, his head or his stomach. All of the food he had eaten the past week had shot right through him. His lack of digestion was making him weaker every day.

There'd been a lot of snow during the past week and through the window flap, Hank noticed it was another gray day. It was a long seven days, plenty of time to think. There was the avalanche that descended down the southwest face of Everest and partially buried the advance base camp. Privately, he thanked Miyolangsangma that no one was there when it happened; still, it had been a major effort to dig out and re-establish the camp. The expedition had also survived two episodes of climbers falling through snow-covered crevasses. In both cases, the men were properly roped off and extricated themselves with minimal bruising. Also, everyone at camp dealt with some form of numbness in their extremities; the cold had taken its toll.

Hank knew if the snow didn't abate soon, it might get too cold to climb. He thought about all the hardships, the back and forth scaling of the mountain; it had worked. There was no effort now to breathe at base camp. Everyone who had ventured back to Periche, or even further to Namche, commented that the air felt "heavy" and "thick" to breathe. The acclimatization had been so successful that camps one and two were visited regularly throughout the month. And he was relieved the night gagging for air, and dreams of drowning had stopped.

"Good morning," came Doctor Mel's voice as she peeked into his window. "How are you feeling?"

"Too many trips to the toilet Doc."

"Mmm. Could be an intestinal bug. I'll get you something."

"I need to get to the communications tent for the latest report. Wait a minute, I'll be right out." It took him barely three minutes before he was suited up and standing next to Mel. The cold had trained him to move quickly, lest he freeze in one spot.

"Can we talk for a minute?" Not waiting for a response, she added, "Over here," and walked to the supply room. Hank stepped down into the cavernous room that was constructed on three sides with stones and small boulders and had a large blue tarp roof.

"This is difficult for me to have to tell you, but Matt has rib problems," Mel said bluntly. "I believe he's torn some cartilage and one rib may be fractured."

"What? How?"

"It's his coughing, he hasn't been able to shake off the bronchial virus and the coughing fits have done damage to his rib cage. He's been in a considerable amount of pain for a long time." Hank was stunned by the news. In all their interactions, he'd never let on. "I have bound up the damaged area for now but you must know, his condition might endanger all of you when you get high up on the mountain. It goes against my convictions to break confidentiality," Mel added, "but I can't let him endanger the rest of you." She paused for a long moment and then said, "And . . ."

"And he won't say anything," Hank finished for her.

"Will you talk to him?"

"I'll hear what he has to say, and then decide if he should go."

"He thinks he needs to be your bodyguard," Mel said. "He told me how much he wants your mission to succeed."

"I don't think I'd be here without him, and frankly I'd feel a lot safer with him up there, but I will talk to him I promise." As Hank pondered his options, he crossed the compound to the communications tent. Sara and Dave were inside reviewing weather reports. Lopsang was also there, going over equipment checks with several Sherpas.

"Hello everyone. Hey Lopsang? What're you doing here?"

"I am everywhere important when things happen," he said as he grabbed a coil of rope.

"He's going back to ABC," Dave said. Hank sent a stern look Dave's way. "I thought the weather was no good."

"The light's about to go from red to green," Sara sang. Before Hank could respond, Captain Jim pushed through the tent's flapping door.

"I hear we're a go," he said to Hank, but instead of happiness, there was only a look of quiet determination.

"The report?" Hank questioned Dave who'd been studying wind patterns almost round-the-clock for three days.

"Regionally, there's a major shift in the Calcutta express. Nice big fat window opening up. It's amazing how the world turns." Hank felt like he had a hundred questions to ask, but instead asked only one.

"How much time?"

"Five days, maybe. Everest is a mountain unto itself; just because the wind is calm over Bhutan and Tibet doesn't mean things can't go haywire around here."

"But now's the time?" Jim asked. Dave nodded, affirming the fate of all of those involved.

"I'll go tell the men."

Sara got up, "I'll go with you," she said, and the two of them left together.

Dave turned to Lopsang and barked out, "Lopsang, get on the squawk box and let every one know at the camps above, we start tomorrow morning. And if you want to be a part of this, you'd better get your crew together and get that rope up there."

Lopsang hit the radio and a flood of messages went out over the airwaves to the men scattered among camps one through three. Hank didn't like the way Dave bossed around the locals. Protocol dictated the base camp manager maintains control, but his approach was excessive and unnecessary. Hank, although pissed, kept it to himself for now.

"So what kind of time frame are we looking at?"

"You'll arrive at ABC tomorrow afternoon," Dave began. "Get an early start the next day, and climb to camp three. Get as much rest as you can there because the next day you'll have to traverse over to four and stay there until 10 or 11p.m. before you go on to the summit. It'll take you a full night and part of the next morning to get within reach, and then you'll need just as much time to get back to camp four before nightfall. After that you'll probably need all of day five to get yourselves down the Lhotse Face; don't forget you'll be hauling a body down with you."

"I haven't forgotten." It was his time to confront Dave about the coordinates and his suspicions. Lopsang had gotten up from the radio and went out into the night; they were alone.

"Dave, we know he's dead, you marked the position, right?" Hank took out the folded paper Mel's sister had given him and passed it to Dave. "So look at this."

"This isn't right," Dave shook his head in confusion. "I know the degrees, minutes and seconds by heart; these aren't them."

"I know they aren't; I know the position by heart as well. The problem is, these coordinates were taken over the body and they're different. Not by much granted, a few seconds maybe but still, how do you explain it?"

"Someone's equipment must've been off," Dave reasoned.

"Maybe; or maybe not." Hank had an unusual calmness to his demeanor, like that of a professional interrogator.

"I've never had much faith that electronics could work very well at such high altitudes."

"Except for the cell phone you brought, so your celebrities could talk to their dads." Hank stared down at his seated camp manager. Dave returned the gaze.

"Maybe my mind slipped when I took the reading. As you'll soon find out, it's not easy to keep your thoughts clear up there." Hank looked at

Dave and decided not to say anything. He learned that sometimes to get the information you wanted, you didn't have to say anything at all. Seconds passed. The only sound in the tent was the static coming from the radio and the wind flapping the entranceway cover.

"Maybe while I was descending I mixed up some of the coordinates. I had to keep it in my head until the next day, before I could finally write it down."

"Tell me more about when you left him."

"When I left him? What does that mean Hank? You want to know how it was?" Dave stood from the chair. "Heavy snow was falling, the wind was whipping up and down the ridge. I'd seen the storm coming and was frantic to get everyone off the top. Everyone's moving, struggling to breathe and find their way; visibility was dropping fast."

"And Aaron's not moving," Hank chimed in, wanting to move Dave to the point.

"No, he was slumped over a boulder, about a hundred yards down from the summit. I had to go to him because the wind was too loud to shout over."

"And when you got there?"

"I yelled, loud, and in his face; grabbed him, and tried to get him up."

"Back in DC you said he was already dead when you reached him."

"He was."

"Then what was the point in trying to pick him up? To carry him?"

"If there was any possibility that he might've been alive . . . I thought trying to get him up would've promoted a response."

"You tried to pick him up because you thought he might still be alive?"

"Yes."

"What made you think he was alive?" Hank watched as Dave turned his gaze away from him and looked down at the ground. He could see that Dave was trying to recall the event.

"There was a possibility he was still breathing," Dave confessed. Anger swelled up in Hank as he grabbed the front of Dave's parka and shook him.

"Still breathing means, he wasn't DEAD!" Hank pushed Dave back into the chair. He paced the tent, not knowing what to say next.

"You can't know if someone is dead at such a high altitude."

"What the hell is that supposed to mean?"

"It's almost impossible to diagnose death that high up," Dave said solemnly. "I was in no position to drag Aaron back to camp, warm him up, and see whether or not he would come back to life." Hank frowned at trying to understand the medical axiom.

"So what you're saying is he was mostly dead?"

"Last stage Hank. He was headed to his maker. And I was in no condition to bring him back," came Dave's tepid reply.

He now understood the scenario of a comrade dying and not being able to do anything about it. Matt had taught him that. "I'm sorry Dave, for not trusting you."

"I don't need yours, or anyone else's sympathy." Hank was tired; he sat down beside Dave. Side by side, they stared at the plywood platform.

"Why are you here?"

"Just trying to right a wrong. Doesn't the criminal always return to the scene of the crime? I'm that person; scarred for life by this mountain and the decisions I made, and people I lost as a result."

"What crime did you commit? There are forces of nature that dominate this part of the world; you didn't cause Aaron's death, and you can't undo it."

"I knew he wasn't dead, and the different coordinates confirms it. In the end he did get up—didn't he? He didn't get very far, but he tried." Dave ran his hands through his hair while he paused to think. "If I'd stayed there with him, we'd both be dead. I know that."

"Yeah, you would be."

"If there was any way he was going to get off the mountain, he needed to show me that he could at least get up and walk. There was no way I could've dragged him out of there."

"Of course," Hank tried not to appear curt. It all made sense, logically, but not emotionally . . .

"It's funny that fate would have me at 29,000 feet, in a freezing snow storm, with a man, incapacitated and in pain; at the same time, a friend whose been the cause of so much pain in my life."

"How has Aaron . . ." Hank didn't finish.

"They carried on for years, Hank. It wasn't long after we were married that I found out Tracy and Aaron were still in touch. At first, it seemed innocent enough; some e-mail correspondence and a Christmas card to let him know how we were doing. But then came the phone calls, and soon after that were the 'girlfriend get aways'. I suspected they didn't involve any girlfriends. I hired a detective to confirm it. And as the years went by, I made it into a game. When I knew she was going somewhere, like France for example, I'd work up an assignment for one of my magazines and then request Aaron get the assignment. Lo and behold we'd find out he was already in Paris and could easily get to the photo shoot."

"You never confronted her?"

"Nah. She knew I knew." Hank heard the sadness. "But I couldn't talk about it. Angry as I was, I was also terrified she'd leave me. I love her so much, it was better to have her most of the time than not at all." Hank was surprised, but he understood. "The fact that Aaron wasn't where I said means I didn't kill him. Besides, the motive for getting rid of him wouldn't have been because he was sleeping with my wife."

"No?" Hank was incredulous. "It would've been for me."

"But I'm not you. In fact, the best part of my marriage was the weeks that followed one of her 'away' trips. Tracy would be all happy and things between us would be great, if you know what I mean."

"I think I do."

"If I wanted to kill Aaron, it would've been for what he's done to Tracy." Hank saw the tears in Dave's eyes.

"Because he ended it?"

"Because he was committing himself to another woman; to the other Traci, and his daughter.

You saw her in DC, right? She's drinking it up and there's nothing I can do to stop it, nothing."

"So you did have motive. You could've murdered the man, but instead you let the mountain do it for you."

"No, he was too far gone when I reached him. And I didn't want Tracy to lose both of us at the same time."

What a soap opera! "So why are you here, Dave?"

"Guilt perhaps, maybe duty. I did leave him there, and if there's a chance to retrieve him . . . You're not the only one who needs to say goodbye to Aaron."

"You need to?"

"No, but Tracy does."

"I'll tell you Dave, I had major concerns on your effectiveness at relaying correct information to us once we're up there, whether you really wanted us to succeed."

"You thought I'd sabotage the mission?"

"When I got those coordinates, I had my doubts." Hank was blunt. "Now that you've told me the whole story, I understand why you're here."

"I won't let you down."

At that moment, Matt came through the tent's flap opening.

"I hear we're a go." Hank and Dave acknowledged with nods. "It's about time we . . ." Matt broke off and turned away to cough.

"Dave? I need to go over a few things with Matt, will you find Sara and make sure she's in on the loop?" Dave grabbed several spiral notebooks off the table and quickly left. Hank turned to Matt.

"How are you feeling? Can't shake that cough?"

"Yeah, I'm real sore from the coughing, but I'm okay."

"Uh huh."

"And I'm freakin' cold. The doc told me all my fat is gone from being here a month. I've lost twenty pounds!"

"Anything else?"

"No, I guess I'm in the same boat with everyone else going for the top." Matt coughed again. Hank could see him wince.

"I think you're worse than you're letting on. You want to tell me everything, or should I bring in Doc to give me her opinion."

"No, no, no, you don't need to do that." Hank waited for Matt to decide how to phrase his next sentence. "Doc thinks I've got a busted rib. I think it's cartilage strain, but she's overly concerned."

"I'm going to let Sara know, and you're going to swear to me on all things holy that if she decides that you're in no shape to continue, you'll abandon the mission and descend." Hank waited for Matt's reply. Matt looked up at Hank who was startled to see moisture in the big man's eyes.

In almost a whisper he said, "I swear."

"Good." Hank looked at his watch. "Time for sleep; we get up in six hours."

Chapter 32

Getting Close

IT WAS A windless day, only 5 a.m. and the group was just about ready to move up the mountain. Fog-smoked breath danced between halogen lights as the crew ran a final check on the equipment. While they were busy, Hank decided to pick up a few extra blessings at the Stupa. And then to complete his circle of protection, he pulled out the cross from beneath his parka, kissed it and said a silent prayer.

The climb from base camp to advanced base camp took the entire first day. They arrived just a few hours before the sunlight descended behind Nuptse, plunging them into frigid darkness.

Dinner was served early and everyone hunkered down right after that.

When Hank awoke, he looked first at the clock, 4 a.m., then at the little thermometer clipped to his parka, five below.

"Matt," he called to his cocooned friend. "Time to wake up, buddy." Already, Lopsang and some of the Sherpa crew could be heard moving about the campsite, but he doubted the fire crew, Captain Jim or Sara were up yet.

"It's fucking cold," Matt's hoarse voice groaned when he unzipped his bag and reached for the first layer of polypropylene underwear. He began to shiver vigorously, firing a round of expletives.

Hank laced up his boots and strapped on his headlamp. "I'm going out to check on things, meet me outside when you're ready."

"Give me a few minutes, I'll be right out," Matt said.

Hank noticed that the wind had picked up. He turned his back, flipped up his hood and quickened his pace to the dining tent.

"Hey," Sara said, holding a steaming mug of tea with both hands. "Did you get any rest?"

"Some," Hank replied. "How we doing on time?"

"I think everyone's up and about. I was just about to call down to base camp to check on the weather." Hank reached for the Motorola. With a seven-mile radius, the walkie-talkie could easily reach back down to base camp or up to the summit.

"Base camp—this is ABC, over." There was a short pause before Dave's voice crackled through the line.

"*Mornin,' ABC. How do you read?*"

"I read you 'five by five'."

"*Wind's kicking up, you're going to have to watch it up there on the Face.*"

"Already noticed," Hank said. "Will it get worse?"

"*You'll know before I know.*" Hank handed the walkie-talkie to Sara.

"Base camp? Looks like we're on schedule for an o-six-hundred departure."

"*Ten-four; signing off.*" Sara returned the radio to its charging base. She put on her headlamp, handed Hank an ear microphone and a portable radio. "Clip this on. You're on point."

"Me?"

"You've been up there before, you know where to go."

The slope of the Western Coom gave way to the bergschrund that delineated the Khumbu Glacier's upper end. Hank and his expedition snaked toward the sloping field and arrived shortly after dawn.

It was a challenging climb at first, but now they were all ready for the recovery to truly begin.

"See you at camp three," Hank said, as he clipped on his ascender. It was only an hour into the climb when Hank looked back and discovered the other climbers much farther below; only Lopsang kept up. The march up the face had got tougher as the wind's intensity increased. When he got to the third tie off, he dug his spiked crampons firmly into the ice-covered ground. He dropped onto his knees and with wooden fingers attempted to transfer his safety line from the top of the anchored rope to the bottom of the next section. *What am I supposed to do?* Disoriented, he stared at the safety line until he heard Lopsang shout from below.

"Mr. Henry, clip on to the next rope. Clip on!" Jarred back into reality, he secured the line, just as an enormous shadow descended from above him. Lopsang cried out, "Avalanche!" Hank dropped, with lightening speed, onto the slope, and hammered his axe into the ground. Every muscle in his body tensed, waiting to be hurtled down the side of the mountain, but the moment never came. He lifted his head above the snow, above his half buried body, and surveyed the damage.

"Lopsang?" Hank called out. "Lopsang?" Hank looked over his shoulder and was relieved to see his climbing sirdar right behind him. Lopsang smiled and gave a thumbs up. Sara's voice crackled over the radio.

"Thanks for the heads up, Lopsang. We're lucky that was a small one."

Hank reached for Lopsang and pulled him next to him. The two of them lay on their sides and watched as the wind carried the displaced snow off the steep slope.

"That ever happen to you before?" Hank asked.

"Yes," Lopsang yelled back, over the noisy wind. "Three years ago, on North side of Sagarmatha. Four porters there carrying supplies, two carried away. One my cousin."

"That's it for today guys," Sara's voice broke in over the radio. "Everybody descend to ABC, now." Hank knew she was right. They had been through enough for one day.

At camp two, everyone had a story to tell about how they pressed themselves to the face of the mountain and hung on for their lives, when the snow broke loose and raced down the mountain; almost taking them with it. Matt looked worn, more so than the others, and Hank had his doubts if he should even continue.

"Look Matt, God knows I wouldn't have made it this far without you, but I refuse to lose another friend to this mountain."

"And you won't," Matt said hoarsely. "I can make it. But maybe you'd better have another talk with the powers that be; do some apologizing or something. If we're dealing with female powers that run the show around here, we must've done something insulting." Matt paused as a fit of coughing interrupted his thought.

"You think it might've been a warning?"

"Well, maybe she threw the snow at us to let us know we shouldn't have tried to go any higher today. Maybe she's not ready yet; not on a first date."

"Well, that's a positive spin on a near death experience."

As the team ate in silent defeat that evening, Sara stood up and delivered a team speech.

"I'm glad we went through that extra avalanche training before heading up here. We were lucky today, but let's not forget how unpredictable Everest is. We can use today as a reminder; we started out with a favorable weather report and ended up in a maelstrom of wind and freezing temperatures—then an avalanche. But you came through like champs. You're first time climbers and every one of you acted with clear, quick responses, as if you'd been doing this for a long time. You should be proud of yourselves and each other." Hank stood up to face everyone and then spoke.

"I've gotten to know all of you pretty well and I consider you friends, but when I recruited you, I didn't realize it was going to get this bad. So, if anyone wants out, it's okay. Just let me know." A chorus of "no's" and "no ways" cut Hank off. One by one, the men depicted their own past life-threatening escapades and finished with an agreed upon, "piece of cake," comment. So, it was decided, the men would continue; they would climb, find Aaron and bring him down off the mountain.

Hank listened to the testimony of the men he had picked, and the brave things they had accomplished. When everyone had the chance to speak, Hank turned to Matt and asked, "Matt? What about you?"

"I've been in worse situations than this. I'm good."

"Yeah?" Ed trumpeted. "Like what?"

"S.E.A.L. 'Hell Week'".

"This mission is not over. Let's keep going." Sara got back up and with a smile said, "We've got much better weather for tomorrow. Base camp reports that the winds will abate, so we'll get started early and get ourselves up to camp three."

The next day, once again, Hank had out-paced the rest of the crew, except of course for Lopsang, who stayed just above him. The wind was hardly noticeable now, and the bright sun had kept the frigid chill at bay for most of the sunlit morning. Foot by foot he continued to climb until he saw the cluster of blue tents perched up on the face above.

It had taken four-and-a-half-hours to make it to camp three, and it was only halfway up Lhotse. Next, they'd move on to the summit, which was still almost a vertical mile away.

Chapter 33

Camp IV

AS THE FIRST to arrive at camp three, Hank chopped the ice to melt for the others who would soon arrive dehydrated, in desperate need of water. Lopsang and the support crew were already en route to camp four, and for the first time, Hank and the team were on their own.

It was about forty-five minutes before Hank felt the first spasm rip across his colon. The axe hit the ground. *Oh man, of all places!*

Hank surveyed the slope for a place to relieve himself before the next wave of pain sent him scrambling for paper. Time was running out and there wasn't a single roll in sight. *Shit!* Then he had remembered Dawson had given him a headband.

"Here, take it," Dawson urged. "It brought me good luck whenever I climbed. I'm sure you can put it to good use." He'd stuffed it into his backpack and forgotten about it, until now.

Hank scaled the steep pitch to an abandoned platform and ripped off everything that stood between him and relief. He groaned. As the cold wrapped itself around his exposed butt, he wondered if he would have the courage to tell Dawson the headband did come to good use.

"Hey Jack, remember that headband you gave me? Well I . . ." and then he stopped talking and grunted as the floodgate evacuation of his bowels began.

He was in his tent and had just finished replenishing lost fluid when Sara and Pete appeared. The rest of the crew followed shortly after, all except for Matt, who was the last to make it to camp.

"You okay Matt?" He passed him a water bottle.

"How much further?" Matt asked, just before a coughing fit racked his upper torso.

"Another mile, or so. Tomorrow we go up and over. After that, it's the big push."

"I was built for power and speed, not this. In the service, you get in and out." Matt's head shook from side-to-side. Poor guy was wiped out.

Hank left Matt to get some rest and went to find Sara. Sara was bent over a burner melting ice for water.

"I may need you to help me with Matt."

"Whatever you decide, I'm with you," Sara replied. "But if I didn't love the big knucklehead so much, I would've sent him packing two weeks ago."

As the sun began to disappear over Pumori ridge, Sara made some announcements.

"Listen up everyone." The tired group focused on Sara. "You're all doing a great job, but we're going to have to make a few changes now, to ensure a safe and successful completion. The last time we were here we didn't use oxygen, but tonight we'll sleep with it. The masks may be uncomfortable, but it's mandatory, so do it." A few grumbles and nods and the group quieted down again. "Up until now," Sara continued, "we've more or less traveled at our own pace, but starting tomorrow, we climb as a team. Stay within one hundred feet of each other at all times." Hank and the others gave a variety of small affirmatives to her command. "Make sure you check each other's regulators tonight; one liter of gas per hour. Take extra canisters, you'll probably have to change in six or seven hours. We kick off at 0900 tomorrow." The men broke in to small groups, and headed to their tents. Only Sara, Hank and Matt remained.

"Matt, you're struggling. I can't have the crew waiting around in subzero winds while you try to catch up."

"Yes, Ma'am."

"I don't think you should go tomorrow."

"Let me see how it goes tonight, please?" Matt asked. "If I get some sleep . . . Then, if anyone passes me on the line, I'll pack it in."

"Fine," Sara said. "Tomorrow I'm on point and I've got Pete bringing up the rear. You guys can take anywhere in between."

"Roger that," Matt replied.

"Time to snuggle," Sara said with a grin. The three made their way to the tent.

"Will this be your first threesome?" She asked Matt.

248 | Adam A. Wilson

Hank added to the fun, "Hey, hands off, I'm a married man."

Matt gave a rueful look.

The next morning, when Hank woke, the tent was already bathed in sunlight and his two companions were outside. He climbed out of the waist high shelter and looked around.

It's a good day. Hank grabbed another oxygen canister and attached his regulator to it.

Thank you, Miyolangsangma, for your inexhaustible generosity.

"Good Morning," Matt said with a cheery disposition. Hank was elated to see Matt fit and ready. It was a far cry from the ravaged state he'd been in just the day before.

"How're you feeling?"

"M-u-c-h better. Still coughing, it's manageable."

"Okay, we'd better get moving."

Hank had some trail mix and washed it down with two cups of melted ice. From another melting pot he poured half a bottle full and stuffed it inside his wind suit. He checked his pocket thermometer, 4 below. Strapping on new oxygen canisters, Hank and Matt made their way over to the climbing route and waited until Captain Jim had gotten a safe distance up the slope before the next climber went.

"Remember, keep an eye out for falling rocks or anything else that might come whizzing down from above," Hank said to Matt.

Matt nodded, strapped on his oxygen mask, and dropped his heavy goggles down over his eyes. He turned around to let Hank adjust his regulator and Hank followed suit.

Clipping on to the rope, Matt started to climb. After he made his way up, it was Hank's turn. From this point, he had known the mountain and had become intimate with it. Now he was headed into new territory.

Climbing now with oxygen was a strange sensation and took some getting used to. "Stay calm, just breathe," he said hoarsely through staggered breaths. Sara told him that the ascent to the South Col was one of the most strenuous and draining parts of the climb, especially crossing the Yellow Band and the Geneva Spur. A sense of panic crept within him that he might not be able to go any farther, much less get to the next camp, and then to the summit. *Whatever you do,* he said to himself as he slid the ascender up the fixed rope, *keep moving.*

An hour later he ascended the Spur's mound of black schist and slatty rocks that looked like tiles from a roof. Waiting for him was Matt, who was seated and enjoying the view.

"You waiting for me?" Hank inquired, as he held his mask out from his face.

"I wasn't going to let you pass me," Matt said, "so I humped hard to get here. But looky here," he pointed. "Now it's downhill to the South Col." Hank saw that the slope dropped down over a hundred feet to the broad rocky expanse where their final camp had been established.

"I can't believe," Hank began, "that I'm here right now, at one of the highest places on Earth."

"Twenty-six-thousand-feet up," Matt said. "Three-thousand to go."

"We're almost there!" Matt pulled himself up using his ice axe for leverage. Strapping their masks back on, they began the long, unroped walk to the South Col.

Hank was surprised to see how expansive and flat the high plateau was. Several hundred yards wide and long, the notch between the ramparts of Lhotse and Everest was an austere place littered with debris from previous expeditions. Side by side, several bodies lay prone on the windswept rocks. Hank thought of Aaron at that moment, somewhere higher up and his remains exposed to the elements.

"A reminder of our own thin hold on life up here," Matt said, his voice muffled by the breathing apparatus. Hank nodded and they moved on.

As those behind Hank and Matt made their way to the camp, the wind's velocity began to increase. Although some tents had been erected, a few more were still needed for the climbers coming into camp. The Sherpa guides had gotten their own and a supply tent up, but three more were needed to accommodate those plodding their way in.

They were scheduled to depart in another eight hours. If the wind was blowing this hard on the Col, he could only imagine what it was like up above. Hank finished securing his tent and watched as Matt and Captain Jim dove inside. Instead of joining them, he made his way to the supply tent, which also housed the communications center. Lopsang had the small gas stove fired up for a pot of tea, while Sara was working the satellite radio, trying to reach base camp.

"Hello, base camp? This is four checking in. Are you there?" Hank un-strapped his oxygen mask, seated himself on the floor, and accepted a mug of lemony tea from Lopsang. The heat from the stove helped him relax. He was grateful.

After Sara's sixth attempt, the tinny static voice of Dave Horton came back at them.

"Base Camp to four—copy?"

"Sara here, we've arrived without casualty; tents are up and the wind's blowing."

"*Roger that,*" Dave said. "*Hate to be the bearer of bad news, but looks like recovery attempt will be delayed.*"

"Ten-Four," Sara acknowledged. Everyone listened to the wind as it rifled past their nylon shelter, their only source of protection from the tempest storm. Hank peered out at the blizzard conditions that had now lay siege on the South Col.

"What's the plan?" Sara asked Dave.

"*Let me talk to Lopsang first,*" the voice from the radio responded. Lopsang pointed to Hank to take over the stove.

"Lopsang here."

"*How many cylinders do you have at the camp?*"

"Sixty."

"*Stand-by, I need to calculate.*"

Hank looked first at Sara and then Lopsang. He knew what they knew, Dave was figuring how much they had for the attempt and what reserves there were if they had to wait another day. Hank did a little math of his own.

"We don't have enough, do we?" Before they could respond, Dave radio'd back in.

"*Okay, it looks like tonight's assault is out, copy?*"

"Yes. Ten-four."

"*Sorry,*" Dave continued, "*front's passing through and winds are too high.*"

"Ten-four," Sara said.

"*You can stay up there for one extra day, but you'll have to spend the night and the better part of the morning off the gas.*"

"Can we?" Hank asked Sara.

"Copy that; stand-by, base. The short answer is yes." Sara took a moment to gather her thoughts. "It'll depend on how acclimatized each of us are, but we should be okay, at least until we get the weather report tomorrow. If we don't have good news by 11 am, we descend." Sara went back to the radio. "Base, we copy. The gas is off for the night."

"*I'll leave the radio on and update you at 0600. Over and out.*"

They now had to gamble with lives as they calculated the risks involved for an unplanned extended stay in The Death Zone. Hank knew if they had doubts he should call the whole thing off.

Sara began, "We're not going anywhere at the moment, not with this storm brewing."

"Once up here two days," Lopsang said. "Not easy, but we do it."

"I think," Sara added, "we'll have to see how everyone feels in the morning and check the status of the weather before we make any decisions."

"We've come so far," Hank added, "we can get through the night."

"It's going to be a miserable night," Sara said. "I doubt we'll get any rest." Hank thought about the crew. *These guys have been in plenty of tough situations, I know they can handle it.* Then it dawned on him that he was possibly the weakest link to the team. Sara smiled at Hank and said, "We'll be fine. You tell everyone in your tent." Then she turned to Lopsang. "You tell the guides, and I'll pass the word to the other tents. No oxygen from 1800 tonight until 1100 tomorrow. Let's go." With a clap they dispersed.

Hank was the last to leave, fastening and zipping before he stepped back out into the storm.

Sara was right. Hank didn't sleep at all. The wind gusted with such fierceness that Hank imagined he and his companions would be blown off the Col right into Tibet.

By morning, the snow had stopped. *Well that's a good sign.* Captain Jim and Ed Casey donned their protective suits and made their way to the supply tent for breakfast. Hank crawled over to Matt, who was still sound asleep. He was impressed that Matt had been able to find a way to get the needed sleep he wished he could have had, so he let him be.

All those who had squeezed into the supply tent had versions of their own horror stories about trying to get through the night with the storm and no air. Many of the firemen had dreams of being trapped in burning buildings and running, looking for a way out.

It was 6 A.M. when Hank re-established contact with base camp.

"*Great news, it looks like we've got a change coming,*" Dave said. "*Storm's passing through and looks like a window's opening up.*"

"Yes, we can tell the wind is receding." Hank looked at the faces of his crew. They were battered and worn, but they smiled at the news.

"That mountain has some left hook," Ed said.

"But didn't even knock us down," Rusty added.

"*Let's hope for no wind in another 12 hours. I'll get back to you with another report at noon.*"

"Roger, camp four out." Hank clicked off and looked at Sara.

"I've checked on everyone," she announced. "No physical complaints other than the usual headaches and tiredness. Just a lot of bitching and moaning."

"I can imagine," Hank said.

"How are you feeling?"

"Exhausted. I may have gotten about five winks the whole night."

"Where's Matt?"

"He's back in the tent sound asleep. It's amazing." Sara flashed a look of concern.

"You sure 'bout that?"

"Yeah. Snoring like a baby."

"Well that's great, but I'll go check on him in a little while, just to make sure."

"What time do you think we'll leave tonight?" Hank asked.

"Earlier than planned." Sara did a quick calculation in her head and said, "Originally I wanted to get to the Balcony by 7 or 8 A.M."

"The Balcony is how high?"

"Twenty-seven-thousand-six," Sara said. "I figured if we were there by then, we'd be up at the summit by early afternoon. But since everyone's had more rest, we can leave earlier and get to the Balcony by dawn."

"I'm sure everyone will be anxious to go," Hank said.

"What it means though is we'll be doing sixteen-hundred-feet of climbing in darkness. Some of it's tricky and it'll be damned cold." Lopsang suddenly burst into the tent agitated and out of breath.

"Mr. Henry! You must hurry," Lopsang managed to say between gasps of breath. "Mr. Matt very sick!"

"What? I just left him a few minutes ago. He was sound asleep."

"Porter guide Tendi Sherpa heard him in tent. Very sick, come quick." Hank dropped his nutrient bar and rushed back to where he'd left his friend sleeping.

When he got there, the guide was kneeling just inside the tent's flapping door. Matt was sitting up, but his eyes were closed and he was slumped to one side. On his knees, he came head to head with the man and said, "Matt! Matt, can you hear me? You okay, man?" Hank sat back on his haunches and watched as Matt tried to respond. He lifted his head up high enough to look at Hank and broke into a smile.

"Hey 'jere good buddy. We're u've been?" Before Hank could respond Matt lowered his head again and appeared to slump back into sleep.

"Matt! I need to know if you're okay!" At first Matt did not respond. Then he looked up once more and said, "Izz okay, Lieutenant. I'll go get those men out."

"Oh shit! He's delusional. Sara and Captain Jim climbed into the tent.

"How is he?" Sara asked.

"He sat up, but seems strange, and he's talking funny." Hank and Jim watched as Sara managed to get Matt's attention and ask him a few questions. She also shook him slightly from the shoulders several times and took off her gloves to feel his face and pull up his eyelids to check his pupils. After a few minutes, she gently put him down on his side and reached for the small black bag she brought with her.

"He needs to descend, now; he's got altitude sickness. I don't know if it's cerebral edema or not, but he's done as far as the climb is concerned." Sara opened the bag and pulled out a syringe and a small bottle. "This is dexamethasone," she announced. "It's a powerful steroid that should get his adrenaline going. We've got to get him mobile so that he can descend to camp three."

"On his own?" Hank asked.

"I doubt that," Sara replied as she pulled part of Matt's pants down and jammed the needle into his hip. Hank flinched, but Matt didn't even react.

"We're going to need two of the team to go with him. One can short rope him and the other can belay." Before Hank could say anything, Captain Jim spoke.

"I'll go." Hank was surprised, and even more amazed when Tendi volunteered to go, too.

"Big man great friend to Nepalese climbers," Tendi said in his static English. "I make sure he get to base camp." Hank looked at Jim and said, "Are you sure?"

"Both Tom and Ed can take charge. They can see you through this." Hank saw something else in the Captain's eyes.

"I have to admit," he began, "I've been concerned that I wouldn't make it all the way, maybe even endanger the mission. Now I have a better mission; I can get him out of here. Once I get back, I can help coordinate things when you do get to your friend. I'm sorry Hank," Jim confessed, "but I've spent a lifetime gambling with my life. I've been lucky, only broke an arm once, but with all this time to think . . ."

"You don't have to explain," Hank said sympathetically. "I understand . . ."

"I thought this could be my last hurrah," Jim interrupted. "One more time with the men and then I could walk away forever from the duty, the danger and the sacrifice. But I've seen the bodies littered around this place. Death's everywhere and I don't want to become a part of it. I'm gonna be a grandfather in three months." Hank stared at the frightened man.

"Jim, if you can get Matt safely out of here, you've done your duty." Hank could see relief in the man's eyes.

"I'll go tell the men," Jim said. And then he crawled out of the tent. Tendi watched the Captain go and made room for Lopsang to crawl in.

"Lopsang," Hank called out, "Matt's sick and we've got to get him to descend. Tendi has volunteered to escort him down to base camp."

"Yes, he is good choice," Lopsang responded.

"Matt?" Hank said. "How are you feeling?"

"What do you mean? I feel fine, I think." Before he could say anything else, Sara chimed in.

"Matt. You're in no condition to climb. I'm sending you back down."

"Back down? Where?" It was obvious to Hank that Matt had no idea where he was. His behavior was like a drunk. His speech slurred and even though he was seated, his balance was off.

"Camp three," Hank said.

"No. I have to stay with you."

"I'll go get a couple of 02 canisters," Sara announced. "I'll be right back."

"You gotta go. You've been a great help until now, but I can get the rest of the way myself."

"Listen," Matt struggled to sit up, "if you just let me rest, I'm sure . . ." Hank cut him off.

"Matt, you're sick and the only cure is to descend fast." Hank listened to the pleas that were more whispers than forceful declarations. The man was a shell of his former self, shivering, with sunken eyes and peeling skin. He shook his head and privately cursed himself for what he'd done to this great man, this brother-friend.

"Listen to me," Hank leaned in and was face to face. "If you go on you'll endanger the mission. We are getting you down to a lower camp soldier, and you're going."

Matt's heavy lids lifted up. "Yes sir." Hank lowered himself to Matt and gave him a hug.

"Thank you," Hank's muffled words filtered through the goose down jacket Matt wore.

"Go get your man," came Matt's winded reply of concession.

The three men disappeared towards the Yellow Band and Spur and the rest of the morning was designated to the revision of plans for the launch that evening. Sara checked with base camp and was relieved to hear the weather reports were good.

After getting back on oxygen, Hank tried to rest, but couldn't. He was anxious; worried the weather wouldn't hold and his friends, in their attempt to descend, would perish in an avalanche or storm. He prayed to the goddesses of the mountain, asking for a safe return for his men before he went back to the radio and waited for the next report. Sara joined him a short time later.

"How are you feeling?" Sara asked as she removed the oxygen mask from her face.

"I'll feel a lot better when I know Matt, Jim and Tendi are safe."

"*Camp four, how do you read?*"

"Five by five," was Sara's reply.

"*I'm getting a lot of static down here. Check your squelch,*" Dave said. Sara adjusted a knob on the top of the radio and keyed the mike once more. "Better?"

"*It'll have to do. How is everyone?*"

"We're on O2 and hunkered down. Weather is calm; cold, but tolerable with the radiant in the tents."

"*Yeah, well enjoy it while it lasts. You'll be looking at subzero temperatures when you climb tonight.*" Hank gestured for the radio and Sara handed it to him.

"Any news on climbers headed to three?" He asked.

"*We've got a visual on them from the Sherpas I sent up from two.*" Hank could see the relief on Sara's face. She looked like he felt.

"*I've got them on the other frequency. They're moving slowly, but should be at camp in another half hour.*"

"That's good news," Hank said. *Thank you, Miyolangsangma, for your kindness in helping my friends down the mountain,* he prayed in gratitude.

"*Hank? We have a visitor here; says she's your wife.*"

Hank's eyes widened, *Linda?* He looked at Sara. *What is she doing here? How'd she get here?* He heard the click and then, "*Hank? Can you hear me?*"

"Yes, I read you loud and clear."

"*Are you okay?*"

"It's awful up here. We're cold and tired, but we're hanging on. Where are the girls?"

"*With Mom. They miss you.*"

"How did you get here?"

"*It's a long story, but to make it short, I got a lot of help from Umesh when I told him I was coming. He hooked me up with Al, who flew me most of the way, then I hired a guide and walked the rest of the way.*"

I've been following your web site. I took the same route you did."

"Are you okay?" Hank asked. He figured that his last dispatch wasn't too far back. If she had decided then, she'd have to have busted her ass with little time to acclimatize in between.

"*I'm tired, Hank. I've got a wicked headache and some nasty blisters on my feet. I've got a pretty good sized cut on my shin from falling on some rocks while crossing a stream.*" Linda paused. "*Your doctor here has been very helpful. She's taking good care of me.*" Hank knew battery time was limited and they couldn't talk for much longer; he had to know.

"Linda, why are you here?" Hank put the walkie-talkie to his forehead, closed his eyes, and waited for the answer.

"*I'm here because you're here, Hank. I didn't want you to think there was no reason to come back. I still think you're insane, but I'm here. I know we were in rough shape when you left, so I decided to come and tell you that you do have a home to come back to—when you're done.*"

Hank brought the microphone to his lips and whispered, "I love you, Linda."

"*I love you, too.*" There was a pause. Dave's voice interrupted.

"*Base camp, signing off.*"

"Camp four, out."

"I had no idea. All this time, you never said a word. Why?" Sara asked.

"It hurt too much. And for now, my focus had to be Aaron and everyone here who signed on to help. Come on, it's time to get some rest, before we finish up, so we can all go home."

Chapter 34

The Road to Sagarmatha

THE NEWS CAME that Matt, Jim and Tendi had arrived safely at camp three. Captain Jim reported Matt was doing better, but his limited mobility made for a difficult descent.

Linda's fantastic appearance created a quiet confidence in Hank. *She came all this way* . . . He had dreaded about what he would have to face when he got home.

With only hours left before they set out again, Hank prayed hard; first, to Miyolangsangma and the need for her ongoing kindness, then to God for the strength he would need in the day ahead. He lay in his sleeping bag, recalling words from the Book of John: "Do not let your hearts be troubled. Believe in God, believe also in me." Hank repeated the quote until nagging doubts were replaced by the understanding that Jesus himself had a troubled spirit knowing he would be betrayed, but still, He reveled in the glory of God. The headache, which plagued him since camp two, began to recede with the light; his eyes closed, and his body relaxed into a sheltering sleep.

"Hey, Hank; wake up, it's show time." Hank opened his eyes to the brightness of Sara's headlamp in his face.

"What time is it?"

"Just after eleven. Weather looks great, so we're kicking off in a half hour." Hank raised himself up. The air was intensely cold, but quiet.

"I'll get ready." Sara patted him twice on the shoulder and crawled out of the tent. Hank took an account of his physical condition. For a man who was about to embark on a climb to the highest point on the planet, he couldn't have felt worse. The headache had returned. It reminded him of the hangover head bangers from college days. There was a muscle-stinging chill through his back and legs. His arms were weak from weeks of rope climbing, and the sensation to his fingertips was only slight; in his toes, it was gone. But in spite of his maladies, Hank still had the motivation to finish the job.

Looking now at the summit ridgeline, the group strapped on oxygen masks and headlamps. The scene of his crew trudging through fourteen-degree-below-zero darkness, looked like men in the tunnel shaft of a coal mine.

From the ice bulge, Sara led the team across a steep snowfield to the base of Everest's Triangular Face. Lopsang identified the fixed rope he and several of the guides had left from a previous climb.

"Okay, from here we clip on and climb." Sara's voice came through the earphones. "Take your time, and don't get too far ahead. You'll only have to stop and wait for the rest of us."

As Sara had briefed the team, the first goal was to get to the Southeast Ridge by dawn. It would take several hours, but they had given themselves an early start and the conditions for climbing were perfect: A full moon for light and only a hint of a breeze. The mask, which Hank had grown accustomed to wearing, presented a further challenge, limited sight. At times he couldn't make out where his feet were going, so he planned a series of steps by turning his head awkwardly to the side in order to chart his direction.

Hank allowed Pete to go ahead of him and now distanced himself from Tom Beckett, who was bringing up the rear. Fixed ropes appeared halfway up the triangular face, but were frayed and worn. Sara had told the team not to hook up on any line that looked suspect. Further up, he noticed a new rope leading over a tricky face of scattered stone and broken limestone. In the meantime, Hank relied on his ice axe for balance as he navigated up the thirty-degree slope.

The lessons he'd learned at the climbing school were being put to good use. Much of the technique involved the use of his custom ice axe. He realized he never would have had a chance of scaling these rocks and deeper snow without it. With a little more luck, he was a few hours from reaching Aaron's remains.

As dawn approached, the rocky terrain gave way to a broad gully of packed snow. Sara, whose bright yellow parka was discernable from the red and black wind suits everyone else wore, was nowhere to be seen. A huge smile emerged beneath the snout of his oxygen mask when he heard her over the radio.

"I'm on the Balcony."

The large nub of snow and rock was the perfect gathering point for Hank's crew to rest and replace almost depleted oxygen tanks with new ones, stored there several days before.

"The toughest part is yet to come," Sara announced. "The ridge going up here is knifelike in certain places and the Hillary Step is sixty-five-feet up and almost vertical." Sara pulled Hank aside from the others.

"I'm losing my voice. The bottled oxygen is cold and there's no moisture."

"So don't talk," Hank said. "Save your vocal chords."

"I will, but I've got one more thing to add." Sara looked back at the others to make sure no one was in earshot of what she was going to say. "Did you see those two bodies back there?" Hank nodded.

"I knew one of them. He's been up here for three years. He died from 'summit fever'."

"What's that?"

"It's when an expedition leader is overcome by the desire to get to his objective. He forgets his scheduled turn around time, ignores the weather conditions, and leaves other members of his team behind in order to make it. That guy back there, sitting up; he made it to the top, but didn't make it back down."

"I understand."

Lopsang joined them. "This part of mountain I know very well. I lead and break trail to South Summit." Sara nodded in approval.

"I stay on right, use snow slope to East Face. Mr. Henry, you come first behind me."

"Sure." Hank looked over at the supply of oxygen tanks that had been placed together by the Sherpa crew and realized it was time to change tanks. Taking off his own, Hank checked the supply and was happy to see the tank was a little less than half full. He would be able to use the tank again if he needed it during the descent. Strapping on a full one, a surge of energy flowed through him as the increased flow eased his ever-present headache and the soreness he felt in his back and legs. He raised his ice axe up to signal he was ready. Others raised theirs in acknowledgement; it was time to push on.

Lopsang broke trail along the upper Southeast Ridge. Hank was amazed at how the Sherpa pushed through the heavy snow that had fallen throughout the monsoon season. The skies were clear and the wind did little more than brush against his down suit as the day dawned on them. He was convinced that Aaron had charmed the Goddess into letting him come for him; *or maybe Miyolangsangma is fed up with him and can't wait to get rid of him.*

"I'm coming buddy, I'm almost there." Hank plodded along the crest of the ridge close behind Lopsang. The pace had slowed considerably as each step required several lungfuls of air.

When he and Lopsang reached the snowy dome of the South Summit, Hank sat and waited for the crew to catch up. The summit ridge and the windswept overhang were to the east and straight ahead was the Hillary Step. Hank checked his watch, 9 A.M.

"Lopsang, how far to the foot of the Step?"

"One hundred meters." The Sherpa guide tied the lead end of a rope around himself and passed the rest of the coiled rope to Hank.

"I go while you wait for others. Be very careful. East side drops ten-thousand-feet to Kangshung Glacier; west side drops eight-thousand-feet into Western Coom. Stay away from overhang, unless roped." Hank nodded and wrapped the high tensile cord around his waist and fed it through his gloved hands. Realizing Lopsang could suddenly slip, he braced himself in case he needed to arrest a fall. Lopsang made it to the base of the pitch at the same time the last team member made it to the South Summit. Without resting, Sara clipped on the now secured rope and started across the traverse. Hank followed and while he found the hard snow easy to cross, he paid close attention to how high he was on the edge. At one point, he pulled his axe out of the snow and found himself staring down onto the Kangshung Glacier. Quickly, he moved further down the ridgeline before it could break off. When he finally made it to the Hillary Step, another great sense of accomplishment filled him.

Several frayed ropes hung from above; Hank pulled three together and gave a tug. They held. He was just about to test them with his full weight when Sara came, waving a finger.

"We're going to set our own static line," her whispered voice came through the radio. She grabbed the three ropes and tossed them off. Lopsang approached with another coiled rope and handed the lead to Sara. She gave Lopsang a hug. Hank realized that Lopsang was giving Sara the ultimate honor; he was letting her take the lead up one of the most famous pitches in all of mountain climbing.

The two watched as Sara first wallowed in the deep soft snow and then gained purchase by pressing her feet against the narrow gap between the rock and the inner side of the adjoining cornice. With Lopsang taking the belay, Sara took her time; she jammed and wriggled all the way. It was a masterful job; Hank clapped. When she disappeared from view, her hoarse voice came over the radio.

"The line's tied off. Come on up." Lopsang extended his hand, palm outward. Hank was next. It was nearly sixty feet, but he did it, in half the time. Sara gave him a hand to leg up the last brow of rock, then the two embraced in celebration of the auspicious occasion.

"The hardest part is over, right?" he said as he stepped back. She shook her head.

"Not yet. For you, it's still ahead."

Lopsang arrived next, and then one-by-one, the men of Engine Company 256 filed in. Hank checked his GPS and searched the vastness of the range. He began to walk. Up ahead, about a hundred feet from the top, just beyond another patch of crested snow, stood a slice of bare ground with a rock shelf that Dave had said was a landmark. The GPS confirmed it. It was the position Dave had given; where he had left Aaron.

Sara, Lopsang and the others were in the distance; they'd let Hank continue alone. He motioned for them to come, but they just stood there, pointing. As he followed the direction and swung around, there it was, a patch of blue and red, about twenty feet up the ridge. *Aaron.*

As the gait in his walk increased, he became winded.

"I made it buddy. I'm sorry it took so long, but I'm here now." He got down on one knee and touched the tattered remains of the nylon shell of Aaron's wind suit. From his torso down, he was covered in a blanket of crusted snow and wind blasted ice. The hood of Aaron's parka was shredded and some of his hair had been torn away, leaving a patch of alabaster white exposed scalp. Hank gasped when he saw Aaron's open eyes, gray and clouded, the remains of a smile frozen on his face.

Hank's emotions were as numb as his toes. There was no relief, as he'd expected no sense of completion; the journey was only half over. Besides, what good would frozen tears be? He was weak enough. His grieving would have to wait, deferred to a later time; when they were home, and everyone was safe; then, he would let loose.

The crew had gathered around Hank. They lifted him to his feet and handed him the radio.

"Base camp? This is Henry Longo reporting."

"Hank? It's Dave. Go ahead."

"We've got Aaron. We're coming home."

"Ten four. We'll pray for your safe return." And with that, Hank signed off. "We'll be here for awhile," Tom informed them.

"We don't need everyone," Ed added. "The fire team knows what to do; we just need some time to get him set for the descent."

"What do you suggest the rest of us do?"

"Take a walk," Ed said.

"Where?" And when both Ed and Tom pointed to the summit, Hank looked at the ridgeline, the highest point on earth. There had never been a thought of the top, only finding Aaron, but he was so close.

Sara and Lopsang stood together; both had heard the semi-order and were staring at the top. Hank remembered Sara's dream, to one day make the summit. And Lopsang's return would also be a milestone, matching an uncle's record of scaling the mountain and summiting for a record third time.

"Go," Tom said. "Come back and tell us what it's like to stand on the top of the world." Hank remembered Satchmo and the little girl back in California who had been promised by her daddy that the doll would reach the top of Everest. He reached to Aaron's hand and pried the little doll out, then waved for Sara and Lopsang to follow. With careful steps they walked uphill, eyeing the prize that lay tantalizingly close, but the pace was slow and the gap was taking longer to close than expected. It was like walking on a deeply inclined treadmill. Hank thought about Aaron.

Instead of trying to descend, in the end Aaron tried to go higher. What was he thinking? And then they were there. No more slope to climb. Hank looked out at the great Tibetean plateau. Lopsang attached some prayer flags to the battered survey pole that had been established on the summit years ago. There were all kinds of artifacts either attached to the pole or scattered around its base. There were some odd items as well: a set of dentures, hair combs and a couple of matchbox cars.

With an outstretched arm, Hank lifted Satchmo up to see the other side of the world. Aaron had promised Hannah that Satchmo would see it. He had come so close. Hank had taken him the rest of the way and Aaron's promise was now fulfilled.

Sara pulled out a small camera and snapped some pictures. She swiveled toward Hank, took his picture along with the little doll, and then satisfied, they all left.

In the meantime the men had pulled Aaron away from the ice bed, gotten him on the sled and strapped down. A gray woolen blanket had been wrapped around his body and secured beneath the ratcheted straps.

"He fits well," Ed said. "It's awful heavy so we're going to slide it as much as we can."

"That's what it was designed for, right?" Hank asked. The crew nodded in confirmation. "Okay," Sara croaked, "Let's get out of here and back to camp four." Hank watched, as the sled was short roped to two of the men in front. Seeing that another rope was tied off to a dead eye in the rear, he picked it up and waited for the sled to be pushed off. When it did, it slid easily enough along the snowy ground and immediately gathered speed. Hank tugged on the line to arrest a fall. It would be a long process, a start-and-stop affair all the way back.

After the long and dramatic process of lowering Aaron down the Hillary Step, The crew huddled together to rest. It took six of the men holding the sled at the top and two belaying from each side to make sure the carrier didn't get hung up on the rocks.

"Thank God we tied off those ropes at the beginning and didn't wait until now," Pete said. "I'm exhausted." They took a considerable amount of time to get down the Step, but still had most of the day to get back to camp four. Hank worried more about the oxygen, which was critical in the descent to the Balcony where they could change tanks again. There were a few half used bottles scattered along the ridge to the Balcony, but it wouldn't be enough if all of them went dry at the same time.

"Heads up," Hank shouted. "The wind is starting to kick up; let's get going."

The weight of the sled was enormous and it took all the expertise the fire crew had to move it along without spilling its cargo or injuring any one. Hank was amazed; the firemen moved with patience and careful determination.

Out in front was Lopsang, breaking trail once again, checking the stability of the snow on the ridge. He moved with uncanny speed, back and forth through the static line, checking to see that the ice screws were secure.

Five hundred feet from the Balcony, Rusty and Colin, dropped to their knees. With the remainder of the crew holding the sled, Hank and Sara made their way to the downed men. Sara reached Rusty first and realized he wasn't getting any oxygen, so she turned up his regulator. Hank dug his crampons into the hard snow and got down close to Colin, who pulled off his mask and heaved for breath.

"Can't breathe," he said as he gulped for air. Hank had him lean forward so he could also get to his regulator. The rubber tubing that led from the tank was blocked with ice. He turned off the regulator and disconnected the hose. From the end of the tubing chunks of yellow, mucus filled ice fell away from the opening. Hank pulled out a Swiss Army knife he had packed.

"Hang on Colin; I'll get you going again." Colin seemed calm, but his eyes said hurry. Hank scraped the ice from the rubber hose and reconnected it to the tank. He turned the regulator up to full and helped the stricken man put his mask back on. After six long breaths, Hank could see that Colin was all right. He leaned over once more and turned down the regulator so Colin would get what he needed, but not deplete his supply before changing over further down the mountain.

Even though Colin was ready to continue, Rusty wasn't. Sara checked and discovered he was out of oxygen.

"Rusty's not going anywhere," she announced. "We have to get him more oxygen."

"I'll go," Hank said. "We'll get him out of the wind and I'll be back with another tank."

"I'll stay with him," Sara replied.

Hank looked at her and shook his head. "No, you can't do that. Let one of the firemen stay if someone has to stay."

"They need to keep moving the sled. They can't spare anyone." Hank looked at Rusty and could see he wasn't doing well. He tried saying something, but his speech was slurred and unintelligible.

"He's borderline delirious," Sara said. "Someone's got to stay with him or he'll walk right off the ridge." Hank didn't want to leave her there, but knew she was right.

"Get yourselves over there. You'll be out of the wind." He pointed to a depression in the snow that was leeward to a large boulder sitting on top of the ridgeline. Sara turned toward the large rock and nodded.

Hank got her to look directly at him; "I'll be back; I promise." With Hank's help they got Rusty up and walking. When Rusty had enough steam to become mobile with only Sara's assistance, he turned and moved past the others and headed down the ridge. When he reached Lopsang, he tapped his bottle and pointed downward. Lopsang nodded and waved him on.

Like a skier, he vaideled from purchase to purchase, making great time in his descent. He was motivated to move quickly, not wanting the two he left behind to end up like the corpses already scattered around the mountain.

It took about twenty minutes to reach the Balcony where he grabbed a tank and was about to start the return climb when he stopped for a second bottle. He had almost forgotten to check his own tank; *empty.* As he strapped on the new tank and turned the regulator up to three liters, he said aloud, "Thank God I didn't forget."

Now, with the additional bottle nestled in his arms, he retraced his steps back up. Despite the added weight and gusting wind, Hank made it to Lopsang and the descending crew in the same time it had taken him to get down to the Balcony. He waved the group on and turned toward the higher precipice, where Rusty and Sara were, but before he could take two steps, there was a pull on his arm. Lopsang waved and pulled off his mask.

"Let me; you go with fireman," Lopsang said. "You go down with Mr. Aaron."

"No Lopsang," Hank shouted through his mask. "You stay with Aaron all the way, right? You don't leave him this time. Remember, you said it was very bad when you went down without him the last time? So this time you stay with him." Hank pointed at the firemen as they struggled to carry the body over a barren part of the ridge covered with rocks. Lopsang looked first at the descending crew and then back to Hank. It was obvious the man was torn.

"I have a fresh oxygen tank, Lopsang. I'll be fine." Before Lopsang could respond, Hank turned and headed back to Rusty and Sara.

Tucked away, out of the wind, Rusty and Sara huddled together, half frozen and trembling. Without hesitation, Hank connected the new tank to Rusty's regulator and helped Sara up to get her moving. Dancing around with arms waving, she attempted to get her circulation going again.

"Sorry it took so long." Sara looked at her watch and gave a "thumbs up" sign.

After a few minutes on the oxygen, Rusty indicated he was ready to go. The two helped him to his feet and continued to hang on to his arms for support.

"God, I feel like shit!" he said as he tried to move his legs.

"You go ahead," Hank told Sara. She shook her head no, but Rusty added, "No matter how far you get in front of us lady, I'm still going to beat you back to camp." Sara looked at the two of them and then looked down the mountain. With no reply to Rusty's bold proclamation, she set off to catch up with the others.

"Ready?" Hank asked.

Hank and Rusty made it to the Balcony and climbed down with the others just below them. When they reached the couloirs above the South Col, they sat-glissaded down several pitches of hard packed snow. Using their ice axes to check their inertia as they slid, they made it through the steepest parts and stood up to walk slowly to their tents. When they arrived, Hank was greeted with a cup of hot tea and the radio, to call into base.

"Base camp? This is four. We made it."

"*Well done,*" Dave Horton answered. "*You've been above 26,000 feet for over sixteen hours. How do you feel?*"

"I don't think I ever understood the word 'exhausted' until now."

"*You've got a lot of people down here breathing big sighs of relief. You have the body?*"

"Yes," Hank said. He looked over at the sled covered with a tarp, secured against the small kitchen tent, and tied down against the increasing wind.

"*Well, we just got the three who left you yesterday.*"

"What?" Matt, Jim and Tendi made it back surprisingly fast. At best, he thought they might have been able to make it to the top of the Ice Fall, but never all the way back to base camp.

"*They just walked in a few minutes ago. They're exhausted, but safe.*"

"Roger that." Hank was elated that Matt wouldn't end up a casualty of his expedition. Now all he had to do was get the rest of them back.

"We're going to get some shut eye, Dave. Tell Linda I love her and I'll see her soon. Signing off."

"*Roger. Base camp out.*"

Hank turned off the radio, headed to his tent, and his sleeping bag. The only remembrance he had of being this tired was during his sophomore year at college, when he stayed up three nights in a row for exams. Once horizontal, his thoughts faded into a void of blackness before his body melted into a dreamless sleep.

Chapter 35

Off The Mountain

"Sit still!" Sara barked.

"I can't see!"

"Stop rubbing or you'll irritate the corneas even more."

"Is it snow blindness?" Hank remembered reading about how the sun's rays could reflect off the snow and cause severe eye pain and temporary blindness.

"Probably; stay calm and I'll get you some eye drops. There's an anesthetic in them, it should reduce the pain." And it did, almost immediately. "Now, try to sleep and we'll see how you are in a few hours."

"Thank you," Hank said, but privately stressed how was he going to get off the mountain without his sight.

Later that morning, Hank had regained partial vision.

Sara heard him stir. "How do you feel?"

"Blurry in my left eye, but I can see a little with the right, although it still hurts like hell."

"We need to get you back to base camp as soon as possible."

"How am I going to climb down when I can't see where I'm going?"

"I'll short rope you and be your eyes."

"Sara, there's something else I need you to do for me. Will you take off my boots and have a look at my feet? I haven't had any feeling in my toes for over twenty four hours."

"Can you walk?"

"Yes, but my left foot hurts pretty bad; especially when I toe-in my crampons."

"Frostbite?"

"You think?"

"Look," Sara began, "if you've got it, taking off your boots won't help. There's nothing I can do and once the boot is off, you'll swell up and not get it back on. The only thing we can do is get you back to Katmandu. So let's get going."

Because of his condition, the firemen insisted Hank get a head start. Their load would slow their pace and they didn't want Hank getting stuck behind them.

"Okay Hank, follow me." Sara walked immediately in front of Hank and her continuous encouragement helped, but the pain in his eyes was intense and would require him to stop and wait for it to subside.

I have to keep going. Linda is waiting for me at base camp and the girls are waiting back in Florida. Hank was determined; he was not going to be Aaron's replacement on Everest.

"We're almost there," Sara shouted. As the tents came into view, Hank put his hand to his chest and tapped three times where his crucifix hung from his neck.

It was a grateful reprieve, the rest at camp three. Hank was given more of the anesthetic eyedrops and some juice the porters had hauled from base camp. A pair of dark glacier goggles was located, which helped, although it was still agony to see.

"How're the men doing with Aaron?" He asked.

"They're way behind. Still at the Spur."

"Should someone go back up?"

"They would've radio'd if they were stuck. I'm sure they're just taking their time and being careful."

"Should we wait?" Hank asked.

"No. I want to get you off the mountain as quick as possible." Hank knew she was right, but was angry with himself that he had become the more important one to get off Everest.

The forecast held; the wind never picked up and the sky remained cloudless, but still the slow climb down took most of the afternoon. The condition of Hank's foot made the descent even more difficult as he had to compensate his weight every time he used his front points to gain purchase. As they approached the advanced base camp, Hank saw something.

"Is it my vision," Hank asked, "or is that fog?"

"Temperature inversion," Sara replied. "The sun's rays produce enough heat to melt part of the Ice Fall. As you get into October the day's end temperatures are a lot cooler. The fog climbs up the valley and is as thick as pea soup."

The porters and kitchen crew, who had manned the advanced base camp, welcomed Hank and Sara with hot tea and soup. Hank had two helpings of each, while Sara entertained the porters with animated conversation about reaching the summit of Everest.

After the meal, Sara and Hank moved over to the communications tent to check-in with base camp. The first news they heard was the firemen had made it to camp three.

"They had a lot of difficulty getting over the Geneva Spur," Dave reported. *"They're okay, just worn out."*

"Can you patch me through?" Hank asked.

"Roger, standby." Hank waited as Dave switched frequencies to hail the others. A few moments later a squawk over the radio indicated they were on.

"Beckett here."

"Tom, it's Hank at ABC. Are you guys alright?"

"Yeah. If it wasn't for Lopsang though, we'd all be dead." Hank shook his head. He transmitted back, "I heard it was tough going at the Spur."

"While we were trying to rope the stretcher over the rocks, Pete lost his grip and Rick couldn't hold his belay. The sled, with us attached, started to slip away. Lopsang got a rope around himself to arrest the fall. Thank God."

It was not hard for Hank to visualize; the weight of Aaron's body, with enough steam behind it, could've dragged them down the side of the mountain.

"Do you think you can continue?" Hank paused and then knew he had to ask, "Or do you want to abort the recovery."

"Nah! We're fine. The hardest part is over."

"Are you sure? I'll call it if you guys think it's too dangerous."

"We're sure. See you at ABC tomorrow. Camp three out." Hank looked at the microphone and then at Sara.

"Do we wait, or move on?"

Before Sara could respond, Dave's voice broke in.

"Hank?"

"Go ahead Dave."

"There've been some shifts in the Ice Fall and your biggest ladder is gone. We've also lost two ladders further down. I have to call down to Katmandu."

"Ten-four." The team had to wait until more ladders were brought from Katmandu to Lukla, and then hauled overland to base camp, unless Dave came up with something else first.

"We could be here for another week," he said to Sara.

"Or longer. All of us could easily climb our way out of here, but not with the stretcher." Hank visualized the Ice Fall and the places where the ladders had been. He knew how torturous it had been climbing up and around those ice towers. It would be impossible without the ladders to get back down with Aaron in tow.

"ABC? Do you copy?" Hank keyed the microphone.

"Right here. We're trying to figure out how much of a delay we're talking about."

"Too long, I'm afraid. We're getting a lot of snow down here."

"I guess we'll just have to get ourselves to the Ice Fall and find a way down."

"I'll see what we can do from this end."

"Okay. Is Linda there? I'd like to speak to her."

"No, she's resting. The altitude's been difficult for her."

"When you see her, tell her I'm all right." Hank's stomach lurched. He yearned to be held by Linda. It was gut wrenching. "Dave, thanks for all you've done. We'll talk in the morning. Over and out."

"I'm tired," Hank admitted. "I don't know if I can make it the rest of the way."

Sara got up. "We're going to win, Hank. Hey, we made it through the Death Zone right?" And then she was gone, through the flap, into the Himalayan dusk.

As he painfully marched towards his tent, Hank knew somehow his faith in God would carry him through. And when he climbed into the sleeping bag once more, he quickly found his way to sleep.

The next day, even though dawn came late to the valley, Hank didn't want to move from the warmth of his sleeping bag. With reluctance, he inched out of the bag to accept his tea and biscuits from the cook who had been calling him.

He could barely chip off a morsel of the biscuit that had been in storage so long. The stone cold pastries were part of the reserve food supply.

"First thing I do when I get back is order a bacon-egg 'n cheese from Einstein's." Hank suited up and made his way to the kitchen tent. Sara looked at him with great concern, obviously noting the limp in his walk as he made his way to the dining table.

"Good morning," she said. "How are you feeling?"

"Not too bad for a guy who lives in Florida, but decides to spend a month on Mount Everest."

"How are your eyes?"

"Much better. The right one still feels a little scratchy, but the left one feels normal again. At least I can see out of one eye."

"Good," Sara said. "And your foot?"

"Well, I hope when I get to Katmandu they let me keep it."

"I was on the radio earlier this morning with the doctor."

"What did Mel have to say?"

"Just get you there fast."

"Dave reported that your friend Al's ready to fly a chopper up to camp one, above the Ice Fall."

"What? How on earth . . ." Sara put her hand up to stop him in mid sentence.

"It's a high altitude flight, but the colonel says he's got a helicopter with a pressurized engine capable of climbing twenty thousand feet."

"Why on Earth does he want to do something like that?"

"Because the consensus is we can't get Aaron through the Ice Fall without the ladders. If we're going to get him off the mountain, we'll need assistance."

"You didn't think I'd want to be involved in all of this?"

"Yes, but you needed the sleep. If we were anywhere else but here, you'd be in a hospital by now. Rest is the only thing you've got going for you."

Hank took another sip of tea and thought about her decision. Even though his authority had been usurped, it didn't matter; what everyone was trying to do was get Aaron off Everest.

"And you made the right call." Great relief washed across her face. "So do we wait?"

"No. We need to get down to camp one and find a place to land a helicopter.

I'll give us until early afternoon to get down the Coom. Maybe a bit longer because you'll need more time walking with that leg. The team at camp three will get here today and won't make the trek down the valley until tomorrow."

Hank started thinking about the logistics. "How are we coordinating?"

"Al will arrive soon after they get to camp one and fly Aaron away. That's the plan. Oh, by the way . . ." Sara got up and went to the corner of the tent. "Lopsang wanted me to give you this. He said you'd need it to get down to camp one." From an equipment bag Sara pulled out a folded umbrella. Hank took it from her and admired its length and maple wood curved handle.

"It's his. He said he's had it on every successful climb." Hank understood the value the umbrella would have keeping the sun off of him as he walked through the Coom.

"Well, if Miyolangsangma is watching over me then what are we waiting for?"

The entourage accompanying Sara and Hank was a small one; mostly porters who were bringing equipment back down the mountain. They began with the sun overhead, but soon ran into the fog they had seen the previous day. Not long into the walk, Hank felt himself heating up once more and shed some layers of clothing he had needed for the upper elevation's biting cold and wind. Wearing dark goggles, holding up the umbrella and limping along, Hank walked with steady purpose.

It was a little after two in the afternoon when they arrived at camp one. Hank sat down to take the weight off his foot, but the pain had intensified so much during the descent, pulsing so hard, that Hank now found himself on the snow covered ground, writhing back and forth, as the torture of stinging needles jabbed through his foot.

"It's bad isn't it?" Sara asked.

"If you had a saw right now?" Hank uttered, "I'd let you take it off."

"I've got something for the swelling. But maybe instead . . ."

"Just give me some water," Hank said in an agonized whisper. "I just have to deal with it." Sara dispatched herself to the small supply tent and returned with a bottle of spring water. Hank sat up again. The pain was making him delusional and he drank to not only satisfy his parched throat, but also to concentrate on something besides the pain. When he finished the bottle, he asked for another. Sara came back with a second one, plus a vial of pills.

"Here, take these."

"Are they anti-inflammatory's?" Sara shook her head no.

"Just take them. They'll help with the pain."

The pills were large and had no markings on them. He wrinkled his eyes and nose in confusion, then looked to Sara for answers. A tremendous sadness showed in her eyes. "I take them to help me sleep. They're for pain."

"What pain do you have?"

"A memory." Sara tilted her head slightly. "I was fourteen. I wouldn't keep quiet when they told me to." Sara looked away. His lips slipped apart as he waited in stunned silence for her to continue. "They beat me. And then they raped me. And then, they beat me again. The doctors don't know how I survived. Maybe because I was fourteen my body found a way to recover from the broken bones, fractured skull, and the damage to my liver and spleen."

"Sara. I'm so sorry." Hank's lips closed tight and his chin lowered, as his head moved from side to side in a slow deliberate motion.

"It's okay." Sara pulled out a rolled up sleeping bag from the boxed supplies and motioned for Hank to lie back down. Hank returned the pills to their bottle and handed it to her as she sat next to him.

"Are you sure? They can make a huge difference." Hank shook his head no and Sara slipped them into her pocket.

"Did they ever catch them?"

"Yeah. One of them is in for life and the others are serving lengthy terms. I sued their families and won a large settlement. I've had years and years of therapy and I've put it behind me."

She's in more pain than me.

"Hank, this expedition has been a triumph for me. You had faith in me to lead this crew and gave me an opportunity to fulfill a lifelong ambition. I made it to the summit of Everest!"

"You believed in yourself." Getting off his feet had helped and the pain in his leg was subsiding. "Now maybe you're ready to conquer a different mountain, those pills." Hank watched as Sara rocked back and forth from her sitting position.

"I don't think I can function without my pills."

"You're relying on something that can never give you freedom. The comfort you get is only fleeting. Now that you have achieved this incredible goal, perhaps it's time for you to believe in something else."

Sara's eyes pointed downward, but Hank could tell he had struck a chord. " . . . Or someone else."

"Like who?"

"*Camp one? Camp two calling.*" Hank recognized the voice. It was Pete Saltus. "*We've made it. We're safe and sound.*" Sara jumped to answer the call, but stopped midway to look back. Hank saw tears mix with a smile, and then she disappeared into the tent. The joy, as she spoke to Pete, was apparent. With his head toward the clouds, he said aloud, "He was not the 'someone' I was talking about."

The firemen left the advanced base camp the next morning with Aaron's body in tow. Lopsang and the climbing crew, who had packed up the equipment, were traveling back down with them. Hank had spent most of the previous evening on the radio coordinating the team's arrival with the helicopter.

"*I think we can wait for a visual on the firemen before letting Al take off,*" Dave said.

"There's been a lot of ground fog up here," Hank replied. "We may not be able to see them until they are almost on top of us."

"We've got a good forecast for the day. They won't be there until afternoon and by then, the fog will have burned off. Even if you have to wait, it won't take long for Al to get there."

"Ten-four. We'll have the landing spot ready."

"Just so you know, he's going to keep the bird running." Sara got on the radio next with a series of questions.

"How are we doing as far as the ladder situation in the Ice Fall?"

"We found some makeshift materials for a new crossing, but I don't think we're going to get the last ladder up there for the two seracs at the top."

"Ten-four. So you advise we climb down that section?"

"Roger that," Dave responded. *"Without Aaron it should be manageable."* Sara took a quick look at Hank. He followed her eyes down the side of his body to his left foot. As if on cue, Mel's voice broke in.

"Sara? Can I talk to Hank?" She passed him the microphone.

"This is Hank. Go ahead."

"Hey Big Foot! How are you doing?"

"Hanging in there, I guess. It's not so bad when I'm off my feet."

"I've got Linda and Matt here with me. We all want you to get back down here as soon as possible."

"As soon as I get Aaron off the mountain I will; even if I have to crawl out of here."

Hank continued talking, but was distracted. He wondered how he would get himself off those gargantuan ice towers without the ladder and without being able to get a toe-hold with his left foot. Linda had a lot to say to Hank, but his responses were short and disconnected. He tried to formulate an idea on how he could make it through the Ice Fall. When he looked over at Sara, he recognized she was doing the same thing: *'how does a climber needing two legs make it down a ninety degree cliff side with only one?'* Hank knew neither of them had the answer.

Hank looked out at the thick blanket of ground fog that once again surrounded them and the gentle slope that wound its way back up toward the Lhotse Face. Sara was putting the final touches on the homemade helipad. The perimeter was square and they used oxygen canisters marking the "L" corners of the landing area. In the middle a large black 'X' had been made from a boiled mixture of animal fat grease, donated by the cook. Now, with the camp about to be dismantled and the preparations all made to disembark for base camp, there was nothing to do but wait.

"*Any sign of them yet?*" Dave said.

"Nothing yet," Hank responded into the portable walkie-talkie he carried. It was almost two o'clock. As Dave had predicted, the fog was lifting.

He pulled up his dark goggles and peered through the binoculars. There it was, the short stick figure he had come to depend on.

"It's Lopsang." Looking again, he could make out a shadowy entourage following close behind his climbing sidar. They moved in a slow and steady pace along the line. Hank immediately radio'd in.

"Base camp, this is one."

"*Go ahead.*"

"I have a visual. They're about half-a-mile out and moving well."

"*Roger that. I'll call Tribhuven. Expect your bird at 1500 hours. Base camp out.*"

"Three o'clock," Sara said.

"I hope he makes it." Hank did not know how much bravery was involved in having Al fly up to them, but assumed it wasn't easy.

"It's been done before," Sara said.

"It'll be good to get Aaron all the way back to Katmandu."

"Yeah, but that may not be until tomorrow." Hank gave a puzzled look. "He's going to do a touchdown at base camp. Dave told me Al wanted to run some kind of engine test before returning to Kat."

"Really? He's going to attempt *two* high altitude landings."

"I don't know Hank," Sara said as she shrugged her shoulders. "That's what Dave said. Can I see the binoculars?" Hank pulled the strap up over his head and handed them to her. He was still confused about Al's itinerary, but lost the thought when she exclaimed, "Oh my God. I don't believe it!" Sara handed the binoculars to Hank.

Out of the mist they came. As the fog lifted around them, the men of Engine Company 256 were no longer dressed in their protective expedition outfits. Carrying Aaron four to each side of the stretcher, they wore the gear of their profession: clothing and helmets, heavy gloves and rubberized boots. They walked in synch with each other, as they followed Lopsang down the sloping trail.

As Hank looked on in amazement, he recalled the negotiations at base camp, between Captain Jim and some of the Sherpa porters, about carrying extra loads. Now, it was obvious that this was what the firemen had planned all along.

The bearers of the stretcher looked exhausted; some walked grimacing every few steps; their faces burned from sun and wind exposure, drenched in sweat as it poured down from their brows. Hank looked at Sara who was crying.

"This is probably the last 'carry out' these men will ever do," he said aloud.

And it's their finest.

Hank limped out to meet the team and Lopsang was the first to receive his joyous hug, soon followed by Sara and several of the porters from camp.

"Well, that was the hardest fucking thing I have ever done in my life," announced Ed as they sipped mugs of tea.

"Thank you for getting him here," a grateful Hank replied.

"If it weren't for Lopsang, I don't think we'd have made it."

"I'm glad he stayed to help you."

"Us too. And because of what he did for us, we've decided to make him an honorary member of the New York City Fire Department; he can run into a burning building with me any day."

"I can't thank all of you enough for getting him here," Hank said. "Now, I hope we can all make it safely the rest of the way."

"Eh!" The lieutenant snorted. "Not having to transport the stretcher will make the last part of the descent a piece of cake!"

"Good. I'm glad you think so." At that moment Hank thought about his frostbitten foot. *I don't know how I'm going to do it.*

"Excuse me, I'm going to radio my Captain." Hank watched Ed go. A month on the mountain had taken a huge toll on his body. He remembered him as a huge, lumbering hulk of a man, but now he looked emaciated, his face sunken and droopy from the loss of body weight. Hank walked over to each of the firemen to say a personal thank you. Each had a story to tell of the harrowing descent and the close calls in the thin crusted snow and ice. All of them reiterated what Ed had said about Lopsang's guidance. If they had not had him up there with them, they never would have made it back.

Hank was the first to hear the "whup-whup-whup" of the helicopter's rotors in the distance below. Several of the fire crew, along with the Sherpa porters, stood on the precipice of the snow cliff waving their arms at the ascending chopper as it made its way up.

The helicopter soared up in front of them, climbing several hundred feet above the camp. A quick scan of the cockpit revealed the colonel was flying alone. The sleek, black fuselage displayed Nepal's air force flag on each side. As it dipped to locate the landing area, Hank spotted the platform on the pilot's side skid.

Al Sampson's expertise landed the helicopter precisely onto the helipad, facing Hank and his crew. He throttled the engine down to slow the rotors, but kept the machine ready, in case he had to suddenly lift off. Al looked directly at Hank and saluted. Hank limped forward and saluted back.

"Let's Go!" Ed screamed above the whirr of the engine. The team gathered to where Aaron's body had been stored. Limping badly, Hank had tried to follow, but fell behind. Sara gave him an arm for support and when they reached the stretcher, he grabbed one corner to help lift it. With each movement, Hank's legs betrayed his ability to keep up; he cried out in agony each time his left foot tried to support his weight. To accommodate him, the team slowed its pace, but when they reached the outer distance of the whizzing blades and began a squat walk, Hank let go so the rest of them could transfer the stretcher onto the helicopter.

They stood together and waited for Al to lift off. "Why doesn't he go?" Hank shouted above the din of the pressurized jet engine.

"He's waiting for you!!" Sara yelled back.

"What?" Hank looked once again at the bubble windshield of the chopper's cockpit. Al sat there staring at him. Sara leaned close and said loudly, "You need to go with him, Hank. You can't make it down the Ice Fall with that foot. He's not going to base camp for an engine test. He's going to take you there."

"I can't leave all of you behind!" He was furious that this plan had been put together without his knowledge. "I'm staying. I climbed up with you and I'm climbing out with you."

"Hank," Sara's eyes were warm with moisture. "You're in no condition to do any more climbing; either up or down." She took a deep breath and put her forehead against his and yelled, "You'll kill us all if you try to get through the Ice Fall with that leg!"

"Please Mr. Henry," Lopsang added, pointing to the stretcher. "You take Mr. Aaron off mountain. Please." Hank looked to the firemen as they lined themselves up. Both Tom and Ed pointed first at him and then swung their arms over to the helicopter. The other's brought their hands up in a salute.

Hank looked at Al who pointed to his watch and then beckoned for Hank to get in. They were right. He turned back to Sara.

"Thank you for everything you've done." Sara gave him a hug.

"Go. Be safe. I make sure everyone get back to base camp," Lopsang said.

Hank turned and made his way toward the chopper. His left foot felt so dead he could barely use it to walk with. When he got within the rotor's blades he bent down on hands and knees and crawled the rest of the way. It was an ignominious end to the long campaign of skilled climbing, but he was grateful to be getting off the mountain alive.

"Welcome aboard," Al said. "Buckle up and hang on." No sooner had he said it, Al throttled up the engine and waited for lift. Hank knew the air was so thin and that the pitch of the chopper's blades would need full camber in order for them to get off the ground. After what seemed like an eternity, the helicopter raised itself a few feet; enough so that Al could turn the vehicle's nose toward the Ice Fall. With trepidation, Hank watched as the view of the huge berg that had been home for camp one, gave way to open air above the Khumbu Ice Fall.

"Hang On!" Al yelled, as the machine dipped and hurtled, headed for base camp. "Nothing to it," he shouted.

As base camp came into view, the helicopter circled twice before touching down on a makeshift pad. Linda and the doctor were leading the group racing toward them. Behind the doctor were several Sherpa men carrying a stretcher.

"Al," Hank began, "thank you man; you saved my life."

"Not done yet. He looked down at where Aaron was laid out. "I've got to get him to Katmandu and on a plane back to the states, and then I'm coming back to get you to a hospital."

"So, I'll see you again?" Hank asked.

"Yes," he said. "Again, and then again." Hank was puzzled by the response, but before asking what Al meant, his seatbelt was unfastened and the lock to his door unbolted.

"Time to go, Hank." Al saluted. Hank took a final look at the man he had known so many years ago. It had been some reunion.

When Hank had limped far enough, he watched the helicopter lift off with Aaron's body latched to its side.

"I told you I had your back," Hank said aloud, as he felt the emotional groundswell of a completed expedition. "Not long now and I'll get you all the way home."

"Hank! Hank!" Linda ran as she shouted.

"Linda!" He was exhausted, slumped against a boulder trying to keep the weight off his leg, but filled with relief as the woman he loved made her way to him. When she got close she stopped and put her hand up to her mouth. Tears overflowed, lips stiffened and the horror of his pain and agony registered as she absorbed his wretched appearance.

"I'm sorry Linda," Hank whispered. He stifled a sob. "I promise, I'll never do this again."

"Oh Hank," Linda rushed forward closing the last of the distance and together they hugged and cried. On so many occasions Hank had wanted to let the tears of his frustrations and pain spill out like a torrential downpour. But he held back, needing to maintain a level of composure to ensure the success of the expedition.

Now, with Aaron off the mountain, his mission was almost complete. He would still have to ride out the safe return of his crew and then get everyone back to civilization. But for now, he was in the arms of the woman he loved the most; the emotional bank he had been depositing into was ready for a withdrawal. A big one. And so the dam burst and the water ran wild.

"Oh God Linda! Aaron's dead."

Chapter 36

Finally Home

THE PRE-DAWN LIGHT had the birds singing. Hank smiled to himself. After months of facing the harsh elements of the mountain, he realized how much he'd missed that simple noise.

A Cadillac hearse waited just inside the iron-gated entrance of Mount Dora Cemetery. From the street Hank could see a large group had already gathered. Linda and the girls were waiting at the gated entrance next to the shiny black vehicle, right where Hank had dropped them before he went to park. Spending a few minutes limping his way along the wet sidewalk, he thought about how grateful he was for Mel's triage work. If not for her, he would have lost more than two toes to frostbite. *Geshe Rimpoche was right, I did lose a part of me in order to get Aaron back.*

Hank took his place at the head of the procession. The men of Engine Company 256 lifted the casket. Sand scraped against tar-covered road, crunching under uniform steps until they turned onto the small grassy hill that led to the back of the graveyard. This is where Aaron's body would be laid to rest, in a plot elevated just enough to receive the first morning sun; a last gift for his friend who had found joy in the simplicity of a sunrise.

Friends crowded together on the left of the apron hole; to the right were Linda and the girls, and next to them, Traci and Hannah. Hank had received a wonderful hug and a big smile when he reunited Satchmo with the little girl.

Linda stood arm in arm with Traci, a gesture which pleased Hank. He hoped Traci would agree to work for him in his new accounting office. And a budding friendship with Linda could only help the situation. As Hank approached the crowd, there was Matt, neatly attired in a suit with a thin leather tie. By his side stood Jenna, who was sporting a beautiful diamond on her left hand.

Sara stood beside Lopsang, who looked out of place in a brown suit and tie. His hair was slicked back and his small tuff of beard had been shaved away. Sara looked beautiful with her hair pulled back, a cute black dress, stockings and black pumps. *What a transformation!*

Many from college were there, the staff of the dorm complex and Al in his dress uniform. Hank was amazed at all of the medals; not only was he a hero to Hank and his expedition crew, but for many others as well.

The fire crew placed the casket on a raised pedestal. Hank looked once more at those assembled. Aaron's mom was seated in a folding chair close to the minister. Ira stood on one side of her and his wife, Lin on the other.

Good. Her dementia would make all of this terribly confusing. *She's with good people. They'll explain it all to her.*

Just beyond the perimeter of the group were Dave and Tracy. Dave stood rigid with his hands clasped in front of him while a stream of tears flowed from beneath Tracy's large sunglasses. Hank hoped today would bring some closure for Dave. He had sacrificed a lot to return to Nepal, and his help was key to the success of the mission. For that he would always be grateful.

Wayne Fishman stood apart from the others with a prayer shawl across his shoulders and a prayer book in his hands. Hank hoped Wayne would find peace today.

"Thank you for coming." Hank took his place beside the grave. "I'm sorry for the early hour, but I knew my friend enjoyed early mornings the most. He shared his best pearls of wisdom at this time so . . ." Hank looked down at the ground. He had seen a few nods of agreement. Some of them had shared the same experiences, but none the way he had.

"I've had a hard time understanding why Aaron is no longer with us, at least in the physical sense. He had escaped so many dangerous moments in his life, why not this one?" Hank looked at the casket. "That's one question, I'm afraid will never be answered, but maybe we can find some comfort in the knowledge that Aaron died living a life he excelled in. His spirit was one that challenged the world; a never-ending searcher of knowledge, seeker of truth, and we are blessed that he's left a part of himself with us; a very beautiful part." Hank gave a smiling nod in Hannah's direction. He walked over to the casket and placed his hand on it. After an elongated breath, he exhaled and said, "I'll bet you're in that '67 Bonneville now my friend, driving down a beautiful open highway."

That was it. There was nothing more to say. There were not even any tears left. They had all been exhausted at the emotional farewell when the helicopter left base camp.

The assembled group took turns bringing private thoughts to the casket. Hank was joined by Linda and his girls. Traci led Hannah to the coffin and Hannah placed one of her little ponies on top. Some laid flowers on as they passed, but Dave and Tracy just watched as the others walked by. Tracy reached for Dave's hand, and together they took the long walk back to their limo. "Nice eulogy." Hank turned to see Sara and Pete standing behind him.

"I know we were hired," Pete began, "for going on the expedition, but I wanted to thank you for the incredible experience. It was the greatest adventure of my life."

"So does that mean next time you'll do it for nothing?" Hank said with a smile. "No way!" Pete replied, waving his arms back and forth.

"Can I talk to you a minute?" Sara asked. Without another word, Hank and Sara headed for the shade tree nearby.

"Do you remember our conversation at camp one, before we got off the mountain?" Hank nodded. Sara reached into the pocket book she was carrying and pulled out a small book with gold leaf trim. Hank saw the cross on the front.

"You're reading the bible," he said admiringly.

"I'm trying." She looked at the book and then back to him. "I got what you said when we talked about my addiction. It wasn't just a throw away line was it? About putting your faith into someone?"

"No," Hank said. "It wasn't. You can be very strong in your life as long as you know there's a guiding force. No matter what, I know I'm protected because I believe in Him."

"Well, I've taken the first step," Sara said. "Pete said he'd help me."

"You two make a cute couple." Sara looked over at her boyfriend and gushed. "He's coming back with me to California."

"Great," Hank said. "Pete and the book, sounds like a better deal than those pills can give you." Sara moved toward Hank and kissed him on the cheek.

"Thank you. I'm a better person because of you."

"Thank you for the decisions you made that saved my life." Hank said. "And helping me get Aaron off Everest."

Hank turned to see Ira waiting for him. He hugged Sara and then walked over to him.

"Ira. Thank you for coming."

"I owed it to Aaron. And to you for the incredibly brave thing you did for him."

"I never thought of it that way." Hank looked down at the ground. "It was a duty based on the love and honor for a friend."

"That's why I wanted to help as well," Ira admitted. "Aaron never judged anyone. As a matter of fact, he went out of his way to root for you if you were an underdog."

"Yes, he did."

"Back in our days at Miami, he would look at the entire staff and figure out who was the 'in' crowd and who was on the fence. He always made sure misfits like me and Al were included."

"Yeah, I remember."

"Aaron didn't care. He made sure we were invited to the party as well." Ira began to cry. "I'm honored . . . to have been his friend." Hank stood there helplessly as Ira continued to cry. He pulled out a handkerchief to wipe the tears from his face.

"I'm honored too Ira. Thank you for your help and for coming today." The two embraced in a comforting hug and then Ira turned to meet up with the others who were now headed for the lined up cars that would take them to a planned reception. As Hank walked back to the gravesite, Lopsang caught up with him.

"Mr. Henry, what amazing journey we have."

"And what lessons I have learned about your country and people," Hank replied.

"Miyolangsangma very kind to all."

"Benevolence," Hank said, "is something every person should pray for."

"You acquire much wisdom."

"Perhaps Lopsang," Hank said smiling, "I've learned it in a previous life and now just remembering." Lopsang smiled, closed his eyes and nodded.

"Mr. Aaron big believer in reincarnation."

"Yes, I know. Lopsang, I am grateful to you for sharing your expertise with us. Without you . . . Well, you know what I'm trying to say."

"You fortunate. Road to Sagarmatha one I know well."

"I'm glad we took it together."

Most of the guests had walked back to their cars before the casket was lowered into the ground, anxious to make their way to the breakfast reception that awaited them at Hank's house.

His mission to bring closure was finally over and he was at peace. They both were. Hank looked around. The ghosts were gone.

Linda called out, "Honey, are you ready to go?"

"I believe I am," he said aloud, although no one heard.